Vivir el Dream

Allison K. García

Vivir El Dream
by Allison K. García

Copyright © 2017 Allison K. García

All rights reserved.

This is a work of fiction.

Published by Allison K. García
Cover Art by Julio Cesar García de Alba

Cactus image credit: www.123rf.com/profile_katjagerasimova/
123RF Stock Photo

ISBN-13: 978-1545567944
ISBN-10: 1545567948

To Grandma Baggott and my parents, who always believed in my writing, and to my husband and son for loving me through thousands of hours of writing and editing.

THE NEW COLOSSUS
by Emma Lazarus

Not like the brazen giant of Greek fame,
With conquering limbs astride from land to land;
Here at our sea-washed, sunset gates shall stand
A mighty woman with a torch, whose flame
Is the imprisoned lightning, and her name
Mother of Exiles. From her beacon-hand
Glows world-wide welcome; her mild eyes command
The air-bridged harbor that twin cities frame.

"Keep, ancient lands, your storied pomp!" cries she
With silent lips. "Give me your tired, your poor,
Your huddled masses yearning to breathe free,
The wretched refuse of your teeming shore.
Send these, the homeless, tempest-tost to me,
I lift my lamp beside the golden door!"

PRAISE

"Through this compelling novel, I experienced the plight of the undocumented in America in a very real way. It opened my eyes and my heart to *la gente*, bringing the music, the food, the culture, and the struggles alive. The book keeps you reading at an unhurried pace and blends diverse characters and languages in a sweet, uplifting tone. Beautiful and inspiring."

— Connie Kuykendall, author of *Love Ain't No Soap Opera*

"A flavorful read with a refreshing voice that celebrates diversity and examines justice, immigration, and faith."

— Emily June Street, author of *Tales of Blood and Light*

"Social mores and cultural clashes take center stage in Garcia's novel. Vivir El Dream is a poignant, heartfelt work of fiction with roots in very non-fiction concepts where characters' faiths are tested far beyond their ability to understand God's plan. Garcia's obvious comfort with the Latino culture allows her to tell a brilliant story of courage through fear, victory over circumstances, and hope in the darkest hours."

— Tamara Shoemaker, author of *Soul Survivor* and the Shadows in the Nursery Christian mystery series

"*Vivir el Dream* is a poignant tale of faith, immigration, and the redeeming love of God. Allison K. Garcia's talent for descriptions will endear the reader from the first page until the last."

- Toni Shiloh, author of *Buying Love*

TABLE OF CONTENTS

Part 1 - Learning the Dream

Part 2 - Living the Dream

Part 3 - Losing the Dream

PART ONE

Learning the Dream

Love your neighbor as yourself
- Mark 12:31

Ama a tu prójimo como amas a tí mismo
- Marcos 12:31

CHAPTER ONE
Corazón Duro[1]

*L*inda Palacios heard a thousand doors of opportunity slam all around her.

The HR manager at Jacobsen Financial looked over her application and shook his head. "You're a very promising young woman, Ms. Palacios, but we're unable to hire you without a Social Security number."

She put on her most confident smile. "I'll only be an intern. You wouldn't have to put me on the payroll. No one would even know I was here."

"I'm sorry. Our agency policy is very strict. We could lose our license if we hire illegals."

The word stabbed her, slicing through the very core of who she was like a paring knife. Illegals. She hadn't done anything wrong. Her only crime was being carried at three years old over the border by her mother. She hadn't had any choice in the matter. Why couldn't Mamá have just stayed in Mexico? What was the point of bringing her here if Linda

---

[1] Hard Hearted, a song by Bronco

couldn't fulfill any of her dreams? Every day things grew harder for undocumented people like her. This summer internship had been her final hope on a long list of eliminated possibilities. Without it, finishing her junior year of college almost felt meaningless, another reminder of how low her chances were of getting a job in her field after graduation. The way things were going, she'd be stuck working at her uncle's shop and the *panadería*[2] for the rest of her life.

Tears threatened to break through her strong façade. She needed to get out of there fast. Her lips trembled as she shook the man's hand. "Thank you for your time."

"Good luck," he said.

She clenched her jaw. Luck? Another slice of the knife. She would need more than luck.

Tim Draker straightened his tie and took a deep breath. He paused in front of the towering office building in downtown Roanoke where he had given his sweat, tears, and long nights for fifteen years. Twelve miserable months had passed since he'd stood in the same spot, shifting a box of his belongings in his arms. Restructuring, downsizing, cut backs. Had they thought changing the words would soften the blow?

His life had fallen into a complete downward spiral. His marriage crumbled, bills ate up his savings, his financial security collapsed underneath him, and it all crashed down on him in one moment. One executive memo and his whole life had spun out of control.

---

[2] Bakery

Swallowing his pride, he continued two blocks down the crowded city sidewalk. He stepped into a four-story concrete office building, checking in with the middle-aged receptionist. First impressions were the most important, so he dredged up his last drops of confidence and smiled. "Good morning, ma'am. My name is Timothy Draker. I'm here to interview for the project manager position."

Her unsmiling eyes peered over her dark-rimmed reading glasses. She pointed a manicured finger at the spacious lobby where twenty other fidgety men and women dressed in dark business suits waited, clutching their résumés in silence. "We've already started interviewing. You can have a seat over there, Mr. Draker."

Tim opened his mouth to ask more information, but she had already touched her Bluetooth and was tackling the barrage of blinking lights on the switchboard. His footsteps echoed on the shiny marble tiles as he walked to an empty chair. His heartbeat pounded in his ears as he mentally rehearsed what he would say. A buzz on the receptionist's phone broke through the vibrating quiet of his surroundings.

"Yes, sir." She hung up and came out from behind her desk, her power suit clinging to her wide, swaying hips. "The position's been filled. Thank you all for coming out."

His heart sank like a balloon losing air. The same scene day after day, for months and months. He couldn't take it. He stared at his reflection in his perfectly shined shoes before closing his eyes, unable to even look at himself. He was nothing. Worthless.

Groaning, he shook his head and stood up, pushing back the lock of light brown hair that had fallen over his hazel eyes. He loosened his tie and followed the noiseless group back outside. As he stepped onto the sidewalk, the sounds of honking horns and people chattering on their cell phones assaulted him. A cool, spring breeze whipped a cloud of grit into his eyes and mouth. Choking on the air, disoriented and lost, Tim put one foot in front of the other, moving in no particular direction.

A Mexican in a hardhat shoveled debris into a wheelbarrow. Tim mumbled a curse under his breath. "Stealing all our jobs." He repressed a strong urge to push the man into the busy street.

Thoughts raced through his head like stock numbers on the news ticker. Where else could he go? He had exhausted the classifieds and job sites. No one was hiring. Desperate, unemployed businessmen quickly flooded the companies who generated want ads. Most were overqualified, which created fierce competition for the few available jobs.

His Adam's apple bobbed nervously. Wendy's nagging had worsened as their savings dwindled. If he went home still unemployed, would Wendy actually take the kids and leave him? She had hinted at it the other day when they'd had to remove their youngest son, Jeremy, from the list for a premiere preschool he had been on since birth, because they couldn't afford the tuition payment.

"Do you want them to end up an office drone like you? Where they can fire you whenever they get into some financial crisis?" Her eyes glaring, Wendy had scream whispered at him while the kids slept down the hall. "I might as well homeschool him at this point. The other area preschools are nothing more than glorified daycares. I should have stayed in Northern Virginia with my parents."

Tim's heart dropped as he remembered her words.

"At least I have options."

Options. The words hung in the air like the Hindenburg, ready to blow at any moment. Every day when he opened the front door, he expected to see her suitcases piled in the hallway. Would today be the day? The day she'd finally had enough of him and his worthless existence? Then one thought pushed out all the others.

Maybe his family would be better off without him.

Juanita stretched her neck as she leaned over her kitchen sink, washing the dishes. Her shoulders ached from hunching over the sewing machine all day, and her eyes were watery and tired. Her boss had received a large order of dresses, and the buyer wanted them delivered by next week. Impossible. She and her coworkers would have to work night and day to make the deadline. They weren't robots, though he sure treated them like that sometimes.

Juanita sighed. The worst part was that their boss was holding their pay until they'd finished the order. Another month late on her family's phone bill. Last time it had gotten cut off, they'd had to pay the deposit and couldn't catch up for months. Maybe it was time for one of those fancy mobile phones her daughter kept pushing her to get. Having grown up almost forty years ago in a small pueblo without electricity, new technology overwhelmed her.

She turned to dry a plate but lost her grip. It shattered on the linoleum. "*Ay*, Juanita." She sighed, rubbing her swollen, arthritic hands. "*Cada día más viejita.*"[3] Some days she felt twice her age. Groaning, she bent to sweep the pieces into a dustpan.

---

[3] Every day a little older.

Keys jingled in the front door. It creaked open, slamming shut a second later.

Juanita's body jerked in response. Eighteen years ago, she escaped a violent marriage, and despite near constant prayer, her nerves never seemed to forget. "*¿Mija?*"[4] she called as her daughter stalked by, her high heels thudding on the thickly carpeted living room floor. "*¿Qué pasó?*"[5]

"*Nada,*"[6] Linda yelled from her bedroom. Another door slammed.

Juanita dumped the broken plate in the trash and made her way to her daughter's door. "Linda?" She poked her head into the room. Her daughter lay face down on her bed, crying and wrinkling the sophisticated, eggplant-colored skirt and matching jacket they had purchased last month at the second-hand store.

"Go away." Her pillow muffled her words.

Juanita smoothed out the comforter and sat on the bed. "*¿Por qué lloras, mi amor?*"[7] She stroked her daughter's long, black hair. "What happen?"

"I didn't get the internship."

"No?" Juanita clicked her tongue. "*Pues, son estúpidos,*[8] to not hire a smart, pretty girl like you."

Linda turned and faced her. Black mascara smudged the caramel skin around her dark chocolate eyes. "They said they can't hire illegals."

Juanita's heart squeezed in her chest. That label. Branded on them from the moment they had stepped on American soil. If only Linda could understand why she'd risked everything to come here. But she

---

[4] My daughter
[5] What happened?
[6] Nothing.
[7] Why are you crying, honey?
[8] Well, they are stupid

couldn't tell her. It was her burden alone, between her and the Lord. There were certain things a child should never know, and though her child was now a young woman, she would never tell her the whole story. If that meant Linda couldn't appreciate all she'd done, it was worth it to limit her suffering.

She sighed, cupping her small hand on her daughter's oval face and running a thumb over a tear on her high cheekbone. "You gonna find something. *No te preocupes.*[9] Memo said you can work in his *taller*[10] this summer. *Necesita ayuda en la oficina.*"[11]

"*Ay, Mamá.*" Linda groaned, sticking out her thick lower lip. "Is that why you came to the U.S.? So I could go to college and work as a secretary in your brother's shop?"

Casting her eyes to the floor, Juanita said nothing. When she could talk, the word caught in her throat. "No." She adjusted her apron and returned to the kitchen. She blinked out a few tears and quickly wiped them away. She grabbed an onion and a cutting board. Her mother had always told her to take advantage of chopping onions. Juanita took out a knife and let the tears flow.

Tim kicked an empty fast-food wrapper as he moved forward in line. He stared at the value menu while his mind pondered other plans. Wendy and the kids would get money from his life insurance if he died, but it'd have to look like an accident. His boys were still young enough that they might not even

---

[9] Don't worry.

[10] Shop

[11] He needs help in the office.

remember him. He didn't hesitate to wonder if Wendy would find a replacement for him. His lip curled in disgust. She might even bring the guy to Tim's funeral.

He shook off the thoughts as he ordered a cheeseburger and passed the teenage girl a crumpled dollar.

Her hand stayed outstretched. "You still owe ten cents. There's tax."

Tim's ears turned hot as he searched through his empty pocket. Gees. Couldn't he do anything right? He grabbed a handful of pennies from the take-a-penny, leave-a-penny container and slapped them on the counter.

"Thanks." She rolled her eyes and handed him the burger, shooting him a half-smile. "Have a nice day."

"Oh." Tim turned. "Could I have a cup for water?"

She sighed as she bent for the cup. "Here you go, sir. Can I get you anything else?" Her fingers drummed on the counter.

At this point, he was just taking up space in the world. Even his simple requests were a burden to people. "No." After filling his cup and grabbing some napkins, he plopped down at a table near a window. Even his reflection was pitiful. His sideburns were overgrown, and his hair was so long even product couldn't keep it from being unruly. The bumpy bridge of his nose, broken by a basketball during a high school game, was now only a reminder of his many imperfections. His empty eyes and crumpled suit matched how downtrodden he felt inside.

How would he do it? He gazed through the window at the same construction site he'd passed earlier. Hadn't he just watched a video where a guy fell into a manhole while distracted by his phone? But what if it wasn't fatal? If he survived, the medical bills would bury them sooner than the gravedigger. Maybe he could lose his balance while crossing the street, and a car would run over him.

Plans floated through his mind as he chewed his lunch without tasting it. Popping the last bite of the cheeseburger in his mouth, he crumpled the greasy wrapper with trembling hands. It was now or never.

He held his head up, standing a little taller, and pushed open the oily-handled door. Just ten or fifteen blocks to the barrio. A white guy in a business suit, he'd stick out like caviar in a *taco* joint. An easy target for some little gangster with a gun. All he'd have to do was offend one of their mothers, and he was done for. Or better yet, he could buy a gun, do it himself, and somehow make it look like an accident.

A dozen blocks later, his shins were tight. A blister was starting to form on his big toe, but he barely noticed, his mind so focused on his goal. A car honked next to him, yanking him back to the present. The rickety Cadillac rolled by, bass thumping and rattling its windows. This drew his attention to a sign across the street: MECHANIC WANTED.

He paused for a moment. Something tugged at his heart, a glimmer of light in his darkness. It'd been years since he'd worked on cars with his dad, but it was worth a shot. If it didn't pan out, there was always Plan B.

Linda waited until Mamá left the room before lying back, her eyes blurry with tears.

What was the use of maintaining a 4.0 grade point average if she couldn't do anything with it? Through all four years of high school and her nearly three years of college, while everyone else had partied, she'd stayed home studying or worked at the *panadería* or at Tío's shop when he'd needed help with the books. Linda's hard work and multiple scholarships were paying for college. That was more than most of her classmates could say. Their parents paid their bills. She had been working at La Panadería Hernandez since she could lift a broom. Until she'd graduated high school, Mamá had put the money into a college savings account for Linda.

The springs creaked as she moved from the bed, and tiptoed out of her room into the hall, listening to her mother's soft sobs. Her shoulders drooped. How could she have been so selfish? It wasn't Mamá's fault U.S. immigration laws were messed up. Mamá just wanted a good life for her daughter.

Linda walked up behind her mother and wrapped her arms around her. She kissed her mother's head, inhaling the fresh scent of Caprice shampoo.

"*Perdóname*[12], *Mamá.*"

"*Ay, mija.* Is okay."

Linda sniffed the air. The heavy scent of thick, fried corn tortillas mingled with shredded chicken drowned in Mamá's famous salsa. "*Sopes?*" Her mouth watered in anticipation.

"*Sí, de pollo.*[13] Your favorite."

Linda gave her a squeeze and reached for a *sope*.

Mamá's wooden spoon connected with her hand.

"Ow!" She rubbed her hand, smiling. "I was just going to take the plate to the table."

Her mother chuckled and wagged her finger. "*Ya te conozco, mija. Siéntate. Yo te sirvo.*"[14]

"Probably a good idea. They smell so good. I

---

[12] Forgive me
[13] Chicken ones
[14] I know you well enough, my daughter. Sit down. I will serve you.

could eat them all." Linda kissed her mother's damp cheek.

"Onions," Mamá said, wiping her eyes.

"*Ya le conozco, Mamá.*"[15] No one else's mom ever cried so much over onions.

---

[15]I know you well enough, Mamá.

CHAPTER TWO
Nosotros Los Pobres[1]

*T*im took off his jacket and loosened his tie, letting a taxi speed by before crossing the street. He took a breath and walked into the garage. Loud music with tubas, accordions, and a lot of brass usually reserved for cheesy Mexican restaurants echoed off the shop's walls.

"Hello?" he called.

A man's off-pitch voice sang with the radio. Well-worn work boots protruded from beneath a beat-up Lincoln, swaying and tapping in rhythm to the music.

Tim walked closer. "Hello?" he repeated.

This time a wrench clinked to the ground, and the man rolled out. His brown skin was smudged with grease on and around his five o'clock shadow.

Pausing, he scanned Tim with a smirk before rolling back under the car. "The highway's three blocks to the left," he said in a thick, Mexican accent.

Tim cleared his throat. "Actually I'm here about the job. The sign says you're looking for a mechanic."

1 We, the Poor Ones – a 1948 Mexican movie starring Pedro Infante

The man slowly rolled out again, sitting up and grinning. He pointed a wrench at Tim. "You look a little fancy for a mechanic."

Tim crossed his arms over his chest. "Can I speak with your boss?"

"I am the boss." He rolled a toothpick with his tongue as he wiped his greasy hands on his already filthy rag.

Oh, great, a Mexican boss. Tim doubted the guy would hire someone like him anyway. They only hired their own, probably another illegal. If they'd all just stayed in Mexico, maybe he would've found a job by now. He wasn't going to beg one of them for work. Plan B came back into focus. "I don't want to waste your time. I see you're busy." Tim gestured to the line of broken-down cars parked outside and the three in the shop already.

"Can you really fix cars?" the man asked, standing.

Tim's mouth twitched. "Yeah."

"When can you start?"

"Anytime," Tim said hopefully. Wendy would kill him for getting a blue-collar job, but it was better than losing their house. "Right now, if you want."

The man chuckled. "In that pretty suit of yours?"

Tim put down his briefcase, took off his necktie, and unbuttoned his shirt, exposing a bright, white tank top underneath.

"Okay." He handed Tim the wrench. "I tell you what. If you can change the oil and clean the carburetor in this piece of junk, you got the job." He motioned to a pair of dark blue-green coveralls hanging on the wall. "My last mechanic just got sent to prison for ten years, so I don't think he'll be needing his stuff anytime soon. This might fit you."

Tim stepped into the coveralls. They were a little short but close enough. He pulled his black socks over his pants to protect them from oil or grease. Taking a deep breath, Tim rolled under the car, the fluorescent lights glinting off his dress shoes.

Linda finished the last bite of her *sope* and leaned back in her chair, letting out a contented sigh. "*Ay, delicioso, Mamá.*[2] You could have your own restaurant."

Mamá frowned and got up to clear the table. "*No te burles de mí,*[3] Linda."

"No, I'm serious. *Usted es una chef.*[4] One day when I have a little money saved up, we can go into business together. You can cook the food, and I'll handle the money."

"It won' work."

"*¿Por qué?*"[5]

"Because you will eat all the food, and then we make no money."

Linda laughed. She stood and gave her mother a hug. Then, holding her shoulders, she turned her and directed her towards the couch.

"*Los trastes.*"[6] Mamá pointed to the stack of dirty dishes soaking in the sink.

"I'll wash them. *No se preocupe.*"[7]

"*Pero, mija, ¿no tienes ninguna* homework?"[8]

"*Bien poquito.*"[9]

---

[2] Oh, delicious, Mamá.

[3] Don't make fun of me.

[4] You are a chef.

[5] Why?

[6] The dishes.

[7] Don't worry.

[8] But, my daughter, don't you have any homework?

[9] Hardly any.

It wasn't true. She had two tests to study for, half a book to read, and a paper to write all within the next five days. But they could wait ten minutes while she washed dishes. Mamá looked so tired today. And Linda was sure her earlier rant had not helped the situation. The circles under her mother's eyes had darkened over the years, and her black hair, pulled into a long *trenza*,[10] grew grayer every day.

The mothers of most of her college friends were in their late forties but appeared years younger than Mamá, who was only a few days away from thirty-seven. But then, none of them had grown up poor in Mexico, picking the fields from the age of six. Nor had they gotten pregnant at sixteen, nor crossed the desert into the U.S. at age nineteen alone with their three-year-old daughters, nor worked twelve hours a day or more in a sweatshop.

Linda shook her head at her earlier anger towards her mother. Mamá had never told her why she'd left her father, and Linda had been so young when they'd left she didn't remember him. Throughout the years her Tío Memo had hinted at a bad marriage, bad enough that Mamá's eyes looked like those of a scared wild animal anytime his name was mentioned. Linda couldn't blame her for wanting a better life for her daughter. If only it were easier for people to cross legally, but the system was flawed and corrupt. Linda sighed as she passed the sponge over a plate.

"*¿Mija?*" her mother called from the living room above the *novela*[11] she was watching.

"*¿Sí*, Mamá?"

"*Tu tío quiere que lo visites hoy en su taller.*"[12]

---

[10] Braid

[11] Short for *telenovela* – soap opera

[12] Your uncle wants you to visit him in his shop today.

Linda groaned quietly. It never took less than half an hour to visit her uncle. Ever since his assistant, Javier, went to jail last month, Tío Memo talked any visitor's ear off. She set the last dish in the drying rack and wiped her hands on the orange, crocheted kitchen towel.

"*¿Mija? ¿Me escuchaste?*"[13] her mother called louder.

Linda walked into the living room and grabbed her backpack. "*Sí.* I'll go now. I'm going to study in the library after I talk with Tío."

"Don' come home too late. Is dangerous."

"Okay, Mamá. I won't."

Mamá smiled and turned back to her *novela*.

Putting on her jacket, Linda kissed her mother on the cheek and headed out the door. The late afternoon air held a slight chill. Linda quickened her pace as she walked down the empty street, planning what she would work on first. It was Monday, and she had a test in Accounting 305 on Wednesday and another in Research Methods & Statistics on Thursday. The book and the paper were due Friday, but she knew it would take a long time to write the essay. Her preference was studying for the tests. She was better at math than literature. Math could be solved and applied to the real world. Literature was less cut and dry. She still got A's but had to work harder for them.

This semester her literature class focused on the works of people who changed the world, either through their books or their actions. They had already read *The Jungle* and an autobiography by Frederick Douglass. Now they were reading a biography about César Chávez. This week's essay would deal with how his demonstrations improved

---

[13] Did you hear me?

things for Latinos in the U.S. and what current organizations or people were making changes for Latinos today.

The trouble was, from where she stood, things hadn't changed much in the last fifty years.

Tim took a deep breath, steadying his hand. "You can do this, Tim," he whispered under his breath. "Don't mess this up like everything else in your life. This is easy stuff. Cake. Twenty years ago you could have done this with your eyes closed."

But twenty years was a long time. Before he'd had to sell his car last month to cover the next few mortgage payments, he used to take it to the dealership for oil changes. He'd gotten lazy over the years and was out of practice.

He spent a good five minutes flat on his back before he remembered the carburetor was under the hood and not under the body. Luckily, the boss had told him to change the oil, too, so he didn't look like a complete idiot. "If I just loosen here," he said, turning the wrench. A few drips trickled out, but he scooted away in time, grabbing a metal pan and letting the oil flow into it. He lay on his back, still beneath the car, watching the shiny, black stream with satisfaction as he wiped his hands on a stiff rag.

Someone kicked his foot, calling out in Spanish. He jumped, rolling into the line of thick fluid. "What the—?" he spurted as he slid out from under the car. Wiping the slippery liquid from his face with a dirty rag, he squinted through his grease-blurred lashes to discover a young, Mexican woman. An industrial fan near the garage bay door blew her shining, black hair around like a model's on the catwalk.

"*Dios mío*,"[14] she cried, her mouth forming an O and her cheeks flushing dark pink. "I'm so sorry. I thought you were my *tío*."[15]

"Your who?" Tim scowled, making his way to the sink, the oily sweet residue still on his lips.

"My uncle. I didn't know he'd found anyone new yet."

Tim found a slightly cleaner rag and wiped his eyes and lips with water. "Yeah, well, it's my first day, I guess. If I don't screw up, that is."

"I hope I didn't mess anything up for you." Her dark eyes held genuine concern.

Tim shrugged. She had kicked him while he was down, but he was used to it from Wendy. At least she'd apologized. "I'm fine; the car's fine. This shirt's a different story." He unzipped his coveralls to show a large, black oil stain down the front. "I think this is officially my work shirt."

"I'm so sorry. I'll put in a good word with my *tío*." She flashed a half-smile.

"Thanks." He nodded.

"See you later . . ." She paused.

"Tim," he said.

The young woman smiled and held out her hand.

He showed her his oil-stained palms.

"Oh, right." She chuckled. "I'm Linda. Nice to meet you."

"It's been a pleasure." He pointed a dirty rag towards the office on the second floor. "I think your uncle's upstairs."

"Thanks." She waved and hurried up the steps.

Tim watched her ascend, her tight jeans hugging her hips. She was pretty hot . . . for a Mexican.

---

[14] Oh my God.
[15] Uncle

Linda frowned, feeling his gaze on her. She brushed it off. How in the world had she thought he was her uncle with such fancy shoes? She shook her head, feeling silly, and knocked on the office door.

"Come in."

"Hi, Tío."

"Oh, Linda, *mi sobrina favorita.*"[16]

Linda stuck out her tongue. "I'm your only *sobrina.*" She kissed him on the cheek.

He chuckled and pointed with his lips to another chair. "Sit."

Linda dropped her bag on the desk and sat heavily in the rusty, metal folding chair.

"*Aguas,*"[17] Tío said. "You might break it. That chair's older than you."

"Sorry, it's been a long day."

"*Sí,* your *mamá* told me you had an interview downtown today for a . . . *¿cómo se dice?* . . . *práctica.*"[18]

"Internship," Linda answered, despair creeping in again. "But I didn't get it. So once school ends in another month, I'll have time to help out here."

"Well, I'm glad you'll be here, but I'm sorry for the internship. Do you have more interviews?"

"*Ay,* what's the point, Tío? No one will hire me *sin papeles.*"[19]

"I can get you some *papeles chuecos,*[20] if you want."

Linda shook her head with a smile. Being here was already a crime, she didn't want to add fuel to the fire. "Thanks, but I want to work under my own

---

[16] My favorite niece.

[17] Careful

[18] What do you call it? . . . internship.

[19] Without papers

[20] Fake papers

name. Besides, that's against the law, and I don't want to get detained or anything."

Tío frowned. "They'll deport you for anything these days. They don't need a reason."

"Don't say that. They're only supposed to deport people who cause major crimes now, like felonies and stuff."

"Yeah, tell that to all our *paisanos*[21] sitting downtown in a cell."

Linda's stomach dropped. She tried to push the thought out of her mind. The fear was constantly there, like an ominous cloud, filling her mind with the dread that any moment she could be incarcerated like a criminal and deported to a country she didn't remember and where she'd be completely and utterly confused and alone.

---

[21] Countrymen

CHAPTER THREE
Mojados[1]

*J*uanita's eyes drooped as a commercial for a new *novela* played, a border-crossing story. Her mind drifted back to her own *cruzada*[2] with Linda eighteen years ago . . .

"Dios mío, ayúdanos,"[3] *Juanita prayed aloud in a raspy voice. Her throat was as dry and cracked as the desert. She followed the line of weary people as she shifted her toddler on her hip. It was their third day in the desert, and three-year-old Linda felt as heavy as a full sack of corn. Juanita's feet blistered in the searing desert sand, and her eyes throbbed from the blinding sun, beating down without mercy. Sand surrounded them in every direction. No trees, no water, no border.*

As the day passed, she grew weaker, and the liter of remaining water sloshed in her container, tempting her to drink it. She fought the desire. She had to save it for

---

[1] Wet ones – a common term for someone who crosses over the border without documentation
[2] Crossing
[3] My God, help us.

Linda. A handful of Maseca,[4] beans, and one tostada,[5] broken into pieces by the long journey, were all that were left of their food supply. When they had first entered the desert in the dead of night, the coyote[6] promised they would arrive at a house in New Mexico the following day, where they would have food and water and a place to sleep. Three days later, they were losing hope.

Juanita had heard stories about people dying in the desert. Hundreds of people, maybe thousands. Searching for freedom and a better life for their families. She had heard other stories, too. Stories about what the coyotes did to women, stories she didn't want to believe were true. She took a deep breath and looked ahead with determination. She wouldn't be one of those bodies lying out for the vultures to find. They were going to make it.

All of a sudden, the old man in front of her stopped, swayed, and dropped onto the sand, dead. She made the sign of the cross over her chest and stepped around him, continuing on.

Tim cleaned the last wrench and used the gritty Lava soap to remove grease from his stained hands, arms, and face. He whistled, studying the vehicle, admiring his work. Really, there wasn't much he could see, but he knew he'd done it right. Though he might have taken less time if he had remembered what a carburetor looked like. Next time he'd be faster. If there were a next time. "That wetback probably just wanted a free day's work," he mumbled to himself.

"Finished yet?" the man called from the office.

---

[4] A popular brand of corn flour
[5] A hard, fried tortilla
[6] A paid guide for crossing the border

"Yeah."

The girl had left minutes ago. Tim wasn't sure how long it'd been since he stepped into the shop. Like in the old days with his dad, he'd lost track of time. His mother had to pry them from the garage for dinner every evening. A waste of time, she'd said. She'd always been so hard on his father.

"Hmm . . ." The man inspected under the hood and nodded. "Looks good. Let's see if it works." He got in the car and started it before leaning over and peering beneath the car. "No leaks." He squinted at the engine. "No smoke." Reaching into his pocket, he pulled out a wad of cash. He licked his grease-stained finger and pulled off two twenty-dollar bills. "Nice job." He handed them to Tim.

"So I'm hired?" Tim stuck the bills in his wallet.

"This ain't no charity, *amigo*. I only give money to bill collectors and my employees."

"What's my salary?"

The man coughed out a laugh. "Salary? You gotta be kidding me. What do you think this is? Wall Street?" He laughed again. "No, you get paid for what you do, a percentage. So, if you wanna make *dinero*, I recommend you work a little faster next time."

Tim smirked. "Yeah, I'm a bit rusty."

"Rusty? An hour and a half for an oil change and a carburetor cleaning isn't rusty, it's slow. But I need the help. See all these cars? We got a lot of work to do, man. Come in at seven tomorrow morning and plan to be here late."

Tim nodded. "Sounds good. Do I have to sign anything?"

A smile spread on the man's face. "Yeah, right next to the line about your salary."

"So, how do I know you won't hire someone else?"

His smile faltered. "I'm good to my word, man."

Tim picked up his briefcase, shirt, and jacket. It was the only option he had. He'd have to trust him. "Yeah, okay. Thanks." He held out his hand, and the man shook it. "See you tomorrow."

"*Tempranito.*"[7]

"What?"

"Never mind." His new boss snickered and followed Tim out, flipping a switch. As the garage door closed, he pulled down an extra security gate and padlocked it. "Knock loud tomorrow. If I don't come, walk around the side and ring the doorbell."

Tim gave him a thumbs-up.

"Where are you parked?"

"I took the bus. Where can I pick up the 55 bus around here?"

"The Tanglewood routes?" The man sucked air through his teeth, staring out into the sunset. "It doesn't come up this far. You're gonna have to get on one of the Campbell Court routes and transfer. You have to walk about ten blocks down. I think it should be on the corner of Fifth."

"Yeah, that's where I got off. Thanks."

"Be careful. I wouldn't put on your jacket until you're past 10th street. Walk strong and don't look at nobody. This is a bad neighborhood, *amigo.*"

Tim's heart beat faster in his chest. "I'm not worried."

The man shrugged. "Whatever you say, tough guy. Don't say I didn't warn you."

Linda yawned and stretched her back against the hard wooden chair. Having read through the second

---

[7] Nice and early

half of the Chávez book, she'd searched through the library computer for information on Latino advocacy groups. So far, she hadn't found anything worth writing a five-page paper about. She sighed and continued clicking links.

"I told you we'd find her in here."

Linda turned around. "Hey, guys."

Five of her friends from the Cultural Club approached. Their white faces shone beneath the fluorescent lights. Linda was the Club's president and one of two Latina members. There were also a Korean guy named Lee, and Fatima, an Egyptian girl, though neither were present today with the group surrounding Linda.

Linda hoped she would meet more students in a similar situation to hers by joining the Cultural Club. The halls and classes were seas of white faces with the occasional African-American and a few of her *gente*[8] sprinkled in. Though many Latinos lived in Virginia, few of them attended this college. Now that she was president of the Club, she tried to reach out to more diverse students, but they were nowhere to be found.

Kevin smiled at her. Linda had been fighting her attraction for him ever since last semester when he'd given an impassioned and intelligent discourse on the importance of preserving the sanctity of Native American land. Plus, he was quite good-looking. His navy jeans and turquoise, tight-fitting shirt showed off his muscles and complemented his eyes beneath his dark, brown hair. "How long have you been hitting the books, Palacios?"

Linda blinked at the time on the computer. "Five hours."

---

[8] People

Kevin's soft blue eyes danced over her face. "You need a break, *chica*. We're heading to the club down the street. Come out with us."

"Dance a little salsa…" Katie danced a few steps.

Brian's deep voice continued. "Drink a little *cerveza . . .*"[9]

"Come on, guys. You know I don't drink. It's against my religion."

"Okay, so maybe you don't drink, but we know you salsa." Hannah twirled her long, auburn hair up into a messy bun. "You just taught us last month. Don't you want to see your pupils shake what their mommas gave 'em?"

Linda chuckled.

"Come on," Kevin begged, leaning in, oozing charm. "It'll be fun." His smirked. "You can make fun of Brian."

Brian hit Kevin's arm. Kevin punched him in the thigh, and, yelping in pain, Brian grabbed Kevin in a headlock.

"Y'all quit it," Becky said in her South Carolina drawl, her blonde locks bobbing as she pulled the boys apart. "So immature. I swear y'all are worse than my ten-year-old brothers."

Linda smiled. She was glad for her fun group of friends, and though it was tempting and she could use a break, she didn't have time for one. She admired how her friends built in time to de-stress, but she rarely could relax. Perhaps it was guilt from seeing Mamá working sixteen-hour days; it pushed Linda to strive for a better life and to show appreciation for her mother's hard work by making the most of her opportunities. She sighed and shook her head. "It's late, guys. I have a class in less than twelve hours."

---

[9] Beer

"An even better reason to stay. Taking the bus home, how long is that? An hour?" Kevin leaned on the computer desk, the woodsy scent of his cologne drifting into her space.

Linda nodded, her heart beating faster.

Kevin ran his thumb over the spine of her Chávez book. "That's two hours of travel time for you. If you come dancing for a couple hours, you can crash at our place and wake up in time for your class. No worries."

Their ideas were starting to make sense. A Holy Spirit alarm bell went off in her mind, along with the image of an irate Mamá discovering she'd slept over at a boy's place. She shuddered, imagining the slap of the *chancla*[10] as it made contact. She knew she had to take a step back. "Convincing argument, Kevin, but I can't go. I told my mom I wouldn't be home too late."

"So, call her." Hannah extended her cell phone.

Linda's face went hot. "I can't. Our phone's cut off right now."

"Oh." Hannah pulled her hand back. "Sorry."

The group was silent. By their designer jeans and fancy bags and nice cars, Linda doubted any of them had to deal with money shortages.

Becky stepped forward, giving her shoulder a quick squeeze. "If there's anything I've learned about the similarities between our cultures, it's that you don't mess with Mama."

The tension broke, and everyone laughed.

Grateful, Linda smiled at Becky, who shot her a quick wink.

"All right, maybe next time?" Kevin flashed his pearly whites.

"Maybe next time." Linda waved goodbye and continued with her schoolwork.

---

[10] Sandal/Flip-flop – often used by Latina mothers to give punishments

Juanita gazed into the night sky, praying for help. These were the same stars she could see from her pueblo in Zacatecas, eight hundred miles away. It was the fifth day. They had lost two more people, one from dehydration and another from a rattlesnake bite. In the bright moonlight, Linda cried for food, her little face dark from nearly a week's worth of sun and streaked with lines of tears over her dry skin. Juanita gazed up into the night sky.

Juanita wondered if she'd made the right choice, leaving everything to come to an unknown land. If she had stayed, he would have killed her, just like his last wife. This was the only way.

She fed Linda another spoonful of near-rancid beans, praying they wouldn't make Linda sick. Giving her a sip of water, she held her little girl close under a thick blanket to keep out the freezing air. She stroked her hair and hummed "La Marcha de Zacatecas,"[11] a tune she had learned from her mother.

"God," she prayed into the wide sky. "Keep us safe and guide us to where You want us to go. Keep us strong and carry us to our destination. If we should die before the night is over, please take us into Your heavenly presence." Before she closed her eyes, a shooting star passed through the darkness—a sign from the Lord to keep hope alive.

As soon as Tim got off the bus in his neighborhood, he threw his greasy tank top in the garbage near the empty bus stop. Buttoning his white shirt, he tucked it in and pulled on his jacket. Wendy wouldn't have to know where he was working. It was only

---

[11] Zacatecas March

temporary anyway. He would continue sending out a stream of résumés and making follow-up calls. In a few weeks, maybe something better would turn up.

He walked the half-mile to his house in an upscale suburban area, taking a few shortcuts through well-manicured lawns. He stepped onto his own unmown lawn, a mixture of emotions flooding him, and walked up the sidewalk made of French-imported stone Wendy had insisted on installing. He unlocked the front door of their Georgian Colonial brick house, practicing his white lie.

The shrill cry of screaming children, the smell of burnt food, and a living room strewn with toys assaulted his senses as he walked through the door. Seconds later, Wendy rushed at him, fuming like a bull out of the gate.

"Where have you been?" Wendy grabbed his arm and dragged him into the bathroom, closing the door. She poked a finger in his chest, using her patented whisper yell. "You should have been home hours ago. Is your cell phone broken? I called you a dozen times, and it went straight to voicemail."

"It's out of minutes." He'd ended their cell phone contract three months ago, switching to a month-to-month plan to save money.

She squinted. "You couldn't find some place with WiFi? What were you thinking? Gone all day without any word of where you've been?"

Tim shrugged. "I really didn't think you'd care."

Wendy slowly dropped the pointed finger, blowing a strand of her light brown hair out of her face. "They sent Nathan home from kindergarten with a stomachache that miraculously healed as soon as he walked in the door, so he and Jeremy have been bouncing off the walls together here, driving me crazy." Her tension returned, along with her accusatory tone. "I hope you at least have a good excuse why you're home so late."

Tim grinned. "I found a job."

Wendy's face lit up, and she relaxed against the doorframe. "Oh, thank God."

"Yeah, but we still have to be tight with the money. No expensive lunches at the country club for a while."

"As long as we pay the dues in the fall." Wendy wagged a finger in his face. "You know how hard it was to get in there. We can't lose those connections. What future will the boys have?"

His stomach tightened as he said what he had practiced. "This job doesn't pay as well as my last one. It's an entry level position, but in time I'll move up and bring in the big bucks."

Distracted, she didn't react. "Oh, honey, you got something on your shirt." She touched a small grease stain and clicked her tongue.

"Must be from the bus." He shrugged, his heart pounding.

"Well, I hope you got it on the way home. First impressions are everything."

Tim's tongue weighed heavy in his mouth. His brain hummed, out of excuses.

She didn't seem to notice, making a "hurry up" gesture with her hand. "Come on, take it off. I'll get it out." Her brow furrowed. "Where's your undershirt?"

"Forgot to put one on, I guess." Tim swallowed.

"I could have sworn I saw you wearing one when you were shaving this morning."

His pulse quickened. "Nope, must have been yesterday."

She examined the stain and wrinkled her nose. "Those buses are so dirty. I can't wait for you to have a car again. I told everyone we're on a new, green kick when they noticed we only had one vehicle." She sighed and reached for the door handle. "Well, let me see about this stain. There's a casserole in the oven, if you're hungry. I burned the broccoli, but I could make you a salad."

"Thanks, I'm starving."

It was a close call. He'd have to remember his story and bring extra undershirts next time. It would only be for a little while, until he found something in his field, something better, something less demeaning. He grimaced as he walked into the kitchen and took the *taco* casserole out of the oven. "I can't get away from those Mexicans."

"What was that?" Wendy called from the laundry room.

"I said I can't wait to eat some Mexican food," he called back.

"Yeah, the boys loved it." She emerged from the laundry room, tossing him a clean t-shirt, and sat at the kitchen table, ignoring Nathan and Jeremy, who ran circles around her.

"Hey, hey, hey," he said, grabbing a son under each arm and carrying them down the hall.

"Put me down," Nathan squealed between laughs.

Four-year-old Jeremy wriggled, trying to tickle Tim.

He dropped them onto their beds. "What's this I hear about you giving your mom a hard time today?"

They hid their faces in their pillows and giggled.

"How come you're not in bed yet?" He checked the clock. Nine fifteen already. Almost two hours for his commute. He'd have to leave the house at five in the morning to arrive on time tomorrow.

"We were waiting for you, Dad." Nathan's little lip stuck out in a pout.

"And I'm not sweepy." Jeremy rubbed his eyes.

"Oh, you're not?" Tim tucked them into their beds. "How about a quick story?"

"Yay," they yelled and clapped.

"Tell us the one about the evil boss," Nathan requested.

"No, tell us about the cubicle fairy."

"How about a new story?" Tim asked, opening his eyes wide.

They nodded with excitement.

"This is the story of Joe the Mechanic, who worked on magical cars in a shop high up in the clouds . . ."

Juanita's lips were split from desert sun and dry air. She touched her tongue to her lips and gasped from the pain. She had never experienced heat like this. It was unbearable.

She fixed her eyes on the scorching sands. The coyote's repeated glances at her sent chills down her spine. The stories were true. She could tell. It was the same greedy way her soon-to-be husband had looked at her on her fifteenth birthday as he paid her father, claiming he would "take care" of Juanita as his wife. Shielding her daughter's eyes from the afternoon sunlight, Juanita shifted Linda on her hip. The tension rose with every arduous step. It was only a matter of time before something happened.

With every extra day, more of their group gave up hope. Her only prayer was to make it to El Paso before anything horrible came to pass. Out of the original eleven, only seven were left: Linda and Juanita, the coyote, two men, and one couple whose baby had died that morning. The woman had cried out when she woke to find the infant cold in her arms. She hadn't wanted to leave him, so she continued to carry her son in her arms, wrapped in his blanket.

"Allí está,"[12] *cried the coyote.*

In the distance, she could see one tree and a small building. Juanita's heart swelled, and she cried tearlessly. The Lord had responded. They were going to be all right. She kissed Linda, who smiled weakly at her.

"Ya llegamos, mija. Somos libres. Ya empezamos nuestra vida nueva."[13] She picked up her pace, summoning her last ounce of strength.

"Oye,[14] *Reynaldo,"* the coyote called when they reached the house.

A dirty, mustached man with bloodshot eyes stumbled out of the small house with a bucket of water and a ladle. The coyote took a drink and passed the ladle to the couple. *"Despacio. Para que no se enfermen."*[15]

The coyote shook Reynaldo's hand, and they spoke in a language Juanita didn't understand. Reynaldo glanced at her, his eyes slits. His upper lip curled.

Juanita looked away, her heart pounding like a deep drum. She grabbed hold of the ladle and let Linda drink a little water. She drank a few sips herself before filling her container with a shaky hand.

Reynaldo and the coyote went inside and came out with bread and meat. They called it a "sandwich." Juanita had never eaten anything like it before, but after a week of old beans, it tasted like manna from Heaven.

The coyote motioned the group inside after they had eaten their fill, pointing out the mats on the floor where they could sleep. The main room had a table, two chairs, a few dirty plates, and several empty bottles of tequila.

The sun had fallen below the horizon, and darkness settled in. Sitting on her mat with Linda tight in her arms, Juanita could feel the men staring at her, though she no

---

[12] There it is.

[13] We're here, my daughter. We are free. We can now start our new life.

[14] Hey

[15] Slow. So you don't get sick.

longer met their gazes. She forced herself to stay awake. Tomorrow they would drive into El Paso, where Juanita's cousin lived. They would be safe.

She didn't realize she had fallen asleep until he was on top of her. The smell of tequila and body odor washed over her. A dirty hand muffled her scream. Feeling around desperately for Linda, she realized her daughter's small body was no longer at her side. Her heart thundered in her chest, and she attempted to escape, knowing she couldn't. She needed to find Linda. What had they done with her? The other man grabbed her flailing arms and kneeled on them. Unable to move, her blurry, tear-filled eyes searched wildly for her daughter. A beam of moonlight shot through the dusty window, landing on one of the chairs at the kitchen table where Linda lay, fast asleep.

She pleaded for help through mumbled screams to the couple behind her, but no one moved. The woman held her dead baby tighter to her chest and stared into the darkness of the night. Juanita's body trembled, fear pulsing through her. Unable to bear reality any longer, she gathered her last bit of strength to focus her mind elsewhere, a technique she'd learned through countless nights when her husband had forced himself on her. She escaped in the only way she could. Closing her eyes, she imagined flying through the air with Linda, away from the pain.

Linda quietly closed the front door. The television lit up the dark house. Her mother, on the couch, groaned and tossed in her sleep.

"Mamá?" Linda touched her mother's shoulder.

"¡*Déjenme!*"[16] Mamá screamed and smacked her hand away.

---

[16] Leave me alone.

Linda stepped back as her mother's eyes snapped open.

Mamá blinked, gasped, and sat up, her whole body trembling. "*Ay*, Linda. *Perdóname.*"[17]

Linda knelt down and wiped her mother's brow with the sleeve of her jacket. "*¿Está bien?*"[18]

"*Sí, sí, mija.* Was only a bad dream."

"Do you want to talk about it?" Linda's heartbeat pulsed in her throat.

"*No, estoy bien ahora.*"[19] Mamá smiled and cupped Linda's face in her hands. "Such a good girl." She kissed her daughter's cheek, standing up on shaky legs. Wrapping herself in a blanket, she walked back to her room.

Linda turned off the TV, sat on the couch in the dark, and cried.

---

[17] Forgive me.

[18] Are you okay?

[19] No, I'm okay now.

CHAPTER FOUR
El Rey[1]

*T*im's wife stood in the boys' bedroom doorway, a pleasant look on her face, devoid of any anger. That was something he hadn't seen for a while. Careful not to make any noise, he rose from his chair between the sleeping boys' beds. Tiptoeing from the room, he closed the door and followed Wendy into the kitchen.

After placing a plate of steaming casserole on the table, she dropped into one of their upcycled, painted wooden chairs—purchased from a hipster boutique downtown—and leaned her chin in her hands. "Tell me about your new job."

He hesitated, focusing on his food. "Not much to tell so far. Mostly paperwork today."

"What will you be doing? The same as your last job?"

"No, it's more menial labor. Checking things, fixing people's mistakes, maybe ordering supplies."

"Oh." She shrugged. "I hope there's room for

---

1 The King – a song by Vicente Fernández

upward movement into management. What's your salary?"

He blew on his forkful of casserole. "Actually, I'm getting paid per job, similar to contractual work, so it depends on how fast I am. I'm going to put in some twelve-hour days for a while. The last person left without giving notice, so work's been piling up. I'll play catch-up and try to make a decent paycheck."

Her left eyebrow spiked. "That's different. What company is it?"

He stuffed his mouth full of food and held up his finger.

"I'm sorry. I'll let you eat."

"Sorry, babe. We can talk more tomorrow." He took another bite. "I'm beat."

"Me too. " She leaned against him as he finished his dinner. "You smell different." She sniffed. "Citrusy."

He tensed. Stupid, gritty soap. "I ate an orange with lunch. Guess it was juicier than I thought."

"I can't keep my eyes open any longer." Wendy yawned and stood up, her hand brushing gently against his.

The hairs on the back of his neck stood up. He had forgotten the electricity of her touch. It made him forget her earlier harshness and gave him hope that things were headed in a better direction.

Linda sighed and rolled over in bed. A stream of sunlight shone through the window. She stretched, feeling relaxed and well-rested. Too well-rested.

Her eyes shot open. "Oh, no." She sat up straight in her bed. The clock read eight fifteen. "Oh, no."

She hopped out of bed and tripped over a pair of

heels. Sliding out of her sweatpants, she jumped into some skinny jeans, struggling to clasp the top button. "*Sopes* . . ." She grunted in exasperation. She finished dressing in record time, grabbed her backpack, and ran down the hall, almost colliding with her mother.

"*Ay, mija, me espantaste.*[2] *¿Qué pasó?*"

"Late for school."

"*Come algo.*"[3]

"I don't have time."

"*Aquí, un panecito.*"[4]

She kissed her mother on the cheek and took the bread. "*Gracias,* Mamá. See you tonight."

"*¿A qué hora?*"[5]

"Not sure. Probably late. I told Doña Hernandez I'd help out at the *panadería* tonight."

Mamá waved her out the door.

Linda ran down the steps and turned onto the sidewalk towards the bus stop, jogging past one of her least favorite people—a boy a few years younger than her named Hector—in a wife-beater and flat-bill sitting on his bicycle.

"Late for school again, Lindita?" he taunted.

"Shut up, Hector, or I'll tell your mom you're skipping school again."

He laughed, pedaling behind her. "She don't care. Says I'm a lost cause. Gave up on me years ago. Besides I'm eighteen now. I'm a man."

Hector was as much a man as she was punctual. "Guess you better get a job. Support your family."

"I got a job."

Linda shook her head. "A real job. Not selling your ADHD meds to kids at school."

---

[2] You scared me.

[3] Eat something.

[4] Here, one little bread.

[5] What time?

"That's good money."

"It's wrong, Hector. People die from that stuff." She paused to catch her breath, leaning on the bus stop pole. She squinted up the road. "Did you see the 81 pass yet?"

"Yeah, like five minutes ago."

She kicked the post. "Shoot."

"Chill, girl. I'll give you ride. Hop on my pegs." Hector flashed a grin, revealing a silver tooth on the top right.

Linda smirked at the bike and crossed her arms. "No way am I getting on that thing, especially not with you."

Hector leaned back and frowned. "What is your issue?"

"My issue?" Linda asked, exasperated. He could get under her skin like no one else. "My issue? I'm pretty sure you know what my issue is."

Hector chuckled. "You can't still be mad about that. It was like four years ago."

The heat of anger rose to her face. "You almost got me deported."

"That was a simple misunderstanding."

"Misunderstanding?" Linda put her hands on her hips. "You straight up told that officer I didn't have any papers."

A smirk played on Hector's lips. Linda fought the urge to smack it off his face. "I wouldn't have had to say anything if you'd just agreed to be my date for the eighth grade dance."

"I was a junior in high school."

"So? I was mature for my age." He straightened, brushing off his shoulder with a cocky grin.

Linda rolled her eyes. "You were lucky he wasn't a 'good ole boy' like some of the cops around here. They arrest first and ask questions later."

Hector shrugged. "Whatever. Nothing happened. You should just get over it."

"You know, Hector?" Years of frustration bubbled to the surface. "This is exactly why I never want to talk with you. You never take anything seriously. You don't take school seriously. You don't take work seriously. All you do is mess around and have fun. You were born here. You could get a good job, something that pays well. But no, you're just another selfish kid who doesn't appreciate the privileges you were born with. Like you said, you're an adult now. Wake up and get serious about something."

Hector's brow furrowed. "I am serious." He wiggled his eyebrows. "About you."

She groaned in disgust. "Just leave me alone."

"Your loss, *fresa*."[6] He pedaled away, shouting back, "Good luck getting to class on time."

A bus approached. The number 81 shone on its front. She clenched her jaw. "Such a little liar." She raised her hand and walked to the curb. In another forty-five minutes, she'd be on campus.

Juanita finished her cup of Nescafé and a *pan dulce*.[7] After the dream last night, she couldn't go back to sleep and decided to go in to work that morning from three to eight. They were behind on the clothing order anyway; the boss didn't care how long it took them and how many hours they worked, as long as they finished the order on time. A handful of others had been there at three o'clock but most people, including her friends Diana and María, had shown up

---

[6] Literally means strawberry – another word for snob
[7] Pastry

closer to five. Feeling her energy draining, she had headed home for a short break but needed to get back now.

She sighed and pushed herself up from the chair. "*A trabajar*,"[8] she said aloud as she walked back out the door.

Her joints complained at the morning air. She gathered her long, black hair, still wet from her shower, into a bun, rather than her preferred *trenza*.[9] It would give her a headache, but it was easier to sew with it up. It got hot in that little room, all those machines and bodies moving. It wasn't too bad now, but in the heat of summer, it'd be torture.

Turning the corner, her heart stopped. Police were parked outside the shop, lights flashing. María, Diana, and the rest of her coworkers stepped outside, hands cuffed behind their backs, with the *oficiales*[10] prodding them like cattle towards a group of police vans. Before an officer pushed her into the vehicle, María glanced at Juanita, her eyes wide, giving the slightest nod. It was their sign. Get away while she still had the chance. Juanita's legs shook as she turned and hurried back home, each step feeling like a thousand.

She knew what she had to do. They had already talked about it. She would drop by Diana's house and María's apartment to let their families know what happened. Her friends would most likely be deported. Virginia wasn't light on *ilegales*.[11]

Why now? She shook her head. They were in the middle of a big order. It couldn't have been the boss. He made way too much money off of them. It was

---

[8] Off to work.
[9] Braid
[10] Officers
[11] Illegals

probably one of the *gringas*[12] down the street. They'd be sorry when their fancy designer dresses cost twice as much.

Juanita knew there were a few of those women on the block. Hate oozed from their eyes when they looked at her, thinking they were better, staring at her like she was an animal or a monster. They never stopped to think about the separated families before they called *la migra*.[13] They only thought of themselves.

The crazy thing was Juanita and other "illegals" made the clothes they bought, harvested the fruits and vegetables on their tables, mowed their lawns, cleaned their hotel rooms, tended their children, and cooked food or washed dishes at their favorite restaurants. Without papers their bosses could pay whatever they wanted, usually below minimum wage. Who could they complain to? They didn't have to give breaks or pay for any work injuries. That's why things were so much cheaper. More hours plus less pay equaled a lower price and a happy customer.

People only saw what they wanted to see. Still, it bothered Juanita that people viewed her as a criminal. She hadn't had the choice to do things the "right" way, the "legal" way. She'd never attended school, and her husband had isolated her from any support or resources. Even if she'd had money for the paperwork and someone to help her fill it out, there wouldn't have been time. He would have killed her with a few more beatings. Escaping with Linda and crossing the border was a miracle in itself.

Juanita lowered her head in prayer for her two friends, unsure what situations they would return to

---

[12] Derogatory term for Americans
[13] Immigration

if they were deported, and then knocked on María's door. A small face appeared in the window, followed by a wrinkled one. María's grandmother smiled as she opened the door, but it quickly faded as her eyes lighted on Juanita's somber look.

"*¿Qué pasó?*" Doña Vasquez asked, ushering her into the apartment.

"*La migra.*"

She gasped. "*¿En dónde?*"[14]

"*En el trabajo.*"[15]

"*Y ¿cómo te escapaste?*"[16]

"*Fui para un café allí en mi casa, y cuando regresé, hubo mucha policía. Las sacaron a María y a Diana y a los demás a esposas.*"[17]

"*Ay, Dios mío.*" Her hands shook as she sat in a kitchen chair.

"What happened, *Abuelita*?"[18] María's daughter, Luz, asked in a small voice.

Doña Vasquez shook her head. Luz had entered preschool this year and knew more English than Spanish now. Doña Vasquez nodded towards Juanita.

Juanita squatted to Luz's height and held the small child's hands in her own, trying to explain in her broken English what she had just told Luz's grandmother. "The police come to our job today."

"Why? Was there someone bad inside?"

"No, *amor*,[19] sometime the police come even when you don't do nothing. Sometime people get in trouble 'cause they don't have no papers."

---

[14] Where?

[15] At work.

[16] How did you escape?

[17] I left to get a coffee over at my house, and when I got back, there were a lot of police. They took out María and Diana and the others in handcuffs.

[18] Grandma

[19] Love

Luz tilted her head to the side. "Like for coloring?"

Ay, to be a child again. "No, like a work visa."

"Did somebody get in trouble?" Luz asked, tears forming in her eyes. "Where's Mamá?"

"She got in trouble for work without visa."

Luz's lower lip trembled. "Abuelita? *¿Donde está Mamá?*"[20] Her wide eyes studied her grandmother who held a tissue to her mouth.

"*La migra la llevó.*"[21]

"No," Luz cried. "Why?"

"*Por unos pocos papeles, mijita.*[22] *Por unos pocos papeles.*"

Before the sun even neared the horizon, Tim kissed his sleeping wife and children goodbye. He carried old clothes in his briefcase, figuring he'd leave them at work each day and wear his suit to and from the shop. The brisk walk through the neighborhood woke him up, and he got on the bus. It was almost empty except for the bus driver and a Mexican woman dressed in a maid's uniform.

He shook his head. Couldn't even escape them on the bus. They were taking over the country, one clean toilet at a time. He snickered. He'd have to remember that one when he got an office job again. They'd appreciate his humor. He missed those times around the water cooler or the coffee machine, cracking jokes, trading the latest news, and going over game scores.

---

[20] Where is Mama?

[21] Immigration took her.

[22] Because of a few little papers, my little one.

With the loss of his job went all his friends, all his security, and all his bonds. The pension had been the next to go. He'd tapped into it after unemployment had run out and had dropped it into their checking account to pay for the mortgage they could no longer afford. Three months ago, he'd had to return his BMW to the dealer, unable to make the payments. It had only been two years old, but they'd had to make choices. Wendy had to stop going to the spa for her monthly facial, Nathan had to discontinue violin lessons, Jeremy had to give up that preppy pre-school that cost thousands of dollars. He wondered what they'd have to give up next.

More people got onto the bus. The closer to downtown they got, the more crowded it became. When he transferred at the downtown hub, blue-collar workers dressed in their uniforms and dirty clothes, talking in a myriad of different languages and accents, surrounded him. They smelled like cigarettes, cheap cologne, and fried foods.

He knew he was better than them. He'd graduated in the top ten percent of his class, interning on Wall Street one summer during college. Sure, his father had been a simple man, working construction until his abrupt death during Tim's junior year of high school, an early end to his sad life. Tim's mother had drilled it into him; he needed to be better than that.

"Don't be like your father," she'd said, time and again, pointing to his picture on the wall after he'd passed. "Leaving your family without anything to shake a stick at after you're gone." She'd cupped her hands on either side of Tim's face. "You're smart. Finish college, get a management job and a pretty wife, and move to the suburbs."

It was hard, but he had done it. Reminders of his failures flew around him like angry wasps. He had almost lost it all. Straightening, he shook off his dark thoughts. He'd find a real job soon. No nickel and dime stuff. Forty dollars for half a day's work. Who was he kidding? Still, it was better than nothing.

Tim pulled the string when his stop neared, pressed himself through the thick crowd, and lost his balance as the bus ground to a halt. He muttered an apology as he crashed into a black kid with a backpack. He excused himself and hopped onto the sidewalk, swearing under his breath. When his stomach growled, he realized he'd forgotten to eat breakfast or pack his lunch.

"Idiot," he berated himself as he stepped into a bakery. "This'll cost me a quarter of my earnings today." He bought a couple of bagels with cream cheese and a strong black coffee. That should hold him the rest of the day. He made a mental note to bring some sandwiches tomorrow.

He shook off his jacket and ate a bagel as he huffed down the sidewalk under the streetlamps. Half an hour later, he knocked on the metal garage door.

"¿Quién es?"[23] a gruff voice called.

Tim stepped back at the incomprehensible words. "It's Tim Draker." After there was no response, he called louder through his clenched jaw, "Your new mechanic." Shouting like an idiot in the middle of the barrio. If Wendy could see him now.

"Oh, right, the *tortuga*."[24]

The light above him flickered on, and the garage door motor kicked into action. The man passed him a key through the steel bars of the roll-down security gate. "I didn't think you'd be back."

Tim unlocked the padlock and lifted the gate.

---

[23] Who is it?
[24] Turtle

The man clicked it open at the top with a broom handle. "It's heavier than it looks."

"You can say that again," Tim said, handing him the key.

"It's heavier than it looks." The man laughed.

"What are we working on today—" Tim paused, realizing he didn't know his boss' name.

"Guillermo," the man said, shaking Tim's hand.

"Gee-er-mow?" Tim raised an eyebrow.

"Close enough. But you can call me *jefe*."[25]

Tim squinted. "What's that mean?"

"Boss." He laughed again.

"All right, *jefe*," Tim said, unsmiling, feeling he had sunk to a new low. "What are we doing today?"

"Well, Tortuga—"

Tim cocked his head. "What'd you call me?"

"*Tortuga*. It means 'turtle.' Get it? 'Cause you was so slow yesterday. I told all my amigos about it. Three hours for an oil change."

"Yeah, yeah, real funny." Tim shook his head and scowled. "Besides, it was only an hour and a half. Let's get to work."

"Yeah, we better start soon. Who knows how long it's gonna take you to actually fix something."

Linda power-walked down the long hallway, stopping to catch her breath and shake off her nerves before entering the classroom.

"Ah, Miss Palacios." The professor squinted over his glasses. "How nice of you to join us."

"Sorry, Dr. Lorenze. The bus was running behind." She squeezed through the aisle to her seat.

---

[25] Boss

He raised a peppered eyebrow. "Where were we?" he asked the rest of the class.

"Exchange rates," Kevin answered. He turned around and winked at Linda.

She blushed and mouthed "Thank you."

An hour later Linda's mind swam with numbers and equations.

"Whoever put this class at nine in the morning should be taken out and shot," Kevin said as he stuffed his bag with books.

Linda sighed. "I don't know. I think it's kind of fun. I know it's dorky, but I love this type of math. Everything has an answer."

Kevin draped his arm over her shoulder and walked her out the door. The pleasant, spicy scent of his cologne circled around her. "That's why I like you, Palacios. Ever the optimist." He squeezed her shoulder before dropping his arm.

Linda suppressed a giggle. She'd never been this close to a boy before. It'd been a while since someone had expressed interest in her, other than Hector who didn't count. The boys in high school had given up when they'd discovered she wouldn't put out. In college she was all work and no play most of the time, except for her activities with the Cultural Club. Commuting definitely hindered one's social life.

"Where are you headed now?" she squeaked out. Why did he make her so nervous?

"Lunch. Wanna come? I'll buy." His blue eyes glowed in the bright morning light flooding through the hallway windows.

Did that make it a date? "Okay. But only for a little bit. I still need to do some work. I have two tests and a paper due this week."

Kevin shook his head. "Man, that sucks. No wonder you didn't want to hang out last night."

"Yeah, sorry about that."

"Hey, no worries. *No te preocupes.*" He handed her a cafeteria tray. "Madam," he said in a deep, English accent.

Linda grabbed the tray. "You're so weird."

"You know you like it."

She bit back a grin, her entire face flushing.

Tim tried not to get any black dust in his mouth as he ate his second bagel. They'd worked nonstop since he'd arrived and had already fixed two sets of brakes and a clutch before lunch. Tim looked at the clock. Twelve thirty. The line of unfixed cars parked along the sidewalk stared him down. It was going to be a long day.

He downed the rest of his cold coffee, plodded up the rickety stairs to the office, and knocked.

"*Entre.*"[26]

Tim waited for a second, unsure if that meant to come in or wait.

"That means 'come in.'"

He walked into the small office, peering down into the garage through its big window. "What's next— " He paused before drawling out, "—*jefe?*"

"I called some people to pick up their cars, so that should help the parking situation. There's about ten more cars out there, and I got a call about fixing an air conditioner on a van. We gonna make some good *dinero* this week."

"I guess you stay pretty busy."

"Depends on the week. Sometimes we were so slow Javier would say he was gonna go out and rip

_____

[26] Enter.

out some parts from people's cars just so we have more jobs." He chuckled. "Man, I miss that guy. But he was pretty *loco*,[27] and I think he scared away some customers. Maybe business will pick up a little now that he's gone."

"You want me to get started on something?"

"No, man, take a break. You're working faster, Tortuga. I might change your name to Conejo."

Tim sat, the chair creaking ominously, and crossed his arms. "What does that mean?"

"Rabbit."

Tim smirked. "Yeah, I'm getting the hang of working on cars again."

A bell dinged, and Guillermo stood. "Okay, break over. We got a customer. I see what they want, and you bring in the red Dodge." He tossed a key to Tim.

The key jangled against its chain as he caught it. Guillermo nodded down to the Mexican in grass-covered jeans and a dirty t-shirt, shouting something in Spanish in a friendly tone. As Tim got into the red Dodge, he eyed the man's truck, parked across the street. The Dodge sputtered to a start, and he inched it from the tiny spot without hitting another car and parked it in the shop.

Guillermo shook the man's hand and clapped him on the back as he exited the garage. He swung the truck's keychain on his finger. "We gotta get that truck done today."

"What's it need?"

"He don't know, maybe a wire loose or something. But let's start with this Dodge." He tapped the hood.

"Let me guess. Spark plugs?"

Guillermo nodded. "Sounds like it. But this guy just wants his radio fixed."

---

[27] Crazy

"Yeah, probably so he doesn't have to hear his engine sputtering."

Snorting, he snapped his finger and pointed at Tim. "I'll call him and see if he wants us to fix that. You're making me money already, Conejo."

A small smile crept onto Tim's lips. Rabbit was better than turtle. It could be worse. He could be sitting in another office with twenty other suits applying for the same position. At least he was making money. But how much? He shook the thought from his head. Anything was better than nothing. Despite the menial tasks, he was enjoying getting his hands dirty. Things buried for almost two decades crawled back to him as the day rolled on.

He opened the panel beneath the glove compartment. Thumbing through the manual, he identified the fuse controlling the radio. He detached the blown fuse. Matching it to a new one, he inserted it and started the car. Loud Mexican rap music blared through the radio. He turned it down, flipped through the stations, and clicked the radio on and off.

Guillermo opened the passenger door. "I guess you got it working."

"Yeah, it was the fuse."

"Jorge loves his music."

"I didn't know there was Mexican rap."

"That wasn't Mexican. That was reggaeton. It's Puerto Rican. You know, like Daddy Yankee."

Tim shrugged.

"You got a lot to learn, Conejo."

Juanita put down the phone at Diana's house. Church members would gather for a prayer vigil at María's apartment that night. Pastor Luis would lead the service, and Juanita and a few *hermanas*[28] would prepare a meal. The clock on the wall ticked. She had six hours, enough time for *tamales*.[29]

She peered into the living room. Hector sat on the couch. Normally so tough, today he looked small in his oversized jersey. She approached and sat down next to him. "Hector, *¿estás bien?*"[30]

He clenched his jaw. "How can I be okay? They're going to deport my mom."

"We don' know yet. Maybe *el juez*[31] decide to let her go."

"Maybe."

Juanita wiped a tear from Hector's cheek, and soon her shirt muffled his sobs. "*No te desesperes, Hector. Dios sabe todo lo que hace.* God has a plan, *aunque no lo vemos.*"[32]

Hector sniffed and pulled back. Juanita handed him a tissue. "*Gracias*, Doña Palacios."

"*Ven.*"[33] She pulled his arm. "You helps me make the *tamales*."

Too nervous to eat, Linda rearranged pieces of lettuce with her fork. Her stomach grumbled.

Kevin munched his burger and fries. "You want one?" he asked, pushing his plate closer.

"No, thanks."

"Help yourself. They're *delicioso*."

---

[28] Sisters – as in church family

[29] Seasoned corn dough stuffed with meat and salsa and steamed in corn husks

[30] Are you okay?

[31] The judge

[32] Don't lose hope, Hector. God knows everything He is doing . . . even though we don't see it.

[33] Come

"*Gracias.*" She dipped a fry in ketchup, her hand trembling. She needed to calm down. It wasn't a date, just one friend buying lunch for another friend. Just an attractive friend who was well-spoken and generous and who had the most amazing eyes that she had never noticed before. She slowly released a breath and took a bite of her salad.

"You want that tomato?" he asked.

"No, you can have it."

"Thanks." He popped it into his mouth.

They sat in silence for a few moments, with nothing but the sound of chewing interrupting the void.

Not wanting lunch to flop, Linda blurted, "I was really moved by your Native American presentation last semester."

"Really?" He ran his hand across the back of his neck.

"Yeah, are you part Native American?" Linda asked.

"Nah, I'm pretty much as white as they come. Mostly Dutch and English," Kevin said. "My paternal grandfather said we had some Cherokee in us, but it turned out he liked to make stuff up."

Linda chuckled.

The silence threatened to overwhelm them again. This time Kevin stepped in. "You really liked my presentation? I was afraid no one did. One teacher told me it was my 'soapbox.'"

"No, it was great. I learned a lot of new information. I never knew about the smallpox blankets. That was messed up."

"The early settlers wiped out entire tribes of Native Americans, their culture and languages lost forever. I mean, here in Roanoke, which comes from the Algonquin word for 'money' by the way, loads of indigenous people lived here before the Europeans showed up. Those First Americans spoke Siouan, Tutelo, and Catawban, but there are no native speakers left."

"Really?" asked Linda. "I thought people spoke dialects on reservations."

"A lot of the tribes were pushed together and only certain languages survived. Back in Connecticut, it's the same thing. Connecticut is a butchered version of another Algonquin word for 'long river,' and the Pequot, Mohegan, and Paugusset lived there before the Dutch settlers arrived. Hardly any tribes are left."

"That's so sad." Linda always had a soft spot for the disenfranchised. Being marginalized herself, she knew how alienating, and ultimately dangerous, it could be.

"You know, that's something I've always admired about Mexico." Kevin's eyes shone bluer as he looked into hers. "They've preserved their indigenous culture. Tribes live where they have for hundreds of years and carry on the same traditions, speaking indigenous languages like Mixteco and Otomí. There's something like fourteen million indigenous people in Mexico, speaking sixty to seventy different languages. It's amazing."

"Wow." Linda was impressed. "You know more about my culture than I do."

Kevin laughed. "Like I said, it's my soapbox."

"All I know is that most Mexicans don't treat indigenous people very well. My friend Celia from high school was from Hidalgo and knew Otomí, but it embarrassed her when her family spoke it. I thought it was cool, because I couldn't understand anything they said until they threw in a word in *español*[34] like

---

[34] Spanish

"television," which didn't exist in native Otomí. People made fun of her in Mexico for being an *indita*,[35] and she didn't want anything to do with that culture. In Mexico, it's really common to get teased for things that make you different. Everyone gets a nickname: *gorda, tonto, negrito*,[36] etc. Instead of celebrating diversity in the media, like we do here, they have programs like "El Gordo y La Flaca."[37]

"What was your nickname?" Kevin asked, leaning forward a little.

"This one kid calls me *fresa*."

"Strawberry?"

Linda chuckled. "Well, yes, but in this instance it describes someone who thinks they are better than everyone else. Like a snob, I guess."

"I don't see that. You seem pretty down-to-earth." He shoved aside his plate, folded his arms on the table, and studied her, his blue gaze unnerving her. "In fact, you don't even need a nickname. *Linda*[38] is a perfect description."

Heat rose to her cheeks, and her heartbeat set a new world record. She returned her attention to the floppy lettuce on her plate. She reminded herself how his conservative Connecticut family would react to a poor, undocumented Mexican girlfriend. Sanity returned.

Kevin finished his last fry. "What are we doing for our meeting this Friday?"

Linda shrugged. "I haven't decided. Actually, I haven't even gotten a chance to think about it."

"I have an idea."

---

[35] Little Indian – disrespectful term used in a derogatory fashion
[36] Fatty, dummy, little black one
[37] The Fat Guy and the Skinny Girl – a popular Mexican talk show
[38] Pretty, kind

"*Dime.*"[39]

"Dinner and a movie."

"Okay . . ."

"The theater downtown is showing foreign films all April, starting this weekend. Maybe we can catch one of those and then eat at some ethnic restaurant."

"That sounds fun," Linda said, enthusiasm crossing her face, ready to enjoy herself after a grueling week of studying. "There are so many good places to eat, and I haven't been to any."

"We'll have to work on that." He flashed his straight teeth.

A laugh escaped her before she could cover it. "You have lettuce or something." She motioned to his mouth.

His ears turned red. He ran his tongue over his teeth. "Better?"

"No. It's still there."

"Sorry." Red splotches formed on his neck.

"I think you got it."

"Thanks." He carefully ran a napkin over his mouth.

Linda's stomach dropped. He'd never want to eat with her again. Shrugging carelessly, she said, "The other day I had blueberries with breakfast, and no one told me I had a piece stuck in my teeth. It was three hours before I looked in the mirror. So embarrassing."

"Yeah, I guess that'd be worse." He chuckled, checking the time on his phone. "Well, gotta get to class. It's almost one."

"Ooh, me, too. I didn't realize it was so late. My next class is across campus." She grabbed her bag and tray and followed Kevin towards the door.

---

[39] Tell me.

"I can give you a ride on my bike if you want."

Linda laughed. "You know, you're the second guy to offer me a bike ride today."

He grimaced. "I didn't know I had competition. How do I compare?"

Her mouth stayed open mid-laugh. Competition? Linda's heart fluttered. Maybe he did like her. "I wouldn't worry. He's been after me since we were little."

"Gosh, I hope I don't have to wait that long." He smiled and squeezed her shoulder. "I'll see you later."

She waved and rushed down the stairs, feeling as if she could fly.

Juanita stuffed Hector's shopping basket with cornhusks, chicken, tomatillos, chiles, a few onions, and two bags of Maseca. "*Con eso.*"[40]

Hector lifted the basket onto the counter.

Norma Hernandez, owner of the *panadería* and one of Juanita's good friends, pushed the buttons on the register. "*Veinte con diez.*"[41]

"*Gracias, Norma. ¿Vas a ir a la vigilia en la casa de María?*"[42]

"*Sí, Juanita. ¿Llevo algo?*"[43]

"*Unos panes, si puedes.*"[44]

Norma nodded. Juanita counted on the Hernandez family to bring some *pan dulce* to church events.

Half an hour later, the chicken was boiling, and the cornhusks were soaking. After she washed the

---

[40] That's everything.

[41] $20.10

[42] Are you going to the vigil tonight at María's house?

[43] Should I bring anything?

[44] Some breads, if you can.

tomatillos for the salsa, Juanita showed Hector how to mix the *masa*.[45] Hector removed his large football jersey, draping it over a kitchen chair. After adjusting his tank top, he continued mixing.

"Here." Juanita tossed him an apron.

He rolled his eyes. "This is for girls."

Juanita shrugged. "*Pues, que te ensucies entonces.*"[46] Returning to the salsa, she smirked as he tied the apron around his thin waist. Hector was a good kid, but lately he'd caused his mother all sorts of problems. Every week Diana came to the factory with a different story. Last week he'd gotten expelled for selling his medicine to other students. Day and night Juanita prayed that her best friend's son would find the right path. Prayer was the only thing that kept the nightmares at bay, so she spent hours a day praying for all her friends, her family, and the world.

She dropped the tomatillos and chiles into a pot and turned on the burner. In a couple more hours, they'd sit the *tamales* in the *vaporera*[47] to steam until they were ready. It was a long process, but the results were always good. Looking over at Hector, Juanita thought maybe it would be a long process for him to be ready, too.

Linda caught the bus back to her neighborhood after her last class of the day. During the ride, she finished her economics homework and reviewed ideas for the paper for her literature class. None really stood out to her. Maybe she'd ask Don Hernandez. He knew

---

[45] Dough

[46] Well, get dirty then.

[47] Steamer

about all that political stuff. All she could think about was her lunch with Kevin.

A blue-green building caught her eye, and she realized she had passed her street. Pulling the string, she jumped out of her seat. Soon she was on the sidewalk, moving in the opposite direction towards the *panadería*. The wind whipped her cheeks as she rushed up the block.

The door dinged as Linda entered. "*Aquí estoy*,"[48] she called.

Don Hernandez peeked his head out from the back. A spot of flour decorated his cheek. "I thought you would be helping your mother tonight."

"For what?" she asked.

"*La vigilia*."

"*¿Cuál vigilia?*"[49] Her stomach dropped.

He pointed towards the door.

Linda walked back outside and read the sign in Spanish saying they'd be closing early for a prayer vigil for María and Diana that night.

"*¿Qué pasó?*"

"*La migra pasó al trabajo*."[50]

"*¿Y Mamá?*"

"*Está bien. Estaba en casa cuando pasó.*"[51]

Linda breathed out a sigh of relief. Mamá was okay. Here Linda had been worrying about some guy, and her mother had almost been deported today. Real life flew at her like a hundred-ton jetliner. Exhaustion and worry crashed over her. "Is it okay if I go home?"

"*No hay problema*."[52]

---

[48] I'm here.

[49] What vigil?

[50] Immigration went to their job.

[51] She was at home when they went.

[52] No problem.

"*Gracias*," she called as she raced down the sidewalk to her house. Minutes later, she stepped into the kitchen, inhaling the aroma of fresh *tamales*.

She put her hands on her hips. There stood Hector, in a pink apron. "What are you doing here?"

He frowned and quickly shed the apron. "Helping your mom make *tamales*."

"Why? Didn't you have anything better to do?"

Hector's dark brown curls, cut into a pompadour fade, fell over his eyes devoid of their teasing sparkle.

She hadn't put two and two together, and realization of Hector's pain in the face of his mother's arrest slammed into her. "Oh, Hector. I'm so sorry. I didn't think." She walked over, placing her hand on his shoulder. "Are you okay?"

He nodded, blinking up at the ceiling.

"I don't know what I would've done if it had been Mamá. I can't even imagine what you're feeling."

Hector sniffed, making a valiant effort to hide his emotions. "I had *tamales*, so I'm feeling a little better."

She nodded. "Mamá's *tamales* make anything better. Where is she?"

"Getting ready for the *vigilia*."

"Thanks." She walked into the hall and then popped her head back into the kitchen. "Pink's a good color on you, by the way." She ducked as the apron came flying in her direction.

CHAPTER FIVE
Los Olvidados[1]

*F*ive cars later, Tim was losing steam. He definitely needed something more than bagels tomorrow. His stomach rumbled as he stretched his aching back. He had forgotten what physical labor was like after so many years in that cubicle.

"We still have to fix the truck, and then we're done for today." Guillermo cleaned his hands on a rag. A metallic telephone rang loudly, echoing in the quiet garage. His boss walked to the mustard yellow phone that looked like it was transported straight out of 1970 and picked up the receiver. "*¿Bueno?*"[2] He chatted in Spanish for a few minutes.

Tim rested his tired body against the truck bumper. "Another repair?" he asked as his boss hung up the phone.

"No, my sister. She invited you for dinner."

---

[1] The Forgotten Ones – a Mexican film from 1950

[2] Well? – a common way for people to answer the phone in Spanish. Similar to saying "hello" in English.

Tim wrinkled his brow. "But she doesn't even know me."

"Yeah, that's the point. You eat food, you talk, then she knows you."

"I have to get home to my wife and kids."

"Invite them, too. There will be plenty of food."

Tim's stomach dropped. "Oh, I think they have a thing tonight."

Guillermo tapped Tim's shoulder with his fist. "Perfect. You were gonna eat alone anyway. You need to eat something other than bagels, *hombre*."[3]

Tim's mouth twitched into a smile. "I am pretty hungry."

"All right, then. Let's bring in this truck, finish it, and go eat some *tamales*."

Juanita pulled one of her Sunday dresses over her head and sat on the bed. She asked the Lord the question that had haunted her all day. *God, why them and not me? Please be with María and Diana and their families. They must be so scared. Fill them with peace and understanding, and watch over them so nothing bad happens. Fill those around them with love and kindness, including the judge who will decide their case. Thank you, Lord, for sparing me so that I could stay here with Linda and take care of her. Amen.*

Someone knocked. Juanita wiped her tears and adjusted her dress. "*Entre.*"

"Mamá?" The door creaked open.

"*Ay, mi Lindita. Ven acá.*"[4] She opened her arms, and Linda buried her face in Juanita's chest.

---

[3] Man
[4] Come here.

"When Don Hernandez told me about *la migra*, for a second I thought they had taken you." Her voice quavered. "I'm so glad you're safe."

"*Yo también, corazón.*"[5]

"I don't know what I'd do without you, Mamá." She pulled back and wiped the tears from her eyes with the back of her hand. "*Pobre Hector.*"[6]

"*Estaba llorando cuando fui a visitarlo.*"[7]

"Hector? Crying?" He'd always seemed tough, like he didn't let anything get to him.

"*Sí. Por eso le invité para hacer los tamales. Estaba tan triste.*"[8]

"But he caused so many problems for his mother."

"Maybe is why he feel so sad."

Linda flashed back to their earlier interaction when she'd yelled at him for not being serious enough. He knew how to push her buttons like no one else could, and he enjoyed doing it. Still, imagining him sitting alone and crying at his mom's house tugged at her heartstrings. It must have taken something of this magnitude to break through to him. Glancing at the clock, Linda sighed and stood up. "I'm going to take a shower and get ready."

"*Rapidito, mija. Ya son las cinco.*"[9]

"Okay, Mamá. *No te preocupes.*"

Tim knew he should go straight home, but his stomach told a different story. Another hour and a half without food, and he might pass out. Giving in to

---

[5] Me too, honey.
[6] Poor Hector.
[7] He was crying when I went to visit him.
[8] Yes. That's why I invited him to make tamales. He was so sad.
[9] Hurry up, my daughter. It's five o'clock already.

his hunger, he picked up the phone, which was covered in greasy fingerprints. Wendy answered on the third ring.

"Hi, it's me. Just wanted to let you know that my boss invited me out for dinner, so I'll be home later than I thought."

"Oh, that sounds great. I guess you made a good first impression after all."

"Yeah. Sorry about dinner."

"You said you'd be putting in extra hours, so I figured you'd grab something downtown. I took the boys out for Thai. You know how the kids love that satay sauce."

He frowned. He didn't know. It had been a while since they had done anything as a family. The last year was a blur of applications, follow-up calls, budgeting spreadsheets, and whisper fights with Wendy, with the occasional story time or Netflix movie mixed in.

"Hello?"

Tim dragged his mind back to the present. "Yeah, I'm still here."

"We ran into one of Nathan's friends from school at the Thai restaurant. We're over at their house right now."

"Okay," Tim said, glad he hadn't gone home to an empty house with an emptier stomach.

"Is this your work number?"

Tim tensed. "Uh, no, it's a pay phone. I don't have an office line yet. Not until next week, I think they said."

"A pay phone?" The line was silent for a second. "I didn't know they had those downtown anymore."

"Hipsters," Tim grunted. "It's retro."

"And no one let you use their office phone?" she asked, sounding incredulous.

"Didn't think about calling you until I walked out the door. Oops, gotta go, honey. Someone else is waiting. See you tonight."

Tim hung up before she could pelt any more questions at him and released a sigh. Sweat beaded his brow, more than he had worked up on the job that day. He adjusted his tie and picked up his jacket. It seemed heavier. He reached into a pocket and pulled out a wad of cash.

"You did good work today, Conejo," Guillermo called from the top of the stairs. "Don't get used to *dinero* like that every day, but today we did some good business, *amigo*."

Tim counted. Two hundred and fifty dollars. Maybe this job wasn't so bad after all.

Linda let the hot water pour over her head. The last bubbles of shampoo dripped from her dark locks down to the drain. After she turned off the faucet, she wrung out her hair and stepped onto the bathmat. She wrapped one towel around her head and another around her body. Wiping off the mirror, she studied her reflection.

Mamá always told her she'd gotten her eyes and her father's nose. Her father was a Nahuatl Indian with a long, flat nose and black eyes. That was one of the only things Mamá had ever said about him. Some of Linda's cousins in Texas had mentioned stories they'd overheard, but Linda didn't know if they were accurate. Tío had told her a couple things she hoped weren't true: her father drank too much and liked to fight. Linda tried not to think about it, but every time she glimpsed her nose, she was reminded of whom she'd come from.

Shaking off her thoughts, she tweezed her eyebrows and combed her thick, black hair. She had lifted a leg up on the toilet lid and was rubbing in lotion when the door opened.

She screamed. Hector covered his wide eyes, swore, and closed the door.

Embarrassment-fueled fury pulsed through her. She banged her fist on the door, screeching. "Don't you knock? What is wrong with you?"

"I'm sorry. I didn't know you were still in there," he called from the hall.

He'd probably done that on purpose. The little jerk. At least she'd had the towel on. Imagine if . . . She shuddered as she pulled on her clothes.

Any earlier feelings of sympathy towards him were replaced by memories of years of his relentless harassment. She opened the door and, ignoring his wave of apologies, slapped Hector on the cheek. His mouth dropped open, and he held his hand to his skin.

Linda went straight into the kitchen. "*Mamá. Hector entró sin tocar y me vio casi desnuda.*"[10]

"*Ay, pero, mija. No creo que lo hizo a propósito.*"[11]

"*Fuera,*"[12] Linda yelled at Hector, pointing him out of the room. He stepped back and sat on the couch.

Mamá's soft voice continued. "You be nice, *mija*. Hector is all alone right now."

Linda, hands shaking with rage, released a long, deep breath. She dragged the last bit of patience from the depths of her soul. "I guess I can deal with him for a couple more hours."

"*Bueno, pues . . .*" Mamá hesitated. "*Le dije que se quedara con nosotros por un ratito.*"[13]

---

[10] Hector walked in without knocking and almost saw me naked.

[11] I don't think he did it on purpose.

[12] Out.

[13] Well, so . . . I told him to stay with us for a little while.

Her patience exploded in a cloud of angry disbelief. "What? No way," Linda said in a loud whisper, her hands smacking the air with every word. "I don't want that jerk sleeping in the same house as me."

Mamá didn't flinch. Her face held the same calm amusement it had when Linda used to throw *berinches*[14] in the grocery store. "*Se quedará en la sofa, y ya. Puedes laquear la puerta de tu cuarto, si te hace sentir mejor.*"[15]

It'd been her and Mamá alone for so long. The thought of having another person, especially someone she didn't trust, in the house pulled away her comfortable safety net. "That's not the point. I don't want to lock my door. I want to feel safe in my own house."

"*Ay, mija,*" Mamá pinched her cheeks. "*No te estreses.*[16] You are safe. Hector would not hurt a mosquito."

"It's 'fly,' Mamá. 'Wouldn't hurt a fly.'"

Frowning, Mamá held her head high. "Is what I said." She called for Hector. "*Ven, muchachito.*[17] Use those big *músculos,*[18] and carry this *tamalero.*"[19]

"*Sí,* Doña Palacios. And I'm sorry. I didn't do it on purpose."

Linda scowled at him, eyes narrowed. "If you ever do that again, I'll tell Tío."

Hector's eyes widened for a moment before they changed to his usual playful expression. He crossed

---

[14] Temper tantrum

[15] He will stay on the sofa, and that's the end of it. You can lock your bedroom door, if it makes you feel better.

[16] Don't stress yourself out.

[17] Child

[18] Muscles

[19] Large steamer for tamales

his heart. "I promise I'll knock on every door I walk through from now until I die."

Linda let out an exasperated sigh. "*Vámanos.*[20] Now."

A crowd of Mexicans carrying food and candles walked in front of Tim down the sidewalk. "Is it a Mexican holiday or something?" Tim asked his boss.

Guillermo sighed. "Conejo, why your *gente*[21] think everybody with brown skin is Mexican? See that guy? He's from El Salvador. And that lady? Colombian. That man? Okay, he's Mexican, but you get the point."

"Sorry." Apparently he'd said something wrong. He couldn't tell a Mexican from a Puerto Rican just by looking at them. What was the difference anyway? They were all the same. "What's with the candles?"

"They're going to a prayer vigil for a couple of ladies in the neighborhood."

"Did they die in some drive-by shooting?"

"My neighborhood's bad, but it ain't Compton." Guillermo shook his head.

Judging by his boss' reaction, mentioning gang violence was not the best choice. He regretted his decision to follow someone he'd just met into the middle of the ghetto, even if the man had invited him for dinner. Still, his curiosity piqued as more people with food and candles headed in their direction. "Just natural causes then?"

Guillermo stopped in his tracks, confusion on his face. "What the heck you talkin' about?"

---

[20] Let's go.
[21] People

"The prayer vigil. I thought they were for people who died, like for soldiers or national tragedies."

"Or drive-by shootings?" Guillermo offered, a smile playing on his lips. "Nobody died. We have *vigilias* for lots of things. You'll like it. There's always lots of good food."

Tim stopped. "Wait. I thought you said we were having dinner with your sister."

"No, I said my sister invited us for dinner."

Tim spun around and stomped in the other direction. "Forget it. I'm going home."

"Chill, man, can't you smell those *tamales*? Only a few minutes away. Oh, there's my sister now."

Groaning, Tim turned back.

"I think you already meet my *sobrina*,[22] Linda. And this is my sister, Juanita."

Obviously Linda hadn't gotten her looks from her mother. Juanita's dark, round face was covered in scars. He shook their hands, glancing at the little gangster behind them in baggy pants and a jersey, who struggled with a pot almost as big as him.

"You need some help there, kid?" Tim asked.

"Nah, I'm cool." The curly-haired hoodlum readjusted his grip, the thick, gold chain around his neck clinking against the pot.

"This is Hector."

Hector lifted his chin in a nod, a sneer on his lips.

Tim smirked. Little punk. He searched for an escape route. Maybe he could heat up a can of soup and eat one of Wendy's yogurts. No, if she got home early with the boys and found him, she'd be even more suspicious. Why had he let his stomach do the talking today?

He followed the group through the side door to

---

[22] Niece

Divine Promise Church into a crowded room. The air was thick with the smell of corn and tomatoes and some indefinable spices. His stomach grumbled in response. He sneered at the sea of Mexicans, or whoever they were, packed like sardines.

A man near the front of the room closed his eyes and said something in Spanish, raising his hand in the air. Those around him bowed their heads.

He groaned and put a hand on his rumbling stomach. Couldn't they eat first and pray later? He counted how many different pairs of shoes clustered around him. Everything from sneakers to stilettos to sandals to work boots. He counted fifteen different kinds of shoes before the man stopped praying.

"Here." Guillermo offered him a headset.

"What's that for?" asked Tim.

"Interpretation."

Tim smirked. "I'm good." He was there to eat, not learn anything.

"Nah, man. Put it on," Guillermo urged.

Not wanting to offend his new boss, he forced a pleasant expression and thanked him, placing the headset over his ears.

"We live in a broken world," a female voice stated. "Paul reminds us in Romans 13 to submit to governing authorities, but Peter incited rebellion in Acts 5:29 telling the Sanhedrin we have to obey God above man. So, what happens when man's laws directly contradict God's law?"

Obscure Bible verses? The Sanhedrin? What kind of church was this? What was his boss thinking taking him to a prayer vigil for dinner? He would listen for a few minutes in case *jefe* asked him what he thought.

The voice continued: "Before Jesus shared the parable of the Good Samaritan, an expert in the law summed up God's commandments in two categories: loving God with your heart, mind, soul, and strength and loving your neighbor as yourself. But in that same breath, the man, a sinner as we all are, asked Jesus whom he needed to consider his neighbor."

Tim rolled his eyes. He couldn't stand any more of it. He wasn't a sinner. There was that one thing, but that was a long time ago, and he'd paid for it. He was fine the way he was. And he certainly didn't need to hear how he was supposed to treat these people like neighbors; he didn't even want to be in their neighborhood.

After making sure Guillermo wasn't looking at him, he turned the dial, searching for another station. Baseball season was approaching. But there were no games, only the droning voice of the interpreter. He clicked off the sound and went back to counting shoes.

Linda wrapped her arms around her mother's shoulders, leaning on her. Hector set the pot of *tamales* on the floor behind her. She tried to concentrate on the *vigilia* but found it difficult. So many thoughts buzzed through her head that they drowned out the prayers.

She hadn't eaten anything since lunch. Her stomach tightened and gurgled with voracity. *Lord, let me concentrate on the words today. Please let all the other thoughts drift away.*

She tuned in to Pastor Martinez as he preached on immigration and how it fit with God's word. He referenced a few unfamiliar verses that spoke of caring for the foreigners in your land. His words hit home when he mentioned the struggle undocumented

Christians felt by breaking American laws while trying to follow God's laws.

Even though Linda hadn't chosen to cross the border, she'd had to lie more times than she wanted to admit to avoid sticky situations where she could've gotten in trouble for not having papers. Lying had arrived after Eve's first bite of that fruit and was prohibited not long after. "Do not bear false witness," the ninth commandment reminded them. Half of her life was a lie. But she didn't know what to do about it. All she knew was to pray for guidance and to follow God's word the best she could.

"Like the expert in the law, we want to justify ourselves," Pastor Martinez preached in Spanish. "Who is my neighbor? Not those Mexicans. They came here to steal the jobs I would never work anyway."

The group chuckled.

Pastor Martinez continued, his face growing serious. "Not that black gang member. How can I love someone like that? Not that senator who voted for those deportation laws, right? Not the lady who calls me names as I pass by her house?"

God tugged at Linda's heart. Her biggest prejudice was against people who were prejudiced. It was a struggle not to judge them, one she often failed.

"We only want to love those who love us back, but that's not what God calls us to do. Jesus asked which person acted as a neighbor to the injured man: the people like him who left him to die or the Samaritan who was despised by the Jews? 'The one who had mercy on him,' the expert answered. 'Go and do likewise,' Jesus told him.[23]

---

[23] Luke 10:37

"We are called not to hate the ones who want to deport María and Diana but to love them by showing them mercy. The only way to find that love and mercy is through connection with our Lord and Savior."

The power of this statement hit Linda hard. Loving those who hated her had never been her strong suit. Her mind drifted to her earlier fight with Hector. Slapping him had been over the top. Instead of showing him mercy, she had kicked him while he was down. She owed him an apology but dreaded giving him the upper hand again. Between waking up late, fighting with Hector, and shaking through her lunchdate with Kevin, she'd been spinning through a whirlwind of emotions all day.

Was lunch considered a date? she asked God. A parade of questions had been eating at her all day. *And what did Kevin mean by Hector being competition? Does that mean he's interested in me? What if he asks me out on a real date?*

This was new territory for her. All the guys interested in her before had only wanted one thing. None of them had come close to what she was looking for. Still, she was pretty sure Kevin wasn't a Christian, and that was dangerous ground.

Lord, guide me and help me know what to do. She listened to the silence in the room and opened an eyelid. Tío's new mechanic in front of her shifted comfortably. *Pobrecito.*[24] He probably didn't even speak Spanish. This evening's overload of Latino culture would shock his senses, and he wouldn't want to come back. Her mother pinched her arm.

Linda tuned in to the prayers for another minute as the room finally echoed with amens. Bodies

---

[24] Poor guy.

rustled, pots clanked, and soda fizzed into cups. The smell of her mother's *tamales* mixed with the fresh scent of cilantro, salsa, *empanadas*,[25] and *pan dulce*. The mechanic looked completely bewildered. Tío was nowhere to be found; he had left the poor guy alone.

She pushed through people and grabbed his arm. "Come on, we gotta get in line."

He flinched and glared at her for a moment before softening his gaze. "Sorry, didn't recognize you for a second."

"Yeah, there's a lot of us here." Leading him to the side of the room, she tried to talk over the noise. "I bet we all look the same to you."

"Not you," he said with a grin. "You're much prettier than anyone else."

She dropped his arm in disgust. Ugh. What a creep. He was at least ten years older than her and had a ring on his finger. Maybe she had misunderstood, thinking back to the situation with Hector and not wanting to make a similar scene. The mechanic probably hadn't meant it in a bad way. Besides, if God wanted her to show mercy, she needed to start somewhere. She changed the topic. "Did you understand anything that was going on?"

He shrugged. "I only speak English. And a little Latin from high school."

"I wish someone would have given you a headset. The pastor's wife interprets for English speakers."

The man's face flushed. "Uh, your uncle gave me one, but it didn't work right."

"You should've asked for another one."

He avoided her gaze. "I didn't think there'd be so much talking before we ate."

---

25 Corn dough formed into half-moons with meat or cheese in the middle and fried

Linda laughed. "Yeah, welcome to Latino culture. We take our time on stuff. We were praying for a couple of ladies who worked with my mom. The *migra* came to their workplace and arrested them for working without visas. They might get deported, so we were praying for the courts to be lenient."

"I guess that's what you get for working illegally."

Linda defenses jumped up. "They only came here to take care of their families."

"That's what I'm trying to do, too, but somebody keeps stealing all the jobs."

This mercy thing was harder than she'd thought. She decided to go with the rational approach. "You've found a pretty good job with my uncle. And since I do his books, I've noticed he's paying you under the table, so what's the difference?"

The man lifted his chin a bit higher. "The difference is I'm a citizen."

Linda narrowed her eyes, and then let it go. Perhaps if he had understood the sermon, it might have opened his mind to a more pleasant interaction, if not a change of view. His prideful expression told her that now wasn't the moment to have that conversation. She knew her temper and didn't want to slap another person today, so she whirled around, some of her long hair smacking into him, and left the line. She walked over to her mother, grabbed two *tamales*, and left for home.

She'd finally decided on the topic for her paper.

Juanita put on her nightgown and finished the last sip of her *manzanilla*.[26] She looked forward to

---

[26] Chamomile tea

sleeping in tomorrow. She hadn't done that in years.

She sighed as she lay down and pulled up the covers. Wide awake, despite the overwhelming exhaustion, she wondered where she could find another job. They had probably shut down the factory by now, and even if they hadn't, she couldn't take the risk. Immigration knew that places like a sewing factory couldn't get American citizens to work there for such low pay, so another group of undocumented workers would sit in front of the machines within the week—perfect timing for another *redada.*[27]

She considered her options. She could cook, sew, clean, and care for children. Sewing was probably out, which, given the state of her hands, might not be a bad thing. She could always make *tamales, empanadas,* or *tacos* and sell them at construction sites or at the *panadería.* She knew a few *hermanas* from church who worked at hotels. She could check with them, or she could advertise herself as a babysitter.

She grimaced. It had been so long since she had taken care of a baby. Maybe she would ask about the hotel tomorrow and then buy some ingredients for *empanadas* at the *panadería.* Victor and Norma had asked her to sell her food there a hundred times. It was worth a shot.

Tossing a set of blankets and a pillow onto the couch where Hector had settled, Linda turned around and opened her bedroom door.

"Hey, Linda?" Hector called from the couch.

"Yeah?"

---

[27] Raid

"Sorry again about before. I really didn't mean to walk in on you."

"It's all right." She paused in the doorway, tugging out some of that mercy God was calling her to give. "I'm sorry I slapped you."

"No worries," Hector said. "I probably deserved it anyway."

Some of the tension drained from her body. "Just knock from now on."

"I will. And Linda?"

"Yes, Hector?"

"Thanks for letting me stay here. That's pretty cool of you."

"No problem. Good night."

"Good night."

Linda locked her bedroom door and listened. The sounds of soft sobs drifted down the hall. Maybe he wasn't as hardhearted as she'd thought.

Tim chained the front door and crept upstairs, stepping on at least three sharp toys on the way. He tossed them downstairs in the vicinity of the couch, mumbling a few choice words. He'd have another talk with the boys about cleaning up after themselves.

Though the bedroom light was still on, Wendy was asleep. Her reading glasses had slid down her nose and a book lay in her lap. He tried to undress as noiselessly as possible, but she had always been such a light sleeper.

She yawned and stretched. "What time is it?"

"Almost eleven."

"How'd it go?"

"Not bad." As long as the boss didn't talk with his niece. Judging by the way she'd stormed off, he was pretty sure he hadn't made a new friend. It was too bad, because he enjoyed looking at her.

"That's great. Do you like your new job?"

"It's better than I thought it'd be."

She sniffed the air as he lifted the covers on his side. "Where did you eat?"

"Mexican."

She wrinkled her nose. "You stink. Go shower, or the whole bed will reek."

Tim groaned, exhausted, and headed towards their bathroom.

"Thanks." A small, victorious smile played at her lips as she returned to her book.

In a few seconds, the steamy water invited him into the shower. The hot water massaged his back. His tired muscles reveled in it, and he decided it was probably a good idea to start bathing at night. It'd take less time in the morning, plus it turned out that a surprising amount of oil and grease remained even after a thorough scrubbing at the shop.

"That's much better," Wendy said as he crawled under the soft covers. She put her glasses and book on the bedside table and turned off the lamp. The room was dark except for the one streetlamp that shone through their window. "What time are you leaving tomorrow?"

"Just as early."

"I made you a couple of sandwiches, and I threw in a can of soup."

A grin spread across his face. "That's the best news I've heard all day." He relaxed into the mattress, facing her for the first time in a long time. With her eyes shut, she almost looked peaceful. Perhaps a future together was still within reach.

CHAPTER SIX
La Camioneta Gris[1]

*L*inda grumbled as she changed from her pajamas into jeans and a t-shirt. Sleepiness overwhelmed her, but she had to fight through it. A long day stretched ahead of her. Though her first class wouldn't start until after lunch, Don and Doña Hernandez turned on the oven, which they jokingly called *El Dragón,* at five a.m. and expected Linda shortly after that to help bake *pan dulce* all morning. She reached for her doorknob and did a double-take when it didn't turn.

She grimaced. Hector. Who knew how long Mamá would let him stay? Maybe if her uncle offered him a job, it might hurry things along, help him grow up a little. She unlocked the door and stuck her head into the hall.

Soft snores floated from Mamá's room, but a light shone under the bathroom door. It opened, and Hector stepped into the hall.

"What are you doing up?" she asked.

---

[1] The Grey Truck – a song by Los Tigres del Norte

"Couldn't sleep."

Was it safe to leave him alone with Mamá? She had never known him to be violent, but he sometimes hung around with a pretty tough crowd. Hector walked slowly back to the living room and dropped onto the couch. Her rational side kicked in. He was too depressed to be dangerous.

She walked into the bathroom and then straight back out again, whispering loudly, "Ew, Hector. You didn't flush. And you left the seat up."

"Sorry."

"Gross. You probably didn't wash your hands either." She shuddered, flushed the toilet with her socked foot, and pulled down the lid, locking the door behind her.

Slightly more awake after brushing her teeth and washing her face, she let out a deep sigh and ambled into the living room. She switched on a lamp and sat on the arm of the couch, near Hector's big, bright-white-socked feet. He sat up, dropping the pillow he had been hugging.

"All right," she said, moderating her tone. "If I know anything about Mamá, you'll be here for a while, so we'd better set up some ground rules."

"Ground rules?" He raised an eyebrow and folded his arms across his chest. "Okay."

His attitude ignited her frustration. "First of all, put down the lid, flush, and wash your hands. You're not ten anymore." He rolled his eyes, only fueling her more. "And you better pick up after yourself. Don't leave your clothes or stuff lying around. I'm not going to clean up your mess, and I don't want Mamá cleaning it up either."

"Where am I supposed to put stuff?" he questioned.

"Bring a bag from home and leave it in the corner

over there. Just make sure it's out of the way." She pointed to the handful of wrappers sitting on the coffee table. "And don't be eating all our food, either."

He cocked his head to the side. "Anything else?"

"Yeah." She leaned in closer and watched his eyes widen. "If you ever even think about hurting me or my mom, I'll sic Tío on you."

He smirked. "That doesn't sound very Christian."

"Yeah, well, even Jesus got mad."

"It's been a while since I went to church, but I'm pretty sure He didn't threaten to beat anyone up." Chin raised, he stared Linda down for a moment.

Her stomach knotted. "Mamá's been through enough in this life."

Quicker than he had put it on, his bravado dropped, and he picked at the frayed edge of a sofa cushion. "Listen, I would never hurt you or your mom. I'm not a monster. You don't have to worry about it. I'm cool."

He looked like a scared kid, and she was able to see beyond the tough-guy image he had created for himself. In that moment, he was just Hector, the annoying but good-natured guy she'd known forever. She lowered her guard, upset that she'd let her anger get the best of her once again. She prayed for patience and started over. "I only have one class this afternoon and then I'm going to my uncle's shop. Why don't you meet me there around four, and I'll see if he's got any work for you?"

He shrugged. "Why not? I don't have anything better to do. Beats watching *novelas*."

She stood up and grabbed her jacket before heading out into the pre-dawn morning. "See you at four."

"See ya."

From her bed, Juanita listened to the argument in the living room. Let them figure things out for themselves, she told herself. They were both adults now, not kids anymore. Linda's tone lightened, and Juanita laid her head back on her pillow. The front door closed, and she glanced at the clock. Five thirty. She had slept in long enough.

Tim sipped his coffee as he counted the streetlamps through the bus window. Today he'd brewed his own cup. Why spend five dollars a day for coffee and a bagel when he could make it at home for free? He bit into his second English muffin, and a drop of melted peanut butter fell onto his tie. He shrugged. He'd be covered in grease in a few more minutes anyway.

He'd checked his email that morning, as well as the employment website where he was registered, but his inbox was empty. If he didn't find a better job soon, he'd have to tell Wendy the truth. He shuddered. Her stream of judgmental comments when he had suggested taking her vehicle to a local shop rather than to the dealership had been bad enough. At this point, he'd rather walk out into traffic than tell her he fixed cars for a living. Maybe he could make some calls during lunch.

The bus stopped, and Tim stepped onto the dark sidewalk, considering fessing up. But no matter which way he phrased his story, it only made the situation sound worse and worse. He'd have to keep lying for a little while longer. Hopefully he'd find a job before she found out.

Linda hated to admit it, but Hector had been right. She hadn't acted very Christian. Jesus wouldn't have yelled at anyone for leaving the seat up. Somehow Hector always brought out the worst in her, no matter how determined she was to stay calm. With everyone else she was so polite but one snarky look from him, and she could blow a fuse.

Eyeing the dough in front of her, she tried not to imagine Hector's face as she punched it into form. In the front of the *panadería*, she heard a tap on the glass, and she leaned back to see her mother standing outside the window. Linda waved a floured hand. She quickly shaped the last two *panes* and rolled them in sugar before placing the tray in the hot oven.

She wiped her hands on her apron and unlocked the front door, flipping over the sign to read ABIERTO.[2]

"*Buenos días,*[3] *Mamá.*" She kissed her mother on the cheek.

"*Hola, mijita, olvidé que estás trabajando hoy. ¿Están los Hernandez?*"[4]

"Yeah, they're in the back, *desayundando.*"[5]

"*Gracias, amor.*"

Linda led Mamá through the store into the back room where Don and Doña Hernandez sat at a small card table with plates of *huevos rancheros,*[6] tortillas, and refried beans. The oven timer buzzed, and she

---

[2] OPEN

[3] Good morning.

[4] Hi, my little daughter, I forgot you were working today. Are the Hernandezes here?

[5] Eating breakfast.

[6] Traditional Mexican scrambled eggs with salsa

got up to open *El Dragón*.[7] A wave of hot air and the
aroma of bready goodness blasted her. The deep heat
penetrated the gloves, and a strand of hair clung to
her forehead, sticky with sweat. She closed the door
and laid the tray on a rack to cool.

The visit had put her a few minutes behind, so she
focused on kneading, shaping, and decorating the
next batch. These were her favorites. Sometimes
called *besos*,[8] they were two halves of a circle covered
in coconut shavings and connected in the middle with
a thick, sweet cream after they cooled. She made the
dough into balls, rolled them in pink sugar and
coconut, cut them down the middle with a sharp
knife, and placed them flat-side down on the baking
sheet. Once the tray was full, she put them in the
oven and went to work on the next batch.

La Panadería Hernandez was the most popular
Latino bakery in the area. There were only three in
this part of the city and five in all of Roanoke, so they
got a lot of business, which meant they needed to
make a lot of bread. Don Hernandez told her that in
Guadalajara, where he was from, and in other parts of
Mexico, people ate their *pan dulce* in the evening with
a cup of coffee, milk, hot chocolate, or *atole*.[9] In the
U.S. people ate it in the morning with their breakfast.
That's why the Hernandezes baked twice a day—to
keep the bread fresh and the customers happy.

Linda stuck in the next batch, spread sweet cream
on the flat sides of the half *besos* and kissed them
together. She then mixed up the batter for the *niños
envueltos*,[10] what Americans called a jellyroll, which
was her second favorite. Ever since she was a little

---

[7] The Dragon
[8] Kisses
[9] A hot drink made from sweetened corn dough
[10] Swaddled children

girl, the Hernandezes had let her bake her favorites first, so she could eat one while she was working. Linda had learned in Freshman Psych about Pavlov's dog. Every time Pavlov gave his pup a treat, he rang a bell, and soon enough his four-legged friend was drooling at that ding without any food in sight. She knew it was real, because as soon as she rolled out the dough for the *besos*, even before she imagined how they would taste fresh out of the oven, her mouth started watering.

Over the years, she had been conditioned to love *pan dulce*. She craved the yeasty, sugary scent that filled the air. She enjoyed the process of rolling out, kneading, and preparing the breads. She even reveled in the extreme heat of the room. Doña Hernandez joked that the kitchen was their own personal sauna. Cleaning up was Linda's least favorite part, but if she threw on a little cumbia,[11] time passed quickly as she danced the broom around the kitchen.

Her mother fanned herself as she entered the hot room. *"Ay, Norma, no sé cómo trabajas con este calor."*[12]

Doña Hernandez was right behind her. *"Se acostumbra, Juanita. Se acostumbra. Si no hubiera comido tanto pan, estuviera yo así de flaquita."*[13] She held up her pinky finger.

Linda smiled as she put another batch into *El Dragón*, trying to imagine how Doña Hernandez might look as a skinny woman.

"Linda, *su mamá va a vender comida.*"[14]

"Oh yeah? Where?"

Don Hernandez walked in and answered. "Here."

---

[11] Traditional Mexican music

[12] Oh, Norma, I don't know how you work in this heat.

[13] You get used to it, Juanita. You get used to it. If I wouldn't have eaten so much bread, I'd be this skinny.

[14] Your mother's going to sell food.

Linda gave her mother a floury hug. "*Ay*, Mamá, your food is so good. We're going to be rich."

Mamá waved her hand. "*A ver, mija, a ver.*"[15]

Tim took a bite of his ham sandwich as he flipped through the list of possible employers. His boss had left to pick up some parts at the junkyard on the outskirts of the city, so Tim was keeping an eye on the place. This gave him the opportunity to make an hour's worth of job inquiries.

Forty-five minutes and two sandwiches later, he wasn't anywhere closer to finding a better job. He hung up the phone and balled up his paper bag, shooting it into the trash bin across the garage. "Three points," he said, doing a fake cheer.

Someone cleared his throat.

He spun around to face an older Mexican man with a cane. "Hello, can I help you?"

The man waved him outside and pointed to the grey truck letting off a lot of smoke a block down the road. "You push?" the elderly man asked, miming with his hands.

Tim looked from the shop to the truck. His boss had said not to leave the shop unattended, but if he could see the truck from here, he could see the shop from there. Besides, they had fixed almost all the vehicles and needed more work for tomorrow. He nodded and jogged down the street towards the grey truck. After closing the hood, he opened the driver's side door, held the wheel, and pushed. The rusty Ford inched along, building speed.

It was easier than he had anticipated. Voices

---

[15] We'll see, daughter, we'll see.

behind him chatted in Spanish, and Tim realized the junker was moving so fast because three other guys were helping him push the smoking vehicle. Tim chuckled at his lack of superhuman strength, as they pushed the truck past the old man with the cane and up the small incline into the shop. He parked the vehicle and popped the hood.

Something clinked near the entrance, and he noticed a teenage boy picking up a part. "Hey," he called. "Get away from there."

The boy bolted. The old man tried to stop him with the cane, but he was too slow. Tim grabbed a wrench and chased the kid down the sidewalk, throwing the tool like a fastball. It connected with the boy's back, and he fell to the ground. The construction workers who had helped him move the truck cheered.

"If that's broken, you're in trouble," he told the kid as he lifted him from the ground. The biggest worker grabbed the boy's arm, yelling in Spanish and walking him towards the shop. Tim picked up the wrench and the stolen part, which he now realized was most likely the part needed to fix the grey truck.

The old man shifted from foot to foot, a worried look on his face. The boy rubbed his back.

Tim scrutinized them. Both wore dirty, raggedy clothes that probably hadn't been washed in weeks. "Okay," he said. "If you don't want me to call the police, you'd better tell me what's going on."

The old man and the boy glanced at each other and shrugged. "No English."

One of the construction workers interpreted Tim's statement. Immediately, the boy's eyes widened, and the old man put up his wrinkled hands. *"No policía.*

Por favor."[16] The old man continued speaking in Spanish.

Tim recognized the word *dinero*, but that was all he caught. He turned to the construction worker.

"He say they don' have no money. They live in the truck."

Tim peeked into the bed of the truck, noting several blankets. The extended cab was full of food wrappers and plastic garbage bags, probably filled with clothes and other belongings.

Tim flashed back to a few months after his father had died, when the bank pushed him and his mother out of their home and onto the street. They stuffed everything into big, black trash bags, and his mother, wild with anger, cursed her dead husband, the man from the bank, and God himself in the middle of the sidewalk. Filling the station wagon to the brim and tying the rest down on the roof, they drove hours to his great-aunt's place. If she hadn't taken them in, they would've been in the streets, just like this kid and his grandfather.

A few more months without work, Tim and his family might have been in the same situation, though he doubted Wendy would have stuck around that long with the boys. He sighed and motioned for the old man to have a seat on an empty bucket.

"Tell them I won't call the police, but the boy has to help me fix the truck."

The old man shot him a toothless grin, and the boy stepped forward.

He shook the construction workers' hands before they returned to their jobsite. "Thanks. I can take it from here."

---

[16] No police. Please.

Juanita had bought a dark blue apron at the dollar store on her way home, surprising Hector with it when he returned to help her in the kitchen. *Empanadas* required less effort than *tamales* but they still took time. Norma and Victor had told her to bring them in at eleven, so they had three hours.

Hector helped unpack the grocery bags, putting the ingredients into three separate piles for the different kinds of *empanadas* they would make: cheese, chicken, and pineapple. Juanita explained the process and instructed Hector how to make the dough while she worked on the fillings.

Juanita turned on her ancient cassette player and popped in her favorite mixed tape that Linda had made her one year for her birthday, filled with her favorites. She hummed along as she stirred. Every few minutes she checked on Hector, showing him how to flatten out the dough to be filled.

"Como la Flor"[17] played, and Juanita sang along as she swept up the floury mess on the floor.

The silence behind her pulled her attention to Hector. He stood in the pantry, leaning against the wall, crying.

"*¿Qué pasó, Hector?*"

"That's my mom's favorite song. She used to sing it to me all the time when I was little." He wiped his eyes with his shirtsleeve.

"She's gonna be okay."

"How do you know?"

"*Tengo fe en Dios. Él es más grande que la policía.*"[18]

He sucked in some air through his sobs. "But, *ay,*

---

[17] Like the Flower – a cumbia song by Selena

[18] I have faith in God. He is bigger than the police.

Doña Juanita, I was so bad. The other day, when I got kicked out of school, she was so upset."

"*Sí*, Hector. But she still loves you and believes in you. She always telling us good things you do."

"Really?"

"*Sí*. Last week she say '*Hoy mi Hectorcito me hizo un buen café.*'"[19]

He smiled. "I did make some good coffee last week."

"And other day she say you make her a dinner, very special."

"Yeah, that was the day I was expelled. I felt really bad, so I made her favorite to cheer her up, *coctel de camarón.*"[20]

"*¿Ves? No te preocupes. Te ama muchísimo.*"[21]

Wiping his cheeks with the palm of his dough-covered hand, he nodded.

Juanita chuckled at the white streaks across his cheeks, and he lowered his gaze to his messy hands. He laughed and rubbed his face with his apron.

"*Ven. Tenemos que hacer un montón de empanadas.*"[22]

Linda put the last tray of *pan dulce* on the cooling rack and swept the sugar-covered floor. Don Hernandez walked in and flipped on the CD player. Soon the room was filled with the soft sounds of *cumbia*. Linda smiled and danced with the broom. Don Hernandez grabbed his wife's apron string as she walked by and spun her around.

---

[19] Today my little Hector made me such good coffee.

[20] Shrimp cocktail – a traditional tomato-based soup with shrimp

[21] See? Don't worry. She loves you so much.

[22] We have to make a ton of empanadas.

They laughed and all four of them—broom included—danced around the room, their shoes making coordinated footprints on the dusty floor. Linda stopped and watched her employers. Both in their fifties, they had been together for more than thirty years. She hoped she'd be that happy after she'd been married for thirty years. Linda shook her head. First she'd actually need to go on an actual date.

During her entire childhood and teen years, her mother was very protective of her, and for good reason. At least fifteen girls in her high school class had gotten pregnant between freshman and senior year. Linda supposed Mamá had had her own reasons for keeping her safe, probably related to her own violent marriage, though she'd never told them to her.

So here she was twenty-one years old, and she'd never had a boyfriend. She hadn't even been on a date yet, unless she counted lunch the other day. Bobby Holbert had given Linda her first kiss in middle school, probably another reason why Mamá had become protective early on. Since then, she hadn't kissed anyone. She'd had several crushes, Kevin being the most recent, but once she'd gotten into college, she'd been so focused on her work, she hadn't had time for a boyfriend. During moments like this, she wished there was someone special in her life, someone to dance her around the room and tell her he loved her.

When Tim and the boy, whose name was Geovany, finished replacing the part, the engine roared to a start without any steam flowing out of the front.

Fernando, the boy's grandfather, shook his hand. "*Gracias.*"

Tim nodded. "No problem."

"Sorry," Geovany said as he, too, shook Tim's hand.

"I might have done the same," Tim said.

Geovany cocked his head to the side and frowned.

So much for trying to connect. "Never mind. It's okay." He gave the boy a half-hearted thumbs up and received a smile in return.

He waved as they pulled out and answered the ringing phone. "Hello?"

"*¿Guillermo?*" a woman asked.

"No, this is Tim. Gear-mo's not here right now. Can I help you?"

"*¿Español?*"

"Sorry. I don't speak Spanish."

There was a pause then a loud scraping as the woman called out in a muffled voice. Seconds later the voice of a small child, likely no older than Jeremy, came on the line. "My mommy broke her car. Can you fix it?"

"Yes. Can she drive it here?"

Tim listened as the small voice spoke in Spanish. "She says no. It don't start."

"Okay. Can you call a tow truck?"

Silence.

"Why don't you tell your mom to call back in an hour?"

The phone clicked in his ear, and he put down the receiver. He shook his head. These people needed to learn English.

Looking at the parking lot of vehicles lining the street, he sighed. "Back to the ole grindstone."

❀

Juanita fried the last batch of *empanadas* shaped in perfect half-moons and helped Hector bag the rest. She took the last five out of the oil and placed them on a paper towel. She wrapped them in foil and nodded to Hector. "*Vámonos.*"

"Do you think Linda will still be there?" Hector asked.

"*No creo.*"[23]

Hector frowned and shifted the bags of *empanadas* in his arms.

Juanita smiled. She knew Hector had a crush on Linda. Ever since Linda had shared her *piñata* candy with him at her fourth grade birthday party, he'd followed her around like a puppy. Poor Hector. Linda had never given him a second glance. She could only see the bad in Hector, but Juanita saw beyond that to the sensitive little boy who tried to act tough. If only Hector could drop the act, Linda would open her eyes, and they might actually get along.

"*¿Qué vas a hacer en la tarde?*"[24]

"Linda told me to stop by Memo's shop later to see if he has any jobs for me to do."

"*Muy bien.*[25] Is better than helping me cook."

Hector shrugged. "I don't mind. I kind of like cooking." He wrinkled his brow. "Don't tell anyone that, though."

Juanita nodded. "*No te preocupes.* Your secret is safe with me."

They turned into the *panadería* right as Linda flew out the door.

"Late for class," she cried, kissing her mother on the cheek and running towards the bus stop.

---

[23] I don't think so.
[24] What are you going to do in the afternoon?
[25] Very good.

"*Siempre*,"[26] Juanita said to Hector.

"Yeah, I don't think she goes anywhere without running."

"She is too busy."

"Maybe I can help her out at Memo's garage. I don't have much to do."

"*No sé, Hector. Ella hace el* accounting *para el taller*."[27]

"Oh." He paused. "Guess not. I'm not so good at math."

"*Tal vez no*,[28] but you make a good *empanada*."

He grinned. "Really?" He opened the door for her. "Cool."

Linda jumped off the bus while it was still screeching to a stop and jogged into the mathematics building. Not having studied as much as she would have liked for the test, she was thankful she had a pretty good handle on the theme. Despite her best efforts, she never got as much time to do her homework as she'd hoped. There weren't enough hours in the day. Today after class she needed to spend at least an hour at her uncle's shop and then go to praise band practice. Tomorrow she had to write her essay, and then Friday night she met with the Cultural Club.

"Well, at least I finally picked a topic," she muttered to herself.

As the teacher closed the door, Linda slipped into the room, whispering an apology. She grabbed her seat and scanned over her test. An hour later, she

---

[26] Always.

[27] I don't know, Hector. She does the accounting at the shop.

[28] Maybe not

completed the last answer and put down her pen. Packing away her calculator, she took her exam to her professor's desk.

"Last one in and first one out," Dr. Gregory said.

She was always the first one done with tests. "Yup," she said. "I'm not sure about number fourteen."

"I thought you might have trouble with that one."

"Did I get it right?"

He glanced over the test and winked.

Linda sighed and walked out of the room. She had a couple of hours left before she needed to be at her uncle's. Maybe she could start on the essay.

Following the path worn in the grass from so many footsteps, Linda made her way to the library, her favorite place on campus. It was one of the only places where she never worried about a thing. She could concentrate in its relaxed atmosphere with no *novelas* in the background or *banda*[29] blaring from the house next door. The smell of the books calmed her, and silence enveloped her within its walls. She spent so much time there, it was almost like a second home. Her safe place.

Her preferred spot glowed, like a greeting. She tossed her bag on the plump leather couch. Though she always wrote better longhand, teachers wouldn't accept essays anymore unless they were typed, so she sat at the computer behind the sofa. "Undocumented," she whispered to herself as she searched through online journals.

Ten different sources came up, and she found them in the stacks. Using her jacket as a pillow, she curled up on the couch and flipped a magazine open to one of the articles. The journal described a

---

[29] A common style of Mexican brass band music

movement brought about by undocumented students who had immigrated to the U.S. at a young age and wanted higher education and a career but couldn't obtain them because of their citizenship status. The Dream Act sought a legal resolution where they could obtain visas and a path to citizenship.

Butterflies circled in her stomach and color rose to her cheeks as she read article after article about people just like her. Why had she never heard of The Dream Act before? A whole movement for people specifically in her situation. Unfortunately there had been no solutions yet, but somehow knowing she wasn't the only one struggling helped ease the pain.

Back at the computer, she typed her essay and gathered more up-to-date information online. A website devoted to the movement showed a nearby demonstration scheduled for the month after the semester's end. "Maybe I should check it out," she said under her breath.

"Talking to yourself again, Palacios?" a voice behind her asked.

"Hey, Kevin," she called to him over her shoulder. Act casual, she told herself, her heart racing. "Are you following me?"

"Following you? I don't think that's necessary. This is your permanent location." He threw his bag next to hers on the couch. "What are you working on?"

"An essay for my lit class."

"Yeah, I've got a paper due this Friday for Bio. I haven't even thought about it yet."

"I started mine about five minutes ago. It took me three days to come up with a topic."

"What did you decide on?"

Linda blushed. "Um, it's about The Dream Act."

"What's that?" He hopped onto the couch, using

their backpacks like pillows, his feet hanging off the opposite end.

"Oh, it's a movement fighting for the rights of undocumented students, trying to get them visas."

His brow furrowed. "I didn't realize you could go to school if you're illegal."

There was that word again. Somehow it seemed worse coming out of Kevin's mouth. Her stomach churned as she gathered the courage to talk about the subject. "Actually, they prefer to be called undocumented. Not illegal."

"Oh, sorry. I don't know anyone undocumented."

Or so you think, she frowned. "Yeah, it's kind of offensive to say illegal. I mean, most of the people with The Dream Act came over with their parents when they were little, so they didn't have a choice."

"Really? I didn't realize that. I thought people crossed over the border when they were older."

She smirked. "How did you think all the kids got here?"

He chuckled. "I guess I didn't think about it. I assumed they'd all been born here. Wow, it would suck to be a little kid and have to go through that, especially since it's not even their choice."

"Yeah. People don't think about kids crossing over. The news doesn't report that very often. They just talk about all the immigrants 'stealing their jobs.' They never show all the people who die trying to make a better life for their families."

Kevin rubbed the back of his neck. "If it's that dangerous, why don't they do it the right way?"

The hairs on the back of Linda's neck stood up. "The right way," she repeated, considering how to reply. The faces of her undocumented friends, family, and *hermanos* from the church paraded around her mind. A thousand answers buzzed in her brain.

Unable to decide, she named the reasons as they came to her. "Money. Lack of resources, education, connections, power, time. Illiteracy. Prejudice. Violence. Life or death situations. Many try, but when you spend three month's salary on a visa application and it gets rejected, it's pretty discouraging. You add discouragement on top of suffering, and it leads to hopelessness and desperation. And when you're desperate, you'll try anything, even if it means dying in the desert. And all this for the American dream, that hope that you and your family can make it, despite all the challenges you face once you cross the border."

"See, that's what I don't get." He sat up and wrapped a muscled arm over the back of the couch. "If they know life is going to be so hard when they get here, why come at all?"

Linda sighed. "I think it might be hard for someone like you to understand."

"What do you mean?" he asked, crossing his arms. "Someone like me."

Linda shifted in her chair. This was starting to get awkward. She had never spoken so openly with Kevin before. Her heart thumped, and her mind raced through millions of answers. "Well, you know, someone who has a lot of money."

"What makes you think I have a lot of money?"

"For one, you have a car. And you have nice clothes and your own laptop. You've got that big apartment off-campus, and you go out a lot."

"I never thought about any of that as having a lot of money. That seems like everyday stuff for me."

"Exactly. Sometimes we're so accustomed to things, we take them for granted. It's not a bad thing, but it's hard to understand someone when you haven't walked in their shoes."

Kevin leaned over the couch, his eyes reflecting the nearby lamp. "I'd like to understand."

Linda's heart fluttered. "Today we have to work on our papers, but I have an idea, if you're up for an adventure."

He sat up straight. "I'm always up for an adventure. What'd you have in mind?"

"You can come to my church on Sunday."

He raised an eyebrow. "Church and adventure don't usually go together in the same sentence."

"It does when you go to my church." Linda grinned as Kevin thought it over.

Finally, he shrugged. "Okay, I'm game."

"Cool. You can meet me there." She handed him the address she had scrawled on a piece of scrap paper. "Part of the adventure will be finding a parking spot."

"I've never been to that part of town before."

"Yeah, that's kind of the point." She laughed. "Anyway, let's get back to our papers. I only have one more hour before I have to head to work."

"Don't you ever have a day off?" Kevin asked, shaking his head.

"A day off." She sighed. "Haven't seen one of those in a while. Not since Christmas."

"We may need to work on that." Kevin winked. "All work and no play . . ."

" . . . makes sure the bills are paid on time," Linda continued.

"You're a lost cause, Palacios."

"Hey now. I'm going out with you guys on Friday for dinner and movie."

"Now that's what I'm talking about." He put up his fist. "Pound it."

Linda pounded his fist. What had she gotten herself into?

By two o'clock the empanadas had sold out, and Juanita had made a hundred dollars. She gave twenty to Norma and spent another twenty on the next day's ingredients. Why hadn't Juanita listened to Norma sooner? She'd made the same amount of money as she would have in a ten-hour day at the factory. And it only took four hours to make everything.

"What's on the menu tomorrow?" Hector asked, peeking into the bag.

"*Tacos dorados.*"[30]

"Mmm. That sounds good. Can't wait to help."

Juanita reached into her change purse, pulling out twenty dollars. "Here. *Lo ganaste.*"[31]

"*No gracias, Doña.* You letting me stay on your couch is more than enough for me."

"*Toma.*"[32]

Hector gently pushed her hand back.

Juanita sighed and put the money back in her purse. "*¿Qué hora es?*"[33]

"Two o'clock."

"When you going to see Linda and Memo?" Juanita asked Hector.

"She told me to meet her there at four."

Juanita paused. She dreaded even asking the question. "*¿Primero quieres visitar a tu mamá?*"[34]

Hector's smile quickly faded.

"If we wait, maybe they move her far away to other *cárcel.*"[35]

---

[30] Hard-shelled tacos
[31] You earned it.
[32] Take it.
[33] What time is it?
[34] Do you want to visit your mom first?
[35] Jail

The pastor had been in contact with a local immigration lawyer for both Diana and María. He had offered to go visit them in jail and to take Hector and Luz along. Juanita had decided she would go to support Hector and Luz but would wait outside. Or maybe down the block. A knot formed in her stomach with every uniformed person, police car, flashing lights, or whooping of a siren. After she'd watched her cousin get attacked by police officers in Texas, her heart pounded whenever anyone in uniform was around. Her cousin had been deported back to Mexico only partially healed after three weeks in intensive care for broken ribs and a concussion.

But Juanita had promised Diana she would take care of Hector. She'd take the risk, but she wasn't stupid. She could keep her distance.

"*¿Pues?*"[36] she asked.

He nodded. "Okay."

"*Pastor Martinez va a entrar contigo. Yo me quedo afuera.*"[37]

He swallowed hard. "*Está bien.*"

She patted him on the shoulder and grabbed her coat. "*Vámanos.*"

---

[36] Well?

[37] Pastor Martinez will go in with you. I'll stay outside.

CHAPTER SEVEN
Una Lagrima Más[1]

*L*inda typed the last sentence and leaned back in her chair. "Done."

"No way. You typed an entire paper in an hour?"

"Yup. Once I knew what I wanted to write, it just flowed." She uploaded it onto the class page and put the journals back where she got them. "Well, I'm off."

Kevin frowned. He stood up and stretched. "Should we meet here on Friday around five?"

"Okay, sounds good."

He moved towards her, and for a second Linda thought he was about to hug her. Instead he lightly punched her shoulder. "See ya later, Palacios."

"Bye, Kevin." As she brushed past him, her arm briefly touched his. By the time she reached the door, unable to resist the pull, she looked over her shoulder. His eyes focused on her with intensity. She waved, her heart pounding like Don Hernandez's fists on some tough dough.

---

1 One More Tear – a song by Los Temerarios

Had she really invited him to church on Sunday? What had she been thinking? Mamá was going to have a cow. She grimaced as she hopped on the bus. Also, was it her imagination, or did he almost hug her? She went back and forth for a few minutes and finally told herself to shut up and use the time to study.

Juanita gave Hector a hug and sat on the bench at the bus stop. "*Aquí te espero.*"[2]

Hector shot a half-hearted smile at Pastor Martinez, who put his arm around Hector's shoulders and walked with him towards the jail.

Juanita watched the cars speed by and the people boarding the bus that had stopped in front of her. Her foot tapped on the sidewalk, and she smoothed her skirt. It was strange to sit and do nothing. She could hardly get through her favorite *novela* without falling asleep.

She decided to make a mental list of the foods she could sell at the *panadería*. She had only gotten through a week's worth of ideas before Hector's voice broke her concentration.

"They wouldn't let us see her." Anger clouded his face.

"*¿Por qué no?*"[3] Juanita asked, her heart sinking.

"They said we weren't on the list."

"But your *mamá* know about the list. *Era parte del su plan, ponerte a ti y al pastor en la lista.*"[4]

Pastor Martinez gripped the bus stop sign so hard

---

[2] I'll wait for you here.

[3] Why not?

[4] It was part of her plan, to put you and the pastor on the list.

Juanita was afraid it would bend in half. "I've had this happen before. They say the person doesn't have a list even when they do. Or sometimes they don't even let them know they have the right to visitors."

"*Pero, ¿por qué?*"

"*Discriminación,*"[5] he replied with a grunt. "I'm sorry, Hector. We can try again tomorrow."

"*Tengo una idea,*"[6] Juanita stated.

"What?" Hector said, his brow furrowed.

"*Puedes escribirla una carta.*"[7] She searched in her bag and handed him a pad of paper and a pen.

"But I can't write in Spanish." Hector clenched his jaw. Tears formed in his eyes.

Moments like these dug into her like a tiny shovel in her stomach. She wished she could read and write. Her parents had neither had the money nor the desire to send her to school.

Thankfully, Pastor Martinez stepped forward. "*Ven. Yo te ayudo.*"[8] Juanita patted the spot next to her on the bench, and Pastor Martinez and Hector sat down.

Minutes later, they prayed over the letter, and Pastor Martinez returned to the jail to drop it off. Juanita sat with Hector, holding his trembling hand in hers. Their bus arrived at the same time as the pastor, and they rode home in silence.

"I can't figure out what's wrong with this one." Tim stared under the hood of a grey Buick.

---

[5] Discrimination

[6] I have an idea.

[7] You can write her a letter.

[8] I will help you.

His boss leaned in from the other side of the hood, squinting, and then poked his head under the car. "See that water down there? I think the radiator's cracked."

Tim bent down. "Oh, yeah, look at that."

"I gotta order a replacement part. You know how to take it out?" he pointed to the radiator.

Tim scratched his head. "Maybe."

"We do this one together."

Tim gave him a thumbs up and stepped back. "Okay, *jefe*, you lead the way."

He laughed. "You know you don't really have to call me *jefe*."

"Yeah, I do." Tim faked a frown. "I can't pronounce your name."

His boss' laugh echoed around the garage. "You're funny, Conejo." He pointed to the embroidered name on his jumpsuit.

"Gwill-er-mo," Tim attempted.

Guillermo shook his head. "Ghee. Like guitar. Ghee-yer-mo."

Tim repeated it correctly. *"Jefe's* still easier."

By the time Linda stepped off the bus, she had finished reviewing the chapter for tomorrow's test. She walked in the direction of Tío's shop. Grumbling about having to deal with Hector and that new jerk mechanic, she glanced up from the sidewalk right as Mamá, Pastor Martinez, and Hector got off a bus a few feet away.

Mamá flinched as Linda touched her arm. *"Ay, mija, me espantaste."*[9]

---

[9] You scared me.

"Sorry, Mamá. *Buenas tardes,*[10] Pastor." She shook his hand.

"*Buenas tardes. ¿Cómo te va en la universidad?*"[11]

"*Muy bien, gracias.*"

She lifted her chin at Hector. "Hey, you ready to go?"

"Sure." He kept his head down and stepped towards her.

After she kissed her mother on the cheek, Linda turned to the pastor. "*Nos vemos a las siete.*"[12] With a gentle push, she moved Hector in the direction of the shop. They walked a whole block without Hector saying anything, which was very unlike him. He always had something to say, whether she wanted him to or not. "You're quiet."

"We went to see my mom."

"Oh." Linda studied his face. "How's she doing?"

"I don't know. They wouldn't let me see her."

"Why not?"

"There's a stupid list, and they said I'm not on it."

"That's not fair. You're her son. You should be able to visit her."

He kicked the ground. "I know. The worst part is your mom said Ma knew about the list. They had this whole plan if either of them were detained."

Linda's stomach dropped at the thought that her mother had a plan in case of deportation. She shook off the feeling. "Okay, so what does that mean?"

"It means that either she made a list and they're lying, or they wouldn't let her make a list at all. Or something worse."

"Hey." Linda put her hand on his arm. "I'm sure

---

[10] Good afternoon.

[11] How are things going in college?

[12] See you at seven o'clock.

she's fine. It's probably some redneck *policía*. Maybe you'll get someone nicer tomorrow."

"Maybe." He sighed and stopped walking.

"Don't worry about it. She's not in there by herself. María's there, too. Maybe they're together."

He nodded.

"What are you going to do?" She had no idea what she would do if Mamá were deported. Linda couldn't go back to Mexico. Nothing about it felt like home to her. She had never even been there for a visit. She and her mother knew a few people who traveled to Mexico every year to be with their family, but that happened less and less with every passing year. The risk was too high. Crossing over *mojado* was getting harder and not just because of stronger patrols at the border. There were gangs who would kidnap people who crossed, often killing them whether their family paid the ransom or not.

Hector stuffed his hands into his pockets. "There isn't anything I can do."

"If she has to go back to Mexico, will you go with her?"

He released a heavy sigh and leaned his back against the brick storefront. "I don't know. The only time I've been to Mexico was when my mom sent me to visit *Abuelo y Abuela*.[13] I think I was in third grade. It was forever ago. I have nothing there. I have nothing here," he scoffed, tilting his head back to the wall.

"You have stuff here," Linda reassured him.

"No. You were right yesterday. I haven't taken anything seriously. I never thought anything like this would happen. I was just having fun, doing my thing, you know? And now this happens with my mom, and

---

[13] Grandfather and Grandmother

I need to step up, but I have nothing. Absolutely nothing. Kicked out of school. No job. Sleeping on your couch like a bum." He clenched his jaw. "I'm a total loser."

This was worse than his tough guy act. Linda would take that any day over this. There was always an angry part of her that wanted to see him knocked down a peg, to pay for that time with the police and all the hassles he put her through over the years. But as he stood before her broken, it tore her up inside.

She touched his shoulder. "You are not a loser, Hector. You just don't have it all figured out yet. And there are plenty of people that care about you. Your mom, God, people at church, my mom, me."

He looked down at her, surprise on his face.

"You're okay, you know, when you're not being a jerk." Linda let go of his shoulder and gave it a flick. "You were wrong about that job thing. I'm pretty sure my mom's glad to have you as her sous-chef."

A small smile crept onto his lips. "I do kinda like cooking."

"Come on." She hooked her hand under his elbow and pulled him down the sidewalk. "Tell me about today. Did you make *empanadas?*"

"Only like a hundred." He smirked. "Tomorrow we're making *tacos dorados.*"

"Wow, you're becoming an *experto*[14] in Mexican cuisine."

He shrugged. "I just do what your mom tells me to do."

"That's always the best way to go." She chuckled and let go of his arm as they turned into the garage. "Tío?"

Her uncle poked his head out from behind the

---

[14] Expert

hood of a big car. "*Buenas tardes, muchachos. ¿Cómo están?*"

Linda gave him a kiss on the least grease-covered cheek. "I'm going to work on the books, but I was wondering if you had any work Hector could help you with."

Tío smiled at him. "*Claro. Tengo algunos* parts *nuevos del* junkyard *que guardar. Y siempre se necesita barrer.*"[15] He tossed Hector a broom.

Linda flicked his arm. "Get to work, Hectorcito."

He rolled his eyes and pushed the long broom along the greasy concrete.

Juanita patted out tortillas between her palms to the rhythms floating out of her stereo. The chicken bubbled in boiling water with a few cloves of garlic, half an onion, and a generous helping of salt. She dipped a paper towel in a touch of vegetable oil and wiped it across the hot *comal*[16]. The oil sizzled as she placed the tortillas on its surface and swayed to the music. Tomorrow she and Hector could make the salsa and fry the *tacos* with the shredded chicken in the center.

"*Bidi bidi bom bom,*"[17] she sang. Her favorite memory in Texas was taking Linda to a Selena concert. She'd never heard of Selena before moving to the U.S. The pueblo where they'd lived didn't get electricity until after they'd left and was too far from any city to pick up radio signals. The only music

---

[15] Sure. I have some new part from the junkyard to put away. And it always needs sweeping.

[16] A large, flat skillet used for heating tortillas

[17] A popular Selena song

she'd known growing up was *corrido*,[18] the typical music from her state, though occasionally *bandas* and *mariachis*[19] passed through.

When they'd arrived in Texas in 1994, Selena was everywhere. On the radio, on the television, and live in concert. Nothing had been as beautiful as her little Lindita singing along with Selena on the radio. When she'd learned that Selena was coming to El Paso, she knew they had to go.

Her cousin had known someone who worked at the Coliseum—the concert venue—so he'd gotten them in for free. They'd been so far from the stage, Selena was a sparkly speck, but it had been worth it to see the look on Linda's face. Less than a year later, Selena had been murdered. But Juanita tried not to think about her that way. Whenever Selena's songs came on, Juanita pictured Linda lighting up and singing along with the music.

Linda managed to get her work done and leave before running into the new mechanic. He gave her the creeps. Something about the way he looked at her didn't feel right. Plus, she was still fuming over his comments at the prayer vigil. Knowing she needed to forgive him and actually forgiving him were two separate things.

Linda raced down the sidewalk towards church. She had hoped to be on time for practice but would be late. As usual. It didn't matter too much; they were on *la hora latina*[20] anyway. Half the praise band

---

[18] Traditional Mexican folk ballads
[19] Traditional Mexican music groups with strings and bass
[20] Latino time

showed up late every week, which was often frustrating for the Americans who were almost always on time. They had to explain that in Latino culture relationships were more important than time constraints. The American piano player, in turn, told them she had to leave by eight to put her young son to bed, so as a compromise, practice started right at six thirty with people joining in as they arrived and ending when the pianist headed out an hour and a half later.

Divine Promise Church had people from many different backgrounds, and they had three services on Sundays: one Spanish service called Promesa with a praise band, one English service with a praise band, and one traditional service, also in English, with a choir. Headsets offering interpretation were available for all services, and the church family tried to be together as a church instead of only for separate services.

The beat of the congos reached her before she opened the door. The piano, guitar, bass, violin, and flute joined in the song, soon followed by the singers:

"*Si tuvieras fe como grano de mostaza . . .*"[21]

It was one of Linda's favorite songs. She liked the rhythm and the message. If you have faith the size of a mustard seed, you can move mountains. Songs like this one stuck in her head, strengthening her after a long day. She rushed down the aisle, joining in.

"*. . . y esa montaña se moverá, se moverá, se moverá.*"[22]

Pastor Martinez winked as she hopped on the stage and stood next to the other singers. Eva passed her the maracas, and Linda shook out the rhythm as she let the cares of the day slide away.

---

[21] "If you have faith like a mustard seed . . ." – lyrics from a popular Spanish praise song

[22] ". . . and that mountain will be moved, will be moved, will be moved."

Tim watched another vehicle drive out of the garage, feeling satisfied. Guillermo's greasy hand patted him on the shoulder.

"Good job today, Conejo."

Tim noticed the cash out of the corner of his eye. "Thanks."

"I took out a twenty for that part you gave away for free."

Tim turned around. "Oh, you heard about that?"

"Yeah, man, word travels fast around here with all those *chismosos*."[23]

"I didn't know what to do," Tim said.

"Nah, you did okay, *amigo*. Who knows? Maybe it'll be good for business."

Tim unbuttoned his jumpsuit and moved towards the bathroom. He opened the door. "Whoa, what happened in here?"

"*Ay, ¿qué pasó?*" Guillermo jogged over.

Tim gestured at the sink. "It's clean."

Guillermo grunted and punched Tim's arm. "You freaked me out. I thought Hector broke the toilet or something."

"This clean bathroom might help business, too." Tim laughed and closed the door.

An hour and a half later, he walked up his driveway and rang the bell, knowing how much the boys loved answering it. The curtain moved and a little blue eye peeped out.

"Daddy," Jeremy yelled and flung the door open.

"Hey, buddy." He lifted him into the air as his other son attacked his legs. Tim rustled Nathan's long blond hair and kissed Jeremy on the forehead,

---

[23] Gossips

putting him back down. Each boy wrapped himself around one of Tim's legs. "Wow, my shoes feel really heavy today." They giggled as he lifted them with each step.

"All right, boys," Wendy called from the kitchen. "Let your father get in the door."

"Smells good." He sniffed the air. "What's for dinner?"

"*Pollo*."[24] Jeremy grinned.

Tim laughed. "Where'd you learn that?"

"He's been watching Diego." Wendy sneered. "All day long."

"He'll be bilingual before the month's up," Tim joked.

"I suppose it'll look good on his college transcripts. Besides, with all the Mexicans taking over this area, we'll probably need him to translate for us one day." Wendy jeered. "I saw one moving in down the block. Next thing you know, there'll be a food truck out front selling *tacos*."

Tim's lingering satisfaction from work dropped away. He peeled the boys off his legs and turned them towards the bathroom. "Okay, boys, wash up for dinner."

"You're sweaty." She pointed to his soaked collar.

"The bus was packed."

"Go take a quick shower. The chicken just came out of the oven."

Tim grinned at her as he ascended the stairs, dropping the act as soon as he was out of sight.

He stashed the cash in the back of a dresser drawer inside a pair of socks and then stepped into the shower with a sigh. Every second his lie grew. And the bigger it became, the more likely Wendy

---

[24] Chicken

would find out. Hot water ran over his tired muscles as he washed off the grease and oil and whatever else he was covered with. As he slid his fingers through his wet hair, he watched the soap go down the drain in little grey bubbles.

He toweled off and pulled on pajama pants and an old t-shirt before heading back downstairs. The boys sat at the table, and Wendy spooned some chicken and biscuits onto their plates.

"Ooh, my favorite." He dropped into his chair and inhaled the aromatic steam from the chicken. If she had made his favorite, maybe she was in a good enough mood to be forgiving. But now wasn't the moment. Not with the kids around. It would have to be when they were alone, in case of an explosion. "Nathan, what'd you learn in school today?"

Nathan shrugged and poked at his chicken. "Nothin'."

"Nothing?" Tim asked. "What classes did you have today?"

"Art," Nathan said with a full mouth.

"Did you paint or draw?"

"Paint."

Tim smiled at Wendy. "What'd you paint?"

"A house."

"I painted today, too," Jeremy interrupted.

"Oh yeah?"

Then Jeremy was off to the races, telling about everything he'd done from the moment he woke up through five minutes before Tim walked through the door. Tim waited until Jeremy finished. "That was a very complete history of your day, son."

Jeremy's right cheek lifted in a half-smile, and he moved back to eating his dinner.

"What have you been up to today?" Tim asked Wendy, trying to judge her mood.

"Keeping up with him," she sighed, nodding towards Jeremy, who was now using his front teeth to take tiny bites of his food. "Tomorrow we're going to the d-o-c-t-o-r."

"Doctor," Nathan said.

Jeremy's lower lip trembled. "The doctor?" He dropped his fork and crossed his arms over his chest. "I don't wanna go to the doctor."

"Guess we can't spell stuff out anymore," Tim muttered as Wendy comforted Jeremy.

A few tears and several scoops of chicken and dumplings later, Tim helped Wendy clear the table. He rolled up his sleeves and scrubbed the dishes. "Once we get caught up on bills, the dishwasher is one of the first things I'm going to spend some *dinero* on." It had broken at the beginning of the year, and they hadn't had the extra money to fix it.

"I don't know. I kinda like this dishwasher." Wendy smacked him on the arm as she walked past. "You smell much better now, by the way."

Tim shifted guiltily. He needed to tell her. He'd been making pretty good money the last couple of days. But what if it slowed down again? He couldn't be a mechanic forever. He sighed.

"Hard day at work?" she asked, checking her phone at the table.

"Yeah, I guess so."

"What'd you do today?"

"Nothin'," he replied in a tiny voice.

She looked up from her phone and rolled her eyes. "Ha, ha. No, seriously. What did you do?"

"Oh, a little of this and a little of that. We're mostly catching up still. There's not much to say yet. It's only my third day on the job."

She squinted at the plate in the drying rack. "You missed a spot."

He couldn't even do dishes right. Emotions swirling inside, he picked up the plate and scratched off the bit of food with his fingernail before running it under the faucet again. He could feel her eyes on him with every dish now, judging him, ready to tell him what he was doing wrong. The pressure was palpable.

The boys came running into the kitchen, breaking the tension. "Tickle fight," Nathan yelled, and they attacked.

Linda said goodbye to everyone at practice. As she approached the door, a familiar blonde-haired girl appeared in its frame.

"Becky?" Linda gave her a hug. "What are you doing here?"

"Same thing as you." She motioned up to the front where the worship leader worked out a rhythm with the guitarist. "We had choir practice over in the main sanctuary. We got out a few minutes ago, and I heard some *bachata*[25] and couldn't help myself."

"Oh, yeah, that's the new one the music director came up with. It's fun, isn't it?" Linda hummed the melody and danced a few steps. "This is only our second or third time doing it."

"Well, it sounded great. What are you up to now?"

"Heading home. I left at five in the morning for the *panadería* and haven't been home since."

"Dang, girl, that's a long day."

"Tell me about it." Linda walked out the door. "Where are you parked?"

"There's never any parking. I took the bus."

---

[25] A popular Latino music style

Linda frowned. "*Chica,*[26] this isn't a nice neighborhood to hang out in after dark."

"Got my mace." Becky lifted a small bottle from her purse. "Plus I took that self-defense class last year. Shin, eyes, groin," she called out as she acted out the steps.

"Remind me not to mess with you," Linda laughed. "I'll walk you to the bus stop, unless you wanna come hang out for a bit. My house is only a couple of blocks from here."

"If I didn't have a paper due tomorrow, I'd be all for it." Becky groaned. "I'm so behind, it's not even funny."

"Yeah, that's what I was telling Kevin today."

"Kevin?" Becky asked, a smile crossing her face. "Do tell."

"It's nothing." Linda brushed it off, her cheeks reddening. "He came to the library to study, and we talked about Native American stuff. Or was that yesterday at lunch?"

"Lunch one day? And a study date the next? He is so into you." Becky pinched her arm.

"Ow." Linda rubbed the spot. "He can't be into me. We're so different."

"Maybe that's what he's looking for. He's probably tired of all those cookie-cutter blonde Connecticut girls with trust funds and their own table at the country club." She paused. "I think I just described myself."

"Except you're from Charleston, silly. And you're cool, so it's okay." Linda chuckled.

"Aren't you a doll?" Becky added extra drawl and tossed her hair.

Linda didn't want to ask the question in her mind,

---

[26] Girl

but she didn't have any *amigas*[27] to gab with anymore. Most of her friends from high school were busy with babies or had moved out of town. "What if he's just, you know, slumming? Or making his parents mad by dating someone like me?"

"You mean someone amazing who's smart enough to get a full ride to college, strong enough to work full-time while maintaining a 4.0, and cool enough to teach us dorks how to salsa? Not to mention the whole innocent beauty thing you have going on."

"Thanks," Linda scoffed, "but I was referencing the poor, Mexican thing."

Becky put her hand on her hip. "Yeah, I know, but not everyone sees the world like that, Linda. Sometimes people just like you for you."

Linda considered that. "I sorta invited Kevin to church on Sunday." She bit her lip.

"Well, there's one way to see if he's really into you. If he doesn't get scared away by your mama, he might be a keeper. Oh, there's my bus." She raised her hand and gave Linda a squeeze. "*Adiós, amiga.*"

"*Adiós,*" Linda repeated as the bus pulled away.

She planned the next day in her head as she walked home. Mid-walk, she paused and calculated the date. "*Ay,*" she cried and jogged toward the *panadería*. After a minute of loud knocking, a light came on in the back.

"*¿Linda? ¿Eres tú?*"[28]

"*Sí, Doña. Déjeme entrar. Olvidé que mañana es el cumpleaños de mi mamá. Necesito comprar unos pedazos de pastel de tres leches.*"[29]

---

[27] Female friends

[28] Is that you?

[29] Yes, ma'am. Let me in. I forgot that tomorrow is my mom's birthday. I need to buy a few pieces of tres leches cake. Tres leches – three milk cake (milk, condensed milk, evaporated milk), traditional Latino style of very moist cake

Doña Hernandez opened the door, and Linda rushed in. "*No es necesario, amor. Ya le hice uno pequeño cuando me di cuenta de la fecha.*"[30]

"You're the best," Linda said, kissing her on the cheek. "*¿Está en la refrig?*"[31]

"*Sí, corazón.*"

Linda ran to the fridge and pulled out a tiny, freshly made birthday cake with her mother's name on it. "It's perfect. *Gracias.*"

"*De nada.*"

Linda put it in a small box and let Doña get the door. "*Nos vemos mañana en la tarde.*"[32]

Doña nodded, visible through the door as she locked up.

Linda smiled and walked home, carefully balancing the cake so it didn't slide around in the box. She opened the front door and sneaked a peek into the living room. Mamá was watching her *novela*, and with all the screaming and crying coming from the screen, she guessed it was a good one. This meant Linda had until the next commercial break before Mamá even acknowledged her presence.

She tiptoed through the living room and into the kitchen, groaning as she opened the fridge. It was full of *tacos*. Eyeing the space, she moved a few containers and rearranged enough of them to fit the cake. But she could not squeeze the last plate of *tacos* back in.

"What are you doing?" a deep voice asked.

She jumped and spun around, losing two *tacos* in the process. "Hector. You scared me."

He snickered. "You and your mom are both pretty jumpy."

---

[30] It's not necessary, honey. I already made a small one for you when I realized the date.

[31] Is it in the fridge?

[32] See you tomorrow afternoon.

"Yeah, well, we're not used to having a guy in the house." She knelt and picked up the fallen *tacos*.

"So, what are you doing?" he asked again.

Linda peeked into the living room. Still no commercial break. "Tomorrow's Mamá's birthday," she whispered.

"Oh yeah?"

"Doña Hernandez made her a cake, but I don't want her to see it until morning when I sing her 'Las Mañanitas.'"[33]

"Do you still do that?" He frowned. "I told Ma to stop waking me up so early a few years ago."

"Of course you would." Linda sighed and pushed the fridge closed. It popped back open again.

"Here." Hector bent down next to her, moving one container of shredded cabbage to a different spot. The door clicked closed.

"Thanks."

"*¿Qué hacen allí?*"[34] Mamá called from the door.

"*Nada*," Hector called and lost his balance. Arms flailing, he thudded onto the linoleum.

"Who's jumpy now?" Linda whispered, helping him up.

Tim brushed his teeth and studied himself in the mirror. He'd made his decision. He was definitely going to tell her tonight. He nodded at his reflection and spit out the toothpaste, slurping some water out of his hands. He patted his stomach, lifting his shirt in the mirror. He had to get back to working out.

He turned off the bathroom light and slipped into

---

[33] Traditional Mexican birthday song
[34] What are you doing over there?

bed next to Wendy. His pulse beat in his throat as he tried to pull together words. Before he could think of them, she rolled over to face him.

"Long day." She yawned.

"Yeah, this new job is wearing me out."

"All those long hours." Her elbow brushed against his forearm as she readjusted her pillow. "You must be exhausted."

"Actually, I'm kind of enjoying it. It feels really good to be working again, no matter what I'm doing."

Wendy blinked sleepily. "That's good, dear."

"Wendy?" His heart pounded.

"Yeah?" She opened her eyes. "Are you okay? You're breathing really fast."

"Actually, I thought maybe—" He paused, considering his word choice.

She groaned. "Not tonight, Tim. I'm too tired for anything physical right now. Maybe this weekend."

Tim's mouth dropped open. Anything physical? Her misinterpretation of his statement opened a branch of their relationship that he thought was dead. The possibility of intimacy floored him. It'd been months, maybe even a year. So long he almost couldn't remember. His desperation drained any thought of uncovering his lie; he was like a thirsty man on a desert trek. "Okay." He tongue stuck to the roof of his mouth. "Maybe this weekend." His confession would have to wait a little longer.

CHAPTER EIGHT
Las Mañanitas[1]

*L*inda's alarm went off next to her head, and she pressed random buttons until it stopped. In a daze, she groaned and squinted at the clock. Why had she set the alarm for five? Realization struck her, and she sat up. Beaming like a kid on Christmas morning, she hopped out of bed.

"Birthday," she said in a sing-songy voice, pulling on some sweatpants and heading out into the kitchen. She rifled through the containers in the fridge until she found the cake box. Feet padded behind her.

"Hey." Hector rubbed his eyes. "Is it time?"

"Yeah." Linda hummed to herself. She reached in the drawer and found some used candles. She lifted the cake onto a plate and stuck a few into its soft icing.

Hector reached with a lighter and lit them.

"Thanks." She picked up the plate and walked slowly towards the hall, keeping an eye on the candles. "You coming?"

---

1 The Little Morning Songs – the Mexican "happy birthday" song

Hector smiled in the dim light of morning. His big feet thudded on the linoleum as he caught up with her.

She knocked on the door and opened it slowly. Mamá turned over in bed, and they broke into song:

"Esas son las mañanitas que cantaba el rey David. Hoy por ser día de tu santo, te las cantamos a ti . . ."[2]

Mamá sat up in bed, wiping away happy tears as Linda sang the next few verses. After blowing out the candles, Mamá turned on the lamp next to her bed. *"Gracias, mija."*

"Feliz cumpleaños,[3] Mamá." Linda kissed Mamá on her damp cheek.

"Feliz cumpleaños, Doña," Hector bent and gave her a peck, too.

"Ay, gracias, muchachos." Mamá stuck her finger into the icing and licked it. *"Mmm, delicioso."*

"I'll bring the cake to the kitchen, and you can come out in a minute." Linda patted her mother's head and followed Hector out the door.

Hector frowned as Linda pulled out a wrapped package. "I didn't get her a present."

"You can make breakfast." Linda threw him his apron. "We like our eggs scrambled."

Tim whispered a goodbye to his sleeping family and grabbed his lunchbox full of leftover chicken and dumplings, a couple of sandwiches, and a bag of carrots, which he supposed were leftovers from Nathan's lunch since a couple had nibble marks on

---

[2] "These are the little morning songs that King David sang. Today because it is the day of your saint, we sing them to you . . ." – first line to "The Mañanitas" birthday song.

[3] Happy birthday

them. An hour later, he stepped off the bus and decided to try a shortcut he'd noticed that would save him half an hour on his route. As he walked down the sidewalk, his mind wandered. Why had he lied to Wendy in the first place? It was impossible to tell her the truth and not expect a horrible reaction. Once she found out, she would be furious. He shook his head. He'd tell her tonight. He had to. He'd checked his email again this morning, and no new jobs had opened in the region. Not the kind he needed, the kind he was pretending to work for.

A deep bark next to him brought him back to the present. He stiffened as a dog jumped towards him. A heavy chain, the other end of which was attached to the rickety railing of a stoop outside a large apartment complex, caught the animal in time before it reached the sidewalk. "Good dog," he managed to spit out and sped up. The beast snarled after him, metal rattling as it struggled against its steel prison. "Thank God for that chain." He'd hated dogs ever since his grandfather's had bitten him in fourth grade. He'd had to get ten stitches and a rabies shot. He noted to go another route tomorrow.

Looking around, he realized he was the only white person in the area. The sidewalks were filled with black and brown faces, shooting him serious looks. A group of thugs exchanged money for bags, and some druggie was shooting up in an alley. He searched for the clearest way back to a safer neighborhood.

The streetlight above his head turned off as he walked beneath it, and he picked up speed. He could see a bus a block down. As it drew closer, he realized it wasn't the one he needed, but he hopped on it anyway, his heart pounding. He dropped into an empty seat, shaken from the whole experience. This commute was starting to get to him.

Linda breezed through her exam and got a head start on next week's assignments before heading to the *panadería* and then back home. It was an early day for her. She almost didn't know what to do with herself as she walked up the sidewalk at five o'clock. Stepping into the house, the odor of seafood assaulted her.

She wrinkled her nose. "We never eat fish." She poked her head into the kitchen. "*¿Qué huele?*"[4]

Mamá smacked her arm with a dishtowel. "*Oye, cuidado. Hector me cocinó coctel de camarón. Es su especialidad.*"[5]

Linda walked over to the stove and peered into the pot Hector was stirring. She stuck out her tongue and grimaced.

"What?" he said.

Mamá cleared her throat.

"Looks good," Linda lied. The smell alone turned her stomach, not to mention the look of the cloudy pink broth.

"It's not done. This is just the *caldo*.[6] I still gotta add all the good stuff." He gestured toward the counter, where onions, tomatoes, limes, cilantro and avocados were cut into little piles.

Sighing, she leaned against the counter. Hector ladled the seafood soup into three bowls, added the extra ingredients, and then grabbed the ketchup out of the refrigerator, squeezing some into each bowl.

Acid rose from her stomach, and a wave of nausea passed through her. She could feel Mamá giving her

---

[4] What stinks?

[5] Hey, careful. Hector cooked me shrimp cocktail. His speciality.

[6] Broth

the look, so she forced a smile at Hector, grabbed the bottle of Valentina picante sauce, and sat down at the table. Hector served Mamá first before bringing bowls for him and Linda.

"*Huele rico*,[7] *Hector. Gracias.*" Mamá breathed in the steam rising from the soup.

Linda specifically avoided the stinky vapor and added a generous portion of hot sauce, hoping to drown out the flavor of seafood.

"Wow, you must really like Valentina," he said, watching her shake in the deep red sauce.

Linda winked at Mamá, who covered a grin with her napkin. She waited for Mamá to take the first sip.

"Mm," Mamá said, making a yummy sound. "*Está rico*,[8] *Hector.*"

"*Gracias.*"

Linda dipped her spoon in the soup and lifted it to her lips. She put the tip of her tongue in the liquid. "Not bad." She sipped it and decided it wasn't horrible. That was until her third spoonful brought up a very un-shrimplike item. "What is this?"

Mamá held up her spoon. "*Calamar.*"[9]

"Squid?" Linda dropped the spoon into the bowl with a clink. "Gross."

"*Fresa.*" Hector shook his head.

"Just because I don't like your weird soup doesn't make me a *fresa.*"

"I know," Hector said, popping a piece of squid in his mouth. "There are lots of reasons why you're a *fresa.*"

Mamá snorted and covered her mouth.

Linda looked over, surprised. She couldn't

---

[7] It smells delicious.
[8] It's delicious
[9] Squid

remember the last time Mamá had laughed. Mamá's giggles were contagious, and soon they were all cracking up. Her mother wiped away some tears and pulled Linda's soup bowl closer to her.

"Sorry, Hector. I don't really do seafood. At least I tried it," Linda said.

Mamá pointed at the fridge with her lips. "*Hay unos taquitos en el refrig.*"[10]

Thank you, Lord. Linda walked to the fridge and pulled out some leftover *taquitos,* heating them in a skillet. "How did it go yesterday and today with selling at the *panadería?*"

"*Muy bien,*" Mamá said, wiping a drip of soup with her napkin. "*Si solo había escuchado a Norma hace diez años, hubiéramos sido ricos.*"[11]

"Better late than never."

Hector nodded. "Yeah, yesterday she made a hundred dollars, but today we made twice that much. People were already asking what we were going to cook tomorrow."

"See? I told you." Linda patted her mother on the shoulder. "*Una buena chef.*"[12]

Mamá waved off her compliment. "Hector and I are *un buen equipo.*"[13]

Hector gave her a thumbs up and slurped up a big piece of shrimp.

"Yuck." Linda put her *taquitos* on a plate. "What are you guys making tomorrow?"

"*Gorditas,*"[14] Hector answered.

---

[10] There are some taquitos in the fridge.

[11] Very good. If I had only listened to Norma ten years ago, we would have been rich.

[12] A good chef.

[13] A good team

[14] Fried tortillas split down the middle and stuffed with meat, cheese, lettuce, tomatoes, and salsa

"Ooh, *guárdenme unas.*"[15]

"Okay." Mamá started in on Linda's bowl of soup. "*Es delicioso.*"

Linda smiled and crunched into her *taquitos.* "I suppose you're not a bad chef either, Hector."

Hector raised an eyebrow and then smirked. "Thanks."

---

[15] Save me some.

CHAPTER NINE
Ustedes Los Ricos[1]

*S*omehow Tim had gone another day without telling Wendy the truth about his job. Each day he moved closer and closer to telling her. Things at the garage were going well. Apparently, people liked the fact that Tim had helped Geovany and Fernando with their truck and were telling friends and family where to get auto repairs.

Guillermo walked around the shop whistling, often stopping to count the money coming in. He mumbled in Spanish and hardly had time to help Tim fix vehicles with the stream of people calling, picking up their cars, or dropping them off.

Tim was getting good at oil changes and fixing small problems. Guillermo still helped with the more challenging repairs. Tim had always been a fast learner, so anything Guillermo did, Tim learned or relearned by watching. As a kid, Tim had had to be quick, because his dad would only show him something once and expect him to know how to do it.

[1] You the Rich Ones – a 1948 Mexican movie with Pedro Infante

Most days he thought of his father when he was at work. Anything having to do with cars reminded Tim of him, which is why he'd stopped working on cars years ago. The year after his father had died, his mother had remarried a man with enough money to get her out of her aunt's house, leaving Tim to finish his final year of high school with his aging relative. His stepfather had been a philanderer and a horrible drunk. Tim, unable to bear his mother's desecration of his father's memory, had chosen a school on the other side of the country and had never spoken with his mother again. Needless to say, he tried not to think of that time. The last few days, though, every wrench, every spark plug, every oil change reminded him of his former life.

Linda's excitement rose throughout the day. Now that the week's tests were over and she had turned in her paper, it was smooth sailing. Finals would come in two weeks, and she knew the end of the semester would be hectic, which is why she couldn't wait for a relaxing night off.

With the exception of *pan dulce* and the campus cafeteria, she hardly ever ate out and rarely went to movies. She looked forward to seeing her friends and especially to spending time with Kevin. Her heart beat faster every time he crossed her mind.

Finding it harder than usual to concentrate in her literature class, she had completely zoned out before she realized everyone was staring at her. She straightened and shifted her gaze to the professor. "I'm sorry, Dr. Chekov. Did you call on me?"

"Yes, Linda," Dr. Chekov said with her light Ukranian accent. "I asked you to tell the class a little about The Dream Act. I found your paper very enlightening."

"Oh." Linda's face grew warm. She explained the basic ideas of the movement and then added, "There's a demonstration nearby next month. I think I might check it out."

"I don't understand," a particularly disagreeable student named Derrick stated. "If colleges know undocumented students can't do anything with a degree, why do they accept them?"

"Because, Derrick," Hannah stared him down with her bright green eyes, "everyone deserves a chance at a good education, regardless of their immigration status."

"But why do they deserve it?" another student asked. "What about all the immigrants who've waited years and spent money to enter the country legally? It seems unfair for them to have equal rights."

"Did anyone else see that train documentary?" Hannah asked. "People died, a lot of people, including kids. I mean, if you're going to risk your life to come here, I say you've earned a chance to go to school and contribute your best to society."

Derrick turned in his seat, shrugging. "I wouldn't want to take all the effort of applying for college, taking classes, and paying for school if, after I graduated, I couldn't get anything better than a dishwashing job."

"Exactly. That's what The Dream Act's for," Linda replied.

"It's not going to pass anyway," Derrick said. "Why even try?"

"Of course you wouldn't understand." Everyone's eyes widened. Never before had Linda spoken so strongly in class. "When you've had everything given to you all your life, you don't understand the satisfaction of hard work and a job well done. Just because society doesn't recognize something doesn't mean it's not worth fighting for."

Hannah whooped. "You tell him, girl."

"Thank you, Linda," Professor Chekov said. "Any other thoughts?"

Derrick crossed his arms. "What's our school's policy on accepting illegals?" He drew out the last word, giving Linda a pointed look.

Linda clenched her jaw. "As I mentioned in my explanation of The Dream Act, it's 'undocumented,' not 'illegal.' And the college's policy is to accept everyone, regardless of their immigration status."

"I guess that means you could be illegal." He narrowed his eyes at Linda.

Linda's heart squeezed in her chest.

Hannah jumped in. "Or it could mean you're illegal, Derrick."

Derrick snickered. "That's stupid. I can't be illegal. I'm—"

"White?" Hannah continued. "So are all the undocumented Eastern Europeans no one ever talks about. Plenty of white people have come to this country without a visa. Probably some of your ancestors."

"That is a good point," Dr. Chekov said. "In the eighteen and nineteen hundreds, many European immigrants would pay off steamship crew members and stow away. Once they arrived at Ellis Island, only one percent of people were sent back. And it was even simpler to cross over the Canadian border. By 1925, immigration services reported almost 1.5 million immigrants living illegally in the U.S., which meant that, during that time, one out of every hundred people living here was undocumented. Of those undocumented immigrants, about 200,000 obtained amnesty through a process called 'pre-examination,' not unlike what The Dream Act is trying to do."

Derrick sighed and turned back around again.

"Good discussion, everyone. I would like you all to read some articles or books on immigration and answer the following question in three to five pages." Dr. Chekov wrote on the board: *Why do people come to the U.S. without a visa knowing the hardships they will face?* "I want those papers sent to me by Wednesday. Have a nice weekend."

Linda ignored her desire to trip Derrick as he walked past her, nearly hitting her in the face with his backpack. She released a deep breath and packed up her things.

Hannah patted Linda's shoulder. "That guy's a jerk. Ignore him."

"It makes me so mad sometimes," Linda said. "And sad. People don't understand. You know?"

"Yeah." Hannah frowned. "Try not to think about it anymore, until you have to write that paper."

Linda laughed. "Everyone's going to hate me now. A new random assignment because of my essay."

"Actually, I believe it was more due to Derrick's ignorance, so they should blame him."

"Okay." Linda winked. "I'll go with that." She slung her bag over her shoulder. "You coming tonight?"

Hannah's brow wrinkled and then she blushed. "Oh, right, dinner and a movie. Can't make it."

"Oh." Disappointment settled in. The only time she could go out on the town this semester, and one of her favorite people wasn't going.

"Sorry, *chica*," Hannah said. "Gotta go."

Linda watched as Hannah hurried from the room, wondering what her friend was in such a rush to do.

"Hector, *no lo quemes*,"[2] Juanita advised as she looked at the stove.

He peered into the pot and went back to stirring.

Juanita mixed up the dough and formed them into fat tortillas. One by one, she dropped them into bubbling oil, waiting until they inflated like little balloons and turned a golden brown color. She laid them on plates covered in paper towels to absorb the excess grease. Once they cooled down enough to handle, she slit each one open along the edge, creating a pocket ready to be stuffed with meat. She placed them in the warm oven.

She observed Hector as he tasted the salsa and added more salt. They really did make a good team. It was hard to imagine doing all this work without his help. She'd thought it over long enough. She would ask him. "Hector?"

"Don't worry, I'm not burning it."

"No, no." She turned off the burner where the meat mixture boiled. "I wanna ask if you help me cook."

He raised a brow. "I'm already helping you cook."

"No," Juanita laughed. "*Siempre. Como un trabajo.*"[3]

"Oh." He stopped stirring for a moment, his brow furrowed. He shrugged. "Well, it's better than cleaning the toilet at Memo's shop."

"Oh, good. *Me ayudas bastante,*[4] Hector."

He grinned. "*Gracias.* This helps me, too." He laid his spoon on the edge of the pot and pulled Juanita into a hug. "Okay, let's make some *gorditas.*"

---

[2] Don't burn it.
[3] Always. Like a job.
[4] You're such a big help.

Linda stood in the cafeteria with a chicken sandwich and a salad. Becky and Brian sat together at a table near the wall. They noticed her and waved her over.

"Hey, guys."

"I heard you kicked Derrick's butt in Lit class today," Brian said.

"How did you hear that?"

"Hannah posted it."

"*Ay, esa muchacha.*"[5] Linda smirked and ate a bite of her salad. "What else did she say?"

"That you defended the rights of undocumented students everywhere," Becky stated.

Linda coughed out a laugh. "That's a bit of an exaggeration. The teacher asked me to talk about my paper, and I said a few things and then responded to Derrick's ignorant comments."

"I think you can probably leave out 'ignorant,'" Brian said. "All Derrick's comments are ignorant, so it's implied."

Becky laughed. "Ain't that the truth." She traced her finger along Brian's jawline and then kissed him on the cheek.

Linda did a double-take. "Whoa, hold on. Wait, wait, wait. This is new. Are you guys going out?"

Becky grabbed Brian's arm and pulled him close. "Yeah, ever since salsa night. Brian wowed me with his dance skills."

Brian rolled his eyes and snorted. "I think she just felt bad for me. But I'll take what I can get." He kissed her full on the lips.

Linda was beginning to feel third-wheelish. She cleared her throat. "You guys coming out tonight?"

---

[5] That girl.

Brian and Becky grinned at each other. "No, we had plans already."

"Hmm." Munching on her salad, Linda pondered the situation. "You guys never miss activities, and now neither you two nor Hannah can make it. Next thing you know, Kevin'll cancel, too."

"Oh, I don't think that'll happen," Brian laughed.

Becky elbowed him in the gut.

"Ugh. That was a chicken nugget you just hit."

"Ew," Becky said, leaning away from him. "Why am I dating you again?"

Brian grinned and stuffed another chicken nugget in his mouth. "My charm," he said with his mouth full.

Linda scarfed down her chicken sandwich before she had to witness a make-out session at the lunch table. She finished her water and stood up. "Well, gotta get to the library and work on a paper."

"Have fun tonight," Becky said in a sing-song tone.

"Thanks." Linda raised an eyebrow. This was starting to get weird.

Tim popped the chicken and dumplings in the microwave around three o'clock. His sandwiches had disappeared slowly throughout the day, and he was ready for something substantial. He was thankful Guillermo's hot niece had brought her friend to clean up the other day, because he was pretty sure the microwave hadn't been cleaned. Ever. He wasn't too particular, but who knew what Mexicans ate?

The phone rang for the umpteenth time. Five more people had brought their vehicles before lunch, and he and Guillermo had worked on about ten since they'd opened at seven. The microwave beeped, and he pulled out his steaming food.

Guillermo walked by. "Looks good, Conejo."

"Yeah, it's my favorite. Chicken and dumplings." He inhaled the aroma of the food and sat on a rickety folding chair. Blowing on a bite, he tasted the creamy dish.

Guillermo opened a Styrofoam container to reveal what looked like fried *tacos*. "*Gorditas. Mi favorito.*[6] Mmm . . . still warm." He sat on the other folding chair and bit the corner of a small plastic bag of salsa, letting it drip onto the *gorditas*. "I ordered the parts for the Explorer and the Dakota. They should come in Monday afternoon." He took a crunchy bite, some of the loose meat, white cheese, lettuce, and tomato falling onto his lap. "Want one?"

Tim shook his head, wrinkling his nose. "I'm good, thanks."

"You sure? They're delicious. My sister made them. She's selling food at the *panadería* now."

"The pana-what?" Tim mumbled, stuffing a forkful of dumpling into his mouth.

"*Panadería*. It's a Mexican bakery. She made all those *tamales* you ate the other day."

"Those were good." Tim nodded. "I'm glad that little kid caught me before I ate the outside though. I didn't know it was a corn husk."

Laughing, Guillermo held the plate out to Tim. "No corn husks here. Easier."

"Okay," Tim sighed and grabbed the hard shell. "Wait," he said before Guillermo took the plate away. He spooned some chicken and dumplings onto Guillermo's plate. For a second he flashed back to middle school lunches, where he and his friends

---

[6] My favorite.

would trade their apples for oranges and share their cookies or chips.

"*Gracias.*"

"You're welcome. What am I eating?" Tim asked, poking at the meat in particular.

"A *gordita*. It's a fat, fried tortilla opened down the middle and stuffed with meat and cheese."

"It reminds me of the *tacos* Wendy makes sometimes with the hard yellow shells and all the fixings." Tim took a small bite and chewed. "Not bad." He took a bigger bite. "You Mexicans must really love corn."

Guillermo laughed. "As much as you Americans love bread." He poked at the dumpling. "And the Chinese, rice. The Italians, pasta."

"I guess that's true. It's pretty good." Tim finished his last bite of *gordita* and returned to his original meal. "Are we working tomorrow?"

Gullermo shrugged. "If you wanna come in."

"I have bills to catch up on," Tim said. "I could use the extra money."

"I don't work Sunday," Guillermo said, his mouth full of food.

"Sounds good to me."

"Yeah, I got church. You go?"

Tim waved his hand. "Nah, that's not really our thing. Sometimes we go with my in-laws at Christmas, but that's about it."

"No good, man. You should come with us sometime."

He couldn't even handle a prayer vigil without flipping out. What would a whole service in Spanish be like? Probably full of loud music and people jumping around and convulsing in the aisles. Not his cup of tea. "Thanks for the invite, but I think I'll pass."

Guillermo grew serious, leaning forward in his chair. "I used to be like you. Trying to do it all on my own. Then I realized I needed God in my life. I needed his forgiveness."

A smirk crept onto Tim's face. Who did this guy think he was? They weren't anything alike. "We're doing fine, thanks." What Tim needed was a steady paycheck. Only money could solve his problems right now. Besides, certain things were unforgivable, like what had happened with that girl his freshman year of college. He hadn't touched a drop of alcohol since then, and his stepfather had covered up the situation with money, but nothing could erase what he'd done.

Guillermo shrugged. "Your funeral, man." He took a bite of the creamy chicken. "Your wife's a good cook. Does she work in a restaurant?"

Tim laughed. "No, just in our kitchen. She takes care of the house and the kids."

"She don't work?"

Tim shook his head. "Not since we had Nathan. That's our first kid." He put the lid back on the empty container and stuck it in his lunch bag.

"How many you got?" Guillermo asked, tossing his Styrofoam container in the trash and wiping his hands on his jumpsuit.

"Two. Nathan's six and Jeremy's four. You?"

"One. She lives in North Carolina with my ex."

Tim nodded. "That's hard."

"It's not too bad. She comes up for a week or two at Christmas and a few more weeks in the summer."

Tim sighed, thinking how sad it would be to see Nathan and Jeremy only a few weeks of the year if he and Wendy divorced. He shoved the thought away and stood up. "Ready to start on the Kia?"

The *gorditas* flew out of the store in groups of five or ten or even twenty. Thank goodness Juanita had left a few in her brother's kitchen before going to the *panadería*. She placed vegetables in her basket along with a few spices. The rest of tomorrow's ingredients would have to be purchased from the market down the street.

Hector passed Norma containers filled with four *gorditas* and a small bag of salsa.

"*¿Qué va a cocinar mañana, Juanita?*"[7] Carlita asked. Carlita was, by far, their best customer. Her purplish-red-dyed hair was pulled into a ponytail. Her dress was at least two sizes too small and stretched so tight over her thick body that Juanita feared it would split in two.

"*Menudo.*"[8]

"*Ay, qué delicioso,*" exclaimed Carlita. "*¿Y el domingo?*"[9]

"*No cocino el domingo. Es el día del Señor, un día de descanso.*"[10]

Carlita frowned. She was not a regular church attendee. A day of rest that didn't involve *tacos* was apparently not appealing to her. "*¿Y el lunes?*"[11]

"*No sé. Hector, ¿qué piensas?*"[12]

Hector handed another happy customer a container. "For Monday? Maybe *chiles rellenos?*"[13]

Carlita's arm fat jiggled as she clapped her hands. "*Sí, eso, por favor.*"[14]

---

[7] What are you cooking tomorrow, Juanita?

[8] A soup made of cow stomach

[9] And Sunday?

[10] I don't cook on Sundays. It is the Lord's day, a day of rest.

[11] And Monday?

[12] I don't know. Hector, what do you think?

[13] Stuffed peppers.

[14] Yes, that, please.

Juanita lifted her basket onto the counter. "Okay."

"We should make a menu for each week, Doña," Hector suggested. "I can bring in this little chalkboard I have at home."

"*Me parece bien,*"[15] Norma agreed. She counted up the containers. "*Sólo hay tres ordenes más.*"[16]

"*Yo los compro,*"[17] Carlita said, raising her hand.

Hector smirked and passed them over to Carlita, who paid Juanita.

"*Buen provecho,*"[18] Juanita said.

Her heels clunking on the tiles, Carlita marched to the door, waiting until Hector opened it for her. After buying eight orders of *gorditas,* she had her hands full.

Linda heard Kevin's heavy footsteps treading the library's worn carpet. Before he could say her name, she logged off the computer, turned, and greeted him. "Hi, Kevin."

"Hey."

She frowned when she saw his khakis and nice shirt. "Oh, no. Was I supposed to dress up?" She glanced down at her jeans, blouse, and ballet flats. Thank goodness she'd chosen a blouse over a t-shirt today.

"You look great." He flashed a nervous smile.

Why was he acting weird? She packed up her bag and stood up. "Is everyone meeting here?" She stretched on tiptoes, straining to see the door.

---

[15] Sounds good to me.

[16] Only three orders left.

[17] I'll buy them.

[18] Bon Appetite.

"Actually," he said, rubbing the back of his neck, "no one else could make it."

"Hmm. Do you still want to go out then? If it's just me."

He smiled, his cerulean eyes catching the last sunlight shining through the library's windows. "Definitely."

"Okay. Oh." Linda paused. "Oh." Oh no. She realized now why Becky and Hannah had acted so strange earlier. This was a date. Like an actual date. Her first date. The pressure rose, her stomach did some backflips, and she suddenly felt as awkward as he was acting.

"The movie starts at eight. We should get to the restaurant soon, so we have plenty of time."

Linda followed him outside. "So . . ." she started, unsure of what to say. "Where are we going for dinner?"

"Where do you want to go?" he asked.

She shrugged. "I never eat anywhere except the caf and home. I don't really know any places around here."

He shoved his hands in his jacket pockets. "There's an Ethiopian place a couple of blocks from here that's pretty good."

"Ethiopian?" Linda raised an eyebrow. "What kind of food do they eat?"

"Oh, it's good. It's kind of like Indian food."

Linda suddenly felt pretty uncultured for being head of the Cultural Club. "I've never had Indian food either."

Kevin chuckled. "Well, you're in for something different, then. They eat lots of greens, lentils, and vegetables. It's good. They have this bread called injera. It's kind of like a fermented tortilla. It looks like a sponge and feels like skin."

Linda grimaced. "That does *not* sound good."

"Oh, come on, where's your sense of adventure?"

"All right, why not?" She shrugged.

"Cool," he said. "It's fun, 'cause you get to eat with your hands."

"I'm good at that. We eat with tortillas all the time."

They walked in silence for a block or so. "Here it is." Clearing his throat, he opened the door for her.

"Thank you." The hairs on Linda's arms stood up as his hand grazed her back, guiding her into the restaurant. She breathed a little faster.

"Table for two, please," he said.

They followed the waitress to a small booth in the corner. Linda chose one side, and Kevin sat across from her.

"Tonight's special is Doro Wat, which is chicken and hard-boiled eggs in a red pepper paste. We also have a curry soup." The waitress handed them the leather-bound menus. "Can I start you with something to drink?"

"Thank you." Linda glanced at the menu. Fifteen dollars for a meal? Good thing she brought that extra twenty from her money jar. "I'll have water."

"Me, too," Kevin said. The waitress left, and Kevin pointed at the menu. "If you want, we can get the Dinner for Two and try all different things."

It cost about the same as everything else. "Sure."

"Do you like spicy stuff?"

Linda smirked. "Are you questioning my Mexicanicity?"

He laughed. "You crack me up, Linda."

Her heart warmed as he said her name. This was the only time he had called her by her first name. It sounded nice coming out of his mouth.

Linda let Kevin pick out the different dishes that

came with dinner, since nothing sounded remotely familiar to her. Twenty minutes and a pleasant conversation later, their food arrived on a big, round tray. A spongy, grey, circular bread topped with brightly colored unknown foods lay on the tray like an off-color pizza. The only food Linda recognized was the salad in the middle.

She leaned forward and took a whiff. At least it smelled good.

Kevin raised his water glass. "To new adventures."

"To new adventures." Linda lifted her own glass, clinking it with his.

"I'm going to work late again today," Tim said, the phone line crackling loudly in his ear.

"It's really hard to hear you," Wendy sighed. "Why don't you use an office phone?"

"The boss doesn't like us to use our phones for personal business."

"Fine, but next time find a quieter place to call from. Borrow someone's cell phone and go to the storage closet or something." There was an edge to her voice.

"Okay, I'll be home around eight or nine. I just wanted to let you know."

"You're working a lot of hours over there. I hope they pay overtime."

"They do. Don't worry."

"When do you get paid?"

"Can we talk about this tomorrow?" Tim sighed.

"Fine," she said.

He knew that was woman-code for "not fine," but he didn't want to deal with it at the moment. "All right, I'll be home as soon as I can."

Click. She had hung up on him before he could even say goodbye.

Juanita and Hector prepared the ingredients for *menudo*, so it'd be ready for tomorrow. *Menudo* took a long time to make, and she wanted to get a head start. After an hour of preparation, they sat at the kitchen table.

Hector stood up again. "Hold on." He walked to the living room and came back with a small chalkboard and some colored chalk. "I found it stuffed in the back of my closet." At the top he'd written MENU and on the left were the next week's dates. He pointed to a word next to each number. "Did I spell them right?"

"*No sé. Nunca fui a la escuela.*"[19] Juanita shrugged.

"You never had to go to school?"

Juanita frowned. "Is a privilege to go to school. *Mis padres,*[20] they had no money to send a girl to school."

"You wanted to go to school, but they didn't let you?"

Juanita nodded.

"Why didn't you start school when you came to the U.S.? Weren't you a teenager?"

"*No hubo tiempo.*[21] All day working, working, and then taking care of Linda."

Hector screwed up his face in concentration. "I have an idea."

"*¿Pues?*" Juanita cocked her head.

---

[19] I never went to school.
[20] My parents
[21] There wasn't time.

"You teach me how to cook, and I'll teach you how to read and write."

His excitement won out over any embarrassment she felt. She didn't want to hurt his feelings. *"Está bien. Empezamos el lunes."*[22]

"Okay." He picked out a piece of blue chalk. "Now let's figure out what we're cooking next week."

"I'm so full." Linda leaned back in the booth. "That weird bread really fills you up."

"But it's good, right?" Kevin asked, grabbing a piece of injera and picking up the last of the greens.

"Yeah, I have to admit. It's pretty delicious."

"Told you."

Linda smiled back at him. The initial nervousness had worn off, and they'd been chatting comfortably for the last hour or so. Eating with your hands really broke down barriers. "What time does the movie start?"

"Eight. Why? What time is it?"

Linda shrugged. "Don't know. I don't have a watch."

"Oh, is that why you're always late to class?" Kevin's eyes flashed.

"No, we call it *la hora latina*."

"¿La hora latina?"

"Yes, my *gente*[23] put more emphasis on relationships than on time frames. So, if someone shows up at our house for a visit, but we have an appointment, we visit for a few minutes and then go late to the appointment."

---

[22] All right. We start on Monday.
[23] People

"What kind of people are showing up at your house before our 9 a.m. math class?"

Linda laughed, covering her mouth. "Okay, that day I overslept. But the rest of my argument is valid."

"I get it. You've got the collective culture, and we're all individualistic. That must be tricky. Either way you end up making somebody mad. If you forgo the collectivism and skip out on a visit, they'd feel disrespected, but if you stay, then the Americans feel disrespected. It seems like you might have adapted by now, though. Haven't you lived in this country your whole life?"

"Pretty much," Linda said. "But like all of us, I'm still heavily influenced by my surrounding culture. You'll see when you come to church on Sunday."

Kevin sighed. "I haven't been to church in a long time. Just thinking about it is giving me acid reflux."

"It might be the pound of spicy lentils and beef you just ate."

"Nah." He smirked. "Definitely the church thing. Well, we should probably get to the theater. It's a bit of a walk, but it's easier than trying to find a parking spot."

"I wouldn't know." She grabbed her purse and pulled out her wallet.

Kevin touched her arm and reached into his back pocket. "It's on me."

For a second she'd forgotten it was a date. Now she felt awkward again. "Thanks, Kevin."

He smiled and dropped a few twenties on the table. He held out his hand, and she took it. She thought he'd let go once they were standing, but he didn't. Her head swam as his ocean blue eyes focused on her face. "This was nice."

She wondered if he could hear her heart pounding like mad. "Yeah."

They stood still staring into each other's eyes for a moment until the waitress walked over, killing the magic. "Do you need a box?" she asked.

Kevin dropped Linda's hand and shook his head. "Nah, I think we're good."

Linda eyed the half-eaten food. "Well, if it's okay, I'll take it home."

The waitress left and returned in seconds with a take-home box and a plastic bag to carry it.

Linda rolled up the injera and folded it into the box, along with the leftover foods. She closed the box and followed Kevin outside.

"Sorry," Kevin said. "I should have asked."

"I hate seeing good food go to waste." Linda smiled up at Kevin. "It's so cold." She grabbed Kevin's arm and wrapped her hand around it. He stiffened. "Sorry. Was that okay? That's kind of a Latino thing, too."

"Yes, you just took me by surprise. It's very okay." He leaned into her and ran his hand over her fingers. "Your hands are freezing." He covered them with his warm hand. "You want my jacket?"

"No, I always have cold hands."

"Cold hands, warm heart."

"What?"

"My grandmother used to say that. Anyway, my hands are always warm. Must be a sign."

Linda chuckled and breathed in his cologne. "You smell nice."

He cleared his throat. "Thanks. It's Axe. You smell nice, too."

"Thanks, I think it's eau de injera."

He burst out in a loud laugh. Several people turned around in front of them.

"Shh," Linda said, giggling. "They're going to think we're drunk or something."

"Drunk on Ethiopian food," he said, cracking up again.

After the laughter wore off, they walked in comfortable silence for a few minutes. Linda enjoyed the warmth of his arm against hers. They walked slowly, enjoying the evening air.

They found the theater, and Kevin paid for her ticket. Once Linda sat down, Kevin reached for her hands and warmed them. Linda found it hard to concentrate on the movie with Kevin so close, running his thumb over her hand. From time to time the shadows from the screen reflected on his fair face. Even with her gaze straight ahead, she felt his eyes burning like beams of sunlight through the clouds on a hot August day. Sometimes they caught each other staring at the same time, grinned with trembling lips, and quickly glanced away. Kevin whispered comments to her during the film. His breath in her ear and on her neck raised goose bumps.

"That was a really good movie," Kevin said. "I didn't realize that was his son until the very end. A good twist."

"Yeah." Linda had no idea what the movie was about, having been so distracted by her company. She fished for something to say. "It's too bad no one else could make it," Linda remarked as they walked down the sidewalk, her arms encircling Kevin's elbow.

Kevin was quiet. "I have a confession to make."

Linda raised an eyebrow.

His ears grew red. "I kind of told everyone not to come."

"I know." Linda smiled.

"You know? Did someone tell you?"

"No. Becky, Hannah, and Brian were all acting weird today, so I put two and two together. We women are very intuitive."

"I was afraid you might say no, and I've liked you for a while. I wasn't sure if you liked me, too, and I didn't want to lose you as a friend." He paused. "I've never met anyone like you, Linda. I hope you're not mad about tonight."

She stopped and lifted her gaze to his. "Not at all."

His stare flittered from her eyes to her mouth. He brushed her hair from her face, leaned down, and kissed her.

CHAPTER TEN
La Semilla de Mostaza[1]

By the time Sunday morning rolled around, Linda's feet had finally landed back on the ground. Now the cold reality hit her like an Arctic blast. She had invited a boy to church. A white boy. A rich, white boy. She would have to tell Mamá about it. And Mamá could read her like a book. Linda waited until they were almost out the door.

"Mamá, *le invité a un muchacho de la universidad a la iglesia hoy.*"[2]

"*¿Sí?*" Mamá studied Linda's face with pursed lips. "*Y ¿quién es?*"[3]

"*Se llama Kevin y es de Connecticut.*"[4]

"Connecticut?" Hector asked. "That's like the capital for rich, white people."

Linda huffed. "Hector, stay out of this."

---

[1] The Mustard Seed – a Latino praise and worship song
[2] I invited a boy from college to church today.
[3] Who is it?
[4] His name is Kevin, and he's from Connecticut.

He smirked and finished buttoning his shirt.

"*¿Es tu novio?*"[5] Mamá narrowed her eyes.

"*No sé,*" Linda replied. Friday's kiss had left her wondering.

"*¿Cómo que no sabes?*"[6] Mamá put her hands on her hips.

"*Pues, salimos el viernes.*"[7]

"*Tú me dijiste que ibas a salir con el Club Cultural.*"[8]

"It's true. It was a club activity, but no one else showed up."

Mamá raised an eyebrow. "*Y ¿qué hicieron?¿Fuiste a su apartamento?*"[9]

"No." Linda's defensiveness kicked in. "We only went out for dinner and then watched a movie. I'm twenty-one, Mamá. I can go on a date without telling you."

Mamá shook her head. "*Te lo dije y te lo digo otra vez. Los hombres sólo quieren una cosa.*"[10]

Hector raised his pointer finger. "That's not always true."

Linda and her mother both told him to shut up, Linda in English and Mamá in Spanish. Hector plopped down on the couch and crossed his arms.

Linda hugged her mother. "Mamá, I know you want to protect me, *pero ya soy grande.*[11] You can't protect me from everything."

Tears formed in Mamá's eyes. "*Yo sé, mija. Yo sé.*"[12]

"Besides," Linda said. "Kevin is a very nice boy. I

---

[5] Is he your boyfriend?

[6] What do you mean you don't know?

[7] Well, we went out on Friday.

[8] You told me you were going out with the Cultural Club.

[9] And what did you do? Did you go back to his apartment?

[10] I've told you once, and I'll tell you again. Men only want one thing.

[11] But I'm big now.

[12] I know, my daughter, I know.

think you'll like him." Linda glimpsed the clock. "*Vámanos. Ya es tarde.*"[13]

Mamá kissed Linda. Wrinkles lined her eyes as she pinched Linda's cheeks. Hard. "*Está bien, mija. Vámanos a conocerle a este Kevin.*"[14] The way Mamá spit his name did not foreshadow a good first meeting.

Tim rolled over in the bed and noticed Wendy's spot was already cold. He squinted at the clock. Almost eleven. He'd slept nearly twelve hours. He yawned, stretching his tired muscles, before slowly sliding his feet into his moccasins.

Splashing cold water on his face, he attempted to tame his unruly hair. He ran his tongue over his freshly-brushed teeth and headed downstairs.

"Daddy," Jeremy yelled, attaching himself to Tim's leg.

"Hey, buddy. Where's Mommy?"

"She's making pancakes with smiley faces."

"Okay, finish watching your cartoons."

Jeremy sang the theme song for Bob the Builder and hopped back on the sofa, getting under his favorite fuzzy Sponge Bob blanket.

Tim chuckled and wandered into the kitchen. He leaned over her shoulder at the sizzling skillet. "Smells good." He gave her shoulder a squeeze. "Where's Nathan?"

"He has some big project he's working on." She nodded at the corner, where Nathan knelt, surrounded by popsicle sticks, Elmer's glue, and cotton balls.

---

[13] It's late.
[14] Let's go meet this Kevin.

"Whatcha making, kiddo?" Tim lowered himself to the floor next to him.

"It's a surprise." Nathan's brow wrinkled, and his little tongue stuck out in concentration as he glued another popsicle stick.

"Oh." Tim kissed Nathan on the top of his head. "Well, it looks pretty cool."

"Yeah," Nathan said. "I know."

Wendy wiped her hands on a kitchen towel. "Nathan, go get your brother. Both of you need to wash your hands. The pancakes are ready."

Nathan shook a cotton ball off his sticky finger and hopped up. "Yay," he yelled. His little, bare feet slapped the floor as he ran through the kitchen.

"Nathaniel Caleb, no running in the house."

"Sorry." Elbows jetting out, he slowed to a fast walk.

Tim pulled dishes from the cabinet and set the table. "Any plans for today?"

"Just relaxing." Steam rose from the pancakes and bacon as Wendy placed them on the table next to the syrup and butter.

"Sounds good. I'm exhausted. I haven't worked this hard since I was a kid."

"You're working a lot of hours, but you've put in overtime before."

"Yeah, but this is different." Tim forked a few pancakes onto his plate.

"How so?" Wendy put one pancake on each of the boy's plates along with one piece of bacon before serving herself.

Tim had decided he'd tell her today. But this wasn't exactly the moment. The boys came sliding into the kitchen. "I'll tell you later."

"Pancakes," Jeremy cried, clapping his hands. "Mine has a smiley face."

Tim glanced at his plate. Blueberries formed a smiley face on each pancake. Looking over at his wife, hopefulness entered his heart. Why was he so worried? What was the worst that could happen?

Linda smiled. Kevin stood outside the church, shifting from one foot to the other, looking into the distance. Everyone eyeing him on their way inside wasn't helping matters.

Finally, he turned in their direction, his shoulders relaxing. He waved and walked towards them. "*¿La hora latina?*" he asked with a grin.

Linda gave him a warning glance, nodding in her mother's direction. "Not quite."

Her mother cleared her throat.

"Hello, you must be Mrs. Palacios." Kevin extended his hand. "*Mucho gusto.*"[15]

"*Un placer,*"[16] Mamá said in a very unpleasant tone.

Kevin pointed to Hector. "Is this your brother?"

"Ew, no." Linda grimaced. "That's Hector. I don't have a brother. I'm an only child."

Kevin offered a hand to Hector, but Hector stuck his in his pocket.

Mamá smacked him on the arm. "*Salúdale,*"[17] Mamá ordered.

Frowning, Hector stuck out his hand.

"Nice to meet you," Kevin said.

Hector mumbled a response.

The pastor waved them inside, and Mamá and Hector entered the building.

---

[15] Nice to meet you.
[16] A pleasure.
[17] Greet him.

Kevin pulled Linda to the side. "What was that? Do they hate me already?"

"Don't mind Hector. He's been in love with me since he was seven."

"Oh, he's that guy." Kevin rolled his eyes. "But what about your mom? She was piercing me with dagger eyes."

"She's a little protective."

"A little? Mama bears have been friendlier."

Linda covered up a laugh. "I told you it'd be an adventure," she said as they led the way inside.

"*Buenos días.*" Pastor Martinez shook everyone's hands on the way in.

A few rows from the front of the sanctuary, they sat down next to Mamá and Hector in the Palacios' usual spot.

"Do you want an earpiece?" Linda asked. "For interpretation?"

Kevin shook his head. "Nah, I'll wing it. I'll put my six years of Spanish into practice."

"I have to go up to sing. I'll be back." Linda stood up.

"But—" he protested.

"Don't worry. They won't bite." She touched his shoulder as she walked past.

Juanita scanned the pale-skinned, blue-eyed boy sitting one chair over. He smelled like trouble. Why would someone like him be interested in her Lindita?

She didn't worry as much when she looked at Hector. Maybe because she knew him better, maybe because Hector had held a flame for Linda for so many years, maybe because she'd had so many bad experiences with Americans, or maybe the Holy

Spirit was telling her something. She wasn't sure, but she didn't have a good feeling about him. The boy's hands trembled as he flipped through the bulletin. She smirked. Good, he was nervous. She hoped he'd think before he did anything to hurt her precious daughter.

She glanced at Hector. His right heel drummed the floor. She placed her hand on his knee.

"Sorry."

Searching her memory, she tried to recall the last time she had seen Hector at church, other than at the prayer vigil earlier in the week. He'd stopped going sometime in high school, so it'd been a few years. He looked about as uncomfortable as Linda's friend, Kevin. She shook her head. She could tell he liked her daughter as more than a friend.

Juanita found it harder to read Americans. It didn't help that she didn't know the boy's family or where he came from. That might have given her a better idea of what kind of person he was. The language barrier didn't help either. She was pretty sure he didn't know much Spanish, but sometimes those *güeros*[18] surprised her.

Chairs creaked and fabric rustled as everyone stood for the scripture reading. She tried to pay attention to the words but had trouble concentrating. Apart from her distracting thoughts, the boy was attempting to read as fast as the congregation and falling behind. He stumbled over the harder words but could pronounce most of them. Spanish was easier than English anyway.

When the sanctuary filled with music, Juanita focused better and got lost in the songs. Music could always distract her, even in the most difficult times.

---

[18] White people

Tim sat nervously on the couch in his office, his hands pinching his coffee mug in a death grip. Wendy sat at the other end, sipping her own coffee as she scrolled through social media on her phone. Nathan had resumed his project on the kitchen floor, and Jeremy was in front of the television again.

Tim took a deep breath. "I've been meaning to talk with you about something."

"What's wrong?" She flipped her phone over on her lap and eyed him over the edge of her cup.

Nervous energy pulsed through his system, and he took another sip of his coffee before placing the mug on his desk. "Nothing's wrong. I wanted to talk with you more about my job."

"Okay . . . ?"

"You know how I told you I've been working at a big company in the city?"

"Yeah."

"I lied."

Wendy's nostrils flared. Not a good sign. "Then what have you been doing for all those hours?"

"Oh, I got a job. Just not an office job."

"What kind of *job* did you get?" Wendy carefully—too carefully—set her coffee down next to his. She leaned back, crossing her arms.

"I'm a mechanic in the barrio."

Wendy cocked her head. "A mechanic? In the barrio? Are you kidding me right now?"

Heart racing, Tim shook his head. "I saw the sign and got the job once my boss made sure I could actually work on cars."

"I can't even process this." Wendy brushed a strand of hair out of her eyes. "What are you getting paid?"

"I get a percentage of every car I work on, which is going really well. I've made well over a thousand dollars this week. My boss calls me 'Conejo' because I'm fast like a rabbit."

"Your boss is a Mexican? This just keeps getting worse. What am I supposed to tell the girls at the salon?"

"The truth. That your husband is an excellent mechanic and making good money."

"Oh yeah, that'll go over well. It'll be the talk of the town soon enough. This is so embarrassing." She stood in a huff. "I can't handle this." And she walked out of the room.

"At least she didn't hit me," Tim mumbled as he took another swig of coffee.

Linda enjoyed watching Kevin from the front of the church. He squirmed a bit during the service, trying to sing the songs and understand the Bible verses. His ears constantly turned brighter shades of red, but he smiled up at her. As she sat down for the sermon, he leaned into her, his body warm against hers. She was glad he didn't try to hold her hand. Mamá would probably have smacked them.

The only thing that ate at her were her questions about Kevin's faith. They hadn't talked about religion, mostly politics and culture and schoolwork. There was so much she didn't know about him yet, but she supposed that was the fun of dating. Getting to know someone. She hoped she liked what she learned about him. His heart seemed to be in the right place, but one could never really be sure.

After church was over, Linda grinned at Kevin. "So what'd you think?"

"Really nice. All the church members were so friendly, the songs were new for me, and what I caught of the sermon was really interesting. It's been a long time since I've gone to church. I'm glad you invited me."

"¿*No va a la iglesia?*"[19] Mamá asked, her jaw clenched.

Strike two. Luckily Kevin answered.

"*Sí, Señora Palacios, voy a la iglesia con mis padres en Connecticut. Pero no encuentro una iglesia aquí.*[20] I liked this. Maybe I'll come back next week." He shot Linda a smile.

Tío walked over and clapped Hector on the back, making him jump. "You did a good job the other day, Hector."

"Thanks."

"You can come over once a week for a few hours if you want. To help out a bit."

"Okay."

"¿*Quién es el güero?*"[21] Tío lifted his chin towards Kevin.

"*Es mi amigo,*[22] Kevin," Linda answered before her mother could. "Kevin, this is my Tío Memo."

"*Mucho gusto.*" Kevin shook Tío's hand.

"Hmm." Tío narrowed his eyes, glancing at Mamá.

A spark of mischief gleamed in Mamá's eye. "*Mija, ¿por qué no le invitas a tu amigo para almorzar en la casa? Ayer hice menudo.*"[23]

Linda grimaced. She could barely stomach

---

[19] He doesn't go to church?

[20] Yes, Mrs. Palacios. I go to church with my family in Connecticut, but I don't find a church here.

[21] Who's the white guy?

[22] He's my friend.

[23] Why don't you invite your friend over for lunch at the house? I made menudo yesterday.

menudo and expected a boy like Kevin would turn up his nose at the sight and smell of the soup. But before she could protest, he accepted the invitation.

"I would love to come. Thank you. It's better than ramen."

"Don't be so sure," Linda whispered to him.

Mamá smirked, and Hector and Guillermo chuckled. Kevin cast a worried glance at Linda.

Linda shrugged. "You can't back out now." They turned and headed home.

Tim washed out his coffee cup, placing it in the drying rack, and walked over to Nathan.

"I'm almost done." He glued the last couple of pieces together. "There. Mommy, Mommy," he shouted. "Come see."

Wendy strode into the room, completely ignoring Tim, and bent to see Nathan's project. "Wow, this is really great Nathan. What is it?"

"It's Joe the Mechanic working on magic cars."

Wendy shot Tim a scathing look.

"See, there's Joe." Joe was represented by G.I. Joe, who stood next to a few matchbox cars. "And there's the magic cars." Nathan pointed to a structure built of popsicle sticks and cotton balls. "And that's his garage. In the clouds."

"That's exactly like his shop." Tim patted him on the back. "You did a great job, buddy."

Nathan beamed but sobered when he glanced at his mother. "What's wrong, Mommy? Don't you like it?" His lower lip quivered.

"No, I love it." She gave Nathan a big hug. "You are one special boy."

"I know." Nathan smiled.

Wendy laughed, and Tim worked up his courage, reaching for her shoulder. She shook it off and stood up, holding the project. "Come on, let's show Jeremy."

"Okay," Nathan squealed and jumped up, leaving Tim alone on the floor.

"What am I going to be eating?" Kevin whispered as soon as Linda led him from the church and out of earshot of everyone else.

"The less you know, the better," Linda replied.

"Your family is terrifying. I'm especially afraid of your uncle."

"And for good reason. He was in a gang for a while."

"Are you serious?" Kevin's eyes widened.

"Yeah, he got in with a bad crowd when he lived in Texas as a teenager."

"Good to know. I'll try to stay on his good side."

Linda's stomach churned. She hadn't wanted Kevin to see their house. It was small and old and, well, Mexican. The walls were painted in bright colors and covered with knickknacks and tapestries her mother had sewn. Not that this was a bad thing. She loved their home. She was used to it, but it wouldn't be normal for Kevin. She pictured him living in an austere home like the ones she'd seen in magazines and movies, where everything was a different shade of beige.

She took a breath and let him in the front door.

"Wow. This is awesome. It's just like the house from that movie we watched in Spanish class the other day." Kevin paused and moved closer to Linda. "I'm really glad you invited me today."

Putting her hand on his upper arm, she gazed up into his bright blue eyes. The front door squeaked open, and she jumped back as the rest of their group walked in.

Mamá barged in and grabbed Kevin's arm as she strode past, leading him to the kitchen. He craned his neck back to look at Linda, his eyes filled with fear. Linda chuckled.

"*Ven, muchacho. Siéntate.*"[24] Mamá sat him in a kitchen chair. "*Yo te sirvo.*"[25]

Kevin tried to stand up, but Tío pushed him back into the chair, stating, "In the Mexican culture, it is polite to serve the *invitados.*"[26]

"Oh, sorry. My mom always told us that God gave us two arms for a reason and to get things ourselves. This is nicer."

Linda got out five bowls and spoons and set them at the table. Tío grabbed a step stool and gestured for Hector to get out of his current chair and sit there. Hector groaned and moved over. While Linda heated up some tortillas on the *comal,* Mamá carried the hot soup and placed it on a woven potholder in the center of the table.

Kevin straightened and peered into the pot. "This is *menudo?*"

Mamá nodded, stirring the steaming liquid.

"Looks good," he said. "Thank you again for inviting me."

Mamá lifted a big, holey, rubbery chunk and plopped it into his bowl.

Kevin stared at it. "What kind of meat is that?"

"*Estómago,*"[27] Mamá answered.

---

[24] Come, youngster. Sit.
[25] I'll serve you.
[26] Guests
[27] Stomach.

Kevin's skin went a shade paler. "Stomach?"

"I warned you," Linda whispered as she passed him tortillas wrapped in a kitchen towel. "If I were you, I'd grab plenty of tortillas." Menudo wasn't her favorite dish either, but now that Mamá and Tío were forcing Kevin to eat it, she felt obliged to have some herself.

Mamá ladled some broth over the spongy-looking stomach chunk and then filled up the rest of the bowls on the table. Hector jumped up and swiftly cut up some limes and onions, setting them on the table, along with a spicy homemade salsa.

Linda threw another batch of tortillas on the *comal* and plopped into her chair. Poor Kevin. He'd probably never want to see her again after this. Pushing away the negative thoughts, she spooned some onions into her bowl and nodded for Kevin to do the same. He followed her example, adding onions and squeezing a few lime wedges into the broth. Linda shook a bit of *mejorana*[28] on top.

"What's that?" he asked.

"It's like oregano."

"Oh, cool."

Linda turned to Hector to ask for the salt, but he held the shaker out to her already. "Thanks," she mumbled, a slight, inexplicable irritation in the back of her mind.

Hector lifted his chin at the marjoram. "What'd you think it was?" he asked their guest, the bravado back. "Weed?"

"No." Kevin furrowed his brow. "I know Linda's really religious, so why would I think you'd have pot around the house?"

Hector grabbed the warm tortillas, throwing on a

---

[28] Marjoram

new batch, and then rolled one up and handed it to Linda before placing the rest in the kitchen towel. "'Cause we're Mexicans. Everyone thinks we're drug dealers."

Tío slurped his soup and held up a finger. "Technically I was a drug dealer."

"*No hables de esto,* Memo,"[29] Mamá said, shaking her head.

Linda added a splash of the salsa to her bowl, warning Kevin. "This is really spicy. You may not want to add too much."

Tío stared Kevin down while adding several spoonfuls to his own dish. "Real men eat spicy food."

Hector grabbed the spoon and added more to his bowl. Narrowing his eyes, he passed it on to Kevin, who ladled some salsa into his own bowl.

"*Eso.*"[30] Tío barked, slapping Kevin on the back.

Kevin stirred the soup and took a deep breath. "Here goes." He sipped a spoonful and coughed. Linda handed him a tortilla, rolling it up into a cylinder. He bit into it, exhaling with his tongue sticking out. "It's good. Spicy."

Linda grinned at Mamá and returned her attention to Kevin as Tío instructed him on how to cut off a piece of the stomach with his spoon. Linda gave him a thumbs-up. "*Sí se puede,*"[31] she encouraged with a chuckle.

Kevin shifted in his chair and held up the spoon, examining the meat. He shrugged and ate it. He chewed a couple of times and swallowed. "It's chewy." He ate the other half of the tortilla.

Everyone stared at him in disbelief as he ate

---

[29] Don't talk about that, Memo.

[30] There ya go.

[31] Yes, you can.

spoonful after spoonful and tortilla after tortilla. Hector and Mamá showed their disappointment with frowns and clenched jaws, but Tío was being really cool.

"You're okay, man," Tío said, patting Kevin on the shoulder. "You ate that like a *campeón*."[32]

"Thanks." Kevin wiped his brow and ran his tongue over his bright, red mouth. "Whew, my lips are burning."

"I can make you a *quesadilla* if you want," Linda suggested. "That might help."

"Nah, I'm okay. But, thank you. *Y muchas gracias, Señora Palacios, por el rico menudo.*"[33]

"*De nada*,"[34] Mamá muttered.

Despite Tim's attempts to continue their conversation, he made no headway with Wendy until after the kids had gone to bed. His stomach was so tied up in knots, he'd had to take an antacid to settle it.

Brushing her hair with more force than usual, Wendy glared at him in the armoire's mirror. "I can't believe you didn't tell me sooner," she scolded with a scowl.

"I was afraid of how you'd react. And for good reason, apparently."

"What did you expect? You've been lying since the day you got the job. I was telling the girls at the club about your mysterious new position at a company downtown and how you'd been working so

---

[32] Champion
[33] And thank you very much, Mrs. Palacios, for the delicious menudo.
[34] You're welcome.

hard. Now I'm going to look like a complete idiot. How do you think that makes me feel? Of course I'm going to be angry."

"I know, and I'm sorry." He tried to move closer, but she took a step back. His shoulders drooped. "I was embarrassed."

"You should be embarrassed." Her words dripped acid as she moisturized her arms. "You have an MBA, and now you're working for some greasy Mexican in the 'hood, playing around with cars all day."

For a second Tim flashed back to his mother screaming at his father in the garage. Wendy's words hit a little too close to home. He shook them off and sighed, feeling defeated. "It's only temporary. I've still been applying online every day. There just isn't anything out there."

"Well, you'd better find something soon. You could get shot on your way to work. Besides, how many cars could there be in the ghetto? Isn't that what the bus is for? For people like that. We are not bus people, Tim. I cannot be married to a bus person. If you stay in that job, with no security or pension or anything, riding the bus all day, I couldn't stand it. I'd leave you. What kind of life would that be for me, for the kids?" She slammed the lotion onto the dresser. "What happens when half the barrio gets deported? You'll run out of work, and then where does that leave us?"

"You're right," Tim said, disappointment flooding him. What had he been thinking? He'd even started enjoying the job a bit. He'd been deluding himself. "Don't worry. I'll find something soon."

She grunted and climbed into bed. "You can make your own sandwich tomorrow."

"Are you sure?" Linda asked Kevin on the front stoop. "I don't mind walking you."

He shook his head, his brown hair flopping into its perfect position "I'm only parked a block from here."

"All right." Linda studied his face, trying to read him. "At least this adventure's over with."

Kevin rubbed the back of his neck. "It was a bit awkward, but nothing I can't handle. Besides, my parents are way more judgmental."

"Really?" Linda asked, feeling relief mixed with anxiety. He didn't seem too flustered over Mamá, but she had hoped his parents would be more friendly and open.

"Yeah, thank God mine are in Connecticut. You won't have to run into them."

Sounded like he wasn't planning on introducing them anytime soon. Linda nodded, unsure of what to say. She thought meeting the family was a standard for dating, but maybe it was a cultural thing. She shrugged it off.

"I promised Brian I'd be back for flag football. We play in the quad almost every Sunday afternoon. You wanna come cheer me on?" Kevin asked, taking her hand in his.

"Maybe another time," Linda said. With all the tension between Mamá and Kevin, she felt like she'd just run a marathon. "I'm pretty tired. It's been a long week."

"No worries," Kevin said. "I'll find you in the library tomorrow. We can have lunch in the caf."

"That'd be great." Linda looked forward to a Monday more than she had in a while.

He glanced around and then leaned in, pressing his lips against hers. "I had fun today."

"Me, too." Though it'd been stressful, it'd sort of been fun watching him gnaw away at the menudo.

"See you tomorrow, Linda." He blew her another kiss and walked down the sidewalk.

She closed the door behind him, letting out a contented sigh. Something sizzling in the kitchen caused her stomach to rumble. After Linda had managed the initial unpleasant spoonfuls of *menudo*, Mamá had finished off most of Linda's bowl. In the end, Linda had only eaten a handful of tortillas with salsa. She sniffed the air and smiled, looking forward to whatever Mamá was cooking for supper.

She was surprised to find Hector at the stove instead. "Oh." She stopped in the doorway. "I thought you were Mamá."

"She's at her Bible Study. I figured you'd be hungry, so I heated up a few *gorditas* for you." Hector gently placed them on a plate, not spilling any of their contents.

Part of her wanted to be mad at him for the way he'd treated Kevin, but the other part understood where he was coming from. Living under the same roof as her and watching her bring home a boy probably didn't top his list of fun Sunday events. "That's really sweet, Hector." She took the plate and caught his eye. "Thanks."

Hector shrugged. "No big deal."

Linda sat at the table and spooned homemade salsa onto the *gorditas*. Hector hesitated by the stove.

"You gonna eat?" Linda pushed out the chair next to her with her foot, inviting him to sit down.

"Sure," he said, bringing his plate to the table.

Linda decided to avoid the Kevin topic altogether. "Have you heard anything from your mom?"

Hector shook his head, swallowing his bite. "I haven't gotten a letter back from her yet, but I was able to add money to her account at the jail, so I know she's still there."

"Wow, that's so hard. I can't believe they're not giving you any more information. Whatever happened to basic human rights?"

"I suppose they don't look at you like you're human. All they see is you not having papers."

All the emotions from her experience with Derrick rose to the surface. "It's like the other day in class. I was talking about The Dream Act, and this kid was acting like it shouldn't even matter."

Hector shook his head. "I never really had to think about it until now. I was born here, and my mom didn't let me in on all the stuff you guys have to go through." He paused. "After what happened with my mom, it made me think about what I did to you, nearly getting you deported. I feel really bad about it now. The same thing could've happened to you." He looked her in the eye. "I'm really sorry."

Linda felt tears rise up. "Thanks."

They both ate in silence.

"Oh," Hector said, "I almost forgot to tell you. Your mom officially hired me as her sous-chef."

Linda clapped him on the shoulder. "Good job. You know, I bet if you got your GED you could go to culinary school one day." She held up the final piece of her *gordita*. "These suckers are really good."

"Thanks." He ran a hand through his hair. "I don't know. I'm not very good at math."

"It might not be as hard as you think. They have some practice tests online and books in the library for studying. If the online test goes well, there's a test you can take at the technical center by the mall, and if you pass it, you take the GED for free. Some of my friends did that."

"Oh, yeah?" Hector piled more of the thick salsa onto his gordita. "I didn't know about that. I guess it's worth a shot if it's free."

"Everything's better when it's free." Linda grinned. "Besides, I could help you study over the summer, if you want."

"Thanks." He sat back in his chair. "My mom would be really proud if I got my GED."

"*Claro*.[35] It's a big thing." Linda looked at the clock. "Speaking of schoolwork, I have a paper to start."

"What's the topic?" Hector grabbed their dishes and went over to the sink.

"Why do people come to the U.S. without a visa knowing the hardships they will face?"

Hector scrubbed the dishes and grinned back at Linda. "You should say: to steal jobs and live off government money."

Linda erupted in a fit of giggles. "Yeah, that'd really throw the professor for a loop."

Juanita stirred in her bed. She'd thought for certain that the *menudo* would have made Kevin run for the hills. His ability to eat *menudo* didn't make her any more comfortable about him dating her daughter. He was nice, but men always seemed nice at the beginning. Her husband had put on a good face for her parents. The coyote had promised her cousin he'd take care of her. Who knew what might be going through this boy's mind?

She turned over and sighed. Linda was right. Her daughter was too old for Juanita to tell her whom she could and couldn't date. Pushing too much would rush Linda into his arms even faster. She could only hope all her advice over the years had sunk in. Too

---

[35] Of course.

many young girls in the neighborhood had gotten pregnant.

Juanita wanted a better life for her daughter. She wanted Linda to finish college and get a good job, to have a husband who would love and understand her, not beat and humiliate her or leave her alone and pregnant.

When Juanita finally fell asleep, her dreams were ridden by traumatic memories, one after the other, of all the men who had hurt her throughout the years.

CHAPTER ELEVEN
Amor Prohibido[1]

*T*he last few weeks of the semester flew by in a love-soaked haze. Linda spent every free moment she had with Kevin, studying together in the library. They cuddled on the couch and ate meals together. She refused to go with him to his apartment as he frequently insisted. Mamá's words floated through her head. *They only want one thing.* She didn't feel this was the case with Kevin, but she didn't want to test the waters. Also, those blue eyes and strong arms. She almost didn't trust herself.

It was now finals week, and they were studying for the economics class they had together. The exam was the next day. They'd already had one final with four more to go. Linda had her English literature exam later in the afternoon.

"Ugh," Kevin moaned, dropping his notebook on the library floor. "I need a break. My brain is fried."

"Yeah. My neck is killing me." Linda stretched to

---

[1] Forbidden Love – a song by Selena

the side, and soon Kevin's warm fingers rubbed her shoulders. "Oh, that's nice." She sighed, closing her eyes and trying to relax as his strong hands massaged her aching muscles. "I had to make extra *panes* this morning."

"Yeah?" he asked.

Goosebumps rose on her skin as he slowly passed his fingers over it. His lips brushed her neck and moved around to her cheek. She turned and kissed him.

"Hey. This area is for studying only," someone said.

Linda pulled away, heart racing, her eyes popping open. Brian and Becky grinned at her. She clicked her tongue and relaxed again against Kevin.

"Dude," Kevin said, shaking his head. "Uncool."

Brian snickered.

"Y'all are very snuggly and cute over here." Becky winked at Linda.

Linda blushed.

"I'm so glad you two finally got together," Brian said. "That means Kevin will finally shut up."

Kevin narrowed his eyes at Brian.

"Oh, really?" Linda asked.

"Every day for three months: 'I saw Linda today. She's soooo beautiful,'" he mimicked in a high-pitched voice, hands clasped near his heart.

"Excuse me a second." Kevin jumped up and punched Brian hard in the chest.

"'And her eyes,'" Brian said in a lovey-dovey voice.

Kevin grabbed him and wrestled him to the floor.

Becky shook her head and dropped onto the couch next to Linda. "Boys."

Linda smiled and watched as they rolled on the floor, trying to one-up each other. "Is that really true?" she asked in a soft voice.

Becky checked out one of Linda's earrings. "Apparently. Brian told me after your first date that Kevin's been pining after you for a while."

"That's what he told me, too, but I thought it was just a line."

"Guess not." Becky lightly pinched her arm.

Linda shrugged. "I still can't believe a guy like him would be interested in me."

"Girl, you need to up that confidence. Remember what I said the other day? You're beautiful, smart, and you can merengue." She danced her shoulders.

Linda chuckled and shifted her focus to the boys, who were winding down. "I'm hungry. Let's go to the caf for lunch. You guys wanna come?" she asked.

"Nah, we just ate. We're here to study. We'll steal this nice couch if you're leaving."

Kevin pushed Brian as he was trying to stand up. He laughed and jumped away before Brian could sweep his legs. "Come on, Linda." He shot Brian a final look before walking out arm in arm with her.

"Conejo, some angry white lady's on the phone for you." Guillermo held out the phone for Tim.

Tim rolled out from beneath a car and wiped his oily hands on a rag. He wedged the receiver between his ear and shoulder. "Hello?"

"What did he call me?" Wendy hissed.

"Nothing." He shook his head at Guillermo and muffled the phone. "It's my wife."

"Sorry, man." Guillermo grimaced, amusement in his eyes. "She don't sound so happy."

"Story of my life." Since he'd told her he was working as a mechanic, the distance between them had grown greater. "What's wrong, Wendy?"

"Nathan fell on the playground and broke his arm. The school nurse took him to the hospital, and I'm on my way. I need you to come and keep an eye on Jeremy."

His stomach dropped. "Is he okay?" This was the first time either of the boys had ever been seriously hurt. Before this it had only been scrapes and bruises and the occasional bloody nose.

"The nurse said he's been a trooper. He's over at CRMH. How soon can you get there?"

Tim muffled the phone again. "Hey, can I borrow your car? My son's in the hospital. He broke his arm."

"*Claro*," Guillermo said, tossing him the keys. "You can bring it back tomorrow if you want. I don't need it tonight."

"*Gracias*." Tim got back on the phone with Wendy. "My boss let me borrow his car, so I'll be there in about twenty minutes, depending on traffic."

"Right now he's still in the ER, on the pediatric side. Check with the front desk in case he's been moved."

"I'll get there as soon as I can." Tim hung up the phone and rushed out the back.

Juanita's little business was starting to pick up. She and Hector worked about eight hours every day—cooking, planning, and preparing. They had gained so much popularity that most days a line would form outside the *panadería* before they even showed up with food.

Today they were making *tamales de raja*.[2] Hector

---

[2] Tamales made with queso fresco and sliced poblano peppers

sliced the peppers and cheese. The *masa* was already made, and now they needed to *asar*[3] the chiles, stuff the husks with *masa*, placing the peppers and cheese in the middle, and then steam them for a few hours.

"*Vas bien,*[4] *Hector.*" Juanita beamed. Every day he did more on his own without guidance.

"*Gracias, Doña.*"

Juanita prepared the filling, and they worked together to make the *tamales.* An hour later, they had filled the *tamalero* with a few inches of water and nearly a hundred *tamales.* Another two hundred were piled in various containers on every flat surface for the next two batches. Hector lifted the heavy pot onto the stove and placed it between the two right burners, since the large pot couldn't fit on one. He put a wooden spoon under one side to prop it up. They'd already surrounded that side of the stove with aluminum foil to prevent scarring. Juanita had learned the hard way the first time she had made *tamales.* She had spent an hour with a Brillo pad and a heavy duty cleaner trying to get the dark burn stains from the surface of the beige stovetop. It had never been quite the same since.

"Want to work on some reading?" Hector asked.

Juanita nodded. She had made quite a bit of progress in the last few weeks. Hector was a better teacher than she had anticipated. Patient, he explained things in a way she could understand. They'd decided to read in Spanish, since the spelling was simpler than English and Juanita realized English would be too hard to start with.

Hector had picked up a free Latino newspaper at

---

[3] Grill, like in a dry skillet

[4] You're doing well.

the *mercado*,[5] and together they scanned the front page. Juanita sounded out the first few lines. *"Hubo un accidente ayer en la carretera 581. Tres personas murieron y quince están en condición crítica."*[6] Juanita shook her head. *"Ay, que triste.*[7] Next time we read something happy."

Hector chuckled. "Yeah, the news is depressing sometimes. Let's go to the library after we sell the *tamales*. Do you have a library card?"

Juanita shook her head. *"¿Cuánto cuesta?"*[8]

"It's free. I think you have to bring your phone bill or something. That way they know you live in the city."

Juanita opened a kitchen drawer, pulled out a few bills, and stuffed them into her purse. Flipping the newspaper open to the entertainment page, she read about her favorite *novela*.

Tim realized halfway to the hospital he was still wearing his jumpsuit. Luckily Guillermo's seats were black leather. He would clean the car and put gas in before he returned it. His hands gripped the soft leather of the steering wheel. It felt good to sit behind the wheel of a car again, driving more than a few feet from the sidewalk and into the garage. But that pleasant feeling fled when he imagined Wendy's face when he would step into the hospital room covered in grease and oil. He cursed.

"Will they even let me into the hospital dressed

---

[5] Market

[6] There was an accident today on highway 581. Three people died and fifteen are in critical condition.

[7] Oh, how sad.

[8] How much does it cost?

like this?" he mumbled. After stopping at a traffic light, he opened Guillermo's glove compartment and pulled out a few napkins. Something shiny caught his eye. He leaned closer and realized it was a gun.

He groaned and shut the hatch, wondering what else was in the car and hoping the police wouldn't stop him. The light turned green, and he wiped his face with napkins as he drove, occasionally peering in the mirror.

By the time he pulled into the hospital parking garage, his face was mostly clean, but his hands were still stained brownish-black without the aid of the Lava soap. He got out of the car, pulled off his jumpsuit, and tossed it on the floor of the front passenger seat. His jeans and white t-shirt underneath were fairly clean. He sighed, his stomach in knots, locked the door, and jogged across the concrete, following the signs for the emergency room.

The automatic doors opened as he neared them. He slowed and approached the elderly woman at the front desk. "My son was brought in with a broken arm. Nathaniel Draker."

She smiled. "Hold on, let me check for you." She clicked her mouse a few times. "Nathaniel Draker?"

"Yes."

"They just moved him. He's in room 304. Would you like someone to help you get there?"

The hospital corridors were a maze, and he'd never been in the pediatric area before. "Yeah, sure."

She gestured to a young woman in a candy-striper outfit, who walked over. "Can you take this man to room 304?"

"Yes, ma'am." Beaming, she sashayed down the hall, head high. "It's my first day on the job."

"Great," Tim said, wishing he didn't have to make

conversation when he was so anxious. "How do you like it so far?"

Until they reached the children's ward, she chattered idly about the day. "It's a few doors down to your left," she said, pointing.

"Thank you." He hurried into the room, his heart beating fast.

"Daddy," Jeremy cried, jumping up from Wendy's lap. "Nathan hurted his arm."

"I heard." He picked up Jeremy and walked over to Nathan, who sat on the bed, a lollipop in his mouth and a cast on his arm. "How ya doin', buddy?"

Nathan shrugged and winced. "It hurts a lot."

"I bet." He pushed his son's soft hair back on his forehead and planted a kiss in its place. "That's a pretty cool cast. I've never seen one that color before." It was a bright neon blue.

Nathan smiled weakly. "Mom says I can bring a marker to school and have everyone sign it."

"That's what I did when I broke my arm," Tim said.

"You broke your arm, too?" Nathan asked, his eyes widening.

"Yup, I was about ten years old. I was climbing a tree in my backyard and fell."

"Did it get better?"

"Yeah, it didn't take too long either."

Nathan sighed. "Good. I wanna play T-ball."

"We'll have to see what the doctor says." Wendy glowered at Tim. "Look at your hands. You're going to get oil all over Jeremy." She nodded to the bathroom in the room.

Tim put Jeremy down and went into the bathroom, closing the door and scrutinizing himself in the mirror. He sighed and scrubbed the remaining grease from his hands and washed his face once more for good measure. His new job wasn't glamorous, but it made him happy. Couldn't she see that?

Linda approached the topic she'd dreaded mentioning the last few days. "When are you heading to Connecticut?" She avoided eye contact with Kevin, making a Zen mashed potato garden on her plate with a fork.

Kevin sighed and leaned back in his chair. "My last final is on Thursday morning, and my internship starts next Monday, so I'll probably leave Friday sometime. The lease on the apartment runs out on Friday anyway, so we have to be out by the end of the day."

Linda frowned. "Will you come back to visit?"

"I'm going to try, but it might be hard. The internship is forty hours a week, and then I'm working a few shifts at this restaurant near my house, so I can save extra *dinero* for stuff I need next year."

"Sounds like you'll be as busy as I will." Linda smushed her Zen garden, clenching her jaw. "I wish I could have found an internship."

"I have an idea." Kevin reached across the table and grasped her hands. "Why don't you come up to Connecticut and see if you can get in where I'm doing my internship?"

"I don't think it'll work." Linda shrugged. "No one wants to take me on."

Kevin's brow furrowed. "But I don't understand. You're in the top five percent of students here, you're friendly, and you're bilingual. Companies would love to get an intern like you."

Linda's stomach flipped. Should she tell him the real reason no one would hire her? What if he looked at her differently after finding out she was undocumented? His blue eyes sparkled at her, but she still couldn't do it. Instead she changed the topic. "I'm putting more minutes on my phone this weekend. I might even convince Mamá to jump into the twenty-first century and get a simple one. I did the math, and it's actually less expensive to buy her a cheap cell phone and add minutes than to get our landline reinstated. My number should be the same. You still have it, right?"

"I don't know if I ever had your number," Kevin said. He scrolled through his phone and shook his head.

Linda punched it into his contact list. "I think I have yours from our club roster. I'll call you as soon as my phone's working again. Then we can keep in touch during the summer."

Kevin stuck out his lower lip and pulled Linda in for a hug. "I'm going to miss you."

"I'll miss you, too." A dull pain entered Linda's heart where she had opened it for the first time and let him in. "We still have three more days to spend time together."

"Studying." Kevin groaned. "When's your last final?"

"Thursday afternoon."

"Maybe you can come over after and hang out."

Linda wagged her finger. "Becky warned me you'd invite me over this week. She said she already got invited to help 'clean up y'all's mess,'" Linda imitated Becky's drawl.

Kevin grinned. "Cleaning is more fun than studying. Besides we can relax and listen to music, maybe watch a movie. You can finally see my place."

Linda squirmed as he ran his fingers over her sides. "Stop, I'm ticklish."

"Oh really?" He scratched lightly. "Right here?"

Linda giggled uncontrollably. *"Ay, no puedo respirar."*[9]

"What's that?" He continued to tickle her. "You're coming over on Thursday?"

"Okay, okay," she laughed.

He pulled his hands back, still in tickle position. "Okay what?"

"Okay, I'll come over Thursday."

"Good." He pulled her chair closer and brushed a lock of hair from her face. "I can't wait."

Juanita and Hector sold all the *tamales* in under three hours, disappointing a few late-arriving customers. Afterwards they bought the chicken and lettuce for the *flautas de pollo*[10] they would make the next day and dropped all the ingredients off at the house before heading to the library.

"We can go on my bike," Hector suggested.

Juanita laughed. *"¿Qué parezco? ¿Una* teenager? *No creo."*[11]

"Okay, do you want to walk or take the bus?"

"El camión," Juanita answered. *"Me cansé con todos esos tamales."*[12]

"Yeah, I'm tired, too. The bus is a good idea."

Juanita walked out the door, locking it behind her. *"¿Has escuchado algo de tu mamá?"*[13]

Hector shook his head. "No, I haven't heard from her since they moved her to the detention center. I

---

[9] I can't breathe.

[10] Chicken flutes – rolled up fried tortillas with chicken in the middle

[11] What do I look like? A teenager? I don't think so.

[12] The bus . . . I got tired from all those tamales.

[13] Have you heard anything from your mom?

only have the one letter she sent from jail. The lawyer told us it might take a week or so for the money to transfer before she can make a phone call."

Diana and María's court hearings hadn't gone well, and last week they had both been moved to a detention center a couple hours away. If things moved anything like with the other people Juanita had known who'd been deported, they'd be uprooted a few more times to different states before being sent back to Mexico City—also known as Distrito Federal, or D.F.—the capital of Mexico.

"Pastor Martinez said he would drive me and Luz down to see them this weekend."

"¿*Y Doña Vazquez?*" Juanita asked. "María's grandmother?"

"She can't take the risk. No papers," Hector explained. "You know José from church?"

"¿*Cuál?*"[14] Juanita asked. There were at least three men named José at Promesa.

"*El alto.*[15] Last year his sister-in-law went to visit his brother in the detention center, and they detained her. She ended up getting deported, too."

"*Ay, pobrecita.*"[16] Juanita shook her head. "¿*Tuvieron hijos?*"[17]

"*Sí,*" Hector said. "Social services took them and put them in foster care. José and his wife petitioned to take care of them, but since they didn't have papers either, they were denied rights. They won't even let them see the kids."

Tears formed in Juanita's eyes.

"Their lawyer told them that with the current administration, it wasn't even worth trying."

---

[14] Which one?
[15] The tall one.
[16] Aw, poor thing.
[17] Did they have kids?

Juanita said a silent prayer for that family, unable to imagine being separated from her Lindita, unsure if she would ever see her again.

Hector and Juanita flagged down the bus. "Anyway," he told her as they sat on the worn seats. "Pastor Martinez warned me the *oficiales* might not let me or Luz see our moms, but I told him it was worth it. Better than wondering if we could have visited and didn't."

Juanita didn't say anything, but she knew both María and Diana had to be suffering. From what she'd learned from the few *hermanos* at church who'd had family deported, neither the jails nor the detention centers were pleasant places. The inadequate food, the crowded conditions, the isolation, loneliness, hopelessness. After a while, it would get to them.

Watching the buildings fly by, Juanita considered what it would be like to be trapped in a cell for hours, perhaps days, weeks, months, especially when her only crime would've been making a better life for her family. She'd escaped her violent marriage, running away to America. María and Diana could always cross over again, but it was increasingly dangerous to do so, and things were getting harder and harder for undocumented immigrants where they lived in Virginia and in other states as well.

Juanita wondered if María and Diana would stay in Mexico City or move back with their families. María was originally from Guanajuato and Diana from Hidalgo, but only a few of their relatives remained in Mexico. Most had passed away or moved to the U.S. years ago. Juanita would have the same problem if she were ever deported. The drink had killed her husband less than a year after she and Linda had left. Her parents had died a few years later.

She had a cousin in Texas, a brother in Georgia, and a sister in California. No one was left in Mexico, except the ghosts of her memories.

As Tim walked out of the bathroom, Wendy asked. "Can you take Jeremy for a while? He hasn't eaten lunch yet, and he's getting restless here."

"Can I go to your work, Daddy? To see the magic cars?" Jeremy jumped up and down, clapping his hands.

Tim shifted his gaze to Wendy, who threw up her hands, looking too exhausted to put up a fight. "Sure thing, buddy," he said, ruffling his son's hair.

"No fair," Nathan whined, his lip quivering and face turning red.

"Aw, don't cry. We can go another day." Tim sat next to Nathan and squeezed his socked foot under the thin hospital blanket.

Nathan sucked in a few sobbing breaths. "Promise?"

"Promise." Tim crossed his heart.

Nathan sniffed and wiped away tears with his good arm.

Tim kissed Nathan's forehead again. "We'll be home for dinner. Should I pick something up?"

Wendy sighed. "That'd be great."

"Nathan, what do you want to eat for dinner?" Tim asked.

Nathan grinned. "I get to pick?"

Tim nodded.

Nathan's face scrunched in concentration. "I want macaroni and cheese. And chicken."

"I'll stop at KFC."

Jeremy and Nathan cheered, and from the corner

of his eye, Tim thought Wendy almost smiled. But she said nothing, plopping down in the rocking chair near the window.

Tim held out his hand to Jeremy. "Ready?"

Jeremy nodded. "Do you think I can meet Joe the Mechanic?"

"We'll see."

Linda finished her final exam and handed it to Professor Chekov.

"I've truly enjoyed having you in my class, Linda." The professor peered over her dark-rimmed glasses at Linda.

Linda adjusted her backpack. "Thank you. I really liked your class, too. It was different than any literature class I've had before. It stretched me to think outside the box."

"Are you going to the Dream Act rally next month?" Professor Chekov asked.

"I was thinking about it."

"I'll be there." She handed Linda a slip of paper. "Here's my cell. Let me know if you need a ride."

"Okay, cool. Thanks. I'll call you next week sometime."

Linda left the room, waving at Hannah on the way out. The test hadn't fazed her, especially since she'd checked online and found out she had received a ninety-three percent on her paper.

"Only three more to go," she mumbled as she stepped onto the crowded bus. After she found a seat, she took out notes to review for her economics test the next day.

She had two tests tomorrow and one on Thursday afternoon before she'd be finished for the semester.

She anticipated A's in most of her classes, though she was prepared for a possible A minus in her literature class, since it wasn't her main subject. If everything went as planned, she would graduate in a year with a major in International Business and minors in both Finance and Accounting. She had no idea what she would do with her degree or who would hire her, but she tried not to focus on that.

Linda imagined what it would be like to walk onto that stage, shake hands with the dean, and hold up her diploma. She pictured Mamá and Tío in the crowd beaming at her with tears in their eyes. She had been the first person in her family to finish high school and the first to go to college. Her cousin in California had finished high school the year after she had, and another cousin in Georgia had started taking classes at a community college last year. That was it out of the twenty or so family members she knew.

She scanned the buildings outside the bus window and realized she'd been daydreaming for several minutes. Two blocks past her stop, she packed up her bag and hopped off at the next corner, heading towards her uncle's *taller*. To her surprise, a small blonde-headed child ran into her as she turned the corner into the shop.

"Hello," the boy said. "My name's Jeremy. What's yours?"

"Linda."

Tim ran towards them. "Sorry." He put a hand on Jeremy's shoulder. "Jeremy, what did I tell you about running outside the shop?"

"Is this your kid?" she asked.

"Yes, my youngest. The oldest broke his arm today, so I'm keeping this one out of his mother's hair for a few hours."

Linda bent to his level. "What have you been doing today, Jeremy?"

"I'm learning to fix a carbinator." Jeremy grinned at her.

"Oh really?" She laughed. "You're cute. How old are you?"

"This many." He held up four fingers.

"Wow, you're a big boy. Do you go to school yet?"

"No. I was gonna, but Daddy lost his job so we had to ecomonize."

Linda glimpsed Tim's face, which had turned a shade pinker.

"Okay, buddy, let's go finish up so we can bring Mommy and Nathan some dinner."

"'Kay," the little boy said, running inside.

"See ya." Tim waved and hurried after his son.

They hadn't talked much since he had started working. Tío said he was an okay guy, but Linda always felt his eyes on her when she wasn't looking. Watching him interact with his son softened her view of him a little.

Linda walked up the stairs to Tío's office and pulled out the pile of receipts for parts and services she'd been totaling on Saturday. Tío was a good mechanic but a horrible bookkeeper. With the recent increase in business, she'd have to come in more often so he didn't get too far behind.

Since Tío had crossed the border a few years after Mamá, he couldn't legally own the business. A friend of his had gotten the business license and signed the forms for taxes every year. Tío paid his friend for the taxes, and it worked out pretty well. That is, as long as Linda did the paperwork.

She sighed as she browsed the new additions to the pile. Tío had been busier ever since he had hired Tim. Though she wasn't exactly sure why, she guessed it had more to do with Javier's departure. He was intimidating on a good day, dangerous on a bad one. Tío had told her once that Javier had gotten so mad at a customer that he'd ripped parts out of the vehicle just to make him pay twice. Not good for business.

She pulled out her calculator and the logbook and got to work.

Juanita handed the librarian her information. The grey-haired woman glanced sidelong at her as she handed her passport back over the counter.

"Do you have a city ID?" she asked.

Juanita shook her head and offered the woman her light bill and gas bill.

The woman glared at them and sighed. "I suppose this is fine. Please fill out this form. When you're finished, hand it back, and I'll give you your card. Can I help you, young man?" She peered over her glasses at Hector, a frown on her face.

"I'm just helping my friend." He indicated Juanita.

Juanita grabbed the paper and sat at a desk near the fiction section. She pulled a pen from her bag and studied the library card application. Hector sat next to her as she tried to decipher the English. She could understand a quarter of the form, which was a quarter more than she'd ever understood before.

"Not bad," Hector said. "Especially since we haven't even worked on reading English yet."

Juanita beamed. After writing her name and address, she handed Hector the pen. "*¿Me lo puedes llenar?*"[18]

---

[18] Can you fill it out for me?

"No problem," he said, filling out the form.

Five minutes later, they stood in front of the grumpy woman again.

"Here's your card. You can keep books for two weeks and movies, CDs, and books on tape for one."

The woman's voice held a certain emptiness, and Juanita felt sorry for her. So much bitterness. Perhaps Juanita would've turned out the same way if she hadn't found Pastor Martinez and Promesa. They had helped her to heal. Juanita had forgiven her father for forcing her to marry the much-older man who had most likely killed his first wife. And she had forgiven her husband for how he'd treated her. She had forgiven the *coyote* and his friend for raping her, and she had forgiven the employers who paid her miserable wages and forced her to work long hours without breaks. There was still much to forgive and pray about; Juanita knew it was a never-ending process. In time, perhaps God would let her forget.

Every day and every night Juanita pleaded with the Lord to erase her bad memories, but for some reason she could not comprehend, He had not done so. She sighed. God had a plan, but there was so much she didn't understand. Maybe she never would, until she met Him face to face.

Library card in hand, Juanita browsed with Hector through the meager Spanish section, found a couple of books with happy themes that were easy enough for her to read, and checked them out.

Juanita inhaled as the air hit her face. The books were only hers for two weeks, but they were the first books she would ever read. People in church shared Bibles, but she hadn't been able to read the words. A small hop in her chest surprised her; she might be having a heart attack. But it was only something she hadn't experienced in a while. Joy.

CHAPTER TWELVE
Si No Te Hubieras Ido[1]

*L*inda grinned as she put down her pen. Her last final was complete. She stretched and handed in her test. As she left the room, she had a sudden urge to skip down the hall. The test was easier than she had anticipated. She was fairly confident she'd done well enough to get an A for the semester.

Checking a clock in the hall, she remembered she'd promised to help Kevin clean his apartment. Butterflies fluttered in her stomach. What if no one else was there when she arrived? Would he have asked the others not to come? She doubted this would happen, since Becky had said the apartment was a real pigsty and that they needed all the help they could get. Still, she didn't want to be alone with him. Well, a part of her wanted it, and that was the part she didn't trust in the presence of those bright blue eyes. Who knew what might happen if they were alone? She didn't want to find out.

---

1 If You Hadn't Left – a song by Marco Antonio Solis

The afternoon sun hit her face as she stepped outside. Breathing in the spring air and admiring the pink cherry blossoms on the trees, she walked off campus towards the apartment complex where Brian, Kevin, and a couple of their friends lived. Blocks later, she knocked on their front door. Loud music pumped from the other side. She knocked louder, and the music stopped.

Someone opened the door and almost barreled over her. "Whoa, sorry," the brown-haired jock apologized, putting up his hands.

Linda recognized him as one of Kevin's friends. "Is Kevin around?"

"Yeah." He yelled into the house. "Kevin. It's your girlfriend."

Linda's cheeks got hot. They hadn't exactly defined things yet. But Kevin didn't blink an eye. He jogged out of a back room. "Hey, Linda." He kissed her.

Linda wrinkled her nose. She could taste stale beer. She'd tried one beer at a high school party once, but she hadn't liked the taste or how it had made her a bit dizzy. What she liked least was the *chanclaza*[2] she'd gotten from Mamá as soon as she'd walked in the door. Her friends had given her gum, but Mamá had always been sensitive to certain smells, alcohol being one of them. In the end, it had provoked one of Mamá's crying spells, which was worse than the *chanclaza*. Knowing she had caused Mamá such sadness—and later finding out her father had died from drinking—she returned to the commandment to honor thy father and mother, and she'd never done it again. Though she didn't enjoy the smell either, judging was also a sin, so she let other people's

---

[2] Spanking with a chancla (sandal/flip-flop)

drinking go most of the time unless she was worried about them becoming an alcoholic. In Kevin's case, she'd never been to his apartment, and she had no history to create a cause for concern.

"Hey," she greeted, still in her post-final glow. "How'd your last final go?"

"Good. Yours?" he asked.

"Really good. I think I aced it."

"Sweet." He hugged her and closed the door. "Let me give you the tour."

Linda took in her surroundings. There were food wrappers, plastic trash bags, and cups everywhere. Furniture was flipped upside-down and stained. The entire place smelled like a dumpster.

Becky walked into the room and stopped, putting her hands on her hips. "I know it's hard to believe, but it was worse before I got here."

Linda opened her mouth and closed it again, not unlike the goldfish that floated in a small, grungy tank in the corner. Sometimes it was better not to talk. Her mother had always told her if she didn't have anything nice to say, not to say anything at all.

"This is the living room." He moved her down the hall. "These are the bedrooms. There are four. This one's mine." He opened the door.

Wrinkled clothes, books, papers, and unidentifiable objects, which Linda guessed were either food, a science project, or both, covered the floor. The smell was overpowering. She breathed through her mouth, unsure what to say. Even Hector wasn't this messy. She'd never seen a place so dirty before, except maybe Tío's house a couple of weeks after his wife had left him.

"This is the kitchen." Kevin guided her in the opposite direction. It didn't look any better than the rest of the house. "And the bathroom's over there."

"Hope you went before you came," Becky said.

Linda chuckled.

"I'm not kidding." Becky opened the door.

Linda reeled back. It smelled like a convenience store bathroom. Maybe worse, if that were possible. A port-a-potty on a construction site came to mind. "Oh my."

"Yeah, and Brian wonders why I don't visit more often."

"Hey, it's not that bad," Kevin said.

"Compared to what?" Becky asked. "A truck stop?"

"This is going to take a long time." Linda shook her head, unsure where to start, her earlier excitement wearing off.

"Yeah," Becky said. "Did you guys clean at all the whole two semesters you were here?"

"Yes." Brian grabbed Becky around the waist.

"When?" Linda asked.

"Parents' weekend."

Linda raised an eyebrow. "Wasn't that in October?"

Kevin glanced at Brian. "Has it been that long?"

Becky and Linda exchanged frowns.

"Well," Kevin sighed, handing Linda an empty trash bag, "the gang's all here. Let's get to work."

"Linda and I will work on the living room. You boys clean your own rooms. Y'all are nasty."

Linda smirked and followed Becky to the living room.

"Here." Becky handed her a pair of kitchen gloves. "Who knows what kind of germs are living in here?" She pushed a button on the stereo, turning down the volume as an 80s metal ballad hit the air.

Thankful for the gloves, Linda put them on and tossed a few soda cans in her bag. It was full in less than fifteen minutes, so they dug into the next layer of garbage covering the floor. They filled up another bag and took a break to dance to Becky's favorite Latino song, "*Danza Kuduro*."[3] Their laughter filled the room and must have been loud enough for the boys to hear, because soon they joined the girls.

Kevin grabbed Linda's gloved hand and twirled her around, avoiding the overturned furniture and the mountain of stuffed, black garbage bags. He pulled her close as a new song came on and slowed their speed. Dancing merengue and salsa was one thing, but slow dancing was another. Linda's face grew warm, and she pulled back a little.

"What's wrong?" He lifted her chin.

She shrugged, not sure how to explain. This was a slippery slope. One false footing, and she could slide down the mountain.

He spun her a few more times, then released her. Gyrating his arms in mini circles, he danced salsa to the slow mariachi song.

Linda laughed and stepped back. "That's the most ridiculous thing I've ever seen."

He grinned and wiggled his eyebrows, sticking his thumbs in his belt loops and doing cowboy kicks.

"*Ay ay ay,*" Brian yelled in a falsetto voice and joined in. They linked elbows and spun in circles, yipping and yelping. The music stopped; they high-fived each other and bumped chests.

"How do you dance to that song anyway?" Becky asked Linda.

"Oh, I don't think people really dance to that. It's more of a drinking song."

Brian smiled. "That's more up my alley."

Linda sighed. She hoped they didn't start

---

[3] Kuduro Dance – a song by Don Omar. Kuduro is an Angoran style of music and dance.

drinking. It always made her feel uncomfortable. "Okay, back to work." She picked up two brooms and tossed one to Becky.

Tim lifted Jeremy up the steps onto the bus and handed him the fare. "Put it in that box there."

His little face beamed at the bus driver as he let the coins drop into the slot and clapped. "This is fun."

Tim nodded to the driver, picked up Jeremy, and carried him to an empty seat.

Jeremy's feet dangled wildly as he gawked out the window. "Wow, Daddy, this is great. Do you get to do this every day?"

Tim laughed. "Yup."

"Is this bus magic, like Joe the Mechanic's bus?"

"No, this is just a regular bus. The magic bus is invisible, remember?"

"But if it's isvisible, how come Joe can find it?"

"His magical wrench."

"Oh." Jeremy nodded. "Okay."

Over the last few weeks, Tim had really been enjoying his job. He still sent out a résumé or two every week, but if he was being honest, he didn't want to leave Guillermo's shop. The money was good, there was something satisfying about figuring out a problem and fixing it, and he didn't even mind all the Mexicans and their Spanish anymore.

The only problem was Wendy. She was making his life miserable. Her nagging him to find a different job and her insults towards his current one had reached an unbearable level. Her behavior towards him today was the best it'd been since the day of the smiley face pancakes, and that wasn't saying much. Nathan and Jeremy were his reasons to come home every night. They were the glue holding their family together.

Tim smiled and pulled Jeremy in for a hug. "You were a good helper today at the shop."

Jeremy grinned, showing his missing front tooth. "Yeah, and now I'm gonna help buy the chicken."

"That's right." Tim searched the passing scenery for the restaurant. He'd passed it every day for the last month, but he couldn't remember which block it was on.

Several minutes later, Jeremy pointed a grimy finger out the window. "There it is, Daddy."

"Okay, pull the string," Tim said, holding him near the top of the window so his son could reach it.

Jeremy tugged it. They high-fived each other, tottered down the aisle, and hopped onto the sidewalk. Twenty minutes later, carrying two bags of KFC, they boarded another bus and headed home.

"Mommy, Mommy!" Jeremy called as they walked in the door. "I got to pull the string on the bus and give the money, and, and, and, I got to see Daddy's work."

"Did you see Joe the Mechanic?" Nathan asked.

Tim kissed Nathan on the forehead. "Not today. He had a special mission to go on. Maybe I can tell you guys about it tonight."

"Yay!" they both yelled.

"Okay, boys, go wash up for dinner," Wendy said. She walked into the kitchen and set the table.

Tim followed and emptied the bags onto the table, lifting out the containers of warm food. "It's still pretty hot," he said.

Wendy touched one container. She shrugged. "It's fine. I'm too tired to heat anything up anyway."

Tim opened the container of mashed potatoes. "Sit down. I'll finish this."

She sank wearily in a kitchen chair. "Thanks, hon."

For the first time in weeks, her voice wasn't laced with bitterness. His heart throbbed in his chest, tears nearly forming in his eyes. Maybe she was getting over it. Perhaps if he brought enough money in, she could accept his job. Hope flashed through his mind.

He finished setting the table. Realizing it was too quiet, he went to check on the boys. The bathroom door was closed. He knocked and heard a giggle on the other side. "What's going on in there, boys?"

"Nothing," Nathan said.

Not a good sign. He opened the door. The boys had splashed water all over the mirror, sink, and floor. "Nathan, Jeremy," he said, sternly. He handed them each a towel. "You clean this up right now. You know better than to make a mess."

"Sorry," they mumbled as they began to wipe down the various surfaces.

Tim sighed and helped, so it'd go faster. Also, he didn't want Nathan to get his cast any wetter than it already was. "All right, good enough." He motioned towards the kitchen. "Let's go get some chicken. No running."

They slowed down from their all-out sprint, and he let out a sigh. Things were starting to feel almost normal again.

A little before midnight, Linda and the others had cleaned up the trash and scrubbed the hardwood floors the best they could. Luckily there were no rugs, because they would've been stained beyond repair. Layers of filth in the kitchen and bathroom had been bleached off. The few pieces of furniture that had come with the place were wiped down. The cabinets were emptied of expired food, and leftovers were boxed up for trips home. Except for Linda, everyone lived out of town. Brian was from Maryland and Becky from South Carolina. They were both leaving the next day along with Kevin. The other two roommates were packing up to leave in a few minutes.

Linda sniffed the air. The house smelled less like sweaty clothes and spoiled pizza and more like Pine Sol and Clorox. "Much better."

"What?" Becky bumped her with her hip. "You didn't like the scent of eau de bachelor?"

Linda chuckled. "Aw, I'm gonna miss you guys this summer."

"I know," Becky said, plopping into the chair next to Brian's. "Four whole months without us. What will you do?"

"Work, work, and more work, if I know her at all." Kevin wrapped his arms around her and kissed her ear.

Linda giggled and squirmed away. "It won't all be work. Professor Chekov invited me to drive to Blacksburg for The Dream Act rally next month. That could be fun."

"I suppose that depends on your idea of fun." Brian raised an eyebrow.

Becky kicked him under the table, and he winced.

"You guys wanna watch a movie?" Kevin asked.

"I think we're gonna go out on the town, just the two of us." Becky kissed Brian on the nose.

"Linda?" Kevin asked.

"I could watch a movie," she said. "I haven't sat down and relaxed much at all this week."

"I'm sure you didn't. I reckon they've named a wing of the library after you by now," Becky said.

Linda clicked her tongue at her.

"I can order some Chinese," Kevin suggested.

Linda wrinkled her nose. "That nasty stuff I threw out today turned me off from Chinese food and pizza for the rest of the summer, maybe even my whole life."

Kevin's ears turned red. He scratched the back of his neck. "Yeah, sorry about that. Thanks for helping."

Linda jumped up. "Okay, I have an idea." She browsed through the boxes of non-expired food. "I think I might be able to make something out of this stuff."

"More power to ya, girl." Becky pulled Brian out of his chair. "We're heading out. Aw, I'm gonna miss you, *chica*." She squeezed Linda in a big hug. "Take care of yourself this summer. Try to have a little fun."

Linda squeezed back. "You, too, Becky. I'll call you when my phone's back on."

"See ya." Brian towered over her, giving her a short hug before Becky tugged him out of the house.

As Linda waved goodbye, she realized she was now alone in a boy's apartment at midnight. The trouble was, she was too exhausted to care about the repercussions, and besides, it would be their last time together for a while. Promising herself she would make good choices, she called to Kevin, who had walked halfway down the hall. "Where do you think you're going?" She beckoned him with her finger. "You're helping cook."

Juanita rolled over in bed. It'd been a long day, and she hadn't heard Linda come home yet. She squinted at the clock. Almost midnight. She'd awakened from another nightmare, this one from her childhood. She squeezed her eyes shut, struggling to erase the images. Her uncle was one person she had never been able to forgive. She hated remembering what he'd done to her as a child. In her pueblo, no one had believed a young girl over an adult male. Not even her own mother.

Getting up to shake off the thoughts, she sipped water from the glass on her dresser. The shadows on the walls disappeared as soon as she clicked on her small lamp. A prayer on her lips, she took a deep breath and let it out slowly. After a while, her body stopped trembling enough for her to pull out her Bible and read aloud until she fell back asleep.

Linda hummed as she added another ingredient to the pot.

"What exactly are we making?" Kevin asked, squinting at the food cooking in the pan.

"They're called *sobras*,"[4] Linda said with a smile.

He raised an eyebrow. "What are *sobras?*"

"You'll have to wait and see." She stirred the food, tasting a spoonful. "Not bad. A few more minutes." Maybe she could be Mamá's sous-chef if Hector ever left. She wrinkled her brow. It was strange, but she had gotten used to him being there, like he was part of the family now, and the possibility of Hector not being there anymore caused her stomach to churn.

Kevin sniffed the pot and shrugged. "Smells okay."

Linda put the lid on the dish and turned down the heat. "Where did we put the paper plates and forks?"

Kevin frowned and scratched his head. "Ugh, so many boxes." He opened several until he finally

---

[4] Leftovers

raised a package of plates above his head in triumph. "Found 'em."

"What about napkins?"

Kevin put up a finger. "Hold on, got an idea." He left the room and came back in a few seconds with a roll of toilet paper.

"Better than nothing," Linda said. With a hand towel, she lifted the top of the pot. "The food's done."

After she spooned the *sobras* onto their plates, they sat down at the table. Linda grabbed Kevin's hand. "Is it okay if I say grace?"

He closed his eyes and bowed his head. Linda did the same. "*Dios Todopoderoso, gracias por darnos lo que vamos a comer. Oro que proteges a mis amigos mientras conducen a sus casas. Te agradecemos por todo lo que nos das, aunque no lo merecemos. Amén.*"[5]

Kevin squeezed her hand. "I love when you speak Spanish."

"I never really learned to pray in English." Linda picked up a plastic fork.

He examined the food before taking a wary bite. "Hey, this is pretty good. What'd you put in it?"

"Oh, a bit of this, a bit of that. *Sobras* means leftovers, so you just kinda throw stuff together."

He laughed. "My mom does that sometimes. She calls it goulash."

After they'd finished eating, Linda caught a glimpse of the time on Kevin's phone. One o'clock. "Whoa, I had no idea it was this late. I don't think I can stay for the movie."

He whimpered and leaned his head on her shoulder. "Please?"

She kissed the top of his head and stood. "I can't."

---

[5] All-powerful God, thank you for giving us what we are about to eat. I pray you will protect my friends as they drive home. We thank you for all that you give us, even though we don't deserve it. Amen.

Kevin sighed. "At least let me drive you home."

"Okay." Linda agreed. The buses stopped running at ten, anyway. She would've had to get a taxi, and she needed to save her money for more important things.

"Let's go." Kevin grabbed his keys. "Hold on." He jogged down the hall and knocked on a door. "Yo."

Linda leaned against the wall and watched.

The roommate who'd almost plowed into her stepped into the hall and sniffed the air. "Dude, what's that smell? I'm starved."

"There's some left if you want it," Kevin said. "Listen, I'm taking Linda home, so I might not be here when you leave."

"Cool," his roommate said. "See you next year."

"Yeah, have a good summer. Don't do anything I wouldn't do." Kevin winked.

They laughed and punched each other on the shoulders.

Linda stepped into the living room and shook her head. Men were so strange sometimes. Kevin put his arm around her shoulder, and they walked out the door.

Three hours later, they were still parked in front of her house, talking. "I really gotta go," Linda said for the hundredth time that night.

Kevin sighed, his eyelids heavy. "Yeah, I'm about to pass out." He pulled her close and kissed her. "Linda?" he asked, his voice soft.

"Yeah?" Her lips left his for only a second.

He pulled back and framed her face with his large hands. His blue eyes were illuminated by the only working streetlight on the block, and his face was serious. "I think I'm falling for you."

Warmth radiated from Linda's heart. "Me, too."

In the dark car, Linda could see his lip twitch into

a smile as he gave her one last kiss and hug. "I'll miss you," she said and opened the car door. The brightness of the overhead lights made her squint.

"I'll miss you, too. Call me as soon as you can."

"I will. Drive safe." She closed the car door and nearly floated into the house.

PART TWO

Living the Dream

But he wanted to justify himself, so he asked Jesus,
"And who is my neighbor?"
- Luke 10:29

*Pero él, queriendo justificarse a sí mismo, dijo a Jesús: "¿Y
quién es mi prójimo?"*
- Lucas 10:29

CHAPTER THIRTEEN
Tu Camino y El Mío[1]

*L*inda checked her cell phone for the umpteenth time that day. It was less than a week before the fall semester would begin, and she hadn't heard anything from Kevin in three days. She couldn't wait to see him. Every evening for the first month, they had talked on the phone late into the night, but the last couple of weeks their phone calls were getting shorter and shorter. He'd acted distracted, and she wanted to be able to speak with him in person. She had a sinking feeling she'd done something wrong.

Pushing away her thoughts, she browsed through pictures on her phone. A favorite from the summer captured Professor Chekov pumping her fist and screaming among a sign-carrying crowd of Dreamers at the rally for immigrant rights in May. It'd been Linda's first rally, and after it she'd joined a local group called Virginia Organizing that helped give voice to injustices in their community.

---

[1] Your Path and Mine – a song by Vicente Fernandez

Nearly every day during the summer, she'd hopped the bus to the city library to keep up with the latest news. Sometimes Hector had joined her to work on GED prep. It'd turned out that he did need a little extra work on his math, so Linda had kept her promise to help him study. On Saturdays, she'd wake extra early to bake the *pan dulce* so she could attend the Virginia Organizing meetings held at noon every Saturday. Seeing her enthusiasm, the leaders had asked her to help with some of the planning for the march downtown in September.

Still no calls. She had to get out of the house. She was driving herself crazy. Grabbing her backpack, she stepped into the hall.

Hector wandered past in his pajamas. "Morning. I started some coffee. It should be ready any minute."

"Sweet," she exclaimed. She needed to jolt her mind from Kevin. Or maybe the coffee would make her thoughts race on more about him. The aroma of hazelnuts wafted through the air, and she decided she'd chance it. "I'll get out some *panes.*"

"Be back in a minute," Hector said, closing his bedroom door. Mamá had cleaned out her old sewing room after Hector had moved in permanently near the beginning of the summer. Somehow he'd managed to squeeze his bed and all his stuff into the small space. Hector had picked out the most important items from his mom's place and had sold the rest at the church fundraiser. Juanita and Linda refused to take rent money, deciding his money would be better spent on a lawyer.

Unfortunately, the lawyer hadn't made much of a difference, and Diana and María had been deported in July. Hector, Mamá, Linda, and Doña Vazquez had scraped together what was left after the legal fees. With the help of some *hermanos* from Promesa, they'd financed a simple one-bedroom apartment near the center of Mexico City, also sending money for food, clothes, and necessary furnishings. For a hundred and twenty dollars a month, the place wasn't pretty but it was safe and comfortable and was something María and Diana could afford on their own once they'd found jobs.

Since then, Hector had been moping around the house. He'd wanted to go visit his mother in Mexico, but she'd made him promise to get his GED first and then save for the trip. Diana would call him on Sundays from a payphone on a loud street and could talk for only five minutes, so Hector had wired money for her to get her own phone. But phone calls weren't enough. Linda understood. There was nothing quite like a mother's hug.

In the kitchen, Linda frowned. Where had she put the bread? After searching through the fridge and cabinets, she planted her hands on her hips in frustration. Maybe she'd forgotten to bring any home last night. She'd been so focused on Kevin, she couldn't remember what she baked at the *panadería*.

"*Mija, ¿qué andas buscando?*"[2] Mamá asked as she entered the kitchen, passing her apron over her head.

"Didn't I bring *pan dulce* home last night?"

Mamá pointed to the table. "*Ya lo saqué.*"[3]

Pastries sat on a plate in the center of the table.

"*¿Qué te pasa, Lindita? Te veo bien distraída.*"[4] Mamá felt Linda's forehead. "*¿Te estás enfermando?*"[5]

"No, I'm not getting sick. *Estoy bien.*"[6] Except she wasn't okay. Her heart was full of worry.

---

[2] What are you looking for?
[3] I already took it out.
[4] What's wrong with you, my little Linda? You seem so distracted.
[5] Are you getting sick?
[6] I'm okay.

Mamá clucked her tongue. "*Siéntate, corazón. Te traigo un cafecito.*"[7]

"*Ay*, Mamá, I'm fine. I can get my own coffee. *No se preocupe.*"

Mamá stared her down, hands on her hips, reminding Linda of a *vaquero*[8] about to duel in an old Mexican movie.

Maybe Linda would take her coffee to go.

Hector marched into the room and saved the day. "*Siéntese, Doña.*[9] I'll make you a nice cup of coffee."

"*Gracias, Hectorcito.* So polite." She glared at Linda with pursed lips as Hector guided Mamá to a kitchen chair and pulled it out for her.

Hector winked at Linda as he moved towards the coffeepot.

"Thanks," Linda whispered, handing him a mug.

"No problem. She's like a dog with a bone sometimes."

Linda covered a giggle.

"*¿Qué dicen allí?*"[10] Mamá called.

"*Nada*,"[11] they said in unison, smiling.

Mumbling to herself, Juanita put a *concha*[12] on her napkin. Like a dog with a bone? She wondered what else people had been saying about her behind her back all these years.

"*Gracias.*" She inhaled the sweet, nutty aroma of hazelnut as Hector placed a mug in front of her.

---

[7] Sit down, honey. I'll bring you a coffee.

[8] Cowboy

[9] Have a seat, ma'am.

[10] What are you two talking about over there?

[11] Nothing.

[12] Shell – a popular type of pan dulce, rounded with lines of sugar on top

The kids sat down at the table with their own cups, soon munching on their favorite *panes* and sipping coffee.

Hector reached for a second *niño envuelto*. "My mom called while I was getting dressed."

Juanita put down her coffee. "Oh, *¿sí? ¿Qué dice?*"[13]

"They're working more hours at Suburbia now. Everyone's getting ready for next month."

Diana and María had both found jobs in a department store called Suburbia near the Zócalo plaza in the center of Mexico City, only one metro stop from their apartment.

"What's next month?" Linda asked between bites.

"*El Diez y Seis, mija,*"[14] Juanita replied, frowning. It wasn't like Linda to forget about the Sixteenth of September, Mexico's Independence Day. Something was bothering her. Probably that boy. Through the walls, Linda's muffled voice had traveled into her bedroom, chatting away for hours every night, but not the last couple of weeks. Not a good sign.

"She said María's saving up to cross over again, hopefully by Christmas, so she can be with Luz and her grandmother."

Juanita shook her head. If she were in María's shoes, she might do the same thing. But she wouldn't want to experience those horrific days in the desert again. "*¿Y tu mamá?*"[15]

Hector pulled apart his bread and dipped it into his coffee, sighing. "I think she's staying. She likes it in D.F. All the museums, Aztec ruins, and good food. I have to admit, it sounds like a cool place. I only wish I could be there with her."

---

[13] What does she say?

[14] The Sixteenth, my daughter.

[15] And your mom?

"Are you thinking of moving?" Linda asked. Noticing anxiety in her daughter's voice, Juanita studied her face. It was hard to read.

"She won't let me. She wants me to finish my education and make my own life here. Sometimes I think—" Hector's voice caught in his throat "—that maybe she got tired of dealing with me. I put her through too much. I was so stupid." His foot tapped quickly under the table.

"Don't even think that, Hector." Linda placed a hand on his shoulder as his lips trembled and tears salted his coffee. "Your mom loves you, and she's really proud of you. She can see how well you're doing, how you've turned your life around, and she knows you have a chance to make a good life for yourself here. It's not that she needed a break from you. If she could, she'd be sitting right here at this table, eating *panes* and drinking this delicious coffee you made."

"She does love her coffee." Hector chuckled and wiped his tears. "Maybe if I save up enough money, I can go see her at Christmas."

Juanita patted his arm. She couldn't imagine getting separated from Linda. And she never wanted to.

Later that day, Linda stretched as she stared at the computer screen at the downtown library. She'd chosen her courses and filled out her financial information for the semester. All that was left was buying books. The list grew longer every year, and professors wanted the newest editions, which were harder to find online. She would have to purchase the rest in the campus bookstore at an inflated price.

Sighing, she typed the book titles into the search bar. Four out of the ten books for her classes were available at a fraction of the cost. She calculated the total price for the other six books through the campus bookstore's site, and the numbers began to add up. Six hundred and fifty, plus a hundred for the other four. She shook her head. Her "full-ride" scholarship didn't cover books, food, or housing, so she worked extra hard during the summers and school year.

Now that the lawyer fees and start-up cost for Diana and María had been covered, Hector had started chipping in on the rent and food. It eased her and Mamá's burden a bit. But the books still killed her every semester. Seven hundred and fifty dollars was a lot of *dinero* for someone making seven-fifty an hour. A hundred hours worth, to be exact. Money was tight, but she got by with a lot of hard work.

Her cell phone vibrated next to the keyboard. It was a text from Becky. "I'm back in town. Meet for lunch? We gotta talk. ASAP."

Tim lowered the box of kitchen appliances onto the front lawn next to the rest of the yard sale items. He straightened and rubbed his lower back. Although he and Guillermo were taking in a lot of money at the shop, Nathan's medical bills had sucked up a large quantity of their budget. Tim hadn't realized how much his insurance plan had covered until he was uninsured and had to pay out-of-pocket for the ER visit, the x-ray, the cast, and all of the follow-up appointments. Three thousand dollars and counting.

To help pay the mortgage and the bills, he and Wendy had decided to be part of the annual end-of-

summer, neighborhood-wide yard sale. He was
shocked that she'd agreed to even think it. Almost
everyone on the block was joining in, so in the end,
peer pressure won out.

The last time he remembered going to a yard sale
was a few years before his father had died. He,
Wendy, and the kids normally didn't participate in
this ritual. By this time of the summer, they were
usually in the middle of a two-week vacation in a
cooler climate, like Vermont or San Francisco or
Europe.

In fact, Wendy and the boys had only recently
returned from a month-long trip to their
grandparents' place in Northern Virginia, where
Nathan and Jeremy had been enrolled in a summer
enrichment program at an elite charter school in
Fairfax. His in-laws had financed the educational
advancement and had further convinced Wendy to
send the children to a boarding school in England for
the fall to "rid them of the stench of public
education." While Tim felt public school had
provided him with a good start, England was an
amazing opportunity he and Wendy would never
have been able to afford on their own, so they both
agreed to take them up on the offer.

Needless to say, Tim was excited to spend time
together as a family while the boys were still at
home. Over the last week, the four of them had
reluctantly filled boxes with items they no longer
wanted. At first, each discarded toy had come with a
temper tantrum, but the more they'd put into boxes,
the easier it'd gotten. Last night they'd priced
everything, and Tim and Wendy had awakened
before the sun to set items on tables and blankets on
their front lawn.

Tim waved at the other neighbors who were up at

this crazy hour doing the same. Any minute, the early birds would arrive to hunt for the best deals, and a twinge of excitement sprung up at the thought of getting rid of some of their clutter. The rooms were considerably less packed with toys, and Tim could actually walk into their closet without creating an avalanche of shoeboxes.

This was about the only thing he'd been excited about lately. Wendy's initial thawing the day of the accident had stopped after the bills showed up in the mail. She continued giving him the cold shoulder and bothering him about a better job.

But Tim wasn't sure if he wanted to work anywhere else. Never had he encountered so little job stress. Why would he go back to a nine to five? Especially when it turned into seven to seven on the weeks that projects were due. Stuck in a cubicle all day, crunching numbers, talking to unhappy clients, and doing projects for a boss a generation younger than him who would end up taking the credit anyway. Going back to that lifestyle was unimaginable.

Tim was actually starting to appreciate the change. Though Guillermo didn't provide insurance and 401ks, he let Tim take breaks whenever he wanted, and the pleasant chats with Linda whenever she stopped by were a nice change of pace compared to Wendy's anger. He and Guillermo had even found a junker they were working on after hours so Tim would have a car again.

The commute was, by far, the worst part of his job. Having a car would cut down the time from over an hour on the bus to a twenty-minute drive, depending on traffic. The only shortcut was through that sketchy-looking apartment complex, which Guillermo had informed him was "the projects" of

Roanoke; he'd advised him to avoid it in the future. Not wanting to get mugged, Tim chose instead to walk faster on his normal route. If it hadn't been for the free lunch he'd gotten from Guillermo's sister every day, all the walking would have put him in the best shape of his life. The sunshine and air, though not always fresh—especially in the heat of summer— gave him loads of energy, which he channeled into playing with the boys after he got home from work. That is, whenever they weren't up in Northern Virginia.

He set up the last table and watched as the first customer pulled up. "Here goes nothing," he said to Wendy and plastered on a smile.

Juanita held the chalk and carefully wrote out the menu for next week. Hector watched over her shoulder.

"*Perfecto*." He squeezed Juanita's shoulders.

She had become increasingly comfortable with reading and writing, so Hector had moved on to teaching her English. These days she spent her nights with her Bible instead of *novelas*, which Pastor Martinez agreed was a much healthier option.

She stood up to stir the *pozole*,[16] but Hector beat her to it. He tasted the broth and added more spices. Now that he could work more independently, they made twice the food, which greatly increased their sales. Every day they served two separate dishes. Starting around eleven, they set up tables and chairs outside the *panadería*, which were quickly filled with hungry customers.

---

[16] A traditional Mexico soup with large hominy grains and pork.

Memo had inquired about a food truck, so they wouldn't have to carry the food two blocks and could make it to order. Hector could get the license, since he was a citizen. Still unsure what God wanted her to do, Juanita often prayed for guidance. A vehicle would be a big investment, and so far they'd made good money the way they had been doing it.

It was fun being her own boss. The flexibility of making her own hours, deciding what she wanted to do, and getting almost all the profits had been foreign concepts to her. In Mexico, Juanita had worked in the *campo*[17] as a child, picking corn and beans. After she'd married, her husband wouldn't allow her to leave their home, not even for the market or to visit family. The only person she could speak to was their neighbor.

A week before she and Linda had left for the U.S. so many years ago, Memo had gotten her a message through that neighbor. Their cousin in Texas had given Memo the name of the *coyote* and the date and time of his next *cruzada*[18]. Her cousin had gotten word about her dangerous marriage and was able to pay for her journey. Without working, there'd been no other way Juanita could've left her situation.

Early one morning, while her husband had slept off a hangover, Juanita had slipped out of the house, found the bag the neighbor had hidden under a bush, and carried a sleeping Linda through fields and hills to the bus station miles away. She'd handed her ticket to the driver and, heart racing, had stepped onto the road towards freedom.

The sixteen-hour bus ride had taken them to Ciudad Juarez near the border, where they'd met the

[17] Field
[18] Crossing

coyote and the others who were crossing. It was impossible to cross over in the city itself, but navigating to the desert border in New Mexico was a different story. They'd all gotten into the bed of a truck and had driven an hour outside the city into the Chihuahuan Desert, where they'd been given a gallon of water per person and told to follow the *coyote*. Crossing the border should have taken two days, after which they would've gotten a short ride into the city of El Paso, Texas. In the end, it had taken almost a week to get to the shack in New Mexico, and considering what had happened, it had been a miracle she and Linda had even made it at all.

Stirring the *pozole*, Juanita flashed back to the final steps of their journey across the border . . .

After the men raped her, they fell asleep in a drunken stupor in the back room. With shaking hands, Juanita washed off the filth from her scratched and bruised body with a damp cloth. She held back sobs as she observed Linda, still asleep, her little chest rising and falling. As she reached for her daughter, the moonlight illuminated something on the table. Leaning closer, Juanita realized it was a handful of American coins. She stole them, asking God for forgiveness, grabbed her bag, picked up Linda, and snuck outside. It was dark, even with the brightness of the moon. She knew Mexico was behind her, but she didn't know the way to El Paso.

Running a few hundred feet in the opposite direction from where they had come, she knelt, forehead to the sand, and prayed. Linda, awakened by the movement, knelt next to her and imitated her. After concluding her desperate prayer, Juanita opened her eyes, searching to her left and to her right. Nothing was around except a bit of pinkish-orange light in the distance. Drawn to the light, she walked on shaky legs towards it, hoping for at least an hour or two before they'd awake to find them missing.

Soon the bushes and cacti grew bigger, and a few other trees and some grass appeared. The distant, rosy light was her only guide. Her eyes had adjusted to the darkness, and she could see something stretch long in front of her. She squinted and realized it was a road.

"Mira, mija, el camino," she whispered to Linda. "Dios nos ha mostrado el camino."[19]

After six days of wandering, almost dead, in the desert, she had run towards the light and found the path. She walked along the side of road in the direction of the light until something rumbled behind her. She turned, staring into the bright headlights of a large vehicle. "Dios,"[20] she cried, praying it wouldn't be la migra.

She clutched Linda with one arm and waved with the other. The truck slowed to a stop, the exhale of its engine sounding like a sigh of relief. A man rolled down the window and leaned out, saying something in English.

"El Paso?" she asked.

He nodded and opened the passenger door.

"Gracias," she said. "¿Va a El Paso?"[21]

The man pointed towards her guiding light. "El Paso," he said.

"¿Sí?" she asked, nodding in excitement. Tears rose up within her.

"Sí, El Paso." He grinned and adjusted the toothpick he'd been chewing.

Juanita smiled back and placed her daughter on the floor of the passenger seat as she pulled herself into the cab. Linda crawled onto her lap, and Juanita closed the heavy door. The engine rumbled to a start, and Juanita watched as they buzzed by the cacti outside. An hour later, they pulled into a truck stop in El Paso. The man helped them

---

[19] Look, daughter, the road/path . . . God has shown us the road/path.
[20] God.
[21] Are you going to El Paso?

down onto the gravely parking lot. Juanita pointed to a phone booth near the truck stop restaurant and gestured for him to follow her.

She stepped into the booth and handed him her cousin's number and the stolen coins. There'd been only one phone in their pueblo, and she had never used it. The man took the paper, put a coin into the little slot, and pushed the numbered buttons. He held the receiver to his ear and then passed it to her. She listened, jumping at the metallic sound.

Suddenly a voice crackled on the line. "¿Bueno?"

Tears filled Juanita's eyes at the sound of her cousin's voice. God had shown them the road and had brought them to their destination. They were free.

Linda waved at Becky as she walked up the sidewalk.

Becky ran towards her. "Hey, girl. I missed you."

"Yeah, I missed you, too, *chica*. Where are we going to eat? The caf?"

Becky grimaced. "Ugh, I don't want to eat there any more than I have to. Besides, I think it's closed until tomorrow."

"Okay, where then?" Linda readjusted her purse strap.

"I know this great sandwich place a few blocks from here, and I've been dying for one of their steak and cheese subs. We don't have good stuff like that in South Carolina. It's mostly fried chicken and grits."

Linda chuckled. "I'm so glad you called. I needed this. It can't be one of our epic hangout sessions, though. I promised my uncle I'd do some work for him this afternoon." They linked arms and walked up the block. "So, what'd you do this summer?"

"Mostly spent time at my dad's firm. He had this

big trial, so I was making copies for his associates and sorting through evidence and boxes of files."

"That's sounds like fun."

"Yeah, not so much. This one old guy kept hitting on me. Finally, I told Dad, and he sent the man to the other office. Apparently his hearing aid wasn't working when they introduced me as the boss' daughter."

"Oh my." Linda snickered.

"Yeah, for real. Oh, and Brian came up to visit on Fourth of July weekend. He met my family, and we watched the fireworks together. It was great."

Linda frowned. "I didn't get to see Kevin at all. I mean, Connecticut's so far, and I couldn't leave anyway. Summer's when I make most of the money for the school year."

"And I suppose Kevin was too busy to make it down to visit one weekend?" Becky asked, a slight edge in her voice.

"No, he was working too hard at his internship. We talked on the phone a lot, though not as much lately."

"Hmm." Becky opened the door to the shop. "Interesting."

The yard sale was going well. Tim stood nearby as a family bought the last of the boys' used toys. In the first hour, he and Wendy had sold the old dining room set along with their two old televisions and stereos. The exercise equipment had gone next, followed by their old sets of dishes. Wendy's bridesmaids' dresses and shoes had gone before lunch. Only a few watches, books, clothes, and electronics were left, scattered around the yard.

The crowds had died down, but stragglers were still making the rounds. Tim counted the money.

"How'd we do?" Wendy kept an eye on the boys, who were sword-fighting with sticks that had fallen from the oak tree. "You boys be careful."

"Hold on." Tim finished counting. "Wow."

"How much?" Wendy's eyes widened.

"Almost a thousand."

"That's amazing. Why didn't we do this before?" Wendy smirked. "Oh, right, because before you had a normal job with health insurance, and our bills were paid."

Tim ignored the comment and grasped for a positive spin. "Doesn't the house feel so much better already? I'm not tripping over toys every three seconds, and the kids have more space to spread out."

One of the boys cried out.

"Okay, give me the sticks," Wendy yelled. "I told you to be careful."

Tim stood up, glad she'd been interrupted before she went into one of her tirades and embarrassed him in front of the neighborhood. He couldn't stand one more person looking at him like he was a loser. The crunch of dry grass brought him back from his thoughts. Another customer had arrived and seemed to be eyeing the watches.

"Hello there, sir. Anything I can help you with today?" Tim called out above the yelling.

The man scanned the merchandise. "How much for everything?"

"Everything?" Tim did some mental calculations. "I can't sell you the tables. They're not for sale. But for everything else, maybe a hundred."

The man raised an eyebrow. "I'll give you fifty."

Tim shook his head. "That watch is worth fifty. I'll take eighty."

The man shrugged. "All right. Bag it up for me." He handed Tim four twenties. "I'll go get my car. It's down the block."

Wendy approached with the boys nursing scratched arms behind her. "We're about two minutes away from meltdown over here."

Tim wasn't sure if she was talking about the boys or herself or their entire marriage. It was better not to ask, he decided. "That guy bought the rest of the stuff. Boys, can you put the books and movies into these bags?"

The boys skipped over to the table and grabbed some plastic shopping bags.

"That should keep them occupied for a while," Tim said with a wary smile.

Minutes later, the man pulled into their driveway, and they helped him pack the car. "Thanks a lot," Tim said, shaking the man's hand before he drove off with his new treasures. He stood next to Wendy. "Now we don't have to make that trip to Good Will. Plus we hit a thousand dollars with his extra *dinero*." Tim waved the twenties.

"At least that'll cover the doctor's bills." Wendy sighed. "My parents offered again to pay them. I think we ought to take them up on the offer. We could use the money for other things."

Tim clenched his jaw. "I've told you. We don't need them to pay for everything. I can handle it." He already felt bad enough that his in-laws were funding Nathan and Jeremy's schooling. Any more emasculation might send him over the brink.

"I don't know why you're being so stubborn." She narrowed her eyes. "Any news on a job?"

"Not yet."

"It's almost like you enjoy working for that dirty Mexican," Wendy snarled.

"Maybe I do," Tim said with a shrug. "At least there I get a little respect and appreciation."

She stared him down. "I'll give you respect and appreciation when you've earned it."

Tim balled his fists, battling the urge to fight back. "I'll see you later." He folded the tables and grabbed one under each arm. One of the neighbors had borrowed them from a local community center. "I'm taking these back to George, and then I'm going to work."

He groaned under the weight of the tables and his frustration. How long would this go on? It was starting to eat at him. Every day and every night for months. He was tired, and he wasn't sure how much more he could take.

Juanita smiled as the tables in front of the *panadería* quickly filled with families. Saturday was their most popular day. Kids were out of school, and most people were off work.

Hector walked towards her. "Twelve orders of *pozole*, and fifteen orders of *flautas*."

Juanita made up the plates and bowls of soup, and Hector served them to the tables. He put the money in their cash box and called back to Norma. "People want sodas. I'll just write down how many we take. A few want *flan*,[22] if you have any."

"*Sí, tenemos,*" Norma said. "*¿Cuántos?*"[23]

"*No sé,*" Hector said, juggling sodas. "I'll ask."

He opened the soda bottles for the customers and leaned over the tables, talking with them.

---

[22] Mexican custard
[23] Yes, we have some . . . How many?

"*Que milagro, ¿no?*"[24] Juanita whispered to Norma.

"*Ay, sí. Su mamá debe de sentir bien orgulloso de cómo se está portando ahora.*"[25]

Juanita nodded. Hector had left his phone at home while he was at the store the other day, and Diana had called. Juanita had told her how wonderfully Hector was doing and how hard he was working. Diana had choked up on the line when Juanita had told her Hector wanted to make his mother proud and to be a better son.

It was such a dramatic change. He'd even been going with them to church every Sunday. Everyone in the neighborhood could see the difference and were equally surprised at his transformation. Norma and Juanita heard at least three comments per day about his good behavior.

"*Ocho flan,*"[26] Hector said, coming back with empty plates. "And four more *flautas*."

A line of people wrapped around the sidewalk outside the *panadería*. It was going to be a busy day.

"Ooh, I think this is us." Linda's mouth watered as two steaming sandwiches headed their way.

"I gotta talk with you about something," Becky said after the waiter served them their food.

Linda glanced up from her plate and noticed the concern in Becky's face. "What's wrong?"

"I'm not exactly sure how to tell you this." She sighed.

"Are you pregnant?" Linda whispered.

---

[24] What a miracle, isn't it?

[25] Oh, yes. His mother should feel so proud of how he is behaving now.

[26] Eight flan

Becky laughed. "No. Thank God. My mother would have a cow."

"Then what is it?" Linda bit into her sub. "Oh, this is really good."

"Told ya." Becky swallowed. "I'm not sure how to say this, Linda, so I'm just going to lay it on you. Kevin was seeing another girl during the summer."

The sandwich hardened to a rock in Linda's stomach. She opened her mouth, but nothing came out.

"I just found out today. I wanted to tell you before you heard it from someone else. It was some girl at his internship. He told Brian all about it."

"Why didn't he say something?" Linda's head spun in a thousand directions at once.

"Apparently Kevin can be a real jerk sometimes. Brian says he's like a kid at a toy store. He sees something shiny and has to have it; then a few weeks later, he wants the next new thing. Plus it probably didn't hurt that she was the CEO's daughter."

Linda didn't want to think Kevin was like that. All the late-night conversations they'd had about life and the world and what they would do this year fell on her like a brick wall. "So I was just..." Linda couldn't get the words out.

"Something new." Becky frowned, patting Linda's arm.

"I knew something was wrong." Linda picked at the shredded lettuce on her plate, shaking her head.

Becky moved over to Linda's side of the booth and put her arm around her friend's shoulder. "Listen, it didn't have anything to do with you. You are a great, amazing, wonderful person. Kevin obviously has issues if he can't see that."

Linda put her hand over her heart. "I really thought I was falling for him."

"I know. And I know this is the first guy you've ever let yourself feel anything about. Someday you'll find someone who is worthy of that big heart of yours."

Linda hugged her friend and let the tears flow.

CHAPTER FOURTEEN
Llorar y Llorar[1]

*T*im screwed up his face in concentration. Something was leaking from underneath this Nissan, but he couldn't put his finger on it, literally. He'd been staring at the underside of the sedan for what felt like hours, but all he could think about were Wendy's bitter comments. He needed a break.

Familiar clicking heels made their way across the shop, and relief washed over him. "*Hola*, Linda," he said as he rolled out from under the car. His smile dropped as he saw her face. "Hey, what's wrong? Did something happen? Are you okay?"

Linda, eyes red and puffy, shrugged. "I'm fine. I don't want to talk about it." She leaned against the stairs to the office, stepping one heel on the bottom stair, which amplified her well-formed calf. The sundresss she wore was light and airy.

Tim fought his desire to go rip it off and find out what was underneath. He chose instead to let his

1 Crying and Crying – a song by Vicente Fernandez

gaze linger on some of her finer qualities while he washed his hands. "Your mom came by with lunch. I think she brought *tacos* and some strange-looking soup."

She smiled. "*Pozole.*"

He'd almost forgotten what it was like to make a girl smile. If only Wendy were more like Linda. Linda really seemed to care about people. She listened when he shared about his boys and how much he missed them while they were away in Fairfax. "I was just about to take my lunch break. Why don't you join me?"

"I'm not hungry."

"Whoa." Tim showed his clean hands. "You not wanting to eat? Now I know something's wrong."

He was hoping for a laugh, but she broke into tears instead. "I'm sorry," she said, turning away and covering her face.

"Hey, it's okay." Tim walked over and put his hand on her shoulder. Her caramel skin was soft, and she smelled like flowers. Lilacs, perhaps? He tried to remember the last time Wendy had dressed up and put on perfume for him, but it'd been too long. Too long since she'd cared enough to try. Too long since she'd showed him any affection. Too long since she'd let him touch her. He allowed himself to run his thumb over Linda's smooth shoulder for a moment before reluctantly dropping his arm to his side.

Linda took a deep breath and composed herself, wiping her tears with the back of her hand. "Sorry," she repeated. "Guy trouble."

"Tell me about it," Tim said.

Her eyes widened in surprise.

Gears turning, Tim backpedaled. "Girls. I mean, mine is girl trouble. I like girls."

Linda raised an eyebrow.

"Women, obviously," Tim stuttered, his face heating. "My wife in particular. She's the girl. You know, the trouble. So, I suppose it's more like wife trouble."

"I didn't know you guys were having problems."

"You tell me yours, and I'll tell you mine," Tim joked.

Linda shot him a disapproving look.

Recovering, he grabbed a plateful of *tacos* from the fridge and stuck them in the microwave. "Come on, join me for lunch, and we can talk." He gestured to a folding chair.

Linda shrugged. She plopped down on the chair, and it collapsed underneath her.

Tim swore and rushed over, offering his hand. "Are you okay?"

Linda adjusted her dress but not before Tim had seen more than she would be comfortable with. He turned his head and pretended he hadn't noticed.

"I'm fine." She took his hand, and he pulled her up.

"I told Guillermo these chairs were an accident waiting to happen." He pulled over the sturdy stool from the tool bench, toweling off the grease. "You take this one. Wouldn't want you to get hurt. Though there's always worker's comp."

"I don't think that's available when you're employed under the table for family," Linda replied with a smile.

Tim smirked. "But you do the books, so he'd never know."

A gentle laugh escaped Linda's sweet lips. She sat on the stool, crossing her ankles.

The microwave beeped, and Tim placed the food on the old card table that served as their break area.

Linda grabbed one, blowing on it. "These are *flautas*, by the way."

"Same difference. It's all corn and meat fried in oil."

She considered his statement. "I suppose you're right."

"So, what's going on with you and Hector?" Tim asked, taking a bite of his *flauta*.

"What do you mean?" She shook her head. "Hector's just a friend."

"Sorry. You guys hang out all the time. I thought you were a couple."

"No, it's my boyfriend, Kevin. My friend just told me that he's been cheating on me all summer."

"That's rough."

"Yeah, what about you?" Linda asked. "Nathan and Jeremy have always seemed so happy when you've brought them in."

"They are." Tim poked at his *flautas*. I hope the boarding school doesn't change them too much. My in-laws want a better future than we can provide, something with the sophistication and privileges my wife grew up with up in Northern Virginia. Money is the main issue between Wendy and I. Plus she doesn't like my job."

"The long hours?"

Tim got uncomfortable. "That's one of the things." He couldn't tell her the rest of Wendy's reasons without offending Linda, her uncle, or her entire race. "She's really critical."

"You should be proud of what you do. Tío is always going on about how much better you are than Javier."

"I'm not sure that's much of a compliment." Tim chuckled. "And you should forget about that boy. He's stupid if he passed up a chance with you."

"Thanks." Linda finished another *flauta* as Guillermo pulled a car into the garage. "Don't tell my uncle about Kevin. He might try to track him down."

"Don't worry. It'll be our little secret." Tim winked and crossed his heart.

Linda glared at her phone. Kevin was calling for the fourth time that day. She hit the ignore button and lay back on her bed. Someone knocked. *"Entre."*[2]

Mamá came in, closed the door, and sat on the bed next to Linda.

"¿Cómo estás, mija? Te veo muy triste estos días."[3] She frowned, running her hand over Linda's hair.

Linda sighed. *"Rompí con Kevin."*[4] She hadn't told Mamá yet, because she hadn't wanted a lecture about how Mamá was right and she was wrong.

But Mamá didn't take that road. *"Ay, mija. Pero, ¿qué pasó?"*[5]

"He met another girl during the summer."

Mamá's brow furrowed, and her frown turned into pursed lips. *"¿Enviamos a tu tío para hablar con él?"*[6]

Linda laughed. She could just imagine the look on Kevin's face if Tío showed up at his door. *"No, Mamá. Déjalo.*[7] He made his choice."

Mamá nodded. "A stupid choice."

"It's okay." She shrugged. "Now I'll have more time to focus on schoolwork and The Dream Act."

"Y este Dream Act, *¿qué es?"*[8]

"It's to help students who came into the country

---

[2] Come in.

[3] How are you, my daughter? You've been looking sad these days.

[4] I broke up with Kevin.

[5] But what happened?

[6] Should we send your uncle to talk with him?

[7] Leave him be.

[8] And this Dream Act, what is it?

as young kids and don't have papers, the ones who want a better education and a good job."

"*¿Cómo tú?*"[9] Mamá asked with a smile.

"*Sí*, like me."

"*Esto es bueno, mija. Pero ten cuidado. No quiero que te metes en problemas.*"[10]

"Don't worry, Mamá. I won't get into any trouble." Linda held up a finger. "Oh, that reminds me. Daniel from Virginia Organizing is coming in an hour to go over some stuff for the Dream Act rally downtown."

"*¿El hijo de Brenda?*" Mamá asked. "*¿El que se casó hace poco?*"[11]

"Yes, that's the one."

"*Pues, yo voy por unos panes, y le digo a Hector que haga café.*"[12]

"*Gracias.*" Linda sighed.

Mamá kissed Linda on her forehead. "*Te quiero, Linda.*"[13]

"*Le quiero también, Mamá.*"[14] Linda watched her mother leave the room. She waited until Mamá's shoes clicked on the kitchen tiles and then allowed herself to cry.

Juanita sighed and diced the onions for the salsa. She was sobbing by the time Hector came into the kitchen.

---

[9] Like you?

[10] This is good, my daughter. But be careful. I don't want you to get into any trouble.

[11] Brenda's son? . . . The one who just got married?

[12] Well, I'll go for some pastries, and I'll tell Hector to make coffee.

[13] I love you, Linda.

[14] I love you, too, Mom.

"*¿Qué pasó?*" He put his hand on her shoulder.

"*Nada. Son las cebollas.*"[15] She motioned towards the onions.

Hector patted her shoulder. "Okay." He turned and began cutting the tomatoes and chiles.

Juanita put the diced onions in some vegetable oil and cooked them on low heat until they were soft and translucent. Hector added the tomatoes and chiles and a few pinches of salt. They stirred the sauce in silence.

"*Rompieron,*"[16] Juanita said.

"What?" Hector raised an eyebrow. With the time they'd spent reading and writing in Spanish and their time in the kitchen, his Spanish had been improving, but sometimes he still didn't understand her.

"*Linda y ese muchacho.*[17] They—" She put her hands together, then separated them.

"—Broke up?" Hector asked. The spoon he had been using to stir abruptly stilled.

"*Sí.*"

Hector frowned, not saying anything for a moment. "Do you want me to go beat him up?"

Juanita chuckled. "*Gracias, Hector, pero no.*"[18]

"How's she doing?" He nodded towards Linda's bedroom.

"*Muy triste.* She don't show it, *pero yo le conozco a mi hija.*"[19]

"I knew that white boy was bad news."

Juanita clicked her tongue and smacked him with a wooden spoon. "*No digas eso.*"[20]

---

[15] Nothing. It's the onions.

[16] They broke up.

[17] Linda and that boy.

[18] Thanks, Hector, but no.

[19] Very sad . . . but I know my daughter.

[20] Don't say that.

"What? He's a boy, and he's white. What's wrong with that?"

She shook her head with a chuckle. "*¿Cocemos el pollo hoy?*"[21]

"Yeah, that'll save us time, because we can shred it once it cools down. We need to make more tortillas tonight, too. Then tomorrow we just have to fry the *tostadas* and cook the *enchiladas* and the *cueritos*."[22]

"*Me parece perfecto.*"[23] Juanita finally knew what it was like to have a good man in the house, like a son, really. They were becoming a great team. "Linda's friend, Daniel, he's coming to visit in an hour. I will go to the *panadería*. Can you make the coffee?"

Hector turned. "Daniel? Who's that?"

"*Uno de esos* Dreamers,"[24] Juanita replied, and then noticing the look on Hector's face, she laughed. "*No te preocupes, Hectorcito. Apenitas llegó el muchacho de su luna de miel.*"[25]

Hector pulled out a stockpot from the cabinet. "I'll start the chicken." Humming a little rhythm, he gathered ingredients from the refrigerator.

She sighed. One day Linda would open her eyes and realize how much Hector loved her. Then what would Juanita do? Brushing off the thought, she grabbed her purse and headed out the door.

An hour later Linda, freshly showered and dressed, crossed the living room into the kitchen, leaning on the doorway as Hector stood at the stove stirring a

---

[21] Should we cook the chicken today?
[22] Pork skins
[23] Sounds perfect to me.
[24] One of those Dreamers. (People whom the Dream Act would benefit)
[25] He just got back from his honeymoon.

large pot. This no longer surprised her. It was almost stranger not to see him in the kitchen. Stranger still was they had somehow become friends, something Linda wouldn't have bet on in a million years.

So involved in the cooking, he hummed a tune without seeming to notice her. Smiling, Linda recognized the song as *"Por Siempre."*[26] He did a bachata sidestep to check on another pot before returning to the original one, continuing to hum. Putting down the spoon, he danced over to the blender and tossed in a few items.

When the chorus arrived, his humming erupted into a whispered song. "Not a day has gone by."

Her grin widened as she snuck up behind him and sang the next line, "You're always on my mind."

Hector startled, dropping a serrano pepper on the floor in the process, but he recovered quickly. He whirled around and, without missing a beat, gently took her right hand in his and slipped his other around her mid-back, continuing the dance and singing in a warm, slightly off-pitch tone: "My *corazón*[27] needs you."

"I need you." Linda echoed, getting lost in the song and leaving behind her troubles for a moment.

"Without you—"

"—*Sin ti.*"[28] She closed her eyes and sang the chorus' duet. "I wouldn't want to be."

"I've loved you *por siempre.*" Hector's tone was so sincere, she opened her eyes to glance at him. He met her gaze with his own, sweet and intense. It only lasted a second, and then he looked down to avoid crushing the chile he'd dropped.

---

[26] Forever
[27] Heart
[28] Without you.

Linda let out a slow breath, refocusing on the steps and ignoring the electricity pulsing through her. "You're a good dancer, Hector," Linda observed as they made their way around the kitchen to the imaginary beat.

"Thanks." A goofy grin spread over his face. "My mom forced me to take a class one summer to keep me out of trouble. I pretended to hate it the whole time." He let go for a moment and did a perfectly timed turn, continuing to hum.

"You're in an awfully good mood today." Linda chuckled. His moping had mellowed lately, but his spirits seemed higher than normal.

He wiggled his eyebrows and twirled her, pulling her close so her back was against his chest. It all happened so fast, Linda didn't have time to react. Her heart thudded as he leaned in and whispered, "I got my GED," before spinning her out again.

"What?" Linda stopped dancing and clasped her hands together in excitement. "When? Why didn't you tell me you were taking the test?"

"Yesterday," he said. "I didn't want to tell anyone in case I didn't pass on the first try."

"That's wonderful, Hector. I knew you could do it. I'm so proud of you." She wrapped her arms around him and squeezed him in a bear hug.

He stiffened for a moment before relaxing and then gingerly returning the hug. "Thanks."

At that very moment, Mamá walked in the back door, her eyes round with shock.

Juanita stood at the doorway, the bag of *pan dulce* in her hands feeling like a load of rocks.

Linda pulled out of the hug and waved her over,

appearing oblivious to any of Juanita's discomfort. "*Oiga*,[29] Hector got his GED."

Hector's smile had turned wary, and his face flushed. He cleared his throat. "I got it yesterday after I went to the library."

Juanita walked to him, squeezing his arm with a bit too much force. "*Felicidades, Hectorcito. Que responsible.*"[30] She drew out the last word, narrowing her eyes.

"*S—Sí, Doña,*" he stuttered, rubbing his arm. "*Gracias.*"

The doorbell rang. "That's probably Daniel," Linda said, heading for the door. "We'll celebrate later, Hector."

Hector nodded, avoiding eye contact with Juanita.

"*No te tardaste ni un segundo,*"[31] she grumbled.

"What?" Hector asked weakly.

"The coffee," Juanita said. "*No te tardes con el café.*"[32]

Juanita's mind raced as she arranged the *panes* on a serving platter. Dancing in the kitchen? Whispers and hugs? She had waited a full minute before interrupting them. Who knew where things might have gone next? She wouldn't be able to leave them alone in the house from now on.

She eyed Hector, whose hands shook as he poured the ground coffee into the filter. She smirked and carried the tray into the living room.

"*Doña Palacios.*" Daniel greeted her with a bright smile. "*Mi mamá le mandó unos tamales hondureños.*"[33]

"*Ay, qué rico,*" Juanita exclaimed, lifting the foil from the plate to find half a dozen thick banana leaf

---

[29] Hey

[30] Congratulations, little Hector. How responsible.

[31] You didn't waste a second.

[32] Don't be late making the coffee.

[33] My mom sent you some Honduran tamales.

tamales stuffed with chicken, rice, and various vegetables. "*Gracias. Siéntate. Aquí tenemos unos panes, y luego viene Hector con el café.*"[34]

"*Gracias, muy amable.*"[35] Daniel sat on the sofa and picked up a *concha*. "So, Linda, like I said on the phone earlier, we could really use your support at the rally."

"Anything," Linda said. "I'm happy to help."

"I'll be giving the first speech, then Rosa gives hers, and we would love to have you come on stage and talk about your journey as a Dreamer."

Linda winced. "Anything but that. I'm not really comfortable speaking in public."

"*¿No será peligroso?*"[36] Juanita's stomach churned at the thought. She didn't know what she would do if something happened to Linda.

"Thanks." Daniel accepted the coffee Hector handed him. "There is a risk, yes, but we believe that if we stand together, we can create awareness for the situation."

"Like they did during the Civil Rights movement with passive resistance?" asked Hector.

Both Juanita and Linda turned to him, the surprise Juanita felt mirrored on Linda's face.

"What?" he said, mouth full of *pan*. "I read."

"Exactly." Daniel nodded. "It wasn't until White America saw police turning hoses and dogs on crowds of passive African Americans that sympathy for Civil Rights gained some traction."

Hoses? Dogs? What was her daughter getting involved with?

"*No se preocupe, Mamá,*" Linda put her hand on Juanita's knee. "All of The Dream Act rallies have

---

[34] Thank you. Have a seat. Here are some pastries, and Hector will come soon with the coffee.

[35] Thank you, that's very kind of you.

[36] Wouldn't that be dangerous?

been very peaceful, and local government has shown support."

"It is very unlikely anything will happen," Daniel stated. "But if something does, it can only help our case."

Juanita wasn't sure she liked the sound of that. In fact, the whole situation made her nervous. They'd spent a lifetime hiding their secret. Why would they risk things now, when they were achieving their dreams? She turned her attention back to the conversation, watching Linda's face light up with excitement, and realized she needed to let her daughter make her own decision.

"One day I might be able to stand up there," Linda said. "But I'm not there yet. For now, I'm happy to make as many signs and fliers as humanly possible."

"Deal." Daniel shook Linda's hand.

Juanita stared at her uneaten *pan dulce*, her heart sinking. All of the day's incidents—the break-up talk, the bachata in the kitchen, the conversation about the rally—added up to one frightening conclusion. Juanita was no longer in control.

Linda, her little baby whom she had carried for days through the brutal desert, had now grown up.

Tim ate dinner alone. Last weekend, he'd said goodbye to Wendy and their tearful children as the three of them boarded a plane for London. His in-laws, already in England on vacation, had met them at the airport and helped them get settled in at school. Wendy and her parents had spent the rest of the week in London and had returned to Dulles airport almost twelve hours ago. He'd hoped Wendy would already be home, so she could tell him about the trip and how the boys reacted to their new environment.

But the house was silent, and he was left on his own once again with nothing but a can of Campbell's soup and some Ritz crackers to keep him company. He should have brought home those extra *tacos* Juanita had made today. They were amazing. Much better than his instant meal. As the watery liquid dripped from the spoon into his bowl, Tim wondered where she was and how the boys were. Wendy hadn't even sent him a text saying they had arrived safely back in the States. He'd had to check online.

This was getting ridiculous. How long could she stay angry? Why couldn't she just accept that he liked his job and was doing well there?

Sure, the benefits were, well, nonexistent. Unless he counted the free car he was getting—a perk he'd never gotten at the office. But no, Wendy wasn't concerned about that. She cared about the grease under his fingernails and the cash instead of the direct deposits, about the medical bills instead of his free lunches, about their status instead of his happiness.

It was getting worse. Her cruelty level had reached maximum capacity. Prior to the yard sale, she had mostly ignored him and nagged him about getting a job, but before they'd flown to England, she'd kept the boys out of the house for hours, knowing Tim had wanted to spend time with them before they'd left for boarding school. When she had been around, she'd insult him in front of their friends and family. Sometimes she would banish him to the couch, saying he stunk like the garage.

It was humiliating. He'd even gone back to searching online for other jobs if only to pacify her. Though it failed to make a difference, every night and every morning he sent out résumés and filled out applications. With the state of the economy, it was a tough time to be an office drone. But apparently it was a good time to be a mechanic in the 'hood, because he and Guillermo were packing them in there. Their schedule was full for the next two weeks, and people kept coming. It was new for him, and unlike his last job, never the same. No vehicle had the same problem or the same parts, and they all had a mystery he had to figure out. It was simple and entertaining. He loved it, but he also knew that he'd have to leave it and return to an office, or he would lose more than a sweet benefit package.

His phone buzzed. It was a text from Wendy: "Staying with my parents for the weekend. Have fun working."

He leaned back and rested his head against the top rail of the chair, blinking at the ceiling. He covered his face with his hands and wept, the loneliness overtaking him.

Linda's stomach did a few flips as she entered the space in the library that used to be her safe harbor. It was no longer a sanctuary for her. Floating thoughts of long study sessions with Kevin as they'd cuddled on the couch clouded her brain as she walked to the opposite end of the building. Since classes had resumed, she'd tried to do all her research and classwork in the library downtown, but inevitably, she had to make occasional visits here, for the sake of convenience. She hadn't run into Kevin in the last two visits and hoped to be just as lucky today.

She planted herself in front of a computer and logged on. She had to finish the second half of a paper for International Marketing and do some research for a project in her Stats class. This semester she didn't have any classes with Kevin and hadn't seen him on campus. He'd finally gotten the hint last week and had stopped calling.

The library triggered too many memories. She tried to shake him out of her head, but today, she could almost hear him calling her name. Even his scent seemed to swirl around her. She jumped as someone touched her shoulder.

"Sorry," Kevin said. "I didn't mean to frighten you. I thought you were just ignoring me."

Linda glowered up at Kevin. "What do you want? I'm busy."

He sat down in the chair next to her. "I don't like how things ended between us."

Linda set her jaw. "Yeah, me neither." She prayed for the Lord to calm her nerves and anger. The last thing she wanted to do was make a scene. He'd already made her feel stupid enough. She wasn't going to let him get to her this time. "Guess you should've thought about that before you started seeing someone else."

"I never wanted to hurt you." His blue eyes shone under the fluorescent lighting.

She briefly considered making a scene after all. She pushed the idea out of her head and sighed. "Listen, I'm not sure what you want me to say, Kevin. Whether you wanted to or not, you did hurt me. You fell for me one minute and forgot about me the next."

Kevin looked down. "I didn't mean to. It just kind of happened. Besides, we weren't technically exclusive."

"Really?" Linda's anger rose like mercury in a thermometer. "Is that where you want to go with this?"

Kevin winced. "That's not what I meant to say. I meant that . . ."

"Yes?" Linda cocked her head and waited.

"I don't know. It was a mistake, Linda. She didn't mean anything to me. I realize that now."

"What's that supposed to mean?"

"It means I was an idiot. I want to get back together with you."

Her anger thermometer was near explosion. "No, it means your summer romance is too many miles away, and you're looking to slum again."

Kevin frowned. "That was harsh, Linda."

"Maybe it is, but I don't think it's too far from the truth. What you need to do is examine yourself and the things you've done and talk to God." She nodded at the ceiling. "Whatever closure you're searching for can be found there. As for us, we're over *y ya*.[37] That's it. You lost your chance."

"Wow, okay." Kevin remained silent for what felt like an eternity. "For what it's worth, Linda, I'm sorry. I'm really sorry."

Linda's stomach dropped, and the hairs on the back of her neck stood up. She took a deep breath and reinforced the makeshift dam holding back her feelings. "Thanks." Emotion dripped through the cracks. *God, please don't let me cry. Not yet.* "Well, I have work to do, so . . ."

He nodded and rose from his chair. *"Cuídate,*[38] Linda." He squeezed her shoulder and left.

Linda turned back to the computer, but her hands shook so hard, she couldn't type a word. Her face warmed, and she could no longer hold back the tears. Quickly logging off, she grabbed her bag and rushed

---

[37] And that's it.
[38] Take care of yourself

to the bathroom, nearly colliding with a freshman as she pushed inside and hid in a stall. Her sobs echoed off the tiled walls. Careful not to smudge her makeup, she rolled out several sheets of toilet paper and dabbed at her tears. She took deep breaths and prayed for strength, pulling herself together.

After a few minutes, she calmed down enough to leave the stall. She stopped in front of the mirror and frowned. "Great." Mascara ran in dark lines down her cheeks. Grabbing some paper towels, she struggled to fix the damage. She tied her hair into a loose bun and straightened her shirt. She fanned her eyes with her hands and whispered to herself in the mirror. "You've lived through a lot worse. Don't let one pair of blue eyes ruin your life."

She attempted a smile, chin up, and marched out the door.

CHAPTER FIFTEEN
El Pueblo Unido, Jamás Será Vencido[1]

"Undocumented and unafraid!" Linda yelled at the top of her lungs, pumping her fist along with the crowd. The chant filled the air as they marched around the square in the center of the city. "¡*Sí se puede!*[2] Yes, we can!"

She felt alive for the first time in a long time; nearly a month had passed since she'd found out about Kevin. Thankfully, he'd quit the Cultural Club, and she'd only run into him once after their talk in the library. They'd crossed paths in the quad, and her heart had nearly stopped. She'd gathered her courage, met his gaze, and said hello before striding past him.

Becky and Brian had been so supportive since then, and they'd even come with her to the march today. She glanced over at them, hand in hand, shouting slogans in poorly pronounced Spanish.

"This is great," Becky yelled next to her. "I'm so glad you let us come."

---

1 The people, united, will never be defeated – a common phrase called out at protests in Latin America
2 Yes, we can.

Linda gave her a quick hug. "I'm glad you came, too."

They marched for half an hour more around the square, a force of about five hundred undocumented students and supporters. News cameras were there, streaming the event live online, and reporters from the local Latino and city papers were interviewing participants.

The crowd stopped in front of the downtown market, where a podium and some chairs had been set up. Several students dressed in graduation gowns and hats sat in chairs facing the crowd.

"They're so brave," Becky said.

Brian's eyes were wide with awe. "This is the coolest thing I've ever done."

Daniel walked to the podium, and the crowd quieted. "First of all, I want to thank you for coming out today. Undocumented and unafraid!"

The crowd roared and chanted several more times.

He put up his hand and continued by telling the story of his border-crossing when he was nine years old, coming from Honduras and passing through three countries with his parents. "We were escaping the same violence other countries were experiencing, but we weren't considered refugees. We were considered 'illegal.' I entered school, so behind in my studies, not just due to the language but to the poor education system in Honduras."

He clenched his jaw and stood up taller. "I struggled during those first years. After I entered high school, things got even harder. My parents couldn't help me with homework; they had never been to school themselves. I did it all on my own. With the assistance of some really good teachers, I finished high school and was accepted into college, where I worked hard and graduated in May. I got my diploma, but what can I do without a social security number?"

Daniel had just told Linda's story. That would be her by the end of next semester, unless something changed. Linda's face was wet with tears, and Becky put her arm around her shoulder.

"We Dreamers," Daniel called out, "we work as hard as everyone else, maybe even harder, and yet, due to a few pieces of paper, we have none of the opportunities. We need a change."

The crowd cheered.

"Before our senator makes his decision tomorrow about whether or not to pass The Dream Act, we need to let him know how important this is. He has to understand how many of us are struggling through school and being left behind after graduation. I want to hear from you. How many Dreamers do we have out here tonight? Make some noise."

Linda paused. She hadn't told Becky and Brian she was undocumented. What if it changed things? They were supportive now, but how would they react to her secret? Dozens of people around her whooped and clapped their hands. They'd dared to break past their fear, yelling for their freedom.

"Stop being afraid and hiding in the shadows. The world needs to know you exist. Will you come forward? Will you stand up for your undocumented brothers and sisters who couldn't be here? Will you represent those Dreamers who have put themselves out there and have been deported or are awaiting deportation? Will you take that same risk so that your voice can be heard?"

Linda's heart raced as she watched a few Latinos in the crowd step forward. An invisible rope tugged at her insides, pulling her to join them, but the other part of her was screaming in fear. She glanced at Becky, who gave her a teary-eyed nod. In that moment, something in her heart changed, and she understood what God was telling her.

The lack of a few documents didn't make her any less a child of God. She turned her fears over to Him, the fears that had haunted her ever since she could remember. Panic had gripped her whenever a police car passed, whenever a siren blared, and whenever a person in uniform crossed her path. Truthfully, she had lived all her life with an underlying dread that at any moment she could be ripped away from everything she knew. But now she realized God wanted her to rise above that fear and hand it over to Him, and as she did, the heaviness from all those years of terror lifted from her shoulders. She would no longer be burdened by its darkness, at least not for today. Today she would hold her head high. She took a deep breath and stepped out of the crowd, heart racing.

The crowd grew louder, but Becky and Brian's cries rose over the roar. "Go, Linda. We love you."

Linda joined at least fifty Dreamers, standing in front of everyone, declaring their status. She scanned the crowd. Becky and Brian beamed and cheered for her, and so did hundreds of other unfamiliar faces. She recognized some she had seen at the meetings before zeroing in on one face she hadn't expected.

Hector waved and gave her a thumbs-up. Considering how they'd started out last year before he moved in, his support meant the world to her. She returned the wave, and he took a picture with his phone. She knew Mamá would be here if she weren't so afraid. After what had happened to María and Diana, she always looked over her shoulder. María would have been considered a Dreamer, since she had come into the country when she was fourteen and had gone to the local high school. Linda stood for her and for the others whose stories were told at church, in the community, and at the meetings, those who no longer had a voice due to their deportation.

The people next to her grabbed her hands and chanted loudly, "*El pueblo unido, jamás será vencido.* The people united will never be defeated."

Juanita sat at the kitchen table, praying for safety at the march and for nothing bad to happen there. She prayed for her family and her church family. Finally, she prayed for herself. She thanked God for all the people who had shown her love throughout the years—the trucker in the desert, her cousin in Texas, her neighbor in Mexico, and her friends and family.

Though she cringed to think of them, she thanked God for the memories that haunted her, because they never let her forget how coming to the U.S. had changed their lives forever. Juanita didn't have to live in constant terror, alone and empty. Here Linda had the opportunity to go to school, to church, and to walk in freedom. Someday, if the laws changed, Linda would have the opportunity to use her diploma, work, and live her life without fear of deportation.

The house was an empty shell, except for Tim in his cloud of sadness. Wendy was at her parents' house again, this time for a week. Every afternoon, he called England to speak with Nathan and Jeremy for a few minutes, but it wasn't the same as having them in the house. Without the boys playing and watching cartoons, the sound of Wendy on the phone or doing chores, and without voices to break the silence, Tim was alone with his thoughts. They grew negative very fast. How long would it be until Wendy left him for good? What would happen if they got another big hospital bill? If property taxes went up again, would they be able to pay their mortgage? Did the boys even need him anymore? I might as well . . .

He stood up, grabbed his jacket, and left for the garage. Work was the only thing these days that kept him sane. Wendy barely spoke to him, and when she was home, he had a permanent bed on the couch. Things were going from bad to worse.

His only friends were Guillermo and Linda. His boss' niece often brought him *pan dulce* from the bakery and listened to his woes. She was really the only one who listened. No one else cared about him. Trying to concentrate on the scenery as he rode the bus, his worries crept further into his mind. He wondered if Wendy had already spoken with a lawyer, what she had told the boys when he wasn't around, when they would move out forever, if things would change even if he found another job.

He walked, half-distracted, down the sidewalk until a lunging dog awakened him from his thoughts. He jumped back as the animal yanked its chain taut, the snapping jaws an inch from Tim's leg. Drunken laughter pulled his attention to his surroundings. He cringed. He had wandered into the projects.

His insides trembling, he picked up speed and started looking for the bus.

"Yo, where you goin'?" a deep voice asked. "My dog wanna say hi."

There was more laughter, and then footsteps moved towards him. A giant beer bottle shattered on the sidewalk in front of him. His options flashed through his mind. He couldn't fight them. There were too many, and they probably had weapons. If he ran, they'd be more likely to attack him. Instead he turned to face them.

Four young men, faces as dark as old motor oil, were dressed in baggy clothes with thick chains and bandanas and wearing expensive shoes that probably cost more than Wendy's designer heels.

"You're in the wrong neighborhood, son," the one with an aqua Hornets jersey said, his hand reaching for something at his waist. A second later he had a gun pointing at Tim.

Tim put up his hands. "I don't want any trouble. I'm on my way to work. I have a wife and kids."

"Ain't nobody wanna hear yo life story," another with a black hoodie said, taking a swig from a bottle in a paper bag.

The dog owner stepped forward, cocking his head, his face serious. "Hand over your wallet."

Tim's heart sank. He hadn't remembered to put yesterday's cash in the bank. Sighing, he reached for his wallet. It didn't matter anyway. It was just another example of the loser he was becoming. He tossed it to the fourth man, who had a Panthers hat over his bandana.

"And your phone," the dog owner said.

Tim had left it at home. "I don't have one."

"No phone?" The guy in the black hoodie stumbled forward. "You lyin'. Errybody's got a phone."

Tim returned his hands to his pockets and pulled out his keys and a handful of crumpled receipts. "This is all I have."

"Keep the keys," the one in the jersey snickered. "I'll take your ring and the watch."

Wendy would kill him. After returning his keys to his pocket, he took off the watch and threw it over.

"You forgot the ring," the dog owner smirked.

"I can't," Tim said, holding back tears. "You don't understand. My wife, she's about to leave me." He broke down, shaking and sobbing. "Please," he begged, getting onto his knees.

"Yo, that's just sad." The black hoodie wearer finished his paper bag of liquor and threw it at Tim, hitting him on the shoulder.

"I ain't gonna waste a bullet on this loser." The man in the Hornets jersey tucked his gun back into his waist.

"Your wife needs a real man, not some punk," the dog owner said, adding a few unsavory embellishments. "Let's end this."

Tim covered his face as they lunged forward. He felt a fist hit his back, knocking the wind out of him. A foot slammed into the side of his head. Then he couldn't keep track. All he felt was pain and complete and utter humiliation.

A horn beeped loudly, and a vehicle flashed its lights, rolling up onto the sidewalk. The beating stopped.

"Who this sucker think he is?" one of the voices demanded. The sounds around Tim were muffled like he'd stepped out of a loud rock concert.

Tim, lying in a fetal position, peeped out from between his fingers. His vision blurred, he still recognized the grey truck. The same old man sat in the cab and the teenager who'd stolen that part all those months ago stood in the back, holding a baseball bat. The boy pushed up his sleeve with the bat, revealing a tattoo.

The Hornet fan reached for his gun, but the dog owner shook his head. They stepped back from Tim.

"*Ven.*" The boy with the bat waved Tim over to the truck.

No one moved or said anything as they all stared each other down. He rose, inhaling sharply at the scalding pain in his ribcage. Unsure how long this standoff would last, he hobbled as fast as he could to the passenger door and stepped inside, groaning.

"*Vámanos,*" the boy called, tapping on the roof of the cab, and they sped down the road.

Tim strained to remember the names of his saviors. "Geovany and Fernando."

The old man pointed his thumb to his grandson. "Geovany." Then he tapped his chest with a nod. "Fernando." Concern on his face, Fernando reached between the seats and handed Tim a rag, gesturing to his ear.

Hands shaking, Tim touched the rag to the side of his head and winced. Blood soaked into the fabric. A few minutes later they pulled in front of the garage. Geovany hopped out of the back and helped Tim out onto the street. Tim rested his arm on the boy's shoulder, and they made their way to the sidewalk. Fernando assisted from Tim's other side.

Tim shook his buzzing head, his neck throbbing. "It's not open yet. We have to go to the other door."

With their help he limped around to Guillermo's house around the side of the shop and knocked.

"What the heck happened?" Guillermo said, ushering them in.

"*Andaba por allá en los apartamentos,*"[3] Fernando explained, gesturing vaguely over his shoulder.

Tim sat weakly on a kitchen chair.

"I told you not to go over there, man." Guillermo ran some water over a kitchen towel.

---

[3] He was hanging out over there in the apartments.

"I wasn't thinking. I started walking and ended up there." Tim sucked in air as Guillermo tended to his facial cuts. "They took my wallet and my watch." Tim stared at the platinum band on his left hand. "Kept my ring though." In the end, it didn't even feel worth it. She would probably leave him anyway.

They helped Tim get his shirt off, and Guillermo inspected the damage. "You're gonna have some serious bruises, and you got a cracked rib or two and probably a popped eardrum. Nothing you need to see the doctor about, but you're lucky to be alive. A few more kicks and they might've ruptured an organ."

"If it weren't for these two—" Tim started. His swollen lips trembled. "Thank you."

Fernando and Geovany nodded.

"I don't know how we didn't get shot. What was that tattoo you showed them?" Tim asked, eyeing the boy's forearm.

Geovany answered in a thick accent. "Probably didn't even have bullets. Only for show. None of them was in a gang. You can see by the colors they wearing." The boy pushed his sleeve again, showing a large M and S in simple, dark letters. "I was forced into a gang in El Salvador. Is why we left."

"Forced?" Tim thought joining a gang was a voluntary thing.

"I had to join, or they say they kill my *abuelo*."[4] He looked down at the floor. "It was horrible. I did many bad things."

Fernando put his arm around his grandson's shoulder.

"One day I get away, so my grandfather and I, we jump a train and go north to Mexico."

---

[4] Grandfather

"*La Bestia*,"[5] Fernando said.

Tim took a sip of the water Guillermo gave him.

"The Beast," Guillermo explained. "It's a freight train that runs from El Salvador up through Mexico. Covered in refugees."

"What do you mean, covered?" asked Tim. He'd never heard of such a thing.

"You gotta ride on top of the train or on the sides," Geovany replied. "Lot of people died. I don't like to talk about it."

Tim frowned. And he had thought his own life was pretty bleak. He couldn't even imagine going through something like that.

"Do you think you could eat something?" Guillermo gestured to the food on the stove.

The Fruit Loops Tim had eaten for breakfast were already wearing off. He clicked his teeth together. His jaw hurt and his lips were swollen, but the rest of his mouth seemed intact. "Sure, thanks."

Guillermo motioned for Fernando and Geovany to sit, while he got plates out of the cupboard and filled them up with some items from the stove. "It should still be hot. If not, you can microwave it."

"What is it?" Tim eyed the spicy red bits of sausage. "*Chorizo?*"

"Yeah, man. *Ya sabes.*[6] You know your Mexican food now."

Tim smiled. It was true. Before working for Guillermo, his only experience of Mexican food was the Taco Bell variety, which Guillermo insisted was not at all Mexican. "*Gracias.*"

"Your Spanish is better," Geovany remarked.

"So is your English."

---

[5] The Beast.

[6] You already know.

"School. And summer school." He scooped up a load of beans and *chorizo* with a piece of tortilla. "Got jobs, too, and a place to stay."

"That's good," Tim said. Even living in a truck in Roanoke seemed preferable to forced servitude to a gang. Considering what he'd just heard, Tim knew he should be grateful for what he had, but he couldn't pull up any positive emotions. Inside, all he felt was bitterness, hopelessness, and despair.

Guillermo swallowed some coffee. "Oh, that part came in yesterday for your car."

"Mmm?" Tim mumbled, his mouth full of *chorizo* and tortilla and a crumbly white cheese called *queso fresco*.

"Yeah, if you want, we can put it in after work today and see if it'll start for us."

Tim hesitated. "I'm not sure I'll be able to do much."

"Don't worry, Conejo. I'd normally make you do the hard stuff, but I'll take it easy on you today and let you hand me the tools."

"That'd be great," Tim said, trying to sound positive. At least one thing might go well that day.

Becky and Brian gave Linda a big group hug after the rally ended. Linda waved Hector over.

"Who's that?" Becky quietly asked Linda. "He's cute."

Linda raised an eyebrow. "I don't know about that. That's just Hector."

"Oh, my gosh." Becky's mouth formed an O. "You gotta be kidding me. This is the guy you were always complaining about? The guy who's had a crush on you forever?"

"Shh." Linda did not like the sneaky look on Becky's face. She smacked her extra hard on the arm before Hector arrived. "Hey, Hector. These are my friends Becky and Brian."

Hector shook their hands. "Nice to meet you."

Becky glanced over at Linda, a crooked grin creeping onto her face. "We're going to get something to eat, Hector. Would you like to join us?"

"Okay. Thanks. You looked really great up there, Linda." Beaming, he gestured with his phone. "I took some pictures to show your mom."

"Thanks, Hector. I didn't know you were going to come."

"We sold out early today, and your mom said it was okay."

Becky shot Linda a wink.

Linda narrowed her eyes. "Hector works with my mom. They make food to sell at the *panadería* where I work."

"How's business?" Brian asked.

Becky grabbed Linda's arm and pulled her forward. "You guys stand a few feet back now, so we can have some girl talk."

Linda didn't like the sound of that. Not at all.

CHAPTER SIXTEEN
Rayando el Sol[1]

"Okay, so remind me why you don't like this Hector guy?" Becky asked Linda as they made their way through the crowd.

"Well, he's sort of different now. He used to be this little jerk who was always driving me crazy. He would pick on me, trying to be all gangsta with his wife beaters and stupid hats and chains."

"And now?"

Linda struggled to respond. Her feelings about Hector were a jumble of old pain with new friendship and an electric undertone she preferred to ignore. "I don't know. He's okay, I guess." She shrugged, wishing Becky would drop the subject.

Becky leaned in, lowering her voice. "Girl, he's more than okay. He's smokin'."

"Ew, Becky. Gross." She rolled her eyes.

"Do you need glasses? That's a good-looking man right there."

Linda shook her head. "I don't see it. I mean, he's

---

1 Barely Reaching the Sun – a song by Maná

less annoying now, and I guess we've become friends, but to me he's still the crazy little kid who followed me around everywhere."

"Well, he ain't no kid anymore." Becky peered over her shoulder. "Did you see his arms? Those are some spectacular muscles."

"They're probably from lifting all those pots of food for my mom and carrying them two blocks every morning."

"Whatever it is, it's working," Becky said, clicking her tongue.

Her friend's prodding had evoked Linda's memory of the bachata in the kitchen when Hector had held her close. She blocked it out, knowing she definitely wouldn't be sharing that with Becky if she wanted this conversation to end. An uncomfortable scoff escaped Linda's lips. "This is too weird. We need to talk about something else."

"Hmm . . . me thinks thou dost protest too much." Becky smirked and then called behind her. "All right, boys, you can join us again. Girl talk's over."

"Okay, try to start it now," Guillermo called from under the hood.

Tim turned the key. The engine sputtered.

"Give it some gas."

Tim did, and the car roared to a start. He squeezed the steering wheel, a feeling of accomplishment washing over him. Holding his sore side, he stepped out of the vehicle into the garage and reciprocated Guillermo's fist bump.

"You got yourself a working car." Guillermo slammed down the hood and whooped.

Tim ogled the beauty before him and smiled. He

had never worked so hard for anything in his life. It was a 1988 Nissan Pulsar, black, with a hatchback. While waiting for parts to come in last week, they had repainted the exterior and waxed it. Today it shone in the sunlight that poked through the tall windows of the shop.

Considering how it'd looked as the tow truck had tugged it into the shop a few weeks ago, its current state was near miraculous. Someone had stolen its rims, the tires had been bare, the interior ripped and dirty, and the engine wouldn't turn over. In the last couple of weeks, Tim had spent hours replacing fuses, hoses, and parts. Finally, it was finished.

To take something so broken and see it transformed was inspiring. Maybe there was hope for him yet.

Tim dropped into the driver's seat and revved the engine.

"Sounds good, Conejo." Guillermo closed the door. "Take 'er for a spin."

Pushing a button on the dash, music blared from the speakers. Things were looking up.

Juanita sat on her bed, reading her Bible in Spanish, following the sentences with an arthritic finger, whispering the words as she read. For some reason, it was easier to sound out the words than to say them in her head. It was like a whole new world had opened up to her now that she could read. She didn't understand everything, but the sermons made more sense, and she experienced a more intimate connection with God.

At present, she was reading through the book of Mark. The pastor had told her it was the shortest and easiest to understand of all the gospels and meant to be read aloud. Apparently that was what they did in Biblical times, read scripture aloud to big crowds. Now she could continue in this tradition.

She rested the Bible on her chest with a smile. Things were going well for her and her family. Linda had finally gotten over that boy and, though it made her nervous, was involved with The Dream Act. Juanita and Hector had been saving to buy a food truck, and Memo's garage was doing well ever since Javier had left. Things almost seemed too good to be true. Was it actually possible to live the American dream?

"What's wrong with you?" Hector asked Linda as they walked down the sidewalk. They'd said goodbye to Becky and Brian a few minutes ago and were on their way home. The weather was nice, so they decided to walk a little before catching the bus. "You're acting weird."

"What do you mean?" Linda asked. But she knew what he meant. Ever since Becky had pointed out Hector's muscles, Linda couldn't help noticing them.

"You keep staring at me."

Oh, no. He'd noticed. "I don't know what you're talking about."

He huffed. "Whatever."

"How'd you guys do today?" Linda asked.

"Sold out in under two hours. We need to get that truck, because every day more and more people come to eat. We try to make enough food, but we can't keep up. It would be so much easier if we could make it to order."

Linda watched his lips moving, struck by their

shape, their silky thickness tapering off to a sexy quirk at the corners. She struggled to focus on his words. What was wrong with her? He's your friend, she told herself. Like a brother. But even as she thought it, it didn't feel true. She cleared her throat, turning her attention from his mouth. "Yeah, did Tío find anything yet?"

"Not really. He went to see a couple of food trucks, but they were pretty beat up. He's going to check out another one tomorrow, I think."

"Maybe that'll be the one."

He grinned and took a deep breath. "So, what are you doing tonight?"

Ignoring the dimples she had never before noticed, she looked up to the clouds in thought. "I have to go to Tío's shop to finish up something I was working on. But I think I'm going to head over to the library first. I need to write a couple of papers."

"You should buy a computer. You'd save a lot of time and probably money, too."

"Yeah, but then we'd have to get Internet."

"It's probably only thirty something per month," Hector replied.

"There's no room in my budget for a computer."

"I saw some laptops for only a few hundred. How much do you have saved?"

Linda shrugged. "Probably enough, but I like to keep some for emergencies and stuff."

"Maybe we could share it. I'll pay half, and you pay the rest."

"I don't know. That could get complicated."

"Why? I'm not going anywhere." He lightly touched Linda's arm.

Linda tensed at the familiar electric pulse that jolted her. No. No. This wasn't going to happen. She'd just gotten over Kevin. She didn't need another guy weaseling his way into her heart only to break it a few months later. Anger overtook the electricity. "What was that? Did I say you could touch me?"

Hector held up his hands, mumbling an apology. They strolled in silence for another minute.

As the discomfort and guilt from her angry outburst settled, Linda asked herself why her heart had sped up when he'd touched her if she didn't care. She shut that thought down. She could not fall for Hector. It was . . . well, she didn't know what it was, but she didn't want to think about it. "I'm sorry I overreacted. I can't have complications in my life. It's my last year of school. I really need to focus on that."

"Hey, I get it. Don't worry about it."

Linda motioned back to the way they'd come. "I'm going to go to the library now, instead of going home and then coming back."

Hector stopped and turned to her. "Listen, I just wanted to say that it was really amazing what you did up there today. That took guts."

Warmth rushed over her. "Thanks, Hector."

He cleared his throat, shifting nervously. "After you get back from Memo's garage, do you want to watch a movie or something?"

She narrowed her eyes.

"As friends," Hector added quickly.

"I'll think about it."

"Okay."

Before she realized what was happening, Hector wrapped her in a hug. A lingering hug.

Her arms stiffened at her sides. "You smell like *enchiladas*," she commented.

Hector let go, chuckling. *"Es más fácil llegar al sol que a tu corazón."*[2]

---

[2] It's easier to get to the sun than your heart – a line from "Rayando el Sol"

Butterflies fluttered in Linda's stomach, but she shooed them away. Who did he think he was, trying to charm her with lyrics from a Maná song? What did he know? She shot him a sarcastic smile. "Thanks, I'll remember that."

"See you at home," he said with a smirk and walked off.

Juanita stood in her bedroom doorway, watching Hector with curiosity as he organized the magazines on the living room coffee table and fluffed the couch cushions. For a moment, she thought her cleaning habits had rubbed off on him. Until he lit a candle.

Suspicion sparked. She narrowed her eyes and returned to her room, grabbing her cell phone and pocketbook.

She strode past a nervous Hector. "*Nos vemos.*"[3]

"Have fun at church."

She didn't answer but closed the door with a touch of extra force. Small group would have to wait. She had more important fish to fry.

Linda walked into the kitchen through the back door, the buttery aroma of popcorn in the air. "Mamá?"

"She's at a church meeting," Hector called from the dim light of the living room.

Her heart beat a bachata rhythm in her chest. Being alone with him both terrified and excited her at the same time. Her mouth dropped open as she entered the room. A dozen candles glowed on every

---

[3] See you later.

conceivable flat surface. So much for watching a movie as friends.

Hector held up a small bouquet of tall, brightly colored flowers, a shy grin on his face.

"Wow, these are really pretty." Linda received them and sniffed one of the spiraled flowers. A light, floral scent rose from its petals. "What are they?"

"Gladiolus," Hector said. "They represent strength and never giving up."

"Thank you." Linda lifted her gaze to his. His deep brown eyes glimmered in the flickering candlelight. Unable to handle the intensity, she pointed to the array of snacks covering the coffee table. "Hungry?"

Hector ran his hand through his curly hair. "I didn't know what you'd want, so I got a little bit of everything."

"I can see that." Linda stood still for a moment, not sure what else to say. She swallowed the lump in her throat. "I'm gonna put these in some water."

"Right," Hector said. "I shoulda thought of that. I'll get it." He turned for the kitchen and promptly tripped over the foot of the coffee table, knocking over a bowl of cheese balls and landing on top of them with a crunch.

All of Linda's nervous tension burst into a fit of giggles. "Oh my gosh, are you okay?"

Hector rolled onto his back, laughing uncontrollably, pulverizing more cheese balls in the process, which only caused him to laugh harder. His dark blue polo shirt and khakis were covered in neon orange dust. "So many cheese balls," he wheezed, looking around him at the sea of pulverized snacks. "Your mom's going to kill me."

"This rug is so old she won't even notice."

Hector raised an eyebrow. "Your mom? Not notice something?"

"Good point." Linda gently laid the flowers on the couch and knelt on the floor, picking up orange crumbs and tossing them into the bowl. Hector sat up, failing in his attempt not to crush any more cheese balls, and took a large step over the mess. He jogged into the hallway and returned with the vacuum and a vase filled with water.

Linda stood, brushing off crumbs. She placed the flowers in the vase, smelling them again and putting them next to the television. "What are we going to watch?" she asked after Hector had finished vacuuming.

"*Pride and Prejudice.*" He pointed to the DVD next to the television. "I watched it with my mom one time. It's the good one. With Colin Firth as Mr. Darcy."

"I've never seen it. I read it in high school though. I don't think I got through the whole thing. It was long."

"Oh." Hector's smile faltered. "We can watch something else if you want."

"No, I mean, if you like it, I'll watch it." The awkward tension was returning.

"We don't have to."

Linda bit her lower lip and forced herself to look him unwaveringly in the eyes. "I want to."

A giant grin spread across his face. "Cool." He pushed the disc into the DVD player and dropped to the middle of the couch with a sigh, his arms lining the back of it on both sides.

Butterflies circled through Linda's stomach again as she chose the farthest spot on the couch from him. He grabbed handfuls of her favorite snacks, minus the cheese balls, and piled them onto a plate before passing it to her. "Thanks," she said, receiving it with a shaking hand.

A classical song played as the opening credits rolled. Linda thought of her relationship with Hector as the movie progressed. The story took on a whole new meaning. Watching the impact of Mr. Darcy's overwhelming love for Elizabeth—despite the odds, despite the differences, despite the challenges—slammed into her, and she couldn't breathe.

She stole a glance across the couch. Everything, from his tousled hair to his dimpled cheeks and smoothly shaven jawline, screamed out to her. But his spirit, his soul called to her even louder. As a caterpillar morphs into a butterfly, over the last several months, he had transformed into his true self. Her voice shaky, she gathered her courage. "Hector?"

"Yeah?" He turned to face her, his eyes warm.

The front door slammed. Mamá stormed in, grumbling something about Norma chatting her ear off at the *panadería*. She strode over to the couch, squeezed her thick hips past Linda, and plopped down between her and Hector. She forced a bag of smelly pork rinds into Linda's face. "*¿Chicarrones?*"

"*No, gracias.*" Linda buried her head in her hands, embarrassment overtaking her.

"*Nunca entiendo bien esta gente de inglaterra con sus acentos raros. ¿No quieren ver otra cosa? ¿Una película de acción?*"[4] Mamá picked up a candle from the coffee table and blew it out with a smirk. "Fire hazard."

Hector sank into the couch with a groan.

Tim twitched as someone kicked his foot where he lay beneath a Jeep, straining his sore ribs.

---

[4] I can never understand these English people with their weird accents. Don't you want to watch something else? An action movie?

He was still jumpy from yesterday.

"I miss you working in your fancy shoes. They were stylish."

Grinning, Tim tilted his head so he could see out from under the vehicle. A shapely pair of tan calves ended in sexy red heels. He rolled out and caught a glimpse of toned thighs under the red sundress. He'd gotten a pretty good view the other day, too. Plenty to think about during his lonely nights. "Funny." He sat up slowly, trying not to strain himself.

Linda gasped. "This is way worse than Tío Memo let on. Are you okay?"

"I'll live," Tim said.

"Are you sure you don't want to go to a doctor?" Her face was full of concern.

"Nah, I'll tough it out." The physical pain was one thing, but the emotional torment was worse. He had arrived home yesterday, excited to show Wendy the car, but she only berated him for getting beat up. Plus, she'd made him promise not to video chat with Nathan or Jeremy until his face had healed, afraid it would either give them nightmares or the boarding school another reason to look down on them.

She bent down and touched the side of his face. "It looks really bad."

His skin heated beneath her fingers. She smelled like citrus and lavender. It reminded him of the scent Wendy used to wear when they were first dating—Chanel or Armani or another brand that cost a hundred dollars an ounce. A simpler time, when Wendy had cared more about him than about how he compared to her snobby friends' husbands.

"Did you eat lunch yet?" Linda waved a paper bag. "Mamá made *tamales verdes*[5] today."

---

[5] Green tamales

"The green ones?"

Linda nodded.

"Those are good. Pork or chicken?"

"Chicken."

Tim's mouth watered. "I'm starving."

Wendy had stopped cooking completely and hadn't bought any more groceries, so his diet had mostly consisted of Mexican food and bagels. He'd tried bringing some of Juanita's food for dinner once, but Wendy turned her nose up at it, taking the boys out for Thai food instead and leaving Tim to eat the *tacos* by himself.

Most days he didn't even want to go home. No one was there. His sons were an ocean away, and Wendy was generally avoiding his calls, barely communicating through text messages most of the time. He'd even stopped calling the boys every day. They were too busy to talk with him anyway. Why even try?

Linda helped him up, taking his arm in hers, and leading him slowly to the table. He had almost forgotten what it was like to have someone show him a little love.

CHAPTER SEVENTEEN[1]
La Culpa No Tengo Yo

*T*im's heart stopped as he opened the door. He blinked twice to make sure it wasn't a mirage. The suitcases didn't disappear. His worst fears were confirmed. Wendy stomped down the hall and stood with her arms crossed.

"I can't take it anymore." She scowled. "I can't wait any longer for you to stop playing mechanic and get a real job. You're just like your father."

Tim's stomach dropped. "That's a low blow, Wendy. I've been looking. There's nothing out there."

"If you didn't work all those hours at the shop, you'd have time to find one. Besides, I don't want to hear any more excuses. It's been a year and a half since the office downsized. That's plenty of time to find a new position." She picked up the bags. "I'm staying at my parents' summer cottage near London until we sell the house. I called a realtor yesterday. And a lawyer."

---

[1] It's Not My Fault – a song by Los Temerarios

"Wendy," Tim pleaded "Please, don't leave. I don't know what I'll do without you."

"You should have thought of that before choosing that garage over your family." She marched past him out the door, head high.

Tim's legs gave way, and he slid down the wall onto the floor. His hands shook, and the house echoed with his primal scream.

When Linda first walked into the house, she assumed they'd been robbed. Heart racing, she realized it was just messy. Newspapers were spread over several surfaces. "Hello?" Linda called.

"*Ay, mija. Ven acá. Eres famosa.*"[2]

"I'm famous?" Linda raised an eyebrow and walked into the kitchen. Her heart jumped when she saw Hector. They hadn't spoken since the whole *Pride and Prejudice* fiasco yesterday.

"*Mira, Lindita.*"[3] Mamá held up a local Latino paper with a front-page article about the Dream Act march, beaming.

"Cool." Linda peered closer at the paper. She pointed to the left corner of the picture. "There I am."

"*Sí, amor. Hector compró varios periódicos, los que tienen artículos del Dream Act.*"[4]

"Wow, there's so many." Linda stepped back, taking in the sheer quantity of media. Hector must have bought every paper in town.

Hector leaned over the table, his toned triceps flexing beneath his red, short-sleeved shirt. "There's

---

[2] Oh, daughter. Come here. You're famous.

[3] Look, little Linda.

[4] Yes, honey. Hector bought various newspapers, the ones that have articles about The Dream Act.

probably more online, too. Carlos told me there's a video on YouTube."

"Let's just hope it makes a difference." Linda put down the article she'd been studying with a sigh.

"When do they vote?" Hector asked.

"Tuesday," Linda answered.

Hector held out a small binder.

"What's this?" Linda asked.

"I made it for you."

"Thanks." Linda opened the binder. It was filled with pictures from the March and from the first rally she'd attended over the summer. "Hector, this is so nice."

"The back has space for you to add more pictures and articles for all the places you go in the future."

Linda looked into Hector's eyes, overwhelmed by his kindness. "Thank you."

His thick lips quirked into a grin, causing a thermodynamic reaction in Linda's heart as his dimples appeared. Neither of them moved. They stood, staring at each other, until Mamá's voice shook Linda out of her stupor.

"He worked hard to make this for you." Mamá pushed her at Hector. "*Dale un abrazo, mija.*"[5]

Who could understand Mamá? Yesterday her mother was blowing out romantic candles and shoving *chicarrones* in their faces to kill the mood, and now she was pushing Linda into Hector's arms. A pit formed in Linda's stomach. She'd spent years avoiding Hector, and now she didn't know what to do. The trouble was, ever since that *bachata* in the kitchen, something had stirred inside her. Something she wasn't ready for, something part of her still wanted to avoid.

---

[5] Give him a hug, my daughter.

She glanced over at Mamá; her mother wasn't joking. Linda groaned inwardly, not outwardly, or Mamá would have smacked her with the wooden spoon she was holding.

Linda stepped forward and wrapped her arms around Hector's ribcage. Her head leaning against his chest, his heart thumped rapidly in her ear. His body was warm and solid from sampling the *comida*,[6] and a safe, comfortable feeling surrounded Linda as his strong arms encircled her.

"Okay, okay," Mamá said, tugging them apart. "*Ya, ya*."[7]

Linda pulled back and shot him an awkward smile.

"What? No comment about *enchiladas* this time?" Hector asked.

"No." Linda smirked. "Today you smell like *chicharrones*."[8]

They looked at each other and laughed.

"*Ay, niños*,"[9] Mamá said, shaking her head.

Tim rummaged through the pantry until he found what he was looking for: the tequila from a margarita night Wendy hosted a couple of summers ago. He sloshed several ounces into a glass and stared at it for a full minute, considering the situation. He hadn't drunk since the incident in college with that girl, but some situations merited alcohol's numbing effects. Angry bitterness mixed with sadness in his throat. Besides, nothing mattered now anyway. Wendy

---

[6] Food
[7] Enough already.
[8] Pork rinds
[9] Children

hated him, the boys didn't even seem to miss him, even gangsters in the projects thought he was pathetic.

He downed the glass and poured another. He shifted his gaze to a picture of Wendy on the mantel before snatching it up and hurling it onto the Persian rug, grinding into the glass with the heel of his shoe. Half a bottle later, he needed some fresh air. His shiny car glinted at him through the window, and he was overcome with an irresistible desire to drive with the windows down, leaving his troubles behind him. He tested a step or two with minimal stumbling. He was fine to drive, he assured himself. After giving Wendy's picture one last punt, he fumbled for his keys and marched out the door.

Juanita wandered out of the kitchen, trying to remind herself to be happy Linda and Hector were getting along so well. Last night, after feeling a twinge of guilt for ruining their movie night, she'd prayed about it. The Lord had given her peace, reminding her how much she liked Hector and how he would protect her Lindita. Though he was a couple of years younger than her daughter, he was already becoming more responsible, plus he had potential. Judging by the hug she had witnessed, Linda was starting to see that, too.

All she needed to remember was that God had a plan set in motion and that things happened for a reason. At present, it appeared that everything was going in a positive direction for her little family.

Linda hugged her scrapbook as she walked towards her uncle's garage. Hector must have spent hours putting it together, not including the time and cost to buy all the newspapers. She thought more and more about her conversation with Becky after the March yesterday and every moment with Hector since then. She tried not to, but she couldn't get it out of her head. Maybe it was worth it to open her heart to him after all.

She shook the thought from her mind and calculated the figures she needed to add to the books. Since Tío's shop was closed on Sundays, she walked around to his house and knocked on the door.

"He's not home," someone said behind her.

She jumped and spun around. "Oh, hi, Tim. You scared me."

"Sorry. I've been out here waiting for your uncle a while." He closed the hood of his car. His bloodshot eyes drifted slowly from side to side. "Whatcha got there?" he asked, his voice slurred.

Linda pulled the book protectively against her chest, realizing too late it had pulled his attention in that direction. "A scrapbook Hector gave me."

Tim stepped closer and tugged the book out of her hand. Linda could smell the alcohol on his breath as he spoke. "This is really nice. He must like you a lot."

"Yeah, I guess."

"I can see why. You're such a beautiful girl." His wandering gaze had returned to her chest.

Linda took a step backward and grabbed her book. "Thanks. I'm going inside now."

"No. It's a nice day, and we finally got my car working. Let's go for a ride."

"I don't think you should be driving in your condition."

"And what condition's that?" he asked, swaying.

"You've been drinking."

He grunted. "You'd be drinking too, if your wife just left you."

Linda sighed. "I'm sorry about your wife, but I can't go for a ride. I have to work on some stuff for my uncle."

"You can do that tomorrow."

Something told her to get away from him fast. Her heart raced. "No, tomorrow I have to work at the *panadería.*" She turned and used her key with shaking hands to open Tío's door. Tim grabbed her arm and pushed her inside, slamming the door behind him with his foot.

"Let me go!" Linda screamed as loud as she could.

"Shut up," he whispered, clamping his hand over her mouth. "You've been asking for this since we met, parading in front of me with your little sundresses and tight jeans, driving me wild." He pinned her against the door, his eyes like a rabid animal's, his attention moving back to her chest, his face shadowed in the darkening light of dusk. "Don't tell you me you don't want this, too. I know you do."

Linda squeezed her eyes tight against the look and smell of him and sobbed out a desperate prayer.

Juanita, Hector, and Memo sat around the kitchen table, eating the leftover *tacos de chicharrón.* Juanita had just poured them soda when someone banged on the front door. The doorbell clanged several times in a row.

Hector's friend, Carlos, stood outside, panting for breath. "Somebody grabbed Linda and pulled her inside Memo's house. I heard her screaming."

Shock split the air for a single second, and then

Hector and Memo sprinted out the front door. Juanita flew out behind them. Hector and Carlos pulled ahead, disappearing around the corner. Juanita and Memo tried to keep up as best as possible. *"Dios, protege a mi hija,"*[10] she prayed aloud over and over again through wheezing breaths.

"No!" Linda struggled as Tim groped at her. "Please. Don't!"

Bile rose in her throat as he brushed his fingers against the hem of her dress, muttering under his breath, ignoring her pleas. His words blended together. Her mind buzzed in panic and shock. As he reached to loosen his belt, he let go of her wrists long enough for her to yank him down by the back of his head and smash her knee into his face.

Tim doubled over, moaning, his bleeding nose gushing in his hands.

Linda grabbed the door handle, but one of Tim's bloody hands tangled in her hair, and he jerked her back with a curse, throwing her into the kitchen table.

Crying out as her back hit it, she fell to the floor, the wind knocked out of her. Tim came at her, but the door flew open, crashing into him. He lost his balance, staggering to the floor as Hector and Carlos rushed in.

Hector dropped to his knees in front of Linda, reaching for her, his eyes filled with concern. "Linda? Are you okay?"

She nodded, her breaths coming in short bursts. Tío and Mamá tore into the kitchen. Mamá ran over

---

[10] God, protect my daughter.

and helped her up into one of the chairs, hugging and rocking her against her chest.

Hector let out a primal scream and threw Tim against the wall. "What did you do to her?"

He and Tío landed several punches before Mamá shouted for them to stop. Hector let Tim drop to the ground, where he rolled into a ball, holding his face and his side.

"Did he . . . hurt you?" Tío asked, leaning in close and looking in her eyes.

"No, I'm okay." Her whole body shook.

"We need to call the police," Carlos said from where he stood near the door.

"No," Tío spat. "You can't trust them. They might end up taking in one of us instead of him."

"Well, what should we do?" Hector scowled at Tim's huddled body.

Mamá sighed. "*No creo que regrese aquí nunca más. Déjalo ir.*"[11]

Hector and Tío looked at Linda. "What do you think?" Hector asked.

Linda had heard enough stories of corrupt police officers to agree with Tío. They would probably arrest Hector and Tío for assault and release Tim with a warning. Mamá was right. Tim wouldn't come back here after today. He was too much of a coward. "Let him go," Linda answered.

"*¿Estás segura?*"[12] Tío asked.

Linda nodded and leaned her head on Mamá.

Hector lifted Tim onto his feet by his collar. Tim's left eye was swelling shut, and blood dripped from his nose. The cut on the side of his head had reopened. Bloody splotches covered the floor and his shirt.

---

[11] I don't think he'll come back here ever again. Let him go
[12] Are you sure?

Tío glowered at Tim with a level of rage Linda had never seen before. "If you ever step even one foot back in this neighborhood, you'll leave in a body bag. *¿Comprendes?*[13]

Tim nodded weakly.

As Tío stepped back and turned to Linda, Tim hurtled through the door with far more agility and speed than Linda would have expected from anyone so drunk. A second later, a car engine broke through their stunned silence with a roar, and the Pulsar peeled off down the street.

Tim squinted, only able to use his right eye. His ribcage throbbed, and his hearing was muffled again. He pulled a crumpled napkin out of the glove compartment and held it up to his bloody nose. He hadn't been beaten up since middle school and now it'd happened twice in one weekend.

Shaking his head, he spat blood out the window. "What's their problem? I didn't even do anything. It's not like that other girl from college. Linda wanted me. Wearing that dress, touching my face, bringing me food every day."

Tim slammed his fist on the steering wheel. "It's all their fault. If I'd never worked there, Wendy wouldn't have left me. I'd probably have a good job by now. All I have is this stupid car. Because of her, I don't even have a job. If she hadn't led me on, none of this would have happened."

In Tim's inebriated, cloudy mind, an idea formed in a matter of seconds. Clenching his jaw, he pictured the title of the article he had seen in the newsstand

---

[13] Do you understand?

that morning, the one with Linda's face peering out from the corner of the front-page spread, the same article he'd seen cut out and placed in Linda's scrapbook. "Stupid tease," he muttered. "This'll teach you." He picked up his phone and dialed. "Hello, is this the police department?" A few moments later, he swerved onto the highway. "Yes, I would like to report someone working illegally." He gave the officer the information and hung up.

Everything was clear now. He should never have taken the job as a mechanic. He'd made the wrong choice that day. Deep down he'd known it all along. His family would be better off without him.

Wendy had been right; he was just like his father. But now Tim didn't care. In the end, his father had spoken the truth. His final truth before he'd chosen the same fate Tim was driving towards. His father's last words echoed in Tim's head as he pushed the pedal and watched the odometer hit seventy, eighty, and then ninety: "Sometimes you have to give up the fight."

The car shook and seized up. "No more fighting," Tim whispered through gritted teeth. "Back to plan A." He turned sharply and rammed his car into the guardrail.

Juanita held her trembling daughter close to her. Hector opened the front door to their home. Black smoke billowed out in the night. "*Ay*," Juanita exclaimed. "*Las tortillas.*"

"I'll get them." Hector jogged into the kitchen, while Juanita led Linda to the sofa with Memo trailing behind. Hector hurried around the house, opening all the windows and turning on all the fans.

Memo sat next to his niece, rolling his gold cross necklace between his thumb and forefinger. His boot tapped rapidly on the carpeted floor.

Juanita knew if her brother spent too much time thinking, he might leave to go find Tim. Perhaps even kill him. "*Pon agua para unos tés de manzanilla, Memo.*"[14] They all could use a cup to calm down. Soon enough the teakettle clicked to life. She turned her focus back to Linda, who was shaking in jumpy spurts. Juanita whispered to her, reminding her she was safe now. Before long, the teapot whistled and steamed.

In an instant, it all became too much for her—the thick corn smoke, the screaming kettle, the whirring fans. Unable to breathe, Juanita pushed up from the couch and staggered down the hall, running her fingers along the wall. She turned into the bathroom and closed the door with a shaky hand.

Her back hit the linen closet, and she slid to the floor. She squeezed her eyes tightly shut and opened her mouth in a silent sob, pulling at her clothing and ripping her shirt. She muffled her cries with a hand towel and whispered a fierce plea to God, "*¿Por qué, Dios? ¿Por qué? Mi pobre Lindita. Tan inocente. ¿Por qué?*"[15] She repeated the same prayer over and over again, until it was nothing more than an echo of a whisper.

Someone knocked lightly on the door. "*¿Estás bien?*" Memo's voice floated into the bathroom.

Shaking her head, Juanita answered a trembling, "*Sí.*" She rolled onto her knees and pulled herself up, using the bathroom sink. Her legs wobbled, and her head swam. For a moment, she feared she might faint.

---

[14] Put on water for some chamomile teas, Memo.

[15] Why, God, why? My poor little Linda. So innocent. Why?

Sending up another prayer, she turned on the faucet and splashed cold water on her face.

The door creaked open, and Memo's large hand rubbed her upper back. *"Toma, hermana."*[16] The ceramic mug of tea clinked as he placed it on the tiled counter. He handed her a fresh hand towel, and she exhaled as she dried her face.

"Gracias." She picked up the mug with both hands, allowing the warmth to spread through her body and calm her nerves. She breathed in the chamomile-scented steam and took a sip of the soothing liquid.

"¿Ya?"[17]

She nodded, and he guided her back to the living room where Hector sat next to Linda, trying to get her to drink some tea.

Hector's brow furrowed in concern. "I think she's in shock."

Juanita gently touched Linda's shoulder, which jerked in response. *"Cálmate, mija. Dios te protegió. Estás segura."*[18] If only God had protected her before Tim had attacked her, she thought. She pushed out the idea and moved closer on the couch to her silent daughter.

After a few more minutes of comforting and prompting, Juanita and Hector finally convinced Linda to drink some tea. Sipping slowly, Linda stared straight ahead, eyes wide, saying nothing. Sometimes her gaze followed Memo as he paced angrily across the living room.

Juanita knew his temper. If Memo had been anything more than a young teenager when she was married, he probably would've killed her husband.

---

[16] Drink, sister.

[17] Okay now?

[18] Calm down, my daughter. God protected you. You are safe.

She always thanked God for his age at that time in their lives and prayed for his anger.

"*Siéntate, 'mano.*"[19] Juanita handed Memo his mug, and he paused, mumbling a prayer into his drink. Hector refilled Linda's cup, and Juanita prayed aloud constantly, at times whispering praise songs.

Several cups of tea later, eyes were beginning to droop. Balling up on the couch, Memo fell into a fretful sleep. Juanita helped Linda to her bed and lay beside her, wrapping her daughter in her arms. Carrying a kitchen chair into the bedroom, Hector dropped into the seat and leaned his elbows on his knees, burying his face in his hands. He waited in silence until Linda fell asleep and then left without a word to sleep in his room. Staying awake a while longer, Juanita brushed Linda's soft skin with her dry, cracked hands and hummed their favorite Selena songs until she drifted off to a disturbed slumber.

That night Juanita dreamed that a big eagle swooped down upon her and Linda as they walked through the desert. Its large talons gripped Linda, tearing her from Juanita and carrying her away. Waking with a start, she reached for her sleeping daughter.

She glanced at the clock. Almost six. She lightly touched Linda's shoulder. "*¿Quieres ir a trabajar, mija?*"[20]

Linda moaned and rolled over. Her brow wrinkled in confusion, and she sat up, wincing. She rubbed her back, mentioning something about a table.

"*No tienes que trabajar. Puedes descansar hoy. Los Hernandez van a comprender.*"[21]

---

[19] Sit down, brother.

[20] Do you want to go to work, my daughter?

[21] You don't have to work. You can rest today. The Hernandezes will understand.

Linda sighed. "I should go in. It's the busiest day at the *panadería*. Besides I need something to do. Get my mind off things."

"Okay, *mija*." Juanita sat up and reluctantly pushed off the covers. "*Voy a hacerte un té*."[22]

Linda nodded and got out of bed.

Linda kneaded the *masa* for the day's *panes* and purposefully pushed yesterday's events from her mind. She turned up the radio and caught movement out of the corner of her eye. Two policemen peered through the front window at her and pointed to the door.

Shaking, she walked over and unlocked it. A bell dinged as she pushed the handle, sending a small shockwave through her middle. "Yes, officers. How can I help you?"

"Are you Linda Palacios?" one officer asked.

Her heart beat faster. "Yes," Linda said.

"Can we see your visa?"

Linda's mouth dropped open. "I—I don't have it with me." Then she remembered what she had learned at her meetings. "I haven't done anything wrong. I don't have to show you my papers."

The other officer stepped into the *panadería*. "We received an anonymous call last night stating you're working here illegally. That's a crime."

Linda's heart sank.

"Either find your 'papers' or come with us downtown."

Her mind spun in a thousand directions at once. Images of Mamá and Memo and Hector flashed

---

[22] I'll make you a tea.

through her mind. If she went with the police, she
might never see home again. If she could slip out the
back, she might have enough time to get away. "I
need to let my boss know I'm leaving and take the
bread out of the oven."

"We'll go with you." Their shoes creaked as they
followed her to the back.

It was no use. Running was dangerous. People had
been shot for less. She had no choice. She had to go
with them.

Linda put on one oven mitt and dropped the other,
her hands trembling. She took a deep breath as she
leaned over to pick it up, her muscles aching where
she had hit the table. Her mind jolted for a moment
back to last night's trauma. Nausea rose in her
stomach. *Dios, por favor, ayúdame*,[23] she prayed. She
steadied her hands, took the tray of bread out of the
oven, and put it on the cooling rack. She knocked on
the back door and waited for Don Hernandez to come
out.

"What happen, Linda?" he asked.

"Are you Mr. Hernandez?" the officer asked.

"Yes."

"Are you the owner of this establishment?"

He nodded.

"Were you aware that you hired an illegal to work
for you?"

Linda shook her head quickly, pleading with her
eyes. She mouthed "no."

"No," he said.

"Be more careful in the future." The officer took
out a pair of handcuffs. "Okay, Miss Palacios. Let's
go."

She hugged Don Hernandez and whispered

---

[23] God, please, help me.

instructions into his ear. *"Dígale a Mamá que la quiero y que no se preocupe. Y dígale a Hector que hable con la gente del Dream Act."*[24]

Don Hernandez nodded his eyes filled with tears. He and Doña Hernandez had never been able to have children of their own, and she knew she was the closest thing they had to a daughter.

Linda smiled. "I'll be okay." Though fear overwhelmed her, she knew it was true. God had given Mamá the strength to cross an entire desert with her toddler daughter on her hip. He had helped Linda make it all the way to college. No matter where she was, He would be there.

She thought back to the rally, to all the others who had stood in front with her and all those who were too afraid to come forward. Now it was her turn to stand up for them. To show the world they were worth fighting for.

She took a deep breath, held her head high, stuck out her wrists, and watched as they snapped the handcuffs into place. They walked on either side of her to the squad car. Keeping her chin up, she stared into the crowd that had gathered around the shop. Before they pushed her into the back seat, she yelled at the top of her lungs, "Undocumented and unafraid!"

---

[24] Tell Mamá that I love her and not to worry. And tell Hector to talk with the people from The Dream Act.

PART THREE

Losing the Dream

The alien living with you must be treated as one of your
native-born. Love him as yourself, for you were aliens
in Egypt. I am the LORD your God
- Leviticus 19:34

*Al contrario, trátenlo como si fuera uno de ustedes. Ámenlo
como uno de ustedes mismos, porque también ustedes fueron
extranjeros en Egipto. Yo soy el Señor y Dios de Israel
- Levítico 19:34*

CHAPTER EIGHTEEN
Si Tu Te Vas[1]

*F*or the last week, Juanita had been trapped in a haze of confusion and fear. When Norma had come to tell her the news of Linda's arrest, she had fainted. The police had taken away her Lindita in handcuffs in the back of a squad car, perfectly innocent. All because of some "anonymous tip," most likely from the man who had tried to rape her daughter.

Though they'd visited Linda a few times already, it never got any easier. Juanita took a deep breath as the jail came into view. She gripped the bus seat in front her, her knuckles turning white. Hector supported her arm as she stood up on trembling legs. Every day they visited, she worried that they might have moved Linda or that they would decide to haul Juanita in, too.

Her pulse thudded in her throat as they walked through the doors into the cold reception area.

---

[1] If You Leave – both Enrique Iglesias and Juan Luis Guerra have songs with this title

Hector checked them in, and they sat for what felt like an hour, waiting for the officer to bring them to her.

"Juanita Palacios?" a gruff voice called out.

"Yes." She raised her head, wiping the sweat that had formed on her brow.

"You can come back now."

Hector stood, and the officer put up a hand.

"Only one visitor at a time."

Hector's jaw clenched. "But last weekend we both went back."

"Rules change. You'll have your turn."

Clutching her purse like a security blanket, Juanita glanced back at Hector.

"It's okay. I'll be right here." He gave her an encouraging nod.

Juanita turned and followed the blue uniform through the door.

Linda wiped her eyes with the back of her hand as the officer led her mother from the room. A thousand thoughts flew through her mind. She tried to calm them with prayer, but she couldn't concentrate. Ever since her arrest, she had found it harder to pray. A cocktail of anger and bitterness mixed with fear and sorrow drowned out her petitions.

Apologizing to God, she straightened as the buzzer connected to the visitor's door went off down the hall. She wanted to hear what updates Hector had. Earlier in the week she'd given him Becky's number, and he was supposed to call her and let her know what was going on.

She was impressed at how helpful Hector had been. He'd called the school to explain the situation and had contacted The Dream Act organization. She smiled, realizing she was actually looking forward to talking with him. How quickly things had changed.

The door opened, and Hector strode into the room. "Hey." He sat down and placed a notebook on the table between them. His dark eyes were shadowed with worry. "How are you?" he asked, his voice thick with emotion.

Sorrow and exhaustion threatened to overwhelm her. Remembering how God was her strength, she let His peace wash over her instead. "As well as can be expected. My new cellmate's pretty nice."

"That's something I never thought I'd hear you say." His right cheek dimpled.

"Yeah. For real." She chuckled.

The cell they had moved her to yesterday was nicer than the first two she'd been in. The first one she'd heard called "The Drunk Tank." It had been a cold room with a large glass wall. Cold metal benches filled with women sleeping off their hangovers had lined the room. The second had only been big enough to squeeze in one bed and a toilet and sink. It was just as cold as the first cell and was near a rickety elevator that made it sound like the room would collapse around her every time it moved. It had been torture. Each time she'd fallen asleep, she'd been snapped awake again by the elevator's fearful racket. Needless to say, the new cell was pleasant in comparison.

"Did you get a chance to talk with Becky?" she asked.

"I called her as soon as we got home from our last visit. She was really worried when you didn't show up to class."

"Yeah, I think I've only missed two classes in the last three years. One time the bus broke down, and the other time I had the flu real bad."

"I used to miss about two classes every day." Hector frowned. "I was so stupid."

"Hey." Linda put her hand on the table near his. "Don't worry about that stuff. You're different now. Besides, you've got your GED, and you worked really hard for it."

He let out a long breath, his attention on her hand. He lifted his fingers and brushed them lightly over her skin. Shivers raced up Linda's arm, every fiber of her being crying out for his embrace.

"Hey. No touching," the guard warned in a stern tone.

"Sorry." Hector frowned and pulled his hand away. "I guess you're right." He sighed and stretched his arms behind his head.

Linda watched his biceps pop under his tight short-sleeved shirt. She quickly averted her gaze.

The corners of Hector's mouth quirked upwards. He cleared his throat. "Anyway, enough about me. Becky told me she'd call her father, Franklin Abbott. He's some big-shot attorney in South Carolina. She says he knows some people who specialize in immigration."

"Oh, right. I almost forgot about that. She did her summer internship at his firm."

"Sandra from Virginia Organizing called me. They're getting people to sign a petition for your release, but I haven't heard back yet."

"Really?" Linda's face warmed. "Wow. That's, uh…Wow. I don't know what to say."

"You don't have to say anything. I think prayer is the only thing that will help now."

If she could only concentrate long enough to finish one. "Now that's something I never thought I'd hear you say."

He laughed. "Yeah, well, people change."

Tim's face shot into her mind. "I know." Linda dropped her gaze to the table.

"Some of us change for the better."

Linda nodded, still not looking up.

The door behind Hector opened, and the officer stepped into the room. "Time's up."

Hector stood and looked at her with an intensity that overwhelmed her. "We'll see you in court. And remember, no matter what happens, I'm not going anywhere."

Her heart soared, and she swallowed hard, holding back tears.

Juanita sighed as she stepped off the bus. She relaxed her shoulders and shook out her hands. The bus pulled away, and she and Hector headed home. The smell of slowly simmering meats rolled over them in an aromatic wave as Hector opened the front door.

Without Linda, the house felt empty. Every day she had to force herself to cook, clean, and stay busy, or she would be overcome by a surge of tears. Not since her last years in Mexico had she experienced such sadness. Hector did the best he could to cheer her up and encourage her, but she could tell Linda's absence took its toll on him, too. He grew quieter, told fewer jokes, and she could hear him pacing his bedroom at night. The only thing that gave either of them any relief was prayer and staying busy. Whenever she stopped moving, worries entered her mind, and images of what could happen flew around her like a swarm of angry bees.

Juanita went to the kitchen, tied her hair back into a heavy bun, and slipped her apron over her head. She wrapped the straps around her waist and pulled them into a loose knot. Lifting the lid to a pot of boiling chicken, she took a deep breath, a prayer on her heart. A prayer for God to carry her worries about Linda, if only for a minute.

In the small cell, Linda read her Bible to her roommate. The passage was Romans 5:3-5. "Not only so, but we also rejoice in our sufferings, because we know that suffering produces perseverance; perseverance, character; and character, hope. And hope does not disappoint us, because God has poured out his love into our hearts by the Holy Spirit, whom He has given us."

Linda sighed and lay back on her cot, hugging her Bible. She had court today. Questions raced through her mind as she tried to pray. Why did Tim attack her? Why had God let it happen? Why had He not protected her? She failed to see the bigger picture. If she got deported, how would it build her character? Struggling to see God's plan, she turned back to prayers more specific to her court case.

Hector, Mamá, Becky, and Pastor Martinez had been doing all they could to get her released, but she knew such an outcome rarely happened. The judge wouldn't care about the circumstances, about who had called in the tip and why, but would focus on the "crime." Maybe today would be different. She imagined the look on Mamá's face if they dropped the charges and let her go.

Her musings were interrupted by a clink on the bars.

"Palacios, your lawyer's here."

Her prayers had been answered. Becky had come through. She jumped off the top bunk and handed her roommate the Bible. "In case I don't come back. You can have it."

"Good luck, Linda." Her cellmate hugged her.

"Thanks, but I don't need luck, I need Him." She pointed up.

"I'll pray for you."

She followed the guard into a room, where they placed handcuffs on her wrists and attached them to her chair, as if she were dangerous. Several minutes later, a middle-aged, chocolate-skinned man in an expensive suit walked in. She recognized him immediately from the news. He was a prominent civil rights lawyer and had recently won an important trial in California for migrant workers.

"Hello, Miss Palacios, I'm Jackson Brown. My good friend, Franklin Abbott, told me about your case, and I'd like to represent you."

One of the best lawyers in the country, how could they possibly afford him? Linda opened her mouth to speak.

"Just so there's no confusion, I'll be taking your case pro bono."

"For free?" she asked.

"Yes, for free."

Linda's eyes filled with tears. The Lord had most definitely answered their prayers. "I would be honored if you represented me, sir."

He smiled. "You can call me Jackson."

Juanita put on her best Sunday dress and fixed her hair in the mirror. Her fears were attacking her again. What if Linda told her story in court, and they arrested Juanita for bringing her across the border? Pastor Martinez's words about God's plan came to mind, but she didn't understand. How would He let them escape only to have one or both of them sent back? She calmed her fears by reminding herself that if they arrested her, too, at least she and Linda would be together again. Plus since she didn't have to worry about her husband's violence anymore, it was worth the risk.

Hector knocked on the door. *"Ya vámanos, Doña."*[2]

Juanita grabbed her purse and followed him out of the house. Both Hector and Memo were dressed in suits. They got into Memo's car and drove downtown to the courthouse in silence. When they stepped into the courtroom, it was packed full of people. The air was cold, and the wooden benches gleamed under the bright, morning sun that shone through the tall windows on the right wall. The view overlooked the square where, a few weeks before, Linda had marched for the very rights she would be fighting for today.

Hector waved to a group on the right. *"Son los del* Dream Act."[3]

Juanita nodded to them, grateful for their support, and they found their seats in the first row behind Linda and her lawyer. Juanita and Memo leaned forward to hug her. The lawyer shook their hands and introduced himself.

They sat down, and Hector whispered in her ear. "He's a really good attorney. I've seen him on TV."

The man looked familiar. She recognized him from a program that came on after her *novela*. Something about migrant rights in California. Maybe they did have a chance. She exhaled slowly. Tension eased from her shoulders. Memo held her hand, and they stood as the judge walked into the courtroom.

---

[2] Let's go now, ma'am.
[3] They're the ones from The Dream Act.

Linda stood on trembling legs as the elderly judge walked to his bench, sat down, and peered at them over his reading glasses. She recognized him as the same judge who had deported María and Diana. She returned to her seat, fear shocking through her.

Jackson stepped forward. "Good afternoon, Judge Watkins. My name is Jackson Brown, and I will be representing Miss Palacios."

"Oh, I know who you are, Mr. Brown. You've been making quite a name for yourself lately."

"Yes, Your Honor, I have."

"This here's a simple hearing. You'll have no jury to play up to. It's just me. I'll hear from Officer Sheldon and from Miss Palacios, and then I'll make my decision."

Jackson nodded and sat back down. He patted Linda's shoulder. "Don't worry," he said. "This is just what we talked about."

Linda took a deep breath and listened as the officer recounted his side of the story. He'd received an anonymous tip and had caught Linda, *con las manos en la masa*.[4] On the job without a proper work visa. The judge thanked him, and the officer sat back down.

"Miss Palacios, what do you have to say for yourself?"

This was the part she and Mr. Brown had rehearsed. He'd explained that at this level his job was to prepare her to speak at the hearing, file the proper paperwork for further legal proceedings, and make sure they knew she was properly represented.

Linda gripped the table as she rose, not trusting

---

[4] With her hands in the dough (i.e. red-handed)

her shaking legs. She pushed past her fear and held her head up, making eye contact with the judge. "Your Honor, I was brought into this country at the age of three, and I grew up as American as the rest of the kids in this city. I studied hard in school, earned good grades, graduated high school, and was accepted into a good college here in town. I have a 3.9 GPA and have never previously been in trouble with the law."

The judge's face was unmoving, hard like a stone. "I appreciate your life story, Miss Palacios, but you're here today to talk about your choice to work without a visa."

"The night before I was arrested, a mechanic from my uncle's garage, Tim Draker, attempted to rape me. Thankfully, my uncle, my mother, and our friends, Hector and Carlos, found us before anything happened. We let him go, and we believe he was the one who called in the anonymous tip."

"Why didn't you report this to the police?"

"We were afraid they would arrest us instead of the attacker."

"Is this man here to confirm this story, Mr. Brown?"

Linda's heart stopped.

Jackson Brown stood up and shook his head. "No, Your Honor, the police have been unable to locate him for questioning." He returned to his seat.

The judge's lips pursed. He directed his gaze back to Linda. "And were you working at the bakery where Officers Sheldon and Frond picked you up on October third?"

"I was making bread."

"Did they pay you for making this bread?"

"Yes."

"Thank you, Miss Palacios, you can sit down."

Linda's legs nearly gave way as she returned to her seat. Several hands patted her back, and she let out a quiet, deep breath. Her hands shook uncontrollably, and she squeezed the edge of the table to steady them, waiting for the judge's response. Time dragged as the judge studied the papers in front of him.

Finally, he took off his reading glasses and addressed the courtroom. "Despite the circumstances surrounding the arrest, Miss Palacios is here illegally, and she committed a crime by working without a visa. I see no reason to drop the charges."

Angry cries roared throughout the courtroom.

"Order. Order. Everyone quiet down, or I'll throw you all out of here."

After the room quieted, the judge continued. "Mr. Brown, as I'm sure you already know, you can appeal this decision. For now, Miss Palacios will be transferred to the Farmville Detention Center."

Linda turned to her mother and reached for her hand. *"No se preocupe. Voy a estar bien. Él es muy buen abogado."*[5]

Her mother nodded, gripping Linda's hand with all her might, tears streaming down her face. It was the first time she had ever seen her mother cry over anything but onions.

Juanita sat, dazed, as the lawyer spoke with her, Hector, and Memo at her kitchen table. She found it hard to follow the conversation with everything buzzing through her head. Farmville was two hours away, and she couldn't drive. Memo had offered to

---

[5] Don't worry. I'm going to be okay. He's a very good lawyer.

take her, but the lawyer had told them they would be detained, and they needed to be here for Linda when she came back. Besides, who knew when they would transfer her to another center in a state far away like they did to Diana and María?

The lawyer kept speaking, discussing Linda's rights and the processes they had to go through. It was all too technical for her to understand.

"*Espera*,"[6] she said, holding up her hand. "What I wanna know is, can you bring her home?"

He stopped talking and turned to face Juanita, his brown eyes glowing with intensity. He enclosed her hands in his large, warm grasp. "Ma'am, I will not rest until this is resolved. You have my word on that."

Juanita squeezed his hand. "*Gracias*."

"*De nada*," he replied. "It won't be easy, and she could possibly get deported back to Mexico. Virginia's laws are very strict on undocumented persons. If she gets deported, we will not stop appealing. There are many things we can do to fight this injustice. I've filed several motions, I've got my team in California scouring for any loopholes, Virginia Organizing is working on their petition, plus we're filing for a few different visas. I'm not sure yet which one will work, but we're going to do all we can to get your daughter back home."

Hector rose from the table and stirred the *cueritos*.[7] "*Ya están*."[8]

Juanita put the *tostada* toppings on the table. Refried beans, lettuce, onion, *queso fresco*, *crema*,[9] avocado, and salsa.

---

[6] Wait.

[7] Pork skins in vinegar

[8] They are ready now.

[9] Sour cream

"Ma'am, this smells delicious."

"*Gracias. Son tostados de cuerito. Una especialidad de mi pueblo.*"[10]

"*Que rico,*" the lawyer replied, rolling his "r" more than was necessary. "What are *cueritos?*"

"Pork skins," Hector answered, setting the pan of *cueritos* in the middle of the table.

"Mmm." Jackson Brown waved the steam towards his face, inhaling deeply. "My mother used to make cracklin' all the time when I was growing up."

Hector's brow furrowed for a moment. "I think cracklin' is more like *chicharrón.*"

"Same concept." Mr. Brown watched Memo prepare his *tostada,* and he deftly applied the ingredients to his own, imitating him.

Juanita smiled. The man's hands appeared so large, holding that small *tostada.* She was afraid he would crush it in his powerful grip, but he held it delicately, and it survived the journey to his mouth. "You like?" she asked.

He nodded and sighed deeply. "*Perfecto.*"

Juanita sat back, relaxing her shoulders. Having him in the kitchen had increased her hope. He seemed like someone she could trust. Linda was in good hands.

---

[10] Thank you. They are pork skin tostadas. A specialty from my hometown.

CHAPTER NINETEEN
Voy a Navegar[1]

*L*inda picked at the floppy vegetables on her plate. The food at the detention center tasted better than the jail's, but she missed Mamá's cooking. Her new quarters were more crowded, and there was a cloud of hopelessness in the air. She shared her cell with three other women, two of whom she could not communicate with, as one spoke Korean and the other a dialect from Ethiopia. The third woman was from El Salvador.

In the cell most of the day, they were allowed one hour of time in the yard, which consisted of a basketball net and two tables to the side of the court where people played cards or exchanged cigarettes for other items. It was November and getting cold, but Linda still enjoyed the fresh air. The cell stank because of the toilet, which she was pretty sure the guards cleaned less frequently than the toilet in Kevin and Brian's apartment.

Her only comfort was the Bible she got on her

---

1 I'm Going to Navigate – a song by Vicente Fernandez

first day there. She read it constantly and spent time writing letters. To her mother, to Tío, to Becky, to the church, to her friends at Virginia Organizing, and even to Hector. Before she'd been transferred and could still get phone calls and visitors, Becky never failed to mention Hector's untiring efforts to get her released.

She never knew if the letters would reach their destinations or if she would still be there when they sent replies. She wasn't even sure she would stay long enough for Hector to visit before they moved her. She had no sense of security anymore.

Juanita stirred the salsa, her mind somewhere else, drifting back months ago when she and Linda had been together and happy. It'd been two weeks since the court hearing, and they hadn't received any letters or phone calls from her. Even Mr. Brown was having trouble contacting her. Worry constantly churned in Juanita's mind. Perhaps Linda would be deported without their knowledge. How would her little Lindita fare by herself in Mexico City without any documents, any money, or any way to contact María or Diana? Still, Mr. Brown had reassured her that he would know right away if she were deported. Every day she expected that call.

To make matters worse, the police had not been able to find Tim. His house was empty and full of broken glass and month-old garbage. They'd finally been able to track down his wife and children to a town outside of London, England. His family hadn't heard from Tim either, so the police were beginning to look through the John Doe files in the surrounding areas to show to his wife. The lawyer wasn't sure it would change anything, but Juanita didn't like wondering whether he was out there somewhere.

Poor Memo had taken everything really hard, beating himself up for hiring Tim in the first place; plus he had to constantly explain why he was short a mechanic again. Still, he wasn't as hard as Juanita was on herself. Bringing Linda here had been her choice. She still believed God had wanted her to come, but the guilt ate at her, regardless.

Smoke clouded her eyes. Shaking her head, she stopped stirring, turned off the burner, and moved the pot, scraping the inside with a wooden spoon.

The front door opened, and Hector called out, excitement in his voice, "Doña, a letter. *Recibimos una carta de Linda.*"[2]

Juanita dropped the spoon and fell to her knees, crying out to the Lord in praise. As always, He was merciful and answered the prayers of His children. Wiping her eyes with a clean corner of her apron, she took Hector's outstretched arm and sat at the kitchen table. While Hector shut off the oven and finished scraping the salsa from the bottom of the pot, she traced her trembling finger over Linda's familiar, round lettering on the front of the envelope.

Turning it over and smoothing it out on the table, Juanita used a butter knife to carefully open its flap. She pulled two sheets of folded, blue-lined, white paper, imagining Linda's slender hands meticulously writing the letter with a ballpoint pen before forming the careful creases and sliding it into the envelope.

"*Mira,*[3] Hector." She passed him one of the sheets. "This one is for you."

Raising an eyebrow, he took the page addressed to

---

[2] We received a letter from Linda.
[3] Look

him, a smile spreading onto his face. *"Gracias."*
Hector's transformation had not only impressed her
but everyone around him, even Linda. Not only was
he an excellent assistant in the kitchen, he was also
considerate, smart, and wore his heart on his sleeve.
His constant contact with the different groups
helping her Lindita rallied much support and
countless prayers. God had certainly put Hector in
their path for a reason.

Sobs choking her throat, she read her letter
quietly to herself. *"Querida Mamá . . ."*[4]

Linda lay on her cot, her Bible across her chest, her
cheek pressing against the cool concrete wall. Since
her detainment, she'd read the entire New Testament
and now was one page into the Psalms. Previously
they'd done nothing for her, but now every word
spoke to her, as if it were written especially for her.
So far she'd only read six Psalms, and all of them
were relevant, the sixth one most of all.

The third verse caught her attention: "My soul is
in deep anguish. How long, Lord, how long?" Linda
had asked that very same question over and over
again in the dark, lonely nights in the cell. Though
still at the detention center in Farmville, she knew
she could be transferred at any moment. The process
could drag on for months. She just wanted to go
home.

"Marta?" Linda leaned over the edge of the bunk.

Her cellmate opened one eye. *"¿Sí?"*

"Sorry, were you asleep?"

"Not really. Just praying. What's up?"

Linda sighed. "How long do you think we'll be in here?"

"Who knows?" Marta frowned, wrinkles forming on her caramel skin. Born in El Salvador, Marta had been detained first in New York and had been moved four times since she'd been taken into custody. "I've been wondering the same thing for months. *La migra*, they like to keep everyone guessing. You know, moving us around, state to state. That way your families can't visit. Then one day, after waiting forever, they just deport you back to wherever you came from."

"It's too hard, this waiting around. It's like purgatory."

"Which is hell in this analogy? The U.S. or Mexico?"

"Depends on who's asking." Linda smiled.

Marta chuckled. "The thing that bothers me the most is the reason we're here in the first place. I was arrested for jaywalking. What New Yorker hasn't jaywalked? You were arrested for baking bread. Don't even get me started on that anonymous tip business." Marta clenched her jaw and continued. "Over the last five months, I've spoken with hundreds of different inmates. Sure, some of them are here on DUIs or robbery, but most of them were detained for the same reason as both of us, nonviolent crimes. I met one person who was taken into custody for an expired vehicle registration and another for a broken taillight."

Linda twirled the mattress tag, her stomach roiling at the thought of deportation. "I can't even remember Mexico. I was only three when we left."

"Maybe you're lucky. I wish I couldn't remember."

"Was it really that bad?"

"I still have nightmares once in a while. The

things I saw there." Marta shook her head. "I can never erase them from my mind."

"Were you there in the eighties?" Linda asked. Her Salvadoran friends from high school had talked of a bloody civil war that had lasted more than a decade.

Marta nodded. "I was five when it came to our *pueblo*. I remember I wasn't allowed to go outside to play anymore. We could hear the screaming and the gunshots from inside the house. It was safer during the day. Every night my family would run and hide in the mountains." She looked up at Linda. "The soldiers would raid homes and kill people in their sleep. Sometimes they would steal boys to fight in the army. That's what happened to one of my cousins." She lowered her gaze again. "When we would return home in the mornings, we would have to walk past ditches full of dead bodies. Bodies of people we knew. Our neighbors and friends, naked and covered in dark blood. All murdered." Marta turned her head to the wall, wiping the tears from her eyes.

"That's horrible." Linda didn't know what to say. She couldn't imagine living through something like that, escaping, and then being forced to return.

"I can't believe I have to go back there." Marta's quiet tears strengthened into sobs.

"Can you get refugee status? The parents of some of my Salvadoran friends got refugee visas."

Marta shook her head. "We waited too long to leave."

"I'm so sorry." She lowered her arm over the edge of the bed and met Marta's hand, giving it a squeeze. "¿*Oramos?*"[5]

Nodding, Marta closed her eyes. As Linda prayed,

---

[5] Shall we pray?

she wondered how many more stories echoed over these cold walls. Ending the prayer with her favorite passage in Romans again, she sighed, deciding she would have a lot of character by the end of this.

Hector on her left and Memo on her right, Juanita squeezed their hands as Pastor Martinez walked to the pulpit. Waves of emotion had overtaken her since she'd received Linda's letter yesterday. Then the pastor had called her last night; Linda had written to him, too, and he wanted Juanita's permission to read the letter aloud in church. She'd given it, but her nerves were jumping around like *chiles* in a hot skillet.

Nancy, Pastor Martinez's wife, stood by his side, interpreting. Usually she sat in the back doing simultaneous interpreting, but knowing how many of their church members were English-speaking, Linda had written letters both in English and in Spanish.

"As you already know, our sister, Linda Palacios is awaiting deportation at the USCIS detention center in Farmville. Linda is a long-standing member of this church. I can remember when she first walked in that door as a little, six-year-old girl. Her tiny face always brightened my day. And her voice. Oh, what a voice. The praise band hasn't been the same without her."

Memo squeezed Juanita's hand.

"Yesterday we got a letter from her. She addressed it to the entire church, so I'd like to read it aloud to you now." The pastor and his wife both put on their reading glasses. Pastor Martinez continued. "To my brothers and sisters in Christ, I want to start by thanking you for all your prayers and support. They have meant so much to me during this difficult time. Though it has been hard to be away from you all, especially from Mamá, God has put many people in my path here. I have been given a Bible here at the detention center, and I have been reading the New Testament. So many books in the New Testament were written by Paul when he was incarcerated, and this gives me strength, knowing that good things can come out of my experience."

The ache in Juanita's heart grew. She missed Linda more with every word.

"Though I don't understand now the reason for this experience, I have faith that God is with me. It is His will, wherever I go, whether it is back home with Mamá or down to Mexico. Either way, God has a plan. If I am deported to Mexico, which is very likely, I have the assurance that God will place people in my path to guide me and to lead me where He needs me. He is all-powerful and all-knowing. He will not fail any of us."

Tears streamed down Juanita's face.

"Please continue to pray for me. I am finding it hard to be patient. At times it is even difficult to pray; so much anger and anxiety is in and around me. Your prayers are the only things keeping me going." The pastor stopped, unable to hold back tears any longer.

Glancing around her, Juanita noticed the rest of the congregation in the same state.

After a minute, Pastor Martinez continued. "My family also needs support. At least I know that Mamá has Tío and Hector. She is not completely alone. Please remind Mamá that I love her so much. Tío, too. Hector's not so bad either."

Hector chuckled tearily next to her. She grasped his hand tighter and put her head on Memo's shoulder. He hugged her tightly.

"I want to thank each and every one of you. You

have done so much for me throughout the years. I don't know what will happen next, but I do know that all the love I have received from you and the love that God has for me will sustain me for a long, long time."

What Linda had said fit with the verse Juanita had read that very morning in 1 John 4:11-12. "Dear friends, since God so loved us, we also ought to love one another. No one has ever seen God; but if we love one another, God lives in us, and his love is made complete in us." Looking around at her brothers and sisters in Christ, Juanita knew this was true. She was surrounded by God's love.

CHAPTER TWENTY
México, Lindo y Querido[1]

*T*he shrill ringtone pierced the silence of the night, lighting up the dark room with an incandescent glow. A knife seared Juanita's heart. With trembling hands, she picked up the phone. It was Jackson Brown.

Every night since the first court hearing, she had pictured this moment, living it in her dreams. She'd tried to prepare herself. But when the moment finally arrived, her emotions flooded out any rational thoughts she had practiced. Flipping open the phone, she cleared her throat.

"I'm sorry to disturb you at such a late hour, Señora Palacios."

Too afraid to speak, she remained silent, waiting.

"It's bad news, ma'am. Linda's being deported today."

Juanita's cry echoed into the darkness. Seconds later, Hector appeared at the door. He flipped on the

---

[1] Mexico, Pretty and Loved – a song by Jorge Negrete and made more famous by Vicente Fernandez

bedroom light and sat next to her on the bed. He pressed a button on the phone, and Jackson Brown's voice carried through the room.

"In ten hours, she's leaving the Etowah County Detention Center in Alabama, and they're putting her on a plane. She should arrive this afternoon around two o'clock local time at Benito Juárez International Airport in Mexico City. She can't bring anything with her except the clothes she was arrested in and any other possessions that were on her at the time, so she'll need someone to meet her there at the airport."

Hector squeezed Juanita's hand. "I've got that taken care of."

A sigh came through the phone. "I know this isn't what we'd hoped for, but it's not over. Don't give up."

Juanita shook her head. Though she knew where her hope lay, it was hard to hold it, and she felt it slipping through her fingers. In less than twelve hours, her daughter would arrive in Mexico, a country she didn't even remember, with the clothes on her back and nothing else.

Disoriented, Linda searched around her dark cell for anything familiar. It'd been almost two months since her arrest. Since then, she'd been moved three separate times. "Alabama," she whispered to herself, laying her head back on her pillow.

"Linda Palacios?" A gruff voice accompanied a loud banging on the bars of the cell.

Her eyes shot open and a wave of nausea hit her. "*Dios mío, protégeme*,"[2] she cried out.

"Time to go."

---

[2] My God, protect me.

"Where am I going?" she asked, clutching her Bible to her chest.

The guard checked her chart. "Mexico."

Linda slid out of her bed, dropping to her knees. "No, please," she pleaded.

"I don't make the decisions." Opening the bars, the guard stepped into the cell. "Come on now. Don't make a scene. You'll wake everyone up."

Turning to her left, she saw her new roommate, fear plastered on the woman's face. Linda wiped off her cheeks with the back of her hand and slowly stood up.

"You can't bring that with you." The guard nodded to her Bible.

"*Está bien*,"[3] Linda stated, holding her head high. She handed it to the roommate with a smile. "*Aquí lo traigo siempre*."[4] She patted her heart. "I carry His Word with me always."

Juanita stood in front of the television cameras in her best outfit. Memo, moving restlessly next to her in a suit, gripped her hand tightly. Frozen to the world, it was as if Juanita were floating outside her body, looking down on herself. Flashes of lights, clicks of cameras, questions flung left and right—none of them broke through her thick wall of numbness.

Jackson Brown raised his big hands high up in the air and called for silence, jolting her from her daze. He spoke into the microphones with an intensity that made the hair on the back of Juanita's neck stand up. "A travesty of justice has been committed today.

---

[3] That's fine.
[4] I carry it with me always.

Linda Palacios was an upstanding member of our community, our city, and our country. She contributed to our society in many ways, including her active role in her church and with The Dream Act. Without her caring, positive presence here, we are missing out on a stronger future. I will pursue every last thread in this case that the law allows, and I will not rest until this matter has been resolved. Linda Palacios' unfair deportation to Mexico will not be the end to all of this. We will continue the fight until Ms. Palacios has been returned to the country with full rights and documentation." He turned and put his hand on Juanita's back, guiding her through the crowd of reporters and cameras. Memo followed closely behind them.

Linda had urged Juanita to stay here and keep working if Linda were deported, believing with all her heart that Mr. Brown would find a way to get her back into the country. Hector had contacted his mother, so Linda would have a place to stay when she got to Mexico. She would not be completely alone.

Though Juanita knew all these things and believed in God's plan, the empty hole still throbbed where her heart had been ripped from her body.

On an isolated runway, Linda and a dozen other Mexican citizens boarded an unmarked plane, their wrists and ankles shackled and attached by chains to thick, leather belts around their waists. The flight to D.F. would take about five hours. Either Mamá or Hector would call María and Diana and let them know when to meet her at the airport. She had the twenty dollars left over from her commissary account and her uncharged cell phone. Even if she could pay for a cab to María and Diana's place, her friends in the detention centers had told her enough about D.F. to know it wasn't safe for her go by herself. Too many *rateros*.[5]

The engine roared to life, and Linda stared out the window. This was the first time she'd ever been on a plane. A strange sensation gripped her as the jet picked up speed and lifted into the air. It reminded her of the time she went on a roller coaster ride for a school field trip. She watched with tears in her eyes as the bright green trees got farther and farther away, knowing that every mile that passed was another mile between her and her family. She closed her eyes, unable to stand it anymore.

After hours of tearful prayer and reminding herself of her favorite verses, she came to a better place. The clinking of chains caused her to open her eyes. Immigration officers were unlocking everyone's shackles, preparing for landing. She looked out the window at the cottonball clouds below. The entire craft leaned forward into a descent. As they emerged below the clouds, large stretches of land lay before her, lined with rivers and highways and soon the edge of the capital city. Nothing in her experience could compare. Mexico City was the third most populated city in the world. Her eyes couldn't possibly take in the entire metropolis at once. Soon she could make out trees, houses, and cars on the roads.

Before she knew it, the plane bounced onto Mexican soil. Well, Mexican pavement, to be exact. As they stepped off the plane, unshackled for the first time in months, the officers directed them into the back section of the airport where the Mexican

---

[5] Crooks

government checked them for outstanding crimes. She was bombarded with Spanish. She had never seen and heard so much Spanish in her whole life.

After an hour of processing, the official stamped some papers and handed them over. *"Bienvenidos a México."*[6]

Linda stepped hesitantly out of the office. Heart racing, she gripped the entry documents, completely lost and alone. People pushed past her as she gawked at the signs above her, trying to find her way to the exit. She hadn't even noticed that someone had stopped right in front of her until he called her name.

She refocused her eyes and did a double-take. It couldn't be.

Hector smiled. "I told you I wasn't going anywhere."

The tears broke forth. Linda wrapped her arms around him, buried her head in his chest, and didn't let go.

Juanita received Hector's text letting her know he'd safely arrived in Mexico City and was waiting for Linda's arrival. She sighed and continued stirring the salsa for the *birria*.[7] She prayed for God to take away her worries and to fill her with peace. She mixed the sauce with the stewed goat, transferred it to a big pot, and called out for her new assistant, Carlos, to carry it to the *panadería*.

---

[6] Welcome to Mexico.

[7] A spicy stew made from goat

Linda swallowed hard, her heart thumping wildly, as she stared into Hector's eyes. "How did you get here?"

"I packed my bags and took a bus to the airport as soon as Jackson called to tell me you were being deported today." Hector adjusted the strap of his duffel bag. "Got the first flight out. My plane landed about an hour ago. It took a while to get my bags and go through customs. I was worried I wouldn't get here in time. I had to bribe a guard to drive me over in his cart to this section of the airport. I think it might be restricted."

Linda shook her head, too shocked to take in most of what he'd said. "I can't believe you're here."

"I promised your mom I'd look out for you."

"Hector." Linda sighed. "You are something else."

He grinned. "That may be the nicest thing you've ever said to me."

"Well, this is certainly the nicest thing anyone's ever done for me."

He shrugged. "People do crazy things for the ones they love."

The breath caught in Linda's throat, and she couldn't respond.

"Come on, I wanna see my mom. They should be waiting for us outside." He pointed to the exit and handed Linda a bag. "Here's some of your clothes and stuff. Your mom packed it this morning." He waited for Linda to sling the bag over her shoulder before directing her forward and putting his arm around her shoulders.

Linda hadn't felt this secure in months. To be trapped with strangers, not knowing what day might be her last in America, was a completely disorienting experience. Combining this with being deported to a country she didn't remember and then dropped into one of its most dangerous and populated cities had thrown her into a tailspin. Hector's warm presence had erased so much of the fear she'd felt as soon as she'd stepped off the plane.

"I think your mom packed your passport," he said. "It was a good call to get that over the summer at the embassy."

"Yeah," said Linda. "That was Daniel's idea."

"Ooh, a bathroom," he said. "I'll be right back."

While Linda waited for Hector, she leaned against the wall and observed the country she had always wanted to visit. Never in this way, of course. Mamá had barely spoken about Mexico, apart from the occasional recipe. Linda knew she'd lived a very hard life. There was no family left to go back to in Zacatecas, and if there were, she wouldn't want to meet them. She figured if Mamá hadn't contacted them in almost two decades, they couldn't have been very supportive.

"Hey," Hector said a couple of minutes later, pulling her out of her musings.

Linda wiped a tear from her eye. Seeing his familiar face brought her an overwhelming sense of calm. They stepped out the airport door into the sunshine.

"Hector," someone shouted from the crowd gathered on the sidewalk.

"Ma," he cried and ran as fast to Diana as his luggage would allow.

Linda followed quickly behind, keeping an eye on their bags, remembering things her fellow inmates had told her about the *rateros*. She gave María a hug, trying to give Hector a moment alone with his mother.

"I missed you so much," he sobbed. "I'm sorry for everything. I love you."

"*Ay, mijo, todo está bien. No te sientas mal. Te quiero mucho.*"[8] Diana patted his head and wiped tears from her eyes.

"How have you been?" María asked, rubbing Linda's shoulder. "Did they treat you okay in jail and at the detention centers?"

Linda shrugged and plastered on a faint smile. "The food sucked, but other than that, it wasn't too bad."

"*Ay, de veras.*[9] Nothing compared to your mom's cooking."

Linda's stomach dropped. She fought back tears as she thought of how far away Mamá was and how long it would be until she could see her again.

María pulled her in for another hug. "Don't worry. It'll be okay. You'll see her again soon."

Linda nodded, hoping it was true. She sniffed and wiped her eyes with the back of her hand. "You'll have to show Hector and me the ropes here. We've never been to Mexico."

Hector turned to Linda. "No, remember? I've been to Mexico once to visit my grandparents in Hidalgo before they passed away."

"Oh, right." Linda frowned. "I guess I'm the only one here for the first time, then. Well, I mean, the first time where I'm actually old enough to remember things."

"That's okay." Hector slid his arm around her shoulder. "Hidalgo's way different than D.F., so I'm just as lost as you are."

Linda saw María and Diana exchange glances, and her face flushed. Six months ago or maybe even two months ago, Linda would have pushed Hector away

---

[8] Oh, my son, everything's okay. Don't feel bad. I love you so much.
[9] Oh, for sure.

with a force that might have knocked him to the floor. But he had worked his way into her heart. She shook her head. Once Becky found out Hector had followed Linda to Mexico, she would be unbearable.

Juanita sat on her bed, reading her Bible. The house was too quiet now with both Linda and Hector gone. Memo had offered to let her move into his place, but his kitchen wasn't as big, and it would be harder to get the food ready for the business. Besides, during the day Carlos was here being trained as her new "sous-chef," as Hector called it.

Carlos was a third generation immigrant with Dominican and Puerto Rican roots. He hardly knew any Spanish, so Juanita worked hard on her English when they were together. Dark-skinned with thick, neatly buzzed hair, their customers often thought Carlos was black and were confused when he threw out some Spanish. If things went well, Memo would buy a food truck in the next month or two.

Though half of her heart was in Mexico, she knew Linda wanted her to stay here. If Jackson Brown would be able to return Linda to the States and Juanita was in Mexico, she'd have to cross the border again, which was far more dangerous now than it was nearly twenty years ago. She'd experienced so much suffering in Mexico, even thinking about it triggered flashbacks and nightmares. She'd never wanted to go back before, but she was willing to endure a lifetime of nightmares in order to be there with Linda. Still, she needed to stay here, to wait, patiently, on God's timing. In the end, if Linda couldn't come home, Juanita will have saved enough money to give them a comfortable life in Mexico.

Juanita checked the clock. Mexico was an hour behind, but she figured they'd probably be back to María and Diana's apartment by now. She read the instructions Hector had left her for using the calling card. Glancing back and forth with her reading glasses, she followed the instructions on the back of the card and punched the numbers into her cell phone.

Her heart raced as she listened to the metallic ring on the other end. "*¿Bueno?*" someone asked through a layer of static.

"*Soy Juanita.*"[10]

"*Buenas tardes, Juanita. Soy yo, María. Está aquí Linda.* I know you want to talk with her. *Te la paso.*"[11]

"*¿Mamá?*" Linda asked in a shaky voice.

Juanita wept at the sound. "*Te extraño tanto, Lindita.*"[12]

"*Le extraño también, Mamá.*"[13] Linda's own crying sounded a million miles away.

Sniffling and clearing her throat, Juanita asked, "*Mija, ¿cómo estás?*"

"*Estoy bien, Mamá. No fue tan mal el avión.*[14] It was like going on a rollercoaster."

Juanita sighed. "How you like Mexico, *mijita?*"

"*Lindo y querido,*" Linda said.

Juanita chuckled. It was good to hear her voice. "*Y D.F., ¿está tan peligroso como dicen?*"[15]

"María and Diana told us not to go out at night, never to walk alone, and to avoid taxis. They're

---

[10] It's Juanita.

[11] Good afternoon, Juanita. It's me, María. Linda's here . . . I'll pass the phone to her.

[12] I miss you so much, little Linda.

[13] I miss you, too, Mamá.

[14] I'm okay, Mamá. The airplane wasn't so bad.

[15] And Mexico City, is it as dangerous as they say?

going to show us how to use the buses and the metro tomorrow. We're going to the Zócalo to see the Aztec ruins. They're right there in the plaza. It sounds amazing."

"*Ay, qué lindo.*" Hearing her daughter looking forward to something, the aching in Juanita's heart loosened a little. "*Tomen fotos.*"[16]

"We will, Mamá. Will you call tomorrow at the same time?"

"Okay, *mija. ¿Y cómo está Hector?*"[17]

"He's good. I still can't believe he came all the way to Mexico for me."

"He loves you, Linda."

There was a pause. "I know, Mamá."

"*¿Y tú? ¿Cómo te sientes?*"[18]

"*No sé. Me siento algo diferente.*"[19]

Juanita smiled. Her daughter was in good hands.

---

[16] Oh, how nice. Take photos.

[17] And how is Hector?

[18] And you? How do you feel?

[19] I don't know. I feel something different.

CHAPTER TWENTY-ONE
Vivir Sin Aire[1]

*L*inda sat in a courtroom so big that she couldn't see the judge at the bench or the seats behind her. The chair to her left was empty. She was alone at her table. Where was Jackson?

Suddenly a voice called out. "You have chosen to represent yourself, Miss Palacios?"

"No," Linda said. "I have a lawyer. Jackson Brown."

"Mr. Brown has retired your case."

"But—"

"No buts, Miss Palacios. What do you have to say for yourself?"

Linda strained to see the judge, but he was too far away. "I'm not guilty. It wasn't my fault."

"Do you have any evidence?"

"No, Your Honor." Out of the corner of her eye, she saw movement. Before she could turn, someone lunged at her.

In a second, his hand circled her neck. "If you tell them, I'll kill you."

Linda struggled, and his face came into focus. It was

---

[1] To Live Without Air – a song by Maná

Tim Draker. She opened her mouth to scream but nothing came out.

Linda awoke with a start, darkness surrounding her. It had all been a dream. She was still in her cell. Curling into a ball, she started weeping. She jumped as someone touched her arm.

"Linda, are you okay?"

"Hector?" How did he get into her cell? She shook the sleep from her head and realized where she was. "I was having a bad dream. It's so dark in here, I didn't remember where I was."

Fabric rustled and feet slapped against tile, moving away from her. The kitchen soon glowed with a dim light over the stove. *Cucarachas*[2] ran to their hiding places. She sighed. "Thank you."

Like most buildings in Mexico, everything in the apartment was made of concrete, metal, or glass. The walls and ceiling were painted with faded terra cotta colors with the occasional white patch of retouched concrete, and the floors were made of chipped and cracked tile. Small, but cozy, the apartment held various *artesanías*[3] which María and Diana had haggled for at *tianguis*[4] and indigenous vendors around the city.

The modest kitchen held a gas stove, an old fridge, a counter, and a large concrete sink with a *lavadero*[5] for laundry. There was a dining nook with a small glass table and four metal chairs overlooking the city through barred, locked windows. Those windows opened onto a fire escape where the laundry hung to dry over a flowerpot of herbs and an aloe vera plant. The bathroom was large enough for the

---

[2] Cockroaches
[3] Handmade art
[4] Open-air markets
[5] A concrete sink with a washboard

toilet and the shower spigot on the opposite wall. María and Diana shared the bedroom, and the living room held enough space for a wooden coffee table and the sofa that Linda was using as a bed.

Hector came back to the couch and sat on the floor in front of her, where he'd been sleeping. "Do you want to talk about the dream?"

Linda shrugged. "I have them all the time. It was about court and about Tim."

Hector frowned. "We should have called the police that night."

"We couldn't have known all that would happen." Linda hesitated and then reached her hand for his shoulder, lightly tracing the blanket creases on his sleep-warmed skin. "Besides, you know how crooked some of the cops were there. Anything could have happened."

Hector let out a deep breath, his hand capturing hers. He rested his stubbly jawline upon her knee and looked back at her. "If only Jackson could've found him, maybe things would've gone differently."

Linda's heart thudded, resisting the desire to run her fingers through his curly locks. "There's nothing more they could have done. They searched for him everywhere. He just disappeared. For all we know, he's dead somewhere."

"They would have found him if he was dead."

"Who knows?" Linda added. "I've watched enough TV to know that some cases are never solved." She withdrew her hand. It felt cold without his touch.

Hector stretched and yawned. "I haven't gotten much sleep either. I hate cockroaches." He shuddered.

Sleepiness clouded Linda's mind. "You can come up here if you want. I think they're mostly on the floor and in the kitchen."

Hector blinked. "Really?"

Without thinking, Linda sat up and patted the other end of the couch.

He flicked a cockroach off his pillow and stood up. "I'm pretty tall," he said.

"Well, I'm pretty short, so it should work out okay."

Hector shook off his blanket and pillow. "You're sure?" he asked again before sitting on the opposite end.

Shrugging, she replied, "Yeah, why not?"

But in a second, when he'd crawled under the covers, head on the opposite end of the couch, his warm legs pressed against hers, she realized why not. Undeniable electricity.

Linda swallowed, her heart thumping hard in her chest. Perhaps she hadn't thought this through. He was in love with her, he had followed her into another country to be with her, and now she was inviting him into her bed. Would he think it was something more?

She lay still, her breathing shallow, her body tense, listening, wondering. Her answer was his soft, familiar snore. Smiling, she allowed her body to relax and thanked God for this gentle, respectful boy He had placed in her life.

Juanita woke from another nightmare about her past. She got out of the bed and drank a glass of water, praying for the Lord to take the images from her mind. Glancing at the clock, she realized she would need to be up in a few minutes anyway to start the *tamales*. She went into the living room and turned on the television to drown the silence.

After heating up the chicken broth, Juanita set the

cornhusks in some water to soften. She got the shredded chicken covered in green salsa out of the refrigerator and placed it on the counter. After she opened the bag of Maseca, she shook it in equal portions into two large bowls. Pouring warm broth over the flour, adding salt, lard, and a bit of *bicarbonato*,[6] she mixed it with tired hands. Since leaving the factory, her hands didn't ache as much, but she still sometimes had trouble. Splashing in a bit more broth, she worked the *masa* until it was the right consistency. She tasted it and added a bit more salt. Wiping her hands on her apron, she sighed.

The days stretched long without Linda's stories about school and the *panadería*. Juanita missed her voice, singing church songs in the shower. Her head tilted as she recognized a familiar melody coming from the television. She walked into the living room.

There was Selena on stage, performing as Juanita remembered so many years ago. The stadium was different, but the music and the feel of it were the same. She pictured little Linda, singing along in her small voice. She thanked God for reminding her that not every memory of hers was a sad one.

"I have never seen anything this amazing in my entire life." Linda's eyes widened as she stood in the central plaza Zócalo staring at the Templo Mayor.[7] "And to imagine this was here all this time, and they didn't even know it."

"Actually, I think they did know it." Hector raised his pointer finger. "The Spaniards built their

---

[6] Baking soda

[7] Main Temple – part of the Aztec ruins next to the Zócalo

cathedrals right on top of the Aztec temples on purpose to disrespect them."

"Wow. It's no wonder they had such trouble converting them to Christianity with treatment like that."

Hector laughed. "Yeah, for real." He snapped a picture of the ruins with his phone. "I wish I could upload these. I miss the smart part of my smart phone."

"Someone in the detention center told me you can get a new SIM card for a few bucks. That way you can buy minutes for calls and texts plus connect to the free WiFi around the city."

"Cool. We better take more pictures then." He held up his phone. "Here, smile."

"Wait," Linda said. She brushed the hair out of her face and tamed any flyaways.

"You look fine." His lips turned into a crooked smile. "Great, actually."

"All this fresh air." She breathed in and coughed. "Okay, maybe it's not so fresh."

"Yeah, the smog is bad here. Also, it's a really high altitude, so the air is thinner. That makes it harder to breathe, too."

Linda raised an eyebrow. "Where'd you learn all this?"

"I bought this guidebook before I left, and I studied it on the plane ride." He held up a thin, brightly colored book. "I know all the best places to go. We have a busy week planned."

"Oh, do we?" Linda asked, putting her hands on her hips.

Hector snapped a picture.

"Hey, no fair. I wasn't ready."

"Oh, that's a good one. Very . . . you."

"Let me see." She held out her hand.

"No way, you'll just erase it. It's mine now." He held the phone behind his back and dodged as Linda tried to reach behind him and pry it from his hands.

"Ugh, why are you so tall?" Linda asked, pushing her fist into his stomach. "Ow. And bony."

"Hey, that ain't bones, *chica*. What you're feeling is pure muscle." He lifted up his shirt to reveal defined abs.

"Whoa." She traced the ridges with the tips of her fingers. "These are crazy."

"Thanks. I've been trying to work out more. All those *gorditas* were making me *gordito*."[8]

Linda's fingers lingered on his stomach a second too long. Her face flushed, and she dropped her hand, taking a step back. "So, what else are we going to see this week, and more importantly, how are we going to afford it? I'm sure it can't all be free."

"On certain days the museums and other places are free or have discounts, so we're going on those days. El Palacio Nacional[9] has these amazing Diego Rivera murals, and apparently you can spend a whole day at El Museo de Arqueología.[10] Then there's Bellas Artes.[11] Oh, and Teotihuacán,[12] but that might cost a bit more to get there, 'cause it's outside of the city. Speaking of outside the city, we have to go to Xochimilco,[13] too."

"Wow, Hector, you have really done your research."

"I figured you needed a little vacation."

---

[8] A little fat

[9] The National Palace

[10] The Museum of Archeology

[11] Beautiful Arts

[12] Birthplace of the gods - Mesoamerican city with pyramids in the outskirts of Mexico City

[13] A place seeded with flowers – a river/canal city near Mexico City

"That's an understatement," Linda sighed.

Reality flew at her. So focused on the sights, she had forgotten for a moment she wasn't on vacation. It was easier pretending she was here to sightsee. Thinking about living here forever was overwhelming. In those moments, she remembered to trust God and His plan. She certainly couldn't have predicted what had happened so far in her life, so who, apart from Him, knew what the future held for her?

"We have a whole 'nother week before María heads back to be with Luz and Doña Vazquez in the U.S. Once you take over her job, you'll be busy, so I figured we need to make the most of our free time."

Linda considered asking him how long he planned to stay, but she didn't want to imagine him leaving, so she avoided the subject. "So thoughtful." She linked her arm in his, walking with him through the Aztec ruins. "You're becoming quite the gentleman."

He winked down at her and stood a little taller.

Juanita checked the caller ID on her cell phone. "Hello, Mr. Brown."

"Hello, ma'am. How are you doing?"

"*Más o menos,*"[14] she replied. "How are you?"

"I've had better days. Just got some news."

Juanita's stomach dropped. "Is Linda okay?"

"Yes, she's fine. I'm calling to tell you that they found Tim Draker's body."

Juanita sank into the closest kitchen chair.

"He was in a car accident the same night he attacked Linda."

---

[14] So-so.

"But why they don't tell us before?"

"The car he was driving had expired plates, and his body was so badly burned in the crash, they had to go by dental records. He had driven outside the city limits, so they had trouble identifying him. Once they were able to contact his wife, things moved faster."

"Why she din't look for him before?"

"She left for England in early October to be with their children. She and Tim had split up the same day he died. She hadn't realized he was missing until a few weeks ago. She assumed he was angry about their separation, and that's why he didn't call."

"And no one tried to call him?"

"I'm not sure, ma'am. It didn't sound like a very good situation. All the signs point to suicide."

Juanita frowned. Though she hated what he'd done to her Linda, she still pitied him in a way. She knew not to judge another person unless she'd walked in their shoes. She sighed. "What's this mean for Linda?"

"It doesn't change much. It only means we won't ever hear him admit to what he did."

"Any more news?"

"Not right now. I'll give you a call if anything changes."

"Mr. Brown?"

"Yes'm?"

"Don' give up. If anyone can helps, is you."

"Thank you. Don't worry. We'll find a way to get her home."

"*Gracias.*" Juanita hung up and said a prayer as she called Mexico to pass on the message.

Linda climbed the steps to another set of ruins and stopped, her head swimming. "I think I need to sit down."

Hector walked her over to the nearest bench and sat with her, putting his hand on her shoulder. "Are you okay?"

Linda tried to take a deep breath. "I feel like I can't breathe."

"It's the altitude. I can feel it, too. We should get used to it after a while."

Linda faced him, asking the question that had been burning in her mind for the last twenty-four hours. "How long until you go back to Virginia?"

Hector shrugged. "Don't know. Depends."

"Like next week? After Christmas?"

His eyes lit, blazing with intensity. He lifted his hand, trailing his fingers along her cheek. "Linda, as long as you're here, I'm here."

A wave of warmth passed through her, as if she were standing in front of *El Dragón*. Those eyes. They were the color of dark chocolate with a black center. They held the same passion as that day in the kitchen when they'd danced the bachata. She felt the same electricity now, only a thousand times stronger. Unable to ignore it any longer, she leaned forward, watching his eyes widen and then close as she pressed her lips against his.

CHAPTER TWENTY-TWO
Cielito Lindo[1]

*L*inda and Hector walked off the metro hand-in-hand towards the *trajineras*[2] in Xochimilco. Names of women decorated the bows of brightly-colored wooden boats. Linda pointed out one with "Juanita" painted on it.

"*Esa, por favor,*"[3] Hector said to the attendant.

The man took their money and led them to the boat. The *remador*[4] extended his hand, helping Linda and then Hector onto the rickety boat.

They'd been in D.F. for five days now, and so far, Linda had truly enjoyed her time there. She'd tried so many new foods native to the area, foods that weren't in Mamá's vocabulary, having grown up in Zacatecas. At every *taquería*[5] and food stand they ate, Hector watched intently, asking questions as their owners

---

[1] Pretty Little Heaven/Sweet Little One – a song by Quirino Mendoza y Cortés
[2] Mexican gondolas
[3] That one, please.
[4] Gondolier
[5] Taco stands

prepared and cooked the food. He hoped to steal secrets to take home to Virginia later.

They hadn't talked about the kiss, but Linda had let him hold her hand from then on. Often they'd sat together on the couch, her head on his shoulder or his on her lap, talking late into the night. Hector was a good listener and an amazing tour guide. Linda had learned way more than she ever needed to know about Mexican art and history. She loved listening to him prattle on, watching him get so animated. She'd never seen him so happy. Though she'd realized he had a great love for art and history, she believed most of his excitement came from the day by the Aztec ruins where they'd had their first kiss and from their time together since then.

The *remador* pushed away from the dock and paddled with a long oar called a *remo*, very similar to the gondolas in Venice, Italy she'd seen in the movies. The river was full of dozens of boats, some in bright, primary colors like theirs and others simple fishing boats.

"Some of the houses here are only reachable by water, so they have to take a boat to get anywhere. Isn't that cool?"

Linda smiled and wondered how many facts she would learn about Xochimilco before they left.

"*¿Son de los Estados Unidos?*"[6] the *remador* asked.

"*Sí,*" Linda said. "*De Virginia.*"[7]

"*Tengo un primo en Norte Carolina.*"[8]

Linda shot Hector a little smile. Ever since they'd arrived in Mexico, they stuck out like a sore thumb. It was weird, because in America, Linda had never

---

[6] Are you from the United States?

[7] From Virginia.

[8] I have a cousin in North Carolina.

felt American enough, and now that she was in Mexico, she didn't feel Mexican enough. Their accents and clothes gave them away, even before they spoke a word of English.

Linda had never thought she'd had an accent until she'd come here. No one had ever told her. She could hear Hector's accent, because his Spanish, though greatly improved from six months ago, was not very good. Linda had always considered her Spanish as nearly perfect, but she hadn't realized the amount of Spanglish she'd used until she tried to speak with Mexicans who'd never stepped foot in America.

Mamá, Tío, Diana, and María had been in America so long, they understood her Spanglish, but that wasn't the case here. She had to strain her brain to remember words she'd learned in school. Linda hadn't realized how difficult it would be to adapt. She was enjoying herself here, but she'd thought she would blend in a bit more.

"Carlos," Juanita popped her head into the kitchen from the sidewalk, where she waited for her new sous-chef. "You is bringing the *carne?*"[9]

"*Sí, ya voy.*"[10] He held up a large red cooler, filled with the thinly cut steaks they would make into *tortas de milanesa*[11] and *tripitas*[12] for *tacos*. It was their first day with the food truck Memo had found them at the junkyard. He'd worked on it every Sunday for a month. They'd put in a new stove and a small

---

[9] Meat

[10] Yes, I'm on my way.

[11] Sandwiches of breaded, fried steak

[12] Tripe

refrigerator. Don Hernandez had cleared a section of grass next to their parking lot, so they could park the truck there permanently. Since they bought most of their ingredients at the *panadería*, it would be easy to transport it out there to cook the food fresh in the truck's kitchen. They still made some food ahead of time at Juanita's house, so Carlos had purchased a cart at a yard sale, which made traveling the two blocks to the truck an easier feat.

Carlos had picked up the truck at Memo's garage and parked it outside Juanita's back door, so they could fill it with equipment before moving it to the *panadería*'s parking lot. Since he had a license and Juanita had never driven a car in her life, she was glad to let him do the driving.

Buzz had gotten around about their truck. The menu for their first day consisted of *gorditas*, *tortas de milanesa*, *tacos de tripitas*, and *tostadas de cueritos*.

Juanita filled another cooler with chopped onions, lettuce, tomatoes, and avocados, along with salsa, jalapeños, tortillas, and the *cueritos*. Carlos picked up the cooler and brought it out to the truck with the unfried *gordita* rounds.

"Ready for some fun?" Carlos asked, spinning the keys on his pointer finger and grinning.

Juanita sighed. "*A ver.*"[13]

Linda rested her head against Hector's chest. The movement of the water under the *trajinera* rocked them into a certain tranquility. Boats floated by and the wind flicked her long hair around. Something entered her peripheral vision, a boat drifting towards them. She tapped Hector's leg and pointed.

---

[13] We shall see.

"*¿Quieren comer, muchachos?*"[14]

Linda shrugged. They had eaten *plátanos fritos con Lechera*[15] earlier, but she could eat again. "*Sí, gracias.*"

"*Este tiene quesadillas de flor de calabaza.*"[16]

Hector raised an eyebrow. "Squash flower *quesadillas?*" he asked Linda.

"I think so. Sounds interesting. *Sí, queremos.*"[17]

"*¿Cuánto cuesta?*"[18] Hector asked. This was one of his favorite phrases in Spanish. María had told them they could *regatear*[19] with some vendors to reduce the price. They had tried it with several of the souvenirs on the sidewalks.

Linda and Hector had learned, by trial and error, that it was not acceptable to *regatear* in the stores and also that not everyone on the sidewalks was willing to haggle. One time she'd asked an indigenous vendor how much a purse cost, and the woman had answered fifty *pesos*,[20] to which Linda had responded in typical fashion, "*Muy caro.*"[21] The woman had shrugged and said, "*Pues, no la compres entonces.*"[22] Linda had been so embarrassed, she'd paid the woman and taken the purse without another word. Hector had laughed the whole way back to the apartment.

They paid more than they normally would for the *quesadillas*, though by American standards, they were a steal for ten dollars between them, including two sodas.

---

[14] Do you youngsters want to eat?

[15] Fried plantains with sweetened condensed milk

[16] This boat has squash flower quesadillas.

[17] Yes, we want.

[18] How much does it cost?

[19] To haggle

[20] Mexican money

[21] Very expensive.

[22] Well, then don't buy it.

"Mmm. *Son deliciosas*,"[23] Linda said, her mouth full of tortilla, stringy cheese, and the squash flower.

Hector opened up one of his *quesadillas* and peeked inside. "*¿Cómo lo hacen?*"[24]

While the man in the *quesadilla* boat answered, Linda concentrated on her lunch, sipping her Coca Cola, which she swore tasted different than the kind in America.

Linda observed her surroundings. Several other boats floated in their direction. The river market was similar to the outdoor market; if they bought one thing, they were suddenly surrounded by a boatload (literally, in this case) of people trying to sell them stuff. They'd refused jewelry and *tamales* before a boat filled with colorfully dressed *mariachis* approached.

Balancing on the *trajinera* while playing trumpets, violins, and guitars, the *mariachis* serenaded them. Linda caught Hector's glance, and they tried not to laugh. A woman in another boat handed Hector a rose, and he paid her five *pesos*. Hector passed the rose to Linda.

She breathed in its sweet fragrance and sighed, remembering their first disastrous attempt at a date where he had brought her gladioluses. She leaned against him and listened to the words of the famous song: "*Ay, ay, ay, ay. Canta y no llores. Porque cantando se alegran, cielito lindo, los corazones.*"[25]

Hector wrapped his arms around her, his fingers gently brushing up and down her upper arm, sending electricity throughout her body. Linda glanced from the *mariachis* to Hector, and despite her best efforts, she was unable to hold back tears.

---

[23] They are delicious.

[24] How they do it?

[25] Oh, oh, oh, oh. Sing and don't cry. Because, my sweet little one, with singing hearts become happy.

"What's wrong?" Hector asked. "Is it the song?"

Linda nodded. "It's so pretty. I've never listened to the words before."

"Oh." His face relaxed. His thumb gently brushed away a tear, and his soft, full lips kissed where it had been. "So they're happy tears?"

"Yeah, they're happy tears." She leaned her head on his chest and listened to his heart.

Juanita's *taco* truck was now parked securely behind the *panadería* at the tail end of the parking lot. Juanita ran her hand along the smooth, freshly painted exterior. The artwork was a sunset with wispy clouds, and in large letters it read, *Tacos El Dream*. Juanita clasped her hands, beaming as she thought of Linda. "Carlos, you painted the truck so nice," she exclaimed.

He grinned. "*Gracias, Doña.*"

"How is school?" she asked. He was taking courses in visual arts at the community college.

"Okay, so far." He shrugged. "I'm still getting some of the boring classes out of the way."

Juanita chuckled. Carlos was a smart boy, but he was more interested in art than anything else. She'd often find him doodling instead of keeping track of the supplies or counting the money. Still not a very good cook, he mostly cut up vegetables and completed the non-food tasks.

Carlos handed her the small chalkboard she and Hector had used so many times. She wrote up the menu and hung it on a screw near the serving window. With the sleeve of her shirt, she rubbed off a smudge on the glass and then stood back to admire their work. Everything looked perfect.

After flipping the sign on the door to OPEN, she stepped into the truck and started up the stove. Time to make some *tacos*.

The walk back to the metro was silent. Linda enjoyed the comforting warmth of Hector's hand as it held hers. It helped her feel at home in this new place that was so foreign to her. This was their last day before she started work at Suburbia. María had already packed up and would leave tomorrow to cross over to American soil.

The short vacation was nearly over. The enchantment was diminishing, and soon she would need to adjust to life here. Her stomach grumbled at the mere thought. Visiting tourist sites was one thing, making a life in a new country was quite another.

She and Hector squeezed onto the metro, holding tightly to their belongings. Body odor mixed with urine and a thick corn smell sat heavy in the air. A few stops later, Hector pressed her hand, tugging her off the train. Ignoring the man near the entrance who asked if they needed help finding where they were going, they climbed the stairs to the Zócalo.

Crowds had gathered in the plaza, surrounding Aztecs dancing in colorful, feathered outfits. Stopping to watch, they tapped their feet to the rhythm of the drums and flutes. After the song had finished, they clapped and dropped a few *pesos* in a jar. Strolling around the square, they observed children launching long-tailed bouncy balls into the air, serious-faced indigenous vendors selling their crafts, and the American tourists in their shorts and fanny packs clicking hundreds of photos with the cameras.

Hector abruptly stopped walking and turned to Linda, taking both her hands in his and holding them to his chest. "Linda?"

Her head swam. It definitely wasn't the altitude this time.

"Will you be my girlfriend?" he asked.

Linda glanced at his large, tan hands. She slid her fingers through his, stepping closer to him, tilting up her head so she looked him straight in the face, electricity circling around them like a lightning storm. After ten years of trying, he had finally won her heart. "Yes, Hector."

He slipped his arms around her waist, pulling her to him and lifting her off the ground. When he set her back on the gritty concrete of the square, he framed her face with his hands, bent down, and kissed her softly.

A new life together awaited them.

CHAPTER TWENTY-THREE
Bendita Tu Luz[1]

*L*inda and Hector waited behind the roped-off area of the airport. On tiptoe, they scanned the faces coming out of security. Soon two familiar fair-skinned people rolled their suitcases out of the big exit, stepping into Mexico.

"Becky, Brian," she called, waving her arm and hopping in excitement.

Becky lit up, elbowed Brian, and pointed to them. They quickened their pace and joined Linda and Hector. "I missed you so much, girl." Becky squeezed her in a tight hug.

"I missed you, too," Linda mumbled into Becky's puffy winter jacket.

Becky loosened her grip and clapped her hands. "Oh, and Hector, you little Romeo, come here."

Hector grimaced as Becky dragged him by the collar for a hug. He pleaded to Linda with wide eyes.

Chuckling, Linda gave Brian a short hug. "I'm so glad you guys could make it."

---

1 Your Blessed Light – a song by Maná

Brian shrugged. "This is way better than working in my dad's office during winter break."

"Your family didn't mind?" Hector asked, attempting to pry Becky off.

"Nah, not as long as we're home in time for Christmas."

Becky grabbed Linda and gave her another hug.

"Chill, *chica*," Linda giggled. She glanced over at the guard moving towards them with a sub-machine gun. He gestured at them with a gloved hand. "I think we need to clear this area. Hector, do you want to go order a taxi?"

Brian raised an eyebrow. "There are like twenty sitting outside." He pointed as they walked towards the exit.

"Nah, man." Hector frowned. "You can't trust any of those. I don't want to freak you out or anything, but people get kidnapped all the time taking fake taxis. You have to order one from a company to make sure you're safe. Here at the airport, they have these booths. Come with me. I'll show you."

"Keep an eye on your bags," Linda called as they stood in line at the counter.

Becky pulled her suitcase closer to her. "Is it that bad here?"

Linda shook her head. "Not really. You just need to be smart."

A man walked up to them and offered to carry their bags, pointing to the taxis outside the door.

"*No gracias. Les esperamos a nuestros novios.*"[2] Linda pointed to the booth where Hector and Brian were ordering a cab at the window.

He wagged his finger. "Too 'spensive, *amiga*. We have good price."

---

[2] No thanks. We're waiting for our boyfriends.

Linda stood her ground, and the man eventually backed off. "I don't think your blonde hair is helping matters." She flicked a loose strand of Becky's hair.

"I guess they don't get a lot of blondes around here." She threw her hair back with a smirk. "Too bad Brian came. Maybe I could have gotten myself a *novio*."

Linda rolled her eyes. "You're crazy. How are things going with you two, anyway?"

"Much better now that he's not living with Kevin anymore." Becky said the name as if it left a bad taste in her mouth.

"I am so over him." Linda glanced at Hector, who was bargaining for a better price for the ride to their apartment.

"I wonder why." Becky pinched Linda on the arm and eyed Hector with a grin. "I told you he was good for you."

Linda rubbed her arm. "I already admitted it on the phone a thousand times. You were right."

"I know." A smile crept onto her lips. "I just wanted to hear it in person." She picked up her luggage as the boys waved them towards the automatic doors to the streets.

Linda laughed and followed Becky as she sauntered out the door to the waiting cab.

Juanita climbed out of the food truck and plopped into one of the lawn chairs outside, putting her feet up for a few minutes while there was a break between customers. Even though the novelty had worn off, they still had a steady stream of orders every day. They were busiest at lunchtime, but a solid group usually came for dinner as well.

A cold breeze rustled the Christmas bells hanging from the awning. She pulled her jacket tighter around her. It was hot inside the truck, so it was nice to feel the fresh breeze. It hadn't snowed yet, but she could smell it in the air, mixed with the scent of wood burning in someone's chimney. She squinted at the thick, fluffy clouds forming above her.

Footsteps crunched on the gravel lot. She peeked over her shoulder and jumped to her feet. "María," she exclaimed, opening her arms wide to her former coworker and friend. "¿Cómo estás?"

"Con hambre."[3] María winked and pointed her lips toward Juanita's truck.

Juanita called to Carlos to heat up some food before bending down to hug Luz. "You happy to see your mamá?"

Luz's young face shone as she nodded with excitement. She hopped up and down, winding her chubby little arms around her mother and squeezing.

"Siéntense."[4] Juanita arranged a few chairs around a small card table. "Un momento."[5] Grabbing chiles, salsa, salt, and quartered limes, she set them in the middle of the table. "¿Qué quieren? Tenemos tamales verdes, tacos dorados de papa, y pozole."[6]

In the end, they decided to get a little bit of everything. Juanita filled three bowls of pozole and brought out all the fixings: radishes, onions, cabbage, and tostadas. Then she emerged with a plate of tacos dorados and a plate of tamales. "Buen provecho."[7]

"Ay, Juanita. Que rico huele."[8] María inhaled deeply,

---

[3] Hungry.
[4] Have a seat.
[5] One moment.
[6] What do you want? We have green tamales, fried tacos of potato, and pozole.
[7] Bon appetite.
[8] Oh, Juanita. How delicious it smells.

wafting the steam in her direction. As she ate, she told Juanita how Linda was doing in Mexico, stories that were better shared in person than over a crackling phone line.

"*Gracias, María.*" Juanita's voice broke, and tears rose to the surface. "*Gracias por cuidarle a mi hija, de recibirla en tu hogar. Era una bendición.*[9] If you and Diana were not there, if she got there alone...*Ni quiero pensarlo.*"[10]

"*No fue nada.*"[11] María waved her hand. "You did the same with Hector, and look how good things turned out with him."

"*Un milagro, ¿no?*"[12] Juanita chuckled, wiping her tears.

Juanita waited until Luz was distracted with her *pozole* to ask María about her crossing. "*¿Y la cruzada? ¿Cómo te fue?*"[13]

María shrugged. "*No tan mal.*"[14] She explained how they'd crossed over a river about three feet deep and then had hidden inside a small compartment of a freight train for several hours as it had moved farther across the border.

Glad her friend hadn't had to pass through the hardships Juanita had experienced in her crossing, she breathed a sigh of relief and bit into a *taco*. She should have used more *epazote*[15] in the potato filling.

"*¿Qué vas a hacer para la Navidad?*"[16] María asked, taking another slurp of her *pozole*.

---

[9] Thank you for taking care of my daughter, for receiving her in your home. It was a blessing.

[10] I don't even want to think about it.

[11] It was nothing.

[12] A miracle, right?

[13] And the crossing? How did it go?

[14] Not so bad.

[15] A spice similar to coriander

[16] What are you doing for Christmas?

Juanita frowned. She hadn't thought that far ahead. Picturing Christmas without Linda was unbearable. For the last fifteen years, they'd spend the entire week before Christmas cutting out homemade decorations and hanging them all over the house, cooking *chiles en nogada*[17] and *romeritos de navidad*,[18] drinking *ponche*[19] and *atole*,[20] listening to Mexican *villancicos*,[21] and going to Christmas Eve service at Promesa. Every Christmas morning, they would awaken early, open the few presents under the tree, and watch a holiday movie together.

Luz gazed up at Juanita with wide eyes. "Doña Juanita, don't worry. You can come to our house. That way you don't miss Linda too much. And you can bring me presents."

"*Ay, mija.*" María covered her mouth and chuckled.

Juanita laughed and pinched Luz's chubby, cherubic cheek. "*Gracias, amor.*"

Linda giggled at her friends' reactions to the taxi ride. The yellow Nissan Tsuru weaved its way through the chaotic streets of the overpopulated city.

"I think we're going to die," Brian whispered as he gripped the handle above the door.

"Are they even following traffic rules?" Becky strained to see, counting. "There are five lanes and at least six lines of cars between them. And I'm using the word 'lines' very loosely here."

---

[17] Stuffed peppers with a cream sauce and pomegranates
[18] A traditional dish eaten at Christmas with potatoes, rosemary, cactus, and shrimp
[19] Punch
[20] A hot drink made from corn dough, often with chocolate
[21] Christmas carols

Hector chuckled from the front seat.

"¿*Señor*? ¿*Muchos accidentes?*"[22] Brian asked the taxi driver, sweat forming on his brow.

"*Sólo en la noche*,"[23] the man replied as a bus cut them off. He punched his horn and shouted some colorful words out the window.

Brian flinched as the taxi screeched to a stop inches from the bus. "¿*Y en el día?*"[24]

"*Puras raspaditas.*"[25]

Linda snickered.

"What does that mean?" Becky asked.

"Only scratches," Hector replied.

"Oh, gees." Brian squeezed Becky's hand.

Linda chuckled. "Welcome to Mexico City."

"And I thought traffic in Charleston was bad," Becky exclaimed.

They stopped at a red light and were quickly swamped by vendors. With one wagging finger, the taxi driver waved off a teenaged boy with a soda bottle full of soap that the boy was about to squeeze onto the windshield for cleaning. A little indigenous girl offered them *papitas*,[26] a man carrying a box of iced treats walked past and lifted his wares to their attention, and a woman with a blue vest threw a newspaper into the cab onto Brian's lap.

"What's this? Do I have to pay for this?"

"They're free," Hector replied.

"Cool." Brian thumbed through it until the light turned green and the taxi lurched forward again.

Linda decided a little distraction was needed. "Hector, what's that stadium over there?"

---

[22] Many accidents?

[23] Only at night.

[24] And in the day?

[25] Only little scratches.

[26] Potato chips

"Oh, that's La Ciudad Deportiva,"[27] Hector replied. The rest of the ride home was a complete guided tour through Mexico City.

"*Sus platos, por favor.*"[28] Juanita took María and Luz's plates, handing the colorful, plastic pieces to Carlos to wash and prepare for the next customers.

María leaned and stretched. "*Que delicioso, amiga.*"

"*Gracias, María.*" Juanita sighed. Somehow having María here gave her hope that one day soon, she would see Linda again.

"Mamá, I'm cold." Luz shivered.

"Here, you wanna sit in the truck?" Juanita opened the door. She pulled the cushion from the driver's seat and placed it on one of the steps. "*Ven. Siéntate acá, corazón.*[29] Nice and warm." She patted the step, and Luz hopped out of her chair. Plopping down, she was soon engulfed in a handheld game.

"Juanita, your English is so much better." María squeezed Juanita's shoulder.

"*Hector me ayudó bastante.*"[30] Juanita missed Hector's weekly English lessons as much as his help in the kitchen. "*Y este—*"[31] She pointed her lips toward Carlos. "*No habla nada de español.*"[32]

"I think my English got worse." María sighed. "*Y ahora tengo acento de chilanga.*"[33]

Juanita nearly spit out her drink in a spurt of

---

[27] Sports City
[28] Your plates, please.
[29] Come. Sit over here, honey.
[30] Hector helped me so much.
[31] And this one—
[32] He doesn't speak any Spanish
[33] And now I have a Chilangan (Mexico City) accent.

laughter. Though she hadn't noticed it before, it was true. After six months in Mexico City, María now had a slight Mexico City accent. *"No te preocupes. Pronto se te quita."*[34]

"Espero que sí."[35] María sighed. "I hope Linda comes home before she gets one."

Juanita's stomach dropped at the mention of her daughter's name.

"Any news from Jackson Brown?" María asked.

Juanita shook her head and tilted her face to the sky, trying to block the tears that rose to the surface. *"Ay, María. Es demasiado difícil."*[36]

Getting up from her chair, María wrapped Juanita in a warm hug, a whispered prayer on her lips.

As though God was reminding her of His presence in that moment, snowflakes drifted down from the heavens, landing on their faces. María's words flowed over Juanita like a tranquil wave, slowly breaking down her hard exterior and allowing the emotions to pass through. Unable to contain them any longer, her tears rushed out. She reminded herself that God accepted her tears as readily as her laughter and praise. She no longer needed the excuse of onions.

Linda smirked at Becky as they exited the cab.

"Another fun fact is that Mexico City was built on top of a lake, so it's sinking at a rate of one inch per year." Hector's ramblings had distracted Brian and Becky for the remainder of the ride.

"Wow," Becky whispered to Linda as Hector paid

---

[34] Don't worry. You'll get rid of it soon enough.
[35] I hope so.
[36] Oh, María. It's too hard.

the driver. "That is way more about Mexico City than I ever wanted to know."

"He's like a walking guidebook."

"It was very thorough." Becky widened her eyes for emphasis. "He could start charging for that."

"He just got a job at a restaurant, but if that falls through, at least he has options."

"Oh, that's great. Hector, I didn't know you got a job."

He walked past with Brian, carrying their suitcases. "It's pretty recent news. I started two days ago."

"So, Hector?" Brian asked. "How long are you going to stay in Mexico?"

Hector shrugged. "However long it takes for Linda to get her visa. Whether it's a few more weeks or a few more years or forever, I'm not going anywhere."

Becky clasped her hands over her heart and sighed. "I am melting. Oh my Lord, y'all are too sweet."

Linda shot Hector a coy smile. It was true. She melted for him on a daily basis. There was no possible way she could've imagined this scenario a year ago. It was utterly unexpected and wonderful. Without his presence and her faith, she would have entered a deep depression by this time.

Sadness clouded her mind as she remembered Tim's suicide and thought of how alone and desperate he'd become at the end. To see his soul shattered enough to attack her and leave his young sons without a father broke her heart. Where Linda had turned to God and trusted in His will, despite her horrible circumstances, Tim had allowed his anguish to overtake him and had chosen to give up the fight.

Becky's voice drew her back to the present. "And

Linda, you're working at, like, the JC Penney's of Mexico, right?"

Linda nodded, unlocking the door to their apartment. "Suburbia. With Hector's mom. It's not bad. I have a lead on another job, too. At one of those little currency exchange booths."

Brian and Hector dropped the heavy suitcases in the living room. Linda had taken María's old bed, and Hector now had his own bedroom in the corner of the living room, separated by a divider.

"You guys hungry?" Hector asked.

"Starving." Brian rubbed his stomach. "They only gave us this tiny sandwich on the plane. I ate it in one bite."

"We can walk to El Zócalo from here and grab some lunch," Hector said.

Becky opened her suitcase and pulled out a small bag. "Let me freshen up first."

Brian groaned and dropped onto a kitchen chair. "Might as well sit down, buddy," he instructed Hector. "That's girl code for at least fifteen minutes."

Becky punched his arm on the way to the bathroom. She pulled Linda in with her. "So, how are things really going?" she asked after closing the door. She pouted into the mirror and pulled out some makeup.

"It's hard. I miss Mamá so much." Linda sighed. "It's even harder thinking about Christmas coming. I know Jackson is doing his best, but it might be a long time before I'm back in the States. Nothing here is as easy as over there. I didn't realize how spoiled I was until I had to learn to wash my clothes by hand in the *lavadero*. And my brain is so tired by the end of every day from all the Spanish. Don't get me wrong. I love all the culture and the food and the markets, but for me, it's not home."

Becky turned to Linda. "I can't even imagine what you're going through. But I want you to know I'm here for you. My dad said he'd fly me down here whenever you need me."

Sometimes it was nice to have rich friends. "Thanks, Becky."

Becky gave her another tight squeeze before pulling out her toothbrush from the bag.

"Hold on." Linda handed Becky a sealed bottle of water. "That's another convenience I'd taken for granted. You can't use the water here for anything but cleaning."

"Really?" Becky raised an eyebrow. "How come?"

"Well, remember how Hector said Mexico City is sinking? The sewer system has mixed into the water system."

"That's disgusting." Becky poured the bottled water onto her toothbrush.

"Yeah, apparently you can get Hep C from the water." Linda wrinkled her nose. "At least that's what Hector read in his guidebook."

Laughing, Becky rinsed out her mouth before applying another coat of lip gloss and passing it to Linda, who did the same.

"All right, boys," Becky called, sashaying out of the bathroom. "Let's get a move on."

Two blocks later a horn honked to an off-tone rendition of "La Cucaracha."[37] A car flew past with a man catcalling out the window. "Hey, *americana.*"[38]

Becky glanced over at Linda and laughed.

Hector chuckled. "That's never happened before."

"I'm telling you," Linda smirked, "they love blondes around here."

---

[37] The Cockroach – a traditional Mexican folk song
[38] American girl

Brian slid his arm around Becky, pulling her closer with a silly pout. "*Mía*."[39]

Linda glanced at Hector, and they grinned at each other. Hector wove his fingers through Linda's, lifted her hand to his silky lips, and kissed the back of it with a wink.

"Aw, you guys are so cute," Becky cooed.

"Looks like you're in it for the long haul, huh, buddy?" Brian remarked.

"Always have been," Hector stated, pulling Linda tight to his side. "Always will be."

Emotion welled up inside Linda. Though she hadn't understood it before, she now realized why God had placed Hector in her path so many years ago. Despite a history of frustration and annoyance, Hector had never left her. In the last six months, God had formed him into someone responsible, supportive, and loving. Strange as it sounded, she couldn't picture life without him.

---

[39] Mine.

CHAPTER TWENTY-FOUR
La Vida Es Mejor Cantado[1]

*J*uanita sat in church, listening to the announcements. Another member had been arrested and was facing deportation. Before last year Juanita had only heard tales of people being deported, mostly due to drunk driving or committing serious crimes, but lately every other week someone from the neighborhood or a friend's family member were getting deported for little more than a cracked windshield.

Juanita lowered her head in prayer. *Lord, how long will this go on? When will their eyes be opened to see the pain they're inflicting on families? When will the system change so that those who need a better life won't need to cross over mojados only to suffer a lifetime of nightmares and fear?* Juanita didn't receive an immediate answer, but she had faith in God's plan and knew that God's timing was His own and not hers. He knew what He was doing. She had to trust that one day, things

---

[1] Life is Better Singing – a common saying and also a song by Timbriche or Teen Angel

would be different, whether in this world or in the next.

It was a few weeks into the new year. Linda was still in Mexico and would probably remain there for several months or even years. Juanita longed to go and be with her, but she knew Diana and Hector were taking good care of her. Carlos always showed her the pictures Hector uploaded online from his phone every week. Linda looked happy, happier than Juanita had seen her in a while.

Memo had found another mechanic, and his business was back to normal. Carlos' sister helped him with the books, and he made the new guy do the extra cleaning Hector had helped with. Carlos had helped clean for the first few weeks, but he and Juanita were so busy now with the food truck, he no longer had time.

They cooked and prepared every morning for about two hours before walking to the *panadería* around ten thirty. That gave them time to heat the grill before people trickled in around eleven. They had a steady stream until about one thirty, and then they returned home to cook the food for the next day. Financially, they could stay home after that, but eight hours of silence didn't rest well with Juanita, so after a break, they headed back to the truck around four every day and sold until seven. It made for a long day, but it was still the easiest work she'd ever done, and it helped fill the hours where she missed Linda the most.

The strings of a violin captured Juanita's attention, and she tuned back in to the service. She stood and sang along, closing her eyes and listening to the congas and the guitar. She concentrated on the words as she sang. The song was "Salmo 3:1-6,"[2] and it was about the Lord responding to his people's cries for help and lifting them up. The chorus repeated, *"Mas Jehová es escudo alrededor de mí, mi gloria y Él que levanta mi cabeza."*[3]

Juanita raised her hands and lifted her voice and heart to the Lord. A combination of peace and joy filled her. The saying was true: life was better singing.

Linda waved to Hector from her booth at her new job in the *casa de cambio*[4] in the city center. From her bullet-proof window, she could see the restaurant where Hector worked as a cook, under the table, of course. Since there was a limit for six months to visit Mexico without a visa, Jackson Brown had told Hector to apply for a Temporary Resident Visa so he could return with Linda without problems. Becky was helping to gather his paperwork from the U.S., and she hoped to fly out again next month.

Exchanging money, Linda met people from all over the world: Germany, Saudi Arabia, Canada, Bolivia, Japan, and various nations. Other than the currency her professor had brought into class and some *pesos* Tío had given her, she'd never seen foreign money. In the past few weeks, she'd learned how to greet people and say numbers in about twelve different languages. Though it wasn't what she had studied in school, it was the closest thing to her field she could work right now, and she enjoyed it.

---

[2] Psalms 3:1-6

[3] But Jehovah is a shield around me, my glory, and the One who lifts up my head – Psalms 3:3

[4] Currency exchange booth

She had adjusted to life in Mexico and was resigned that she would be here for a while. Jackson was working hard with both the Mexican and United States government to get her back in to the country. He had the help of several immigrant organizations, but even with these things, Jackson had admitted it could take a while. Though Linda missed Mamá, they spoke every Sunday after church and sometimes in between. She, Hector, and Diana had found a good church near their apartment. Linda and Hector had joined the Bible study held on Thursday nights, and they'd attended every Sunday for the last month.

Hector grew closer to her every day. They prayed and read the Bible together, something she had never really shared with anyone before. He was so new to the faith, and like her and everyone else in the world, he had a lot to learn.

Things were very different than she could ever have imagined in her bedroom back at home. God had taken her down a path completely separate from the one on which she had started. For a while, she'd fought against it, thinking her plans were better, but once she'd surrendered to God's will, she realized He had something better in store for her. She couldn't see it yet, but it was going to be more amazing than anything that she could have ever dreamed.

Linda turned up the song on the radio in the corner of her booth. Selena. She couldn't remember the concert, but Mamá had told her the story so many times, she could almost imagine herself there, sitting on Mamá's shoulders, singing and moving to the song's rhythm. She beamed as she spun in her chair, her voice echoing around the booth. Mamá had always told her, "*La vida es mejor cantando.*"[5]

---

[5] Life is better singing.

THE END

Hola, Reader!

What did you think of *VIVIR EL DREAM?*

I would love for you to leave a review of my book on Amazon or Goodreads. Reviews help indie authors like me gain visibility and support.

Gracias!

- Allison K. García

Acknowledgments

There have been so many people who have helped me with *Vivir el Dream*. It has been a five-year process to get to this point.

First and foremost, I have to thank God, because He is the One who put it in my soul to be a storyteller. He never let me give up on my dream, even after I put it away for 10 years. He was there working in my heart, showing me signs and nagging at me to keep writing, even when I wanted to put down the pen and give it up. He placed so many wonderful people in my life to help me on my journey.

I am grateful for my family who have supported me throughout this process. For my husband, Julio, and my son, Miguel, who've loved me through thousands of hours of writing and editing and trips to writing activities. I'm especially thankful for Julio because he did the beautiful artwork for the cover! For my parents, Thomas and Janet Baggott, who didn't give me toooo hard of a time for going to college for Creative Writing. For Grandma Baggott and Uncle John and Grandma Quagliato, who were always willing to listen to my books and were there for an encouraging word. And for my brothers, who didn't bother me for being up writing and editing at insane hours when I went for visits, and for my family in México, who taught me about Mexican culture and delicious foods.

For my friends who have allowed me to gush on about my book and given me ideas to make it better: Leigh, Sandra, Norys, Rose, Tracy, and countless others.

For my great group of writer friends at ACFW and SVW! Without you, this book would not have been possible at all. I am especially grateful for my critique partners and my NaNoWriMo buddies (so many names but the ones that stick out are Anne, Taryn, Maggie, Josette, Rebekah, and Susan) and for my Shenandoah Valley ACFW group: Connie, Regina, and Christine. We're making it!

I want to thank my awesome editor, Tamara Shoemaker, who put up with a thousand (not even exaggerating) FB messages and maaaany emails to make this book the best it could be. I also want to thank Emily June Street, who made this book look so beautiful and for fielding the various formatting nightmares that arose along the way.

I am especially thankful for *mis hermanos* at Alianza, for your faith, your strength, and your love. I have learned so much from being part of our congregration, not only about Latino culture but about how to love. In particular I want to thank the Ruano family, whose unfaltering faith inspired me to write this story. Juan José, thank you also for taking the time to talk with me about your story.

For all the Dreamers out there, for all who live undocumented and in fear, for those who have already been deported, for those tired, poor, huddled masses looking for freedom, for the ones who have passed through trials to get here, who have had to live through experiences that no one should ever suffer, I thank you. This story is for you. Keep hope alive. You are never alone for He is with you.

Learn More, Get Active

Information about Immigration

Dart, Tom. "Fearing deportation, undocumented immigrants wary of reporting crimes." *TheGuardian.com*. Website. March 23, 2017.

Donohue, Brian. "Think your immigrant ancestors came here legally? Think again." *NJ.com*. Website. November 12, 2015.

Duara, Nigel. "Why border crossings are down but deaths are up in the brutal Arizona desert." *LAtimes.com*. Website. October 27, 2015

Fact Sheet. "The DREAM Act: Creating Opportunities for Immigrant Students and Supporting the U.S. Economy." *AmericanImmigrationCouncil.org*. Website. July 13, 2010.

Goldberg, Eleanor. "80% Of Central American Women, Girls Are Raped Crossing Into The U.S." *Huffpost.com*. Website. September 12, 2014.

Moreno, Carolina. "11 Documentaries About Immigrants Everyone Should Watch Right Now." Huffpost.com. Website. January 17, 2017.

Santana, Maria. "5 immigration myths debunked." *CNN.com*. Website. November 20, 2014.

Smith, Tristan & Polo Sandoval. "Life after deportation: What it's like to start over in a country you barely know." *CNN.com*. Website. March 27, 2017.

Resources

Suicide Prevention Services
http://www.spsamerica.org/

Domestic Violence
http://www.thehotline.org/

Immigration Help
https://www.safehorizon.org/

Prayer Line
http://www.klove.com/ministry/prayer/

Organizations for Change

Welcoming America
https://www.welcomingamerica.org/

Virginia Organizing
https://www.virginia-organizing.org/

Sanctuary Churches
http://www.sanctuarynotdeportation.org/

ACLU
https://www.aclu.org/

About the Author

Allison K. García is a Licensed Professional Counselor, but she has wanted to be a writer ever since she could hold a pencil. She is a member of American Christian Fiction Writers, Shenandoah Valley Writers, Virginia Writers Club, and is Municipal Liaison for Shenandoah Valley NaNoWriMo.

Allison's short story, "At Heart," was published in the Winter 2013 edition of *From the Depths* literary magazine, along with her flash fiction. Her work, "You Shall Receive," was published in GrayHaven Comics's 2014 All Women's anthology. Winning an honorary mention in the ACFW Virginia 2015 short story contest, "Just Another Navidad" was published in *A bit of Christmas.* Allison finaled in the 2016 ACFW Genesis Contest for *Vivir el Dream,* to be published May 2017.

Latina at heart, Allison has been featured in local

newspapers for her connections in the Latino community in Harrisonburg, Virginia. A member of cultural competency committees for work and a participant in several Dream Act rallies and other events in her region, she also sings on the worship team and enjoys get-togethers with the *hermanos* in her church. With the help of her husband, Julio, and their son, Miguel, she has been able to nurture her love for the Latino people.

Made in the USA
Lexington, KY
10 October 2018